The Town Without Cheer,
and other stories

The Town Without Cheer,
and other stories

Copyright © 2019 by Philip Boyle

www.philipboyle.vpweb.ie

The
Town
Without
Cheer,
and other stories

by Philip Boyle

Contents

Liberties 1

The Circus Has Left Town 9

The Prizefighter 20

Protest 33

Lone Wolf 52

The Comedian Who Died 62

A Bang On The Head 71

Reversal of Fortune 74

The Miracle of Phibsborough 80

Vonolel...(from the horse's mouth)* 96

The Face In The Wall 101

The Loneliest House In The World 116

31 123

The Moor of Moore Street 129

Slump 152

Pound of Flesh 158

Red Cliff House 164

Interval 176

Black Church 182

A Swim With Two Birds 187

The Fall 197

The Man Who 220

The Town Without Cheer 222

About the Author 238

Liberties

He's in ruins. And that's *before* the sunlight hits him. The curtains are pulled back like a plaster from tender skin, and the wound is still raw. His mother's to blame, but she's a mare without mercy, and doesn't stop there.

'Ah, Ma!'

'Get up, you lazy bollocks. It's near twelve.'

'It's me day off – and what's all that noise?'

'You mean apart from the drink still swilling in your head? That's the parade. You remember the parade? - that thing you were celebrating last night until all hours.'

'Give it a rest, will you?' That's like asking a hungry bear to stop charging. Brady kicks his feet out of bed before she can do her worst. The toilet is ten yards away, might as well be a mile. It's even harder with an audience. '*Please,* Ma – I'm up.' She relents, and slams her way downstairs, still making a point. He reaches the toilet in one piece, but discovers that Saturday night still has something to say. He bids it a final farewell, and it's just as well, because the system can't take much more flushing.

Breakfast is lunch, and she's fetched up a plate-full of burnt-to-hell sausage and bacon – all courtesy of the butchers where he works. He's in danger of keeling, but he fears her wrath more, and manages a mouthful or two. Keeping it down is a whole different matter. If only she had other offspring to worry about, he might have been able to keep the rod off his back. He's eighteen now, about time he was making tracks. She doesn't need looking after, she's as sprightly as an urban fox, and twice as sly. A butcher's assistant doesn't get much of a cut, but to be honest, Bosco is a fair boss, and there's a certain satisfaction in carving joints from carcasses. Bosco, though, is also a robust fifty-something, and won't be visiting the human abattoir anytime soon. Therefore, prosperity is very far off.

She's dressed for the occasion, and ready to leave.

'Clean all that up before you leave – and *don't* go back to bed.'

'I won't. I want to see the parade, too.'

'More celebrating, is it?'

'I didn't drink that much.' He did. 'And I have work tomorrow, don't I?' Which means nothing.

'Well, make sure you *do* get to work tomorrow. We can't afford you losing that job.' *We?* Off she goes, off to church, off to pay her respects to Him Upstairs, as she calls him. Then she'll call into the Clock for a small rum and a natter.

Brady thinks about going back to bed, but his room smells nasty, and he opens a window. The noise from the parade assaults him. What's the saint's name again, the reason for all this fuss? Thomas Street is filling up fast, cheap floats taking their places in the procession before the official kick-off. Suppose he better get down there and show his face. The community needs all the help it can get.

⌒

The slim dandy steals the parade. Brady firsts notices him handing out sweets to bored, antsy kids, instantly settling them, to the shock of frazzled parents. The stranger moves with balletic grace through the crowds, on stick-thin legs, wearing a porkpie hat, and a farmer's jacket. Brady wants to get closer, but the man moves with such stealth that it's hard to get a fix on him.

Under-rehearsed bands play tinny tunes on ancient instruments. The saint, in whose name they're purportedly performing, would be tuning out. Brady's friends are thin on the ground. Those with their own places will likely be sleeping it off, and the rest are probably dead. He'll have to amuse himself, then. The floats are decidedly unamusing, and there's every chance of him being tempted back into the Clock, or Arthur's. He drank there, and elsewhere, the night before, until he fell over, was helped back up, and started all over again. No different to many other nights, except for a nagging doubt that crept up on him late in the proceedings, when he shouldn't have been capable of such reflection. It was a simple thought – *why?* Why was he, and the rest of them, trying to drink themselves into an early grave? It dulled the pain, the boredom, that much was obvious, but wasn't there an alternative? And speaking of his crew, there's Fitzgerald over the road, leaning against the shutters. Brady thinks of calling over to him, but he'd never hear, and Fitz doesn't look like he wants company. Did he even make it home last night?

He carries on towards Cornmarket, where he stumbles upon the stranger, this time doing card tricks for the passing trade, without looking for payment. Brady picks his way through the small crowd until he's directly in front of the magician. The man could be anywhere from thirty to sixty. The hat looks like he was born with it on his head, and as he deals the cards, Brady notices a tattoo on the palm of his hand, a concentric circle that could have been put on with a branding iron. As if he was being marked for identification − or as a warning? His pockets look empty, but he keeps taking objects out of them, the latest being a series of cups and balls, that he proceeds to dazzle his growing audience with. Brady tries to hold the man's gaze, but their eyes never lock.

He drifts back towards home, dismayed by the efforts of the locals to imbue the streets with any spirit of hope or optimism. Not that he's contributed anything himself, he admits. He runs into Farrell, another relic from the night before, who hands him a bottle of beer, and Brady thinks that one can't do him any harm. They barely exchange a word, but God, the beer tastes good. Brady moves away before he gets any more bad ideas.

An orange rolls past him on the pavement, as if it's just out for a stroll. He stops it with his foot, and as it looks fresh and unbruised, he picks it up, and bites into it. Beer and oranges, the perfect hangover cure, and as the light begins to fade, Brady comes back to life. And that's when things really get strange.

The floats have mercifully dispersed, and the cars have returned, and the noise has risen, and the signs are ominous, and things kick off with a mother screaming as her child runs away, and the boy panics, scared to go back, drifting carelessly into the road where a loose horse, with string for reins, clatters into him, and the boy hits the tarmac hard. A crowd quickly gathers, though nobody is terribly anxious to actually go near the boy. Nobody, that is, except the magician, who is about to reveal other talents. He kneels by the boy, and cradles his head in his hands. Brady can see blood on the back of the unconscious boy's head, which spreads to the stranger's hands, but by the time the mother has found her way there, the boy is up and talking, and the blood has disappeared. The stranger stands back, giving mother and child room, and then he fades into the background. Brady tries to follow him, but he proves elusive once more.

He spots his mother enjoying a rare smoke outside the Clock lounge. Best avoid her, she won't look kindly on being interrupted, by her son of all people. He thinks about going home – he has work tomorrow, after all – but there's too much going on for him to leave now. He calls into Arthur's and orders an orange juice, to general amusement. It's sickly sweet, but he stays disciplined, agreeing to a game of darts to keep his mind off the alcohol surrounding him. He's about to throw for the match, but he never gets the chance, as a roar goes up inside about the roar going on outside. He leaves the darts on the table, and follows them out.

A scuffle is too mild a word for it, though it's not quite a full-blown punch-up, yet. Before it gets too serious, the Gardai arrive, and strive to broker a peace. As the duelling factions decide to call it a night, for now, and begin to disperse, Brady sees the magician in the middle of it, looking satisfied at his work being done. This time, however, he doesn't escape, and the police demand a word with him. He offers no resistance, but when asked to turn out his pockets, he unveils an unbroken stream of coloured handkerchiefs. There is contained laugher, as nobody quite knows how to react. He's suddenly told he's free to go, and he slips quietly away, as mysterious as ever.

Brady scans the horizon, but there's no sign of his mother. He's not ready to go home, work in the morning or not. He peers into the Clock, looking for a familiar face, and he finds the magician holding a corner of the lounge captive, weaving a tale of unlikely bravery, featuring you-know-who, moving his hands through the air so that everyone can see the tattoo on his hand, and whatever its meaning, it's working.

One drink won't kill me, Brady reasons, and anyway, he's not leaving until he discovers this man's true purpose.

He sees it, and he'll swear on any bible that it happened - and he's only had two slow pints. The storyteller's tales become more supernatural as the evening progresses, even if time itself appears to stand still. The end of this latest invention – for what else can it be? – climaxes with the man's hat rising an inch above his head of its own volition. But that's not the most extraordinary aspect – it is what's underneath that hat that has those present straining to hold onto their sanity. For beneath the hat lies – nothing, but empty space. Then the hat falls back into place, and the storyteller tips his hat in appreciation, and the rest of his head is exactly where it should be. They had been fooled – a brilliant conjuring of the collective imagination – but Brady's doubts remain. Before serious questions can be asked, the barman calls time, and they're barrelled out into the street, where angry rain is waiting for them.

Angry, and then dangerous. People run for shelter, and Brady follows a small group into the church, mercifully still open for the saint's birthday.

The atmosphere inside is tremulous. The rain continues to strengthen, hammering on the ceiling and doors, demanding to be let in. Brady looks for shelter *inside* the inside, and opens one of the confessionals, where he finds a grunting priest buggering a squealing altar boy. They both quieten, and stare at Brady until he closes the door so they can continue. He staggers backwards, tripping over a footrest, and disturbing a display of lit candles. He rectifies his mistake as best he can, and then his eyes are drawn to an elderly lady praying on her knees in a pew near the back. Her face peeled to heaven, tears roll down her cheek, until she closes her eyes, and falls backward, dead. Brady wants to run to her, but something holds him back. There is an elemental roar as the main doors open, and the stranger enters. He washes his hands in the font of Holy Water, turning it into boiling oil. His features have a darker edge, and he moves intently to a room off to the side of the altar, emerging moments later, decked out in chainmail armour, and mounted on a white steed. He points his shimmering sword to the ceiling, winks at Brady, digs his spurs into the horse's sides, and charges into battle. Brady fears his heart will burst out of his chest – what does it all mean? Has the end come? Is the battle to end all battles raging out there on Thomas Street? And why is he the only one who seems concerned?

He must ask the priest. Damn the consequences, he's going to open that confessional again! The altar boy is now being rocked gently by the priest in a gesture of pure love. Brady can't speak, he can't articulate what's in his head. What *is* in his head? Okay, well, if nobody will help him, he'll have to do it himself. At the very least, he has to get home to his mother, and do what he can to protect her, or just stay with her until the end. He approaches the door, listening for the apocalypse. He can't hear anything. He steels himself, and opens the door…

…to morning. Litter reigns supreme, and the wind is having a field day with it. There are casualties alright, but only of drink, carpeting various doorways in unflattering positions.

Behind Brady, the church is assuredly locked shut. He looks at his watch, and the dials are spinning rapidly, as if speeding through the decades. He feels his face, before finding a window where he can properly reflect on it. He doesn't appear to have aged. He looks at his watch again, and it says ten minutes to eight. Shit, he's due at work in ten minutes, and he needs a shower and a change of clothes, but that would mean facing his mother, and *that* is the greater of two evils.

He needn't have worried. There's no sign of Bosco. Maybe, hopefully, Brady thinks, the butcher was celebrating himself yesterday, and is still sleeping it off. Twenty past eight – he takes the chance, and heads to Carlo's café for a spot of breakfast.

There's a huge black waiter he has never seen in the area before, let alone working in the café. Where's Brenda, or Dickie, for that matter? Never mind – he orders the full fry, and the strongest coffee they can brew. Is that Rex in the corner? He looks younger, somehow, and his nicotine-stained fingers have mysteriously been cleaned. His nails, too, look decidedly manicured. Brady has seen far stranger things over the last twenty-four hours or so, and doesn't give it any more thought.

Breakfast arrives, but there's something wrong. The food is *wriggling* on the plate – it shouldn't be doing that, should it? He's about to ask the waiter, but the waiter has other ideas. For one thing, he's carrying a handful of knives and forks, and he says to Brady:

'Watch!' He proceeds to juggle, the cutlery being thrown higher and higher, almost touching the ceiling. Then the waiter steps aside, and all the knives and forks land on Brady's table, sharps ends sticking them to the surface, and forming a circle, like the one in the stranger's hand from last night.

'Now do you understand?' the waiter asks. Brady wants to say 'no,' but his mouth is full of black pudding. He can't get the food down fast enough, and the waiter pats him on the back, saying 'good boy' before leaving him to it.

Breakfast is on them, Brady's told.

'But why?' They don't answer, and shove him out the door.

It's unseasonably cold, yet everyone he encounters wears light summer clothing. He might be coming down with something. He reaches the butchers, and there's a queue down the block. He's never seen such a queue. Jesus, Bosco will be furious, and happy at the same time. Brady forces his way in, all apologetic.

'Sorry, Bosco. I was here earlier, and thought - .'

'What are you doing here?' Bosco says, shocked to see Brady.

'What do you mean? I - .'

'You shouldn't be here' says Bosco. And then, in chorus, every customer intones, *'you shouldn't be here'.*

His mother is at the kitchen table, her head in her hands. Eyes red from crying, and holding a picture of Brady as a baby.

'Ma? What's wrong?'

It takes her a few moments to realise that he's there. Her first reaction is to make the sign of the cross. Then she struggles to her feet, and starts trembling, with fear or excitement he can't tell.

'What's *wrong?*' he demands to know.

'Have they – *finished?*' she quivers.

'Finished? Finished what?'

'Why didn't they ring me? They let you out already?'

Now it's Brady's turn to start trembling. He knows, deep down, but he can't quite face it at that moment.

His stomach hurts, it really hurts.

'I think I'll lie down for a bit,' he says, and goes upstairs, each step a punch to the gut.

He's in ruins. His insides are a pack of cards being repeatedly shuffled by clumsy hands. The light is blinding, but artificial. He wakes to an audience, feeling like he's been asleep for years – not asleep, as such, but *under*, like drowning, and now he's reached the surface. He hears a distant, muffled voice say, *he's conscious.*

The doctor smiles down at him, reassuring, but still intimidating. He's familiar to Brady. Stick a porkpie on him, and he could be –

'Brady? Can you hear me?- Brady? What did you take?'

Brady can hear, but does the doctor want to hear? Same question, over and over, since he was twelve. *What did you take?* What does it matter? Whatever it is, it's always the same. It always the does the same damage. The names change, but the impact remains the same.

7

'I…'

'Yes, Brady?'

'I took…liberties.'

'What?...what was that, Brady?'

With a mighty effort, Brady lifts his head up, and says,

'I took…*Liberties!*' As good a name as any. Let them figure that one out. Order a search party, issue a public health warning about…*Liberties.*

At the last moment, Brady looks over at the magician in the scrubs, who's now changing his medical garb for chainmail armour, his needle for a mighty sword, and about to mount his white steed, ready to charge into battle, for him.

The Circus Has Left Town

The circus has gone, and left the camel behind. No wonder it's got the hump. Two, in fact. Noel forms an instant dislike for the curious beast, although it's something different to look at other than the usual scrap of derelict land. Every year there's a new plan proposed, one that's never realised, and in the meantime, the weeds grow higher, and the discarded rubbish piles up. The high fence has made little or no difference.

But every once in a while, something comes along, like the circus, to brighten up the area, and cover the mess for a short period. The grass will be mown, the trailers will move in, the tent will be erected, and all of a sudden, Ormond Street is transformed, at night anyway, when the lights and the noise, and the enthusiasm, puts everything else, mercifully, in the shade. Not that Noel has ever gone to the circus, *any* circus, himself. His wife's not one for venturing out, his daughter's too old, and as for himself, well, it's not really his sort of thing, is it.

The problem with the circus coming is that it has to leave eventually, and what remains seems worse, if that's possible, than before.

Seriously, though, what's the deal with the camel? It's not something easily forgotten. It's not like a family pet no longer wanted, one that can simply be abandoned. It wouldn't be too hard to trace the owner of a camel, surely? Maybe Jago knows what's happening. The clown is in the Community Centre right now, doing one last turn for the younger kids. Noel didn't hear much laughter when he passed by the room earlier. Ungrateful bastards, he thinks, they don't appreciate anything these days unless it appears on a screen. They don't deserve the voluntary services of the likes of Jago any more than they deserve the resources of the Community Centre. They don't have to pay a penny, and that's the problem. They think that everything they'll ever want will just be handed to them on a plate. Noel would like to hand them something, all right, a slap of two, teach them respect, teach them a few hard lessons, teach them the truth, that *nothing* is free, at least nothing good.

His ten minute break is well and truly over, but – fuck it, another five minutes won't make much of a difference. Anyway, the moment he sticks his head inside the place, he's abused, from all sides. The kids dismiss him with regular, and obscene, insults, and the staff lay him down on the floor like a mat, and walk all over him. Plenty of time for a second smoke, which he'll draw out as long as possible. Behind the fence across the road, the camel chews on, dreaming no doubt about feasting on tastier stuff than Dublin weeds.

The caretaker is joined at the door by the weary clown carrying his absurdly long shoes.

'Funny to look at,' says Jago, '*not* funny to wear, I tell you.' Noel offers him a cigarette, and a man never looked like he needed one more.

'You finished here now?' Noel asks. 'In Dublin, I mean?'

'Yes!' Jago declares gleefully. 'Off to – what is it called? – yes, *Westport!* You know it?'

'Never been,' Noel admits. Never been much of anywhere. Anywhere except here, and that's been nothing to write home about, has it? 'It's supposed to be nice, I hear. By the way, what's the story with the camel? They're not leaving him there, are they?'

'No. There's a truck coming to collect. Special man, knows how to handle Giorgio.'

'Giorgio?'

Jago points to the animal. 'Giorgio!' he says, laughing.

'Don't they – camels, I mean – get cold over here?' Noel fears being laughed at, and Jago never needs much of an excuse to do that.

'They are tough animals, *tough*. Maybe they do get cold, but we can't ask them, can we?'

Take me with you, Noel thinks. If he was invited, right now, to go to Westport, or anywhere else for that matter, he'd accept, he *would*. No, he wouldn't. He's too fucking scared, not to mention lazy. And there is the family to think about. Not that he likes to think about them much. But he's been doing that more and more lately, *thinking*, about them, about everything. About everything that he has, and mostly what he hasn't.

'I've never seen you without your make-up,' he tells Jago. 'You do take it off, don't you?'

'Sure I do. If I kept it on, I would destroy my face, my skin. At night, alone, I scrape it off, like old paint, only to repaint the next day – ha-ha! Crazy, no?'

'Have you time for a drink?' Noel asks suddenly. A flurry of kids rush past on their way out, pushing the two men together, and Jago's breath reeks of tobacco, and something more exotic.

'Ah, no, I cannot, unfortunately. Time is against me. We are performing tomorrow night. I will get no sleep – yet I have to go on – I have to make them laugh. Only tomorrow, when I fall over, it won't be a performance, it will be exhaustion!'

'Just one? Drink, I mean,' Noel says.

'Now? I cannot. And you – your work? You can leave just like that?'

'No, not like that. I can't leave until everyone else does. But I could slip away now, for a pint, and no one would notice, I'm telling you.' Jago says he wishes he could, but the circus has left, and he must catch up with it.

'And the poor camel?' Noel says.

'That poor camel is stronger than the both of us. He could hold out for weeks, I tell you. Don't worry, I will make a call, and make sure they are coming to collect tonight.' Jago holds out a huge hand, and gives Noel a heartfelt farewell.

'Take me with you,' Noel says under his breath as Jago heads for Cork Street, where he says his car is parked – if it hasn't been stolen already.

Noel puts his fingers through the fence, and the camel reveals a huge tongue that makes him flinch. He looks back at the Community Centre, where there's a steady stream leaving. He'd better show his face, or doubtless one of them will be putting in another complaint. In his pocket, his phone vibrates, but it can wait. It'll only be Etna, wondering what time he'll be home, so that she can have his dinner ready. He has to hand it to his wife, her devotion is never in doubt. Although, there might be news of Rita, their daughter, their *nineteen* year-old daughter, currently lying in a maternity ward waiting for her world, and theirs, to be turned upside-down. Some people at nineteen could be mistaken for thirty, but not Rita. In Noel's mind, she opened her legs for the first boy that came along, and now look at her. And the boy? Nowhere to be seen. She wouldn't even give up his name, let alone attach any blame to him. She's delighted, of course, or *was* until the first cramps came along, and then the morning-sickness, and other associated side-effects of a few moments of ecstasy. Needless to say, the effect of all this on Etna was considerable, to say the least, and the woman was fragile enough to begin with.

Marie is waiting for him at the entrance, agitated as ever, and in no mood for mercy.

'You went on your ten-minute break half an hour ago,' she says. He looks at his watch, as if it will make any difference.

'I'm – sorry,' he says through gritted teeth. He could punch her, and not give it a thought. Just wind her, surprise her, show her he wasn't to be taken lightly. She'd think twice about taking him to task again – if she didn't fire him on the spot, *if* she'd recovered from the blow, that is. And he wants the job, if only because it gets him out of the house.

'We need to have a serious chat over the next couple of days,' she says ominously. *Let's have it now*, he thinks, but she's distracted by her phone, and tells him she has to go.

Finally, fucking alone – and in charge. The care*less* taker enters his domain, wary of stumbling over the odd stray. There's always one, or sometimes two, as when the occasional boy and girl lock themselves in the toilet, and screw like rabbits. He gives the place a cursory run-over, not being in the mood tonight – is he ever? There are no dossers setting up home, no visible rats, though they're clearly there. He checks the locks, and starts to hear the voices. They are dead spirits calling him to order, or calling him home, but he won't answer them, and they haven't betrayed him to Marie yet, as far as he knows. There's more than enough *living* traitors to do that.

The class walls are littered with artistic follies. Therapy through art, they call it, giving the troubled youth a means of self-expression. Noel studies their efforts – *they're just taking the piss*. In his mind, the 'troubled' youth are simply being given a free pass. Whatever they do is excused, and rewarded. He'd reward them in a quite different way. Nothing wrong with a bit of corporal punishment, nothing too extreme, but more than a slap on the wrist, or detention, or a few Hail Marys.

With the heating off, the building quickly becomes a freezer. The voices get louder as the spirits become more agitated. He puts on the alarm, locks the main door, and lights up as daylight fades.

He takes the long way home, which brings him to Echlin Street, in the shadow of Guinness, and the Old Harbour pub. A safe harbour, a haven for lost souls, where the phrase 'just one' is banned, as well as being misunderstood. The quiet is deceptive, the anger and violence is held at bay by regular patrons who know when and where to use them. '*...come in, she said, I'll give you shelter from the storm...*' The lyrics, the only ones he ever recalls, strike him every time he crosses the threshold, but there's a storm inside too, which he, fortunately, is a part of. He isn't so much welcomed as tolerated. There is something comforting about drinking in an establishment that frightens the casual visitor away. Of course, the odd tourist group wanders off the path now and again, and ends up there, expecting a five-course lunch, and the craic. They invariably call during the day, when they're safer, but the food is nothing to write home about, and the atmosphere is more *crack* than *craic*.

A mouldy piper is squeezing out a tune, and squeezing out *of* tune. The addition of a tin whistle does little to improve the musicality, not that anyone cares. One, two, three, in quick succession, goes down so smooth, he hardly even notices, and his whole chest feels warm, and the music is starting to make sense, and Rigsby is digging him in the ribs, as is his wont, and ribbing him about 'mount' Etna. It's the oldest joke in the world, he's heard it a thousand times, yet he always laughs. It's a very different Etna they make jokes about, not the one waiting at home for him. There's a Luke Kelly lookalike adding his voice to the entertainment. He has the red hair, and the beard, but not the voice.

'Another?'

'Go on, then.' Jesus, look at the time. She'll kill him. Except, she won't. The fight's gone out of her in the last couple of years, he's noticed. Between bouts of coughing, she hasn't got much left for berating him. He leaves the last pint unfinished, says goodbye to no one in particular, and no one in particular returns the favour. He has a smoke on the doorstep, lingering as long as possible, glancing up at Guinness, where he used to work, where he thought he'd always work until he retired. He was let go for 'excessive tardiness,' or in other words, for being a lazy bollocks. The proximity of the Old Harbour didn't help, especially in the days when you could smoke as well as drink without having to leave the premises.

Out of smokes, he has no choice but to head home.

Noel met a man once from Pimlico, London, and the comparisons with his own Pimlico, Dublin, made for sorry listening.

The house looks empty, as if she's already gone to bed. It's not that late, is it? There's a plate of cold Shepherd's Pie in the oven, and he hasn't the heart to reheat it. His stomach turns just looking at it. He sits at the kitchen table, and has a quiet smoke, contemplating his upcoming 'serious' chat with Marie. He knows what that means. He also knows what it might mean to have a daughter return home with a bawling, shitting sprog in tow. The bed creaks in the room above him. He prays she doesn't wake, though that rarely happens.

Tomorrow night is quiz night in Arthur's, she's normally up for that, and generally improves the mood between the two of them. That's something to look forward to, isn't it? He's never brought her to the Old Harbour, and he doubts she'd ever want to visit.

She's very much awake, as it happens. He opens the bathroom door to find her squatting on the bowl, the nightdress pulled up around her waist. There are some things a husband never wants to see.

'Why don't you lock the door?' he barks. Even that mild rebuke brings her to the edge of tears.

'Rita was asking for you,' his wife says, taking a handful of paper from the roll. 'She was wondering why you haven't been in?'

'She doesn't want me there,' Noel tells her

'Of course she does,' Etna cries. 'Did you get your dinner? Wasn't too dry, was it?' Time was, she would have hurled accusations like confetti.

'Yeah, it was fine. Now, can I use the toilet, please? If you're quite finished?' She squeezes past him, and, momentarily, intimacy and revulsion collide.

He undresses in the dark, and slips in quietly beside her, knowing it's futile. The moment he turns away from her, and closes his eyes, she kicks off.

'She's not doing well, love. She says she is, but I can see she's not. She wants me in there with her, in the delivery room. How can I do that? I don't think I'm up to it. When I think of her up there now, lying awake, with that baby pushing against her, desperate to get out.'

'Why don't they just take it out?' Noel says. 'What are they waiting for? If she's not up to it, isn't there a danger to the baby to let her have it naturally?'

'Oh, don't say that!'

'I'll go see her tomorrow – during my lunch-hour, though she'll probably have had it by then.' *And that's when the real problems begin.*

'Will you?' Etna asks, delighted. 'She'd love to see you. She was only saying...' His wife settles down, but Noel can't find sleep anywhere. He turns over on his stomach, and gently nudges her in the back. Her hand moves across his torso like a writhing snake, until it finds what it's looking for. Noel holds his breath until the blessed release, and afterwards, he cleans himself off with a tissue which he leaves on the chair beside the bed. It will be hard in the morning, and easier to dispose of. It's an arrangement that suits them both, that came about without any discussion. His increasing reluctance to touch her increasingly skeletal body, not to mention her dentures, and her heavily-stained fingers, made her realise that if she didn't do something, then neither would ever experience anything of that sort again. And so, through fumbling experimentation, a compromise was found, and repeated, perhaps once or twice a week.

'Do you have any money?' she asks him over breakfast. She has a cleaning job of her own, but spends all of her pitiful salary on Rita, and their forthcoming grandchild. Noel hands her a tenner, and she takes it without comment. While he's had two smokes this morning, she's had at least six. She splutters her words, and coughs out the last few syllables. He can hear her chest faltering. He knows how it's going to end for her, she's been warned often enough, and he doesn't want to be there when it happens. And they're about to bring a baby into this cesspit. Rita will foist the child on his wife when things get tough, which will be constantly, hastening Etna's already perilous downward spiral. Noel is the font of all wisdom in his own household. It's only when he steps outside that the world steps on him. Yet he can't wait to get out of there.

'You *are* going to see her at lunchtime, aren't you?' she asks before he leaves.

'I said I would, didn't I?' Hopefully she'll have had it by then, or they'll have pulled it out of her. Thing is, he never knows what to say to Rita. She always looks at him with expectant fondness, but he can't reciprocate. He can't say what he feels about her, because he doesn't know anymore. *Does* he still love her? Probably, but he's definitely disappointed in her, or for her. And she in him.

⌣⌢

Rita, lovely Rita, rotten apple of his eye, putting the load on Etna's slender frame. His daughter's daughter, delivered by caesarean, finally, doesn't have a name yet, and living in a plastic tube for the time being. *Grandad* doesn't sound so grand. Noel crumbles at the sight of Rita, a child herself, and Etna's not much better. The future is here and now, and stretches to bleak infinity. He's next to useless to the two women, or three now, as it is. Rita offers to show

15

him the stitches, in a druggy voice, but she falls back asleep before he can decline the offer. There'll be a scar there, inside and out. He buys his wife a milky coffee in the Coombe's canteen, dying for a smoke. Or maybe just dying. Etna trembles at the prospect of bringing the new-born home.

'We're not ready for this,' he tells her, but she shakes her head, and won't hear of it.

'Where else can she go?'

Nowhere, they both know. Their daughter's finances are, as far as they know, as perilous as their own, but somehow it's all going to work out, as if by magic.

'You still on for the quiz tonight?' he asks. 'Might be the last chance we get for a while.'

'No, I can't leave her. And anyway, I wouldn't be in form, not while she's lying here. *When* will they let her hold her own baby?'

'How the hell do I know? When she's stronger, I guess,' Noel suggests. 'Listen, I better get back to work.'

'You won't be late, will you? You won't go drinking?' There's desperation, not accusation, in her voice.

'I shouldn't be,' he says. He pats her on the shoulder, and heads for the exit. In the harsh light of a late summer afternoon, Noel strikes the match, though he's on his last box, and real ones are becoming harder to find. He better make the most of them. Cigarettes, in his mind, taste sweeter when lit by matches rather than cheap lighters. Back to work it is, then. Some men have all the luck.

⌣

The camel is gone, and has been replaced by an old bathtub, unless God played a cruel trick on the abandoned beast.

The insults ring louder, and cruder, this afternoon, for some reason. And the indifference of the staff is more pronounced, as if Marie has been bad-mouthing him again. Maybe she's told them, inadvertently or not, that he won't be there for much longer. It wouldn't be the first time the poor unfortunate employee is the last to know his fate.

They're playing football with the snooker balls, and writing graffiti on the plaster with the darts. They're splashing the paint around instead of creating with it. They're giving him the finger, and dumping their chip bags right in front of him, trying to provoke. Wankers, each and every one of them. Any half-decent teenager, with an ounce of sense, wouldn't come anywhere near the Centre, for fear of catching something.

No sigh of Marie, thank Christ, but you'd think she could have tidied up before she left. She's supposed to set an example, isn't she? But her desk is tilting to one side with all the stuff piled high upon it, and then there's the floor space, of which there is none anymore. What does she have in all those fucking boxes? How does the scatty mare ever find anything?

'What are you doing in here?' one of the 'creative' volunteers – Violet, isn't it? – asks him.

'I thought Marie was in here. She said she wanted a word with me,' Noel argues.

'Well, she's not here, is she?'

'Then she should lock her door,' Noel suggests. 'And tidy up while she's at it.'

'Don't you have something else you could be doing?' Violet asks aggressively. Yeah, Noel thinks, I could be entertaining you in the staff room, if you'd let me. That is quite a ring on her finger, but she's not bad-looking and he wouldn't say no if she obliged.

'Yes, I have better things to be doing,' he tells her.

They're unbearably slow to leave that leaving, and his resentment festers like an untreated sore. He has an idea, but it's a building without foundations. He needs to give it more thought, and that means a cigarette, or two, but he's not due a break for twenty minutes. Longest twenty minutes he's ever experienced, but they're worth it, because by the time he's outside, smoking as if it's his last, the ideas are steamrolling in, almost lifting him off the ground with excited possibility.

There'll be no sinking at the Old Harbour tonight, or ever, if Rita has her way. He has an unexpected yearning for a glass of rum, or two, just the hit, and the warmth, of it. To steel himself for the coldness of home. And where is Rita, and what's-her-name, going to fit, when all is said and done? There is a room, but it was never intended as a bedroom for two, even though there's a new bed in there. And who'll run when the kid starts screaming? Etna? Walking to Arthur's usually has her complaining about her legs for days afterwards. And he's never seen her run, not even in her youth. Or did he imagine that, her youth?

'Hey, stop daydreaming.' Violet again, informing him that he can lock up.

'Oh, can I? That's very kind of you. Since when did you become the boss of bosses?'

'When I realised what a waste of space you are,' she says bravely. He's at least a foot taller, and several stone heavier, and he could crush her like an insect under his foot, but she's got a set on her, he has to admit. Noel bows, and she stomps away, practically running to her car.

It's no longer an idea, just a fact yet to happen. Not long now, though. He's not waiting for it to get dark, though, because that sky doesn't look like it's in any hurry to leave. He lights one up, and figures on enjoying all of this one before putting the plan into operation. At least there won't be any camel witnesses.

A few things to sort out first, though. Turn off the smoke alarm, and leave the main alarm off. The cameras are nothing to worry about, as they haven't worked for months. Now, where to begin? It's obvious, when he thinks about it. Her own fault, for leaving such an unsightly, and flammable, mess. He imagines it in slow-motion, like a movie, as the match is lit, and falls gracefully onto the mound of papers.

It doesn't quite work out like that. The first match is a damp squib, and his hammering heart is in danger of going before he can light the second.

Success! It happens so quickly, the flames spreading with astonishing speed across the desk and onto the floor, that he wants to take it back but knows he can't. The consequences for him are now set in stone, in flames, and it makes little difference whether it's just her office that's destroyed, or the whole building. He continues to stare as the fire gather pace, and licks at the soles of his shoes.

He reaches the street, and closes the door behind him, carrying a heavy burden that will soon be shared with the whole neighbourhood. There's a flood behind his eyes, through which he looks for his wife and daughter – and granddaughter. He couldn't face living with them, but now they'll have to live without him. Etna won't last a month, and Rita will dissolve into herself, meaning the baby will have to be shipped off to strangers, and probably better prospects.

He listens at the door for a moment, to the snap and crackle. It's getting closer, and there's smoke starting to sneak out through the gap at the bottom.

He heads for Cork Street, in a limping run, with pains in his chest, and a stinging calf muscle. There is orange on the horizon, there is beauty and promise, and hope, and decent people, and – family. But it's too late.

His only thought is to get as far away as possible, as fast as his aging limbs will take him. Crossing Cork Street is the first objective, and he'll take it from there. Will someone in the Old Harbour do him a favour without asking too many questions? Does he know any of them that well? Nobody talks to anyone much in there, not about anything important, anyway.

Cross the road first, then worry about the next part of the puzzle.

Cross, as quickly as possible, and *don't* look back.

Cross Cork Street, without looking, too many other things on his mind…doesn't see, or hear, it coming. But when he does, it's already there, and…*boom.*

The car hits him at speed, at waist height, almost slicing him in two. Noel chokes on his own blood, still dying for a smoke, still dying, and the first responders take no notice of the black smoke pouring out of the building on nearby Ormond Street.

The Prizefighter

It's an unfortunate business that brings him to Dublin for the first time. He steps off the Belfast train, walks through Connolly Station, and out into a city he's too numb to really see. Lennie's here to see his brother, though his brother, sadly, won't be seeing him.

He might have preferred it if the walk to his destination had been longer, to allow him more time to make sense of what's about to happen. What *is* about to happen? It only happens in fiction, to other people, doesn't it? And he has a fight coming up in two days' time, or *did*, until the news broke. He was all set, he was right on the weight, and everything, one hundred and forty seven pounds on the nose, never been in better shape, for boxing, that is. But not this. No one can ever be in proper shape for the likes of this. He could have done with Pauline being with him, but she was having none of it. She was sorry to hear what had happened to the brother, but not even death could overcome years of resentment, not to say outright contempt. And she wasn't the only one, he knew. Lennie, more than anyone, knew his brother's failings. He'd seen them at close hand for over twenty years, so nobody could tell him anything about Derek that he didn't already know in his heart. And now Derek's has stopped beating, and he'll never bother anyone again. She said she'd go to the funeral, but there was no way she was going with him to view the body.

He's early, and he could do with a proper coffee after that swill on the train. He's tempted by the sugary confectionary on offer, especially now that he has no fight to prepare for. He conceded the bout, and the purse, and the ranking points – but what does any of that matter? He's surprised he has any appetite at all, in the circumstances, but he saw both his parents through painful ends, so maybe they toughened him up. He's also tempted by that young woman at the counter. It's always the same around the time of a fight, when he generally abstains from sexual activity, or cuts down anyway. And Pauline, it had to be said, had been giving off strange signals of late. To say things had cooled down in that area would be something of an understatement. Years together, and years of failing to get pregnant, does that to a couple. It's her fault, it's his fault, it's both their faults, but the split could be seismic, and he's been casting a wayward eye in recent months, though he hasn't, as yet, acted on it. He prides himself on being a disciplined athlete, in and out of the ring.

He was early, now he's late. He'd better get a move on, or – what? Will they keep Derek on ice until a relative shows up? If Lennie doesn't show, then the body will be in the freezer until Judgment Day because he's the end of the line, the last of the McSorleys. Unless Derek had fathered children neither he nor Lennie knew about.

This must be the place. It reeks of desolation, and no amount of gleaming surfaces and pastel shades can cover that up. He announces himself to the rather vague girl at reception, who blandly takes note of his details and asks him to take a seat.

He takes a seat, finding it hard to imagine that Derek is through the door there somewhere, behaving himself. That would be a first. His brother was born screaming, and making merry hell, and never changed throughout the course of his short, but eventful, life. Strange emotions are lurking around the corner, and Lennie is aware of them. He has been caught by the odd unexpected blow before, but they've never felled him, only stunned him momentarily, and he's always been able to shake them off. Until now.

A weary-looking man in white medical garb comes into the main office, looking around as if he's lost his dog.

'This is Mr. McSorley,' the girl says to him. He turns to Lennie, and sticks out a hand.

'I'm sorry, Mr. McSorley, but I'm afraid to say that we're not quite ready for you.'

'You mean he's not quite dead yet?' Lennie says dryly.

'What? – no. No, I mean....we have some more...we are a little behind today, if I'm being honest. Short-staffed. I can only apologise. I hope you haven't had to travel too far.'

'Belfast,' says Lennie. 'When *will* my brother be ready?'

'Well, it could be another hour or so. Rather than waiting here, why don't you go somewhere more...comfortable, and we'll call you when it – he – is ready. Would that be okay?'

'I guess it'll have to do, won't it?' says Lennie brusquely.

'I can only - .' Lennie holds up a hand.

'*Stop* apologising,' he tells him.

He goes back to the café, but the second cup doesn't taste the same, and the pastry is sweet enough to make him gag. He keeps checking his phone every other minute, betraying his anxiety. Not even a message from Pauline. Will she still be there when he gets back? Outside, there's a chill in the air that wasn't there earlier. He doesn't want to wander too far in case they call, but on the other hand, he needs to see something more cheerful than the side of the morgue.

He pauses on the steps of Store Street Garda station, considering going in and making a complaint. He also has questions that needs answering. He has a contact name, a detective who told Lennie to give him a call when he arrived. He would, he said, tell him what he could about the events that led to his brother's fatal stabbing. All so…predictable, Lennie thought.

A knife in the belly, a criminal cliché, common as shite among the fraternity of drug offenders everywhere. If Derek had survived the assault, Lennie might have given him a slap just for being so stupid. He veers away from the station, and makes his way towards the river, where the broader horizon gives him a chance to breathe. The stiff breeze off the water knocks a bit of sense into him. He calls Pauline instead of waiting for her to call him, but she's not answering, and he doesn't leave a message. He calls his manager, Monty Foster, to find out if a new fight has been arranged anywhere. He'll fight anywhere, he told him. Lennie *has* fought anywhere, and everywhere, mostly on the east coast of the United States, where he lived for a few years, where every boxer worth his salt has to live if they want to establish themselves. Philadelphia was his favourite spot, though it could be cruel in the winter. He didn't want to leave, in truth, but Pauline was anxious to go home, and *start a family* there, she declared. Start a family – what a success that turned out to be. He never fought a tougher opponent than Pauline in the fits of depression after another false alarm, or phantom pregnancy. She blamed the freezing Philly winter for lowering his sperm count, and he laughed in her face, until she slapped him.

Been everywhere, fought everywhere, except Dublin, and it only two hours down the track, and it being a town with a noble boxing heritage. There had been fights proposed, but the opponents were invariably journeymen slabs of easy meat that Lennie saw no point in taking on, even if the money made it worthwhile. He often wondered if his failure to visit Dublin had anything to do with his family's fervent

Protestant heritage that had, in truth, ended with the death of his parents. It wasn't as if he and Derek had ever shown any inclination to support the cause. His community's determination to protect their religion, by whatever means necessary, always struck Lennie as being absurd, and from his perspective, both sides were equally to blame for prolonging the misery. As for Derek, he only got involved if there was money to be made, making him a mercenary, and something of an oddity, as his circle of 'friends' incorporated everyone from senior IRA figures to Loyalists on the extreme fringes. He was admirably democratic in that way, and Lennie often marvelled at how he managed to survive playing for both teams at the same time.

Dublin is…just there, in front of him, but's it behind glass, he can't touch it. Perhaps he has to give it more than a couple of hours, not that he's particularly enthusiastic about staying longer than necessary. He could come back with Pauline, for a weekend, treat her, and try to bring her back onside.

His phone is deathly silent, in a portent of what's to come, in both his career and his domestic life. He makes a fist with both hands. There's no doubting it, the strength is waning. He's young, in boxing terms, but there's a hell of a lot of a mileage on the clock. Not that he can afford to slow down too much, though the recovery periods between fights have definitely started to lengthen. His face has survived relatively intact, but his abdomen has often resembled a tortured rainbow, and Lennie has sometimes thought the sky would never clear.

He wanders back towards the train station, checking the times of later departures. He won't get back until late, but it's not as if he has any immediate appointments to keep. Arrangements to make, of course, and he'll need Pauline's help with that. There won't be a will, unless Derek had a premonition, and did the necessary. What need of a will, though, if there was nothing to leave behind? He thought he'd be heading back now, and he could still make it if he tried. What difference would it make to his brother now?

He leaves the station before he weakens, and heads straight back to the morgue, and the indifferent receptionist. Her personality hasn't altered in the time he's been away, but he thinks the working environment might have something to do with it. She's an animal at the weekend, he reckons.

'They're ready for you now…I think,' she says, lifting the phone.

They're ready for him, but he's not ready for them – for *him*.

Derek has in death what he never had in life. The chase is over, and he's been caught, but he can finally relax. Lennie almost envies him. The medic and the detective are talking, possibly to him, but he can't understand them. Lennie feels like he's lost a limb, that they've hacked off a piece of him, and brought him in to have a look at it. A butcher showing off his cuts of the day. His brother – his *brother* – they fought like dogs. Took different paths, inevitably. Derek didn't want an older brother showing him the way, because Lennie didn't know the way. And now he's there, he looks happy with what he's found. Lennie will have to wait a bit longer to get there. Maybe Derek had it sussed, take the shortcut, however hairy. He rang Lennie once after a fight, to ask his brother why he hadn't steamed in from the opening bell and buried that black American fucker. Lennie tried to explain, about tactics and such like, but Derek was having none of it. The phone was slammed down, and Lennie didn't hear from his brother for months. He sneaked back into Belfast one Christmas night, and into Lennie and Pauline's house, where they found him next morning, cooking breakfast and looking right at home. He was clean that time, clear-eyed and focused, charming Pauline with his plans for the future, which was something about second-hand cars, but he was gone by lunchtime without a word, and that was it until – now.

He looks like a lightweight on the slab, Lennie thinks, although he can't see most of the torso. Would they show him the rest if he asked? Does he *want* to see it? A single stab in the lower abdomen, is what he was told. How bad can it be? He's seen worse. Remember that bruise he left on Derek when he came into the gym that time? He had doubted Lennie's ambitions to become a professional fighter. So, he struts into the gym one day, interrupting a session, grabbing a pair of gloves, and promising to uncover the fraudulence of his brother's boxing credentials. Lennie indulged him, and danced around the ring as Derek flailed, throwing wild punches and stumbling over his own feet. Lennie patted him around the head a couple of times, but Derek wouldn't give up, not even when he was on his knees dry-heaving and out of breath. Lennie tried to help him, but Derek didn't want his brother's mercy, and stormed out, never to be seen near a boxing ring again. As far as Lennie knew, his brother never watched him fight in the flesh.

Love? Lennie slapped a few bullies on Derek's behalf, if that's what love is. Not that Derek appreciated the help. He'd go straight back into the lion's den, apologising for his brother, and take further punishment.

Lennie used to agree with those who said that Derek was missing something – and they were friends of his. But now he thinks that Derek might have possessed something they didn't have. He was fearless, reckless, stupid, obviously, but he threw himself out without a parachute while the rest were cowering in the plane, *just to see what it was like*. Can he touch him? Did he ever touch him, in affection? Was there a moment when they hugged, for no other reason than that they were brothers? They were united in one cause, at least, against their parents, although they loved them both severely. They loved the people, but not the people's doctrines. Derek burned the Union flag on one memorable occasion, just for a laugh. He was nearly flayed alive for that one, but always said it was worth it. He threw bricks in riots, and charged baton-wielding policemen, without a shred of Christian faith, or political affinity. He was there because it was happening, it was the front line of whatever war was being waged, and he needed to be there, to breathe in the fumes. He'd eagerly have a taste of it, and spit it out afterwards, before moving on to the next dish.

His relentlessly curious and impatient mind couldn't function on its own, though, and medication proved the answer. It was a higher calling he could really believe in, and he quickly became a devout believer. A user and abuser, retailer, wholesaler, he went the whole hog, covering all the bases, and suffered the consequences. Lennie learned all this second-hand. Derek's name was known around the parish, and well beyond. Lennie knew the dangers before Derek did. A series of arrests followed, and the first of several short sentences, but he came out smiling, and stuck his hand right back in the fire. Lennie wouldn't visit him in prison, even at his parents' beckoning. Pauline did, surprisingly enough, declaring her fondness then for Derek despite his flaws. *I thought you were the tough guy*, she said to Lennie, branding him a coward. Lennie suffered in his next fight, hesitating fatally on several occasions, as her words rang in his ears, and he was counted out before the end, the first and last time that ever happened. Derek, meanwhile, lost most of his battles, but kept going back for more…and kept going back for more.

Where's Pauline now, when *he*, Lennie, needs her? Who's the coward now? She changed her tune over the last few years, as Derek's act became an increasingly degrading spectacle. And maybe, just maybe, she suspected there was something of Derek in Lennie. Because what was Lennie but a slightly more refined version of his brother. He was still a brawler, even if he got paid for it.

He could stay looking at his brother forever, and the answers would never be forthcoming.

'Mr. McSorley?' He turns at the sound of the detective's voice. 'Do you need more time?'

'More time for what?' Lennie says. 'That's my brother there, and that's all there is to it.'

'Do you want to get out of here, then? Come on, I'll buy you a coffee.'

Bye, Derek. See ya soon.

⌒

Detective Carroll keeps looking at his watch. Lennie tells him he doesn't need looking after.

'Sorry,' says Carroll. 'Are you heading straight back?'

'Probably,' says Lennie. Why only *probably*? 'Is there any more news about what happened?'

'The investigation is ongoing, as we say. It's early days, but we have a few good leads. They're a relatively small community – the drug fraternity. We know who they are, but it's not always easy pinning anything on them. We just shake a few trees, and wait for the rotten fruit to fall.'

'Had my brother been active here long?'

'No – first time we've come across him. He was obviously looking for new markets, and trod on a few toes.'

'He's been known to do that,' says Lennie.

'The reason I asked whether you were heading straight home or not is that sometimes, victims' relatives think they can help by doing their own investigating – and we like to discourage that kind of thing. I hope you don't mind me being direct, Lennie.'

'I'm not my brother, if that's what you're worried about. We have always followed different paths in life.'

'I'm glad to hear it,' says Carroll. 'I have heard, though, that you can handle yourself.'

'I don't play with knives, detective, or guns, or anything of that kind,' Lennie says firmly.

'Hey, I wasn't suggesting anything of the kind. But it's my duty to point out the lay of the land.'

'I understand,' says Lennie. 'Can you tell me, at least, where it happened? I'd like a picture of it in my mind.'

'Less than a mile from here. On North Strand, as you head out of the city. A fairly grim spot, to be honest. Ossory Road. Like the people who operate there.'

'I thought it might be,' says Lennie. The detective stands up, and tells Lennie they'll keep in touch.

'You'll want to bury him in Belfast, I assume?'

'Where else,' says Lennie, dreading the work that lies ahead in arranging it all.

'Well, you'll receive official confirmation when the body is released,' says Carroll, his job done. 'It shouldn't be long – possibly even today, if they get the paperwork done.'

'I appreciate it,' says Lennie, shaking the detective's hand.

He should be going, so what's keeping him? The station's just over the road. But something's amiss. He should keep his brother company, and not leave him there like that, on his own. There's nothing from Pauline, or anyone else for that matter. Shitters, every one of them. Leave it to Lennie. They'll turn up at the church, all right, shed tears, and share false memories of their beloved lost friend, Derek. He's half a mind to find the nearest crematorium, and throw his brother on the spit.

Lennie shivers, and the sun's out, and people are peeling off layers, so it can't be the cold. He tries the closest bar to hand, Cleary's, and dives into its welcome shadows. Nobody pays him a mind, and he asks for a brandy. It shoots straight to the spot, but he switches to Guinness, and starts to relax. A bowl of soup is next on the menu, and he's quite happy to pass an hour or two there.

The light is gone when he emerges, and the cold is real this time. The morgue is still only a hair's breath away, and he's not ready to leave him yet. Without any luggage, he checks into the North Star Hotel, bemused at his own behaviour. He's a reluctant traveller in a foreign land, climbing under the covers without undressing, and leaving the light on…just in case.

He texts Pauline to say he won't be back. He doesn't try to explain, and she doesn't even call.

Every time he closes his eyes, he doesn't just see Derek on the table, he *is* Derek. And if he does sleep, he might never wake up. Lennie gets up, against his body's wishes, and a feeling of dread overcomes him. There's something in the room with him, or it's just outside the door, or it's waiting for him down in the street. He showers, but he's not alone. There's no choice but to leave. He's hungry, ravenous, but the restaurant is closed, and the hotel bar is too full.

He heads up Talbot Street, finding a fast-food outlet, which he quickly regrets, as the chicken goes down, but refuses to stay down. The toilets aren't for dreaming, but anyway, he manages to get rid of most of it. Back towards the hotel, but he doesn't stop there. If Derek doesn't leave him be, he'll end up doing something stupid.

Cleary's isn't for visiting at this hour of the day, so he goes further, up Amiens Street, and in the direction, he assumes, of North Strand – and the scene of the crime, if he can find it. If he wants to find it.

Less than a mile, the detective said. Lennie's sure he's gone too far. He crosses two bridges, and reaches what he discovers to be Fairview Park. The nocturnal animals are hard at work, some of them human. There is a young man shadow boxing at the edge of the trees, but he doesn't look like a fighter, more like a man with a grudge who's getting in some practice. Wary of asking for directions, Lennie goes back the way he came, trying to remember precisely what Carroll told him. But he may not have been paying complete attention.

He stops just before Newcomen Bridge, and, almost by accident, finds Ossory Road to his left. It doesn't take too long to find what he's looking for, as a length of police tape remains, marking the spot. That could be a stain on the ground, but he could be imagining it. Beyond the low wall lie the train tracks, with several tents spread across wasteland running alongside the water. Nothing good would bring Derek here. Lennie kneels at the spot, looking for his own clues as to his brother's stupidity. There's nothing here, and his head swims as he stands. He looks behind at the row of tiny houses facing the wall. There's an old woman watching him from the doorway, where she stands with a cigarette dangling from her mouth. She waves at him, beckoning him to come over. He stands his ground.

'Come in,' she says, moving back inside, leaving the door open, and offering him a glimpse into a narrow red hallway.

There are no formal introductions as she makes him tea. A skinny dog skirts around her ankles. A lurcher, he recognises, as Pauline's dad used to have one. Two cups rattle on the tin tray as she carries them into the poky sitting-room. She urges him to sit, and hands him the cup, with no milk or sugar in sight. There are leaves floating on the surface, so he sips it, being polite, still unsure why he's there. He owes her an explanation after such hospitality. After all, who invites a stranger into their house in the early hours, and makes them tea?

'I don't sleep,' she says. She has the voice of a much younger woman. 'I don't *ever* sleep. Nothing works, and I have tried everything, believe me. Aah, there he is!' The dog makes an appearance. 'My husband's favourite greyhound, before he passed away. He won several races up in Shelbourne Park – I have the trophies somewhere. We had other dogs over the years, but none like Luke here.'

'He's a lurcher, isn't he?' Lennie says, breaking his silence. The cup falls from the old woman's lap, such is her reaction.

'A *what?* Pure-bred Luke is! How dare you? What would you know anyway?'

'I'm sorry – I thought – someone I know had one, a lurcher, that is. I didn't mean.'

'Lurchers are mongrels,' she declares, 'Monsters!' She grabs Luke in a choke-hold, digging her fingers into his ribs. The dog whines until she lets him go, and then she lifts her cup, and goes to make herself another tea. He should leave, he should never have accepted her invitation. He stands, thinking about slipping out while she has her back to him. But she reads his thoughts, and turns like a ballerina, carrying a cup now overflowing with tea.

'You're not going, are you? Oh, please, forgive me. My manners are appalling. It's just…talking about my husband…I get upset…Will you stay?' Lennie reluctantly sits back down. She moves over next to him on the sofa, putting a hand on his knee. 'When I saw you out there…you reminded me of a young Ernie…the way you were standing…I…'

'My brother…was stabbed there, two nights ago. I'm sure you know about it. You didn't see anything, did you?'

'Oh, no,' she says. 'Boys are always fighting out there.'

'But you didn't see…my brother, did you?' She shakes her head, as if refusing to be drawn into it.

'They knocked on my door, asking me questions. And not for the first time. The *noise* of the ambulance, and the police cars. Why do they have to make such noise? The damage has already been done, hasn't it? So why do they have to wake the whole neighbourhood?'

Lennie puts his cup on the side of the sofa, where it teeters precariously. He tries to stand without knocking it over.

'I have to go. Thank you for the tea.'

'But, you look so tired,' she says. 'Stay a few more minutes. You should rest. You can't carry all that around with you, it's too much. You should give it more time.'

'I have to get back. I have an early train in the morning.'

'Back to Belfast, am I right?'

'You're right,' he tells her.

'I went out with a man from Belfast once. From the Falls Road. I was working up there, just out of college. He was a very serious young man. What past of the city are you from?' He tells her. 'Oh, I don't know that area. Protestant, is it? I thought so. There's something about you that gives it away. You're not offended, are you?'

'Why would I be?' His eyelids are suddenly concrete slabs wanting to fall.

'And you said that was your brother out there? What brought him to the North Strand?'

'Drugs,' Lennie admits, surprised by own candour.

'Oh,' she says in that way of hers. 'And tell me about him? What was Derek like?'

Derek? Had he told her his name?

'Derek was…in trouble most of the time. He never learned from his mistakes. Made the same ones over and over.'

'And you tried to tell him, over and over, I bet?' Her voice has an angelic quality. Her dog now slides over to him, brushing against his knees, but when he tries to pet him, it bares its teeth and growls. 'Now, now, Luke, Lennie is our guest, we must be kind to him while he is with us.'

Lennie? He didn't tell her his name, he's sure of it.

'And now you're the last in the line, aren't you?' she continues. 'Your brother had no family of his own, and neither do you – no children, I mean. His passing means that there's only you left. That must be a terrible burden to carry.'

'How do you know…how could you…' The words dribble out of his mouth, barely having the strength to open his lips.

'Shush,' she says, putting an arm around him. 'Rest…rest.' She stands, and helps him lie down on the small sofa. His feet hang over the end, and his last memory is of her removing his shoes.

He wakes sometime later, alone in the room except for the dog. When he tries to sit up, his head splits open, and the dog launches an attack. He raises his fists to protect himself, but the animal gets through his weak defence, breaking the skin on his cheek, and drawing blood. The dog retreats, but only momentarily. It launches a second attack, but the bite has woken Lennie to the possibility of real danger, and this time he's ready for him. As Luke opens his jaws in anticipation, Lennie catches him with a strong left on the side of the head. The dog is stunned, and Lennie follows up with a second, decisive blow. Luke staggers, and falls, and shudders briefly before going still. Lennie staggers to his feet, the room spinning, and the blood trickling from the wound on his face. He reaches the front door, which is secured with half a dozen locks that appear to have rusted through lack of use. He loses a fingernail in his efforts to escape, and by the time he succeeds, the door is almost off its hinges.

It's dawn, but there's little help in the light as his legs betray him, and he can only manage a few yards, stumbling across the road and falling at the base of the low wall.

⌒

There's a blinding light pointed directly at his eyes. Several figures loom over him, two of them in uniform. They're asking him if he's alive. I think so, he whispers. It takes all of them to lift him, yet he wants nothing more than to be left where he is. They compromise and let him sit against the wall. They give him some water, and ask him if he's been drinking. Not a drop, he croaks, not mentioning the afternoon he spent in Cleary's. He puts a hand to his face, but there's no sign of injury.

'A dog bit me,' he says, his voice coming back. But little sense. Through their legs, he sees the boarded-up house directly in his eye-line.

'What was that?' one of the policeman says. They are soon joined by Detective Carroll, who kneels in front of Lennie.

'What are you doing here, Lennie?' he asks. 'I thought I told you not to get involved? Were you not listening?'

'There was an old woman…she asked me in, and made me tea…had a dog…a lurcher. She said…she said it was…'

Carroll takes Lennie's face in his two hands. 'Did you take something, Lennie?'

'Nothing,' Lennie tells him. 'I've never taken anything…I'm not my brother…*not* my brother. Help me up.' The detective lends a hand, but Lennie doesn't need it, using the wall as leverage. He looks down at the tracks. 'I have a train to catch. I have to get back. What time is it?'

'A little past four. And there won't be any trains for a few hours,' says Carroll. 'Have you anywhere to stay?'

'The North Star,' says Lennie.

'I'll give you a lift,' says Carroll, dismissing the others.

'No, I'll walk,' Lennie insists.

'You sure you'll be okay?'

Lennie looks down at the spot where his brother fell.

'I wanted to feel what it was like…for him,' Lennie says. 'I think I do now.' He rips off the police tape stuck to the wall, hands it to Carroll. 'I don't think you'll need this anymore. It's over. For both of us.'

Protest

Her vocation is in doubt. With each passing day, the commitment to her sister's cause seems increasingly under threat. The lack of progress, after months of unwavering dedication, walking miles over the same small patch of ground, is starting to hurt. The definition of insanity is repeating the same action over and over, and expecting a different outcome each time. If true, then she passed the point of no return weeks ago, and no amount of penance will bring her back. The charms of Kildare Street have long since waned. It is now a symbol of lost hope, and growing despair.

She uncovers the placard, and wedges the plastic bags between cracks in the wall outside Leinster House. The lettering could do with freshening up. She could do with a new sign, a more professional one, but the cost, when she last looked into it, was outrageous. Anyway, the message was clear, at least in her mind. It couldn't be misunderstood, even if few actually took the time to read it. Occasionally, well-meaning souls stopped to ask her why she was protesting, though their interest tended to fade quickly after she began to tell the unfortunate tale of her sister's lengthy, and painful, demise. Mostly, they were intrigued by the use of the word **murdered** on her sign. Perhaps they were looking for a more melodramatic explanation, clear evidence that the Taoiseach himself had pulled the plug on behalf of the government.

She's feeling the heat today, but she's reluctant to remove any layers. Her sister had been so prone to infection that she passed on the fear to Agnes. Her face is barely visible between the hat and the scarves, just the slit of the eyes that suspect everything they see. Vanity, too, is a grave sin in her mind, and she mustn't draw undue attention to herself, not when a grave injustice has been committed. The Garda says good morning, before doing his duty, and warning her that she, or any protester, is free to do so, but *not* if they obstruct the business of government.

'Are you listening, Agnes? Can you hear me under all those clothes?'

'I hear you. And let me remind you that the *business* of government includes murder, in case you hadn't heard.'

'I know the story. I don't need to hear it again. I am obliged to inform you about the laws of the land, and how they must be obeyed.'

Agnes puts a hand on the crucifix around her neck before anger can take hold, and she says something she shouldn't. The man is only doing his job. As she is only doing hers, with increasing frustration. God is with her, of course He is. He would never abandon her, but she's having difficulty understanding what He wants from her each new day. Not long ago, she would never have had cause to doubt herself, or Him. She closes her eyes and says a quick prayer, of supplication and forgiveness. She has obviously strayed from His path somehow, and angered Him. She must find a way back, so that she can hear Him clearly once more, and focus completely on Denise. Her sister's face is beginning to lose its clarity, and Agnes struggles sometimes to remember what she looked like. Not the face of her final few weeks, that was not a human face, as all traces of humanity had been stripped away, leaving the devil to feast merrily on the open wound. No, she's been searching for the sister of her younger days, the one that Agnes followed, in vain hope of replicating. That never happened, of course, as Demise stumbled along her chosen paths, never sticking to one long enough to find her true purpose.

(I'm following her still)

The sign feels heavier today, it won't sit comfortably in her hands. She nearly trips at one point, crossing in front of the gates, but a passer-by prevents her from falling. She's a pest, she knows, to the traffic, both human and mechanical, and it takes immense concentration on her part to ignore the distractions.

"The Govt. murdered my sister. Where is the justice?"

Reading the sign every now and again is vital to the replenishment of her belief. She believes what she has written, with every fibre of her being. There are an infinite number of just causes to be defended, but each individual can only fight their own, and give everything they have to it. She has given everything, or so she once thought…but what if it's not enough, what if there's more she could, *should*, be doing? She has asked, but He hasn't replied. She doesn't want revenge, so that can't be it. There is no eye-for-an-eye in her vocabulary, but justice, surely, is a Christian virtue. She is accusing the State of murder, and how else can it be described? They took money away from a disabled woman who could barely function as it was, forcing her into care, but there too, she was let down, as the cuts were also felt in that area, and Denise, a once vibrant, active woman, became acutely depressed, falling in on herself, and never returning. Agnes, her only relative, fought tooth and nail to give her a reasonable quality of life, but there were limits to what she could do. It took a toll on her own health, during which time Denise moved further out of reach, and death followed soon after. What Agnes couldn't do during her sister's life, she would endeavour to do after it.

Her shoes might need replacing, the soles are wearing down. Her left lower leg has been cramping lately, occasionally in the morning when she wakes, and she has to wait for the circulation to improve. She can't halt the aging process, and the day will come when she can't keep up the same pace – but she's not there yet, and even if that day comes, she will simply stand, against the wall if necessary. A man appears in front of her, raising a camera to his face. She wouldn't mind if they asked her permission. She has an urge to lash out, and smash the camera on the ground. She blushes at the thought, and apologises to God. She will pray for greater strength later, in the Pro-Cathedral, where she goes daily to do penance.

There are hands upon her, and she's been moved off the road.

'Agnes, you'll get run down if you're not careful!' The Garda looks sincere, and she notices the Minister's large black car. Tinted windows shield the occupants from the gaze of ordinary people, as if they were gods that could not tolerate human contact. They are untouchable, she realises, beyond the reach of the likes of her. They are separated by far more than steel and concrete. Her persistence is useless, in its current form – but what other form is there? What alternative means are at her disposal? She has made her case publicly, she has faced down the ridicule, and indifference, of the political class, not one of whom has deigned to speak to her during the long protest. Other protests, and marches, have come and gone, some more violent than others, with missiles thrown, and obscenities hurled, but only she has endured, something she has become aware of, though not with any pride. Those imposters have blown in, and out, full of sound and fury, but signifying nothing. Have any of them succeeded any more than her? Has any protester anywhere ever made any real difference, or is the act important in itself?

She is thirsty, but she's content to wait. She won't faint again, though, not after that embarrassing incident when the ambulance was called, and all that fuss was made, over nothing. Since then, she had made sure to eat a solid breakfast, although she had missed it this morning as she was running late. And that was another thing – she *never* missed her alarm call before, but this morning, nothing could pull her out of the dream, a dream that vanished from memory the moment she opened her eyes.

Her mother's watch tells her it's time to take a break. She adds on the minutes she lost that morning, and heads to the museum café for a soup and sandwich. Forced to leave the sign outside, she worries about it constantly, although who, in truth, would want to steal it? Afterwards, she walks over O'Connell Bridge, on her way to church, her spirits lifting at the prospect of being in His presence for a short while.

⌒

She can't hide her face in a place of worship. She is humbled by her own imperfections, which come into sharp focus when she kneels and bows her head. Denise comes to her then, intensely alive, and eager to tell Agnes about what she's been up to. Agnes giggles at some of the stories, with most being rude and foolish, and she fears the wrath of God. But her sister leaves as quickly as she arrives, before Agnes has had time to ask her forgiveness.

She is numb to the pleas of the man on the ground outside, but she is obliged to offer him a prayer for his salvation. There is a needle on the ground beside him, along with a rolled-up sleeping bag and a toilet roll. She is repulsed by the stink of him, the waste of him. She retrieves the placard from its resting place nearby, and considers striking him with it, ending his misery.

She carries the sign like a cross through the city, slung over her shoulder, where its sharp edge digs into the bone. She laments the carefree attitude around her, the abundant hedonism present in the dress and the language. Yet they look down on *her*, laughing at her for having a belief. Their day of retribution will come, while she lives hers each and every day.

She calls it a day early, the damp creeping under her clothes, wilting in the heat of battle. There's only standing room on the bus, where the sign causes distemper among the other passengers. Agnes presses her face to the window, blurred by the incessant rain. She nearly misses her stop, and her step, but the sign shows its usefulness as a crutch, and saves her from injury.

⌒

Her mother's house, her sister's house, now her house, although she thinks of herself as simply a guardian of their memory until she becomes one herself. She turns on the gas heater, when there's a perfectly good heating system that could warm the whole house. But she's reluctant to indulge, or spend the money, in case indulgence leads to selfishness. And selfishness leads to…*stop!* She slaps herself out of it, attending to more practical matters, like dinner, which tonight consists of her favourite beef stew, unfrozen, with bread and tea on the side. The heater only warms the lower part of her, and it occasionally makes her dizzy. She leaves the empty dish in the sink, meaning to clean it later. She puts on her coat, and settles down on the sofa to listen to an hour of classical music on the radio. She pulls down a book from the shelf – *The Buried Giant*, by Kazuo Ishiguro – determined to press on with it despite her difficulty with the violence inherent in the story. She soon lays it down, and the music fades from consciousness. Is she happy? And does she, or anyone, deserve to be? She once knew her place, and her purpose, but lately, she's been losing touch with it, like a feather drifting on the breeze. She's not doing enough, that's what it is. Her solitude is not a curse but a luxury. She is hiding from the world, not facing it. She has progressively withdrawn over the years, and succeeded only in losing faith, and alienating God. Her sister cries down from the heavens, in sympathy and pain. *It's not enough.*

In her teaching days, in Loreto College, she was feared for ruling with an iron fist, but those girls are doubtless reaping the benefit now. She was accused of cruelty, when in fact she loved her students with a fierceness that made her cry during lunch in the park. She was trying to protect them in later life by exposing them to the harsh realities. Perhaps she strayed over the line now and then, but it was all in a good cause. She broke down, and asked for their forgiveness on her last day. Since then, her contact with the outside world had become restricted to the bus driver and the girls at the supermarket checkout. And she was constantly looking for new ways to reduce even those meagre rations. That's not what He wants from her. That's not what Denise would have wanted, to sacrifice her humanity for a lost cause. And the cause *is* lost, isn't it? - because she's not doing enough. Either that, or give up entirely. Burn the sign, and use it as kindling for the fire she never lights – or start a fire out there. But what can she do but march up and down, and keep her sister's memory alive? She'll sleep on it, if sleep will come.

The shower before bed reveals more than the self-inflicted scars on her abdomen. It shows her losing weight, it shows the pelvic bone pushing out, and the grey hairs of her central region, an area untouched by anyone's hands but her own, and her mother, of course. The thought of a man being anywhere near it always sends a chill through her, and she would listen with increasing horror, and distress, whenever Denise decided to share more intimate details. *'It's the most natural thing in the world,'* her sister would say. *'The human race would cease to exist if everyone felt like you, Aggie.'*

The most *unnatural* thing in the world, Agnes still believes, despite acknowledging the facts of human biology. And not every woman is created with the aim of bringing new life into the world. She would create a monster, she's certain, if she was ever tricked or forced into bearing a child. Denise, on the other hand, dreamed from the time she started bleeding of producing a large brood, but a darker fate intervened, on a quiet Donegal road in the dead of night, leaving her paralysed, and helpless, and in the hands of the State – which proceeded to murder her, slowly.

I am there with her on the road, in that car, telling her to slow down, and turn down the music, and mind the oncoming traffic, but she's too full of energy and painkillers to take any notice of me. I put my hand on her arm, but it goes straight through her – but it's her who's real, not me. I have made this journey a thousand times, and the ending never changes. I can't save her. I climb out of the car before the crash, and crawl back into the fields, where I hide in the heather, and listen.....and listen.

I still can't save her.

She's not doing enough. Those bells are ringing at the breakfast table, deafening in their clamour. They are a call to arms – but where are her weapons?

⌣

She steps outside her front door, and into a hailstorm, which cuts through her layers, blinding her before she reaches the gate. But nothing will stem her flow today, as her veins tingle, her blood boils, with renewed vigour. God spoke to her during the night, when she stopped thinking, and let Him in. He will work through her, using his own just methods, and she must accept them, whatever the consequences.

It is a foul day, tormenting, nailing hopes securely to the ground. She could lift the sign with her mind, it feels so strong. She could make it fly. She bounces on her bruised calves, and welcomes the rain inside her shoes. And she waits, for the next instruction that will lead her towards the path to progress, and justice. The angels sing in the heavens, and Denise is in their choir, lending a hand. Agnes lifts her eyes to the black skies, ecstatic, until a piece of dirt lands in the corner of one eye, breaking the spell. She also realises that she will catch pneumonia if she doesn't take shelter. Buswell's hotel is her only option, although she fears the reception she might receive.

She has reason to fear. She can tell what the waiter thinks before he opens his mouth. He disapproves, clearly, of her appearance, her sign, her whole being.

'I'm afraid you can't bring that in here with you,' he says, meaning the sign.

'Where can I leave it, then?' she asks. She holds her ground until he finds a cloakroom where the sign can be placed out of sight. She then follows him into the bar, where she asks him for a pot of tea, if it's not too much trouble. She finds a seat in the far corner, where she can be as unobtrusive as possible. Unfortunately, it gives the waiter an excuse to ignore her, until she waves at him for attention.

'I ordered a pot of tea?' she says.

'It's on the way,' he says, scurrying off before he has to make any more promises he won't keep. And he doesn't keep the first one. She stands up, and blocks his path when he makes his next circuit of the room.

'Is that mine?' she asks about the tray in his hands.

'Yours is coming, madam,' he says through a grimace.

'You're lying,' she tells him straight. 'What have I done to upset you? Why won't you serve me?' She hates the aggressive sound of her own voice.

'I *will* serve you, if you'll just have patience,' he says, losing his own.

'Why don't I take this one?' she says, reaching for the tray, 'and you can simply get another.' The inevitable happens as they wrestle over the small pot of boiling water. Her hands are washed in the sins of her simmering anger, and she screams in agony as her skin comes under attack. Adding insult to injury, she stumbles back and crashes onto an unoccupied table, with the waiter reaching out too late to catch her. She is, perhaps, fortunate, in being too stunned to feel the full effects of the hot water.

Her hands are red with pain, and the man's words don't sound like any kind of prayer she has ever heard. She is lying down, and floating, with a sense of urgency. She won't confess until she has been accused. She will listen to her Protector, and *He* alone will guide her. She has an image of the sign burning like the cross in her hands. Was it the Holy Spirit making its presence known, sending her a message?

They've stopped. There is a sudden blast of air on her face as the doors are opened, and she's pushed forward into the light.

The man from the ambulance remains at her shoulder in A&E until she is officially registered as a patient. He is unfailingly polite, even cheerful, making jokes in the most absurd situation. Fragments are coming back to her. She vaguely remembers the argument – over *tea!* – resulting in her hands being injured. They sting, in degrees of discomfort which come and go like the tide. *Water* it was that caused this, and surely water is also the cure. Cold water would reverse the damage, wouldn't it? Why won't they come? And who are all these people? She thinks of prisoners waiting to board a ship bound for the colonies, where they will serve out their sentence in the harshest of conditions. And her – what use will she be with no hands?

She opens her eyes, to find her guard gone, and the fluorescent room teeming with gloomy silence. Others are in pain, she recognises, and more so than her. Some have abandoned hope, and scratch the arms of their chairs. Agnes holds up her hands, fascinated by the glowing limbs and her ability to endure without calling out for help. She closes her eyes again, hoping to hear Him, or possibly Denise, but she is abruptly interrupted by a solemn-looking nurse with a long day behind her. Agnes is moved to an armchair, where a dark-skinned doctor with tortured vowels treats her hands roughly before offering instructions to the nurse. She promises Agnes she will return in two minutes, but at least thirty pass before proper help is given, in the form of cream that has an immediate impact, cooling the skin instantly, and bringing joyous relief. She is further comforted by being informed that she should be released in a couple of hours, after the cream has had a chance to do its work.

'Where am I?' she asks the nurse, thinking it might be important.

'The Mater,' the nurse says before escaping to her next emergency.

The Mater? Only a ten-minute walk from the Pro-Cathedral. See, He was only a whisper away, bathing me in the light of His goodness. Across from her, a teenage girl lies in apparent agony in an actual bed. There are tears in the girl's eyes, and she stares at Agnes for sympathy. Agnes turns to the wall, reminded of Denise in the days after the accident, when the well of tears had run dry, with all hope extinguished by the subsequent news of her sister's paralysis. *I cannot give anything to you, little girl – my pity is reserved for someone else, she needs everything that I have to give.*

There is a tap on her shoulder, and a man is standing, then kneeling, beside her chair. He doesn't look like a member of staff.

'I'm sorry to disturb you here,' he says, looking oddly delighted at finding her. 'I lied, and told them I was a relative – not that they're really bothered.'

'I think you've made a mistake,' she says.

'I have your sign,' he tells her.

'My sign?'

'I took it from the hotel. I was afraid they'd throw it out.'

'I don't…' No, she *does* understand.

'I saw what happened,' he says. 'You're okay, I hope? It looked nasty from where I was sitting.'

'First-degree burns,' she tells him. 'Nothing serious. They're letting me out soon, I hope.'

'Do you need a lift somewhere? You probably shouldn't use public transport after what you've been through. Unless you live locally?'

'Conyngham Road,' she admits. Why is she telling a stranger this? 'But, wait a minute…who are you?'

⌒

He's right, she's not in the best condition to travel home alone. He suggests having a coffee, or some food, before she leaves. The canteen smells of nothing but hospital, but she's too tired to refuse. Whatever he is, he's a gentleman, holding her chair out, and carrying the tray to the table. She feels self-conscious wearing the gloves, and the skin underneath still stings, although it's turning into an itch. They have given her a prescription for more cream, which she intends using.

'I cover politics normally,' says the reporter who calls himself Donal Murphy. 'Buswell's has become a second home to me.'

'So why are you here with me?' she wants to know. Being in the company of a man brings added difficulties to an already traumatic situation.

'I told you – I saw what happened. I was concerned about you – and I was appalled by the way you were treated in there.'

'Oh, well…he was busy. I'm sure he wasn't just picking on me.'

'But I think he was,' the journalist argues. 'I've seen you out there, outside Leinster House, making your protest. He *was* picking on you.'

'I have no interest in politics,' Agnes declares. 'I only care about…'

'Your sister,' he finishes for her.

'My sister,' she says with raw emotion. Now it's the turn of her face to burn, with indignation and embarrassment. 'How do you know…about my sister?'

'I wouldn't be much of a journalist, now would I, if I couldn't find out who you were? You've paraded up and down Kildare Street for months. I have no idea how you do that. I admire it, genuinely. And when I saw what happened to you today…well, when the ambulance came, and I saw that you had nobody to accompany you, I decided to follow. I hope I haven't offended you?'

'But you have my sign?'

'I have your sign.'

⌒

She's never been collected from her house before, by a gentleman. Or been driven in a fancy car to a fancy restaurant, and bought lunch. There is a price, however, and it comes in the form of having to tell her story – not her sister's story, but *her* story, Agnes Miller, spinster of the parish, true believer, former teacher, still living in her parents' house, getting by on frugal means, and spending her days in futile protest outside government buildings. She has to tell everything, or he'll find it out himself, or invent it, and she couldn't have that. And why should she be ashamed of the way she lives her life? Her intentions are noble, even if she does fall short.

'I still don't understand – why you need to hear this?'

'I want to tell your story – and her story, Denise's. Be honest, how much progress have you made, if any? You've been out there so long you've become invisible. You are no different than a new tree being planted, or a sculpture being erected. After a while, it becomes part of the landscape, it's accepted, until people no longer notice it. Tell me, Agnes, how much notice has been taken of you, or your sister's case?'

'None,' she admits after a long pause.

⌒

She has listened, and He has answered, albeit in a most peculiar way. She is afraid, though, of what might happen, of what she might do, if she allows herself to be drawn along this path. She feels as if she's been hibernating for most of her adult life, and now she's poked her head above ground – it's intoxicating, if she's honest. She has made human contact, and enjoyed the sensation.

Her hands are like a new-born's, pink, tingling, curious. She uses them to lavish unusual care on her hair, in preparation for the arrival of Donal and the photographer. What was she thinking, agreeing to his ludicrous proposal? Permitting them to enter her home, and take her photograph – it's madness! Her hair won't cooperate, it's being left alone too long. And her only make-up is soap, not that she would ever consider using anything so garish as lipstick. Five minutes, that's all the time he said it would take. Wait till you see, once she lets them in, they won't want to leave. He, especially, will be sticking his nose into every nook and cranny, taking advantage of her kind nature.

She can't eat a thing. Even cereal which is mostly milk won't go down easily. She seeks solace in her crucifix, wrapping her fingers around it, closing her eyes, and looking for confirmation that she's doing the right thing. A knock at the door – *they're here!*

The journalist is different with her today, perhaps because he's brought a friend, the photographer, who gives her a caustic look, as if to say: *I have to photograph this?* She offers them tea, though she wants to get on with it, and hasten their exit. Donal wonders if he can have a look around.

'Why?' she asks, imagining him in her bedroom.

'The light,' Donal says, still rather distant with her. 'For the photograph.'

'I don't see why you have to make such a fuss.'

'What's in here?' he asks, opening the door to the front room. 'Perfect,' he says, calling the photographer in. They both agree immediately, and begin setting up before she has agreed to it.

'But this room is so cold in the mornings,' she argues.

43

'There – on the sofa, I think,' says Donal. 'Agnes, would you mind sitting in the middle of the sofa?' She follows his orders, against her better judgment, and feels distinctly uncomfortable with their eyes, and the lens, upon her.

'Like this?' she asks, bewildered.

'Sit forward, would you? And look straight at the camera. You don't need to smile, or anything like that.' She has no intention of smiling. 'I thought you always wore a cross?' he adds.

'You mean this?' she say, opening her hand to reveal the crucifix.

'That's it. Don't you normally wear that around your neck?'

'Not always,' she says. 'Would you *like* me to wear it?'

'If you don't mind. And – do you have a photograph of Denise?'

'I have several photographs of her,' Agnes says.

'I was thinking you could hold the photograph – she should be in it, shouldn't she?'

'Yes, she should.' *And no one else.* Agnes leaves the room with the idea of not returning. She will lock herself in her bedroom, and wait for them to leave. But when she finds her favourite photograph of Denise, she softens, and returns to the front-room emboldened. She will endure, and soon it will be over, and her life will be returned to her.

'That's perfect,' Donal says about the picture on her return. Agnes sits, and endures, clasping Denise to her bosom, and her heart. The photographer takes over, and takes a dozen or so shots before releasing her from the torment. He leaves before Donal, calming her nerves.

'Is that it?' she says.

'That's one part done, anyway,' he tells her. 'Now, can I give you a lift into town? I presume you're going in today, or are you still not up to it?' She holds up her hands.

'As good as new,' she says.

'Good. So, that lift?'

She yearns for him to leave her in peace, but the thought of that bus journey dismays her.

'What about my sign? You said you had it?'

'I do. But you'll have to come with me if you want it back,' he says, smiling. She gives in, reluctantly.

He turns into Molesworth Street, and stops outside the hotel, suggesting she wait in the lobby while he finds a parking spot.

'In there?' she says, unprepared.

'Yes, why not? I have a surprise for you – two, in fact. Go on, Agnes, it will be fine. I'll be two minutes, I promise. Nothing's going to happen to you, is it?'

It's a trap, she muses, mounting the steps, fearing the worst, feeling her cheeks flush, expecting a horned devil to be waiting for her inside. She doesn't want to take the chance, and waits for Donal to rescue her again.

He escorts her to a corner of the bar, and orders tea for two. The waiter is accompanied by the hotel manager, who offers her a fulsome apology on behalf of the establishment, and places an envelope in her hand.

'What's this?' she asks.

'A voucher, for a complimentary two-night stay – whenever it suits you. It's open-ended, and can be used at your convenience.'

'I have no need of this,' she says, handing it back.

'Please, Madam, we – I – insist. It is the least we can do after what happened.'

'What happened was an accident. And I suffered no serious injury, as you can see.' She shows him her hands. Donal intercedes, taking the envelope, and telling the manager to leave it with him. The manager bows, and makes his farewells.

'That was nice of him, wasn't it?' says Donal.

'I don't want – charity,' Agnes exclaims. 'I just want my sign, so I can get back where I belong.'

'Aah!' Donal cries. 'That's my second surprise – and you have no choice but to accept this one.'

What now, she sighs.

The new sign *is* lighter, she has to admit, and the message is clearer. And he hasn't changed the text, which would have been unforgivable. The old sign is no more, he told her, in a skip, and consigned to history.

Finally left alone, she resumes her protest, although her mind is cluttered and distracted. This is the beginning of the end, she senses, although how it actually plays out remains a mystery. The journalist may have left her for now, but she won't be far from his mind, she suspects. He isn't being kind to her, she has concluded, he is imposing himself on her, using her for his own devices. For a story – but whose story?

My story.

And it should be her sister's.

There it is, in print, proof of her existence, her sorry existence, according to the paper, punctuated by the prominent photograph that gives the impression that she lives inside the pages of *Bleak House*. And yes, the word 'spinster' is used. It's not a lie, but it gives a false impression, it paints a picture of an empty life, a life largely missed by the modern world. And where, *where*, is Denise? She barely merits a sentence or two. She is used as background colour, simply as explanation for the disappointment that is Agnes Miller.

The next day, and the day after, far from the story fading, it grows legs and starts to walk, and then run. She has an audience, she has listeners, supporters, even donors, who offer her money – for what she has no idea. More cameras point in her direction, and then the nadir is reached when a TV crew appear, fronted by a young woman caked in make-up and perfume, pushing a microphone into her face. When she doesn't respond, they become more determined, and aggressive, suggesting she remove her hat so that they can see her face. And no mention of Denise and her unjust demise.

After several unbearable days, and on the brink of giving up, Donal returns, and whisks her away to safety. He's to blame, but he shows little sign of regret. On the contrary, he is positively bursting with self-satisfaction. She refuses to go into Buswell's, and suggests the Natural History museum. He will take her anywhere she wants to go, he tells her.

'Home?' she says.

'What? Home? If you like, but - .'

'The Museum will do for now,' she says. She will be patient, suffer his unbearable vanity for a while longer, and everything he stands for. If she took him to the Pro-Cathedral, would he kneel and pray with her, or would he burn up the moment he stepped over the threshold?

He wants to show her something on his phone.

'You are on Facebook, Agnes. You have your own page. And look – you already have over three-hundred likes. People offering their support, sharing their own stories of injustice.'

'You did this? You did this without asking me? I didn't ask you to do this. And where is Denise? Where is my sister? Why didn't you use her image and not mine? Why are you doing all this?' She stops before she loses her temper. Look what happened the last time she allowed her emotions to overwhelm her.

Donal takes the criticism in his stride, and counters with his own.

'Why do you march up and down each day, week after week, month after month? To highlight your sister's case – and where has it got you, Agnes? I have put a spotlight on you, and through you, they will come to know Denise, and her dreadful misfortune.'

'Misfortune?' Agnes says, her voice cracking. 'They…*murdered* her.'

'Then tell me, Agnes, why *are* you doing all this? If your wish could be granted, if you could get justice, what form would it take? What would make you stop your protest?'

'I…don't know. *He* will tell me that. He will show me, when the time is right.'

They sit in silence for several more minutes, before the journalist's phone alerts him to another story, and he apologises for having to leave her. Agnes follows soon after, finding her mark outside Leinster House, and leaving her hat off for once, brazenly facing the world, and all its obstacles.

⌣

The calm of subsequent days is misleading, like the still darkness before the unpredictable dawn. The tide of publicity doesn't just come back in, it crashes up on her shore.

Tired from her lunchtime trip to the Pro-Cathedral, where He was apparently busy dealing with more urgent cases, she walks into Donal Murphy on Dawson Street, and he grabs her excitedly by the shoulders.

'I have fantastic news,' he exclaims.

'You've found God?' she retorts. Ignoring her odd remark, he ushers her into the monkish quiet of a bookstore, and tells her. 'The Taoiseach has agreed to meet you.'

'The Taoiseach? I don't understand. I don't remember asking to meet him.'

'His office have been on to me. They are upset at the negative publicity surrounding your – sister's – case, and they have agreed to give you a personal audience with the Taoiseach. You will agree to it, won't you? This is what you wanted.'

'Is it?' she asks, still trying to make sense of it.

'Yes,' he insists. 'This is your chance to get some sort of closure on this – and get on with your life. With *your* life, Agnes.'

'Denise *is* my life,' says Agnes.

'No, she *was* your life. You have to live your own, Agnes, Do you want to do this day after day for the rest of your life?'

'If that's what He wants,' she says. He throws his hands up in despair, and turns to leave.

'Okay, okay – I'll meet him. If it will make you all happy – and let me have my privacy back.'

'Just meet him, Agnes, listen to him, hear him out – and then decide if you want to go on protesting. He's not the worst of them, believe me. He's quite a decent man, underneath it all – but don't tell him I said that.'

'And you'll leave me alone – if I meet him? Even if I continue my protest, you won't bother me again, you won't write about me, or call at my house? And you will close down that Facebook page?'

'You drive a hard bargain, Agnes Miller – but I agree.' They shake on it, sealing their fate.

⌒

"But one of the soldiers pierced his side,
And immediately blood and water came out…" JOHN 19:34

With God in one ear, and Denise in the other, Agnes can't really hear what the man is saying – this man, Lorcan Scully, with his light brown suit and schoolboy haircut, this lapsed Catholic, *he's* the leader of the country? She was shown into the ante-room earlier and told to wait. When he arrived, she had expected a certain presence, but he slipped in like a spirit of the air, making little impression. His hand was damp, and limp to the touch. She might have bowed slightly through nerves, but she quickly recovered and took her seat.

She can hear the ticking of the clock. They are both on a tight schedule, with deadlines to meet, and she certainly can't afford to waste the opportunity. She expects to be whisked in and out, so she is pleasantly surprised when the Taoiseach dismisses his assistants, demanding privacy. He also orders tea – perhaps there's more to the man than she thought, and Donal was right. Regardless of the man's decency, her objective remains the same, and all that's left to be decided are the specifics of how it might be carried out. She trusts that it will be revealed to her when the time is right.

She brushes her hands against the light blue material of her dress. She feels naked in it, not worn since her last day as a teacher, when the wolf-whistles drowned out the applause. She has put on weight since then, making her look like a dam about to burst. She should listen to what he's saying, in case He is working through him.

'Let me first offer my sympathies for the difficulties you have faced in bringing this case to my attention. You must understand that my office is overwhelmed with similar cases, which is *not* to diminish your own story, or that of your sister. I have read the details of the – '

'Denise – her name is Denise,' Agnes interrupts.

'Denise, yes of course. As I said, I have read the files, and all I can say is that I can't imagine what she went through – what you both did. It was very unfortunate what happened, deeply upsetting, and nothing I can say here today will ever assuage your grief – or anger. There *was* injustice, I don't mind admitting, but there was no malicious intent on the part of the Government, or anyone in the health service, to make your sister – Denise – suffer in any way.'

'She can hear you,' says Agnes.

'Excuse me?'

'My sister – she can hear you. She's here with us, listening to your false testimony. She can see right through your lies.'

The Taoiseach shifts uneasily in his chair. He clears his throat. 'Let me assure me, Agnes – there is nothing *false* about my testimony, as you claim. I understand your frustration – I do – but I haven't lied to you this morning. Why would I?'

'To ease your guilty conscience. And you are so practiced in the art of dissembling that you don't know the difference anymore.'

'I invited you here today, Agnes, with honest intentions. I wanted to afford you the opportunity of putting forward your side of the story, so that we might learn the lessons from any mistakes made. I had hoped we could have a respectful, polite conversation. If you doubt my sincerity, and are unprepared to accept my word, there is little point in continuing, is there?'

Agnes puts her hands together, and squeezes hard. There is a ringing in her ears, but it is no angelic choir. She has been momentarily abandoned, and is upset and confused.

'I'm…sorry…I…' Tears come unexpectedly, and then he's beside her, putting a hand on her shoulder, reassuring her. There is a gentle knock on the door, and a woman comes in carrying a tray of tea and cake. The Taoiseach moves back to his chair, and Agnes wipes her tears away. Alone again, he busies himself with the chivalrous duty of pouring the tea, and cutting the cake.

'I hope you don't mind,' he says. 'I have a sweet tooth. You won't tell anyone, will you? It's my guilty secret. Even my wife doesn't know. But it's one perk of the office, being able to ask for it, and order them to keep quiet.' He tries a smile that's lost on her. 'Are you okay now? Take your time. Take as long as you like. I'm not in any hurry. Drink your tea. It's the best medicine in the world, isn't it?'

'Apart from prayer,' she says.

'Well, yes, of course,' he says.

'You're not a believer, are you?' she asks. The tea is dark and bitter, and the cake looks at her with devilish temptation.

'I suppose I'm not,' he admits. 'Like most people, I was raised a Catholic, but over the years I've let it slide. But it's clearly important to you.'

'It's more than that,' she says. 'There *is* nothing else. How can there be?'

'But there is…tolerance,' he argues, 'for those who don't share your convictions.'

'And look where that has led us,' she says. 'To this abyss wherein we now reside.'

'Things aren't that bad, surely.'

'You save money in one area so you can spend it in another,' she says. 'You reduce one thing simply to increase another.'

'There are limits to what we, or any government, can spend. That's the unfortunate reality.'

'You can afford cake – but not the money that would allow a paralysed woman to lead a dignified life.'

'You can't compare the two. I know how things can *seem* – we can appear cruel and heartless - .'

'You murdered my sister,' Agnes declares, proud to have finally said it.

'We…didn't murder your sister, Agnes. However terrible it was, it *wasn't* murder.'

'I haven't done enough,' she says. 'Everything I've done for her, it hasn't been enough. It hasn't been anything, in truth. Last night…I was with her again, in that car, on that road, and this time I stayed with her, until the end. I *saw* what happened to her, the agony she endured, and I promised I would never leave her again.'

'I don't know what else I can say to you, Agnes – or do. What is it that you want?'

'*Sacrifice*,' she whispers.

'What?' he says, leaning towards her.

'I said....I think I'd like some cake.'

'Oh, of course. Let me - .'

'No, let me do it,' she protests. Agnes reaches for the cake knife, and cuts herself a slice. And all is revealed. *I will never leave her again.* She licks the cream from the blade, and then moves forward suddenly, thrusting the knife into the Taoiseach's stomach. *'Ugh'* is all he can manage, as he watches the blood pour down his suit and onto his shoes. Agnes puts a hand over the wound, washing her hands in his blood, and staying with him until the end, until she's sure that he's dead. She thought he might have made more noise, bringing them crashing through the door, but he goes quietly, decently, and she is impressed. But not sorry.

Exhausted, she leans back in her chair, and tries the cake, although the cream has turned red, and tastes funny. Here they come, she knows, as there is a gentle knock on the door, and the truth is revealed. 'Sacrifice,' she announces as they enter. 'And, of course, justice.'

Lone Wolf

The steps along Mount Street are a blessing for the weary traveller. More dignified than sitting in the gutter, though when the tiredness comes, beggars can't be choosers. And it's a Sunday, so no need to worry about office workers trying get past him. Time for a breather, and it's only been ten minutes since the last one. It's more than old age, it's more than the hundred and twenty-seven years hanging heavy on his skinny shoulders. Nah, he's a relative youngster amongst his kind, though his kind will show no mercy when the time comes. The light doesn't hurt so much as sting, and it's less than a decade since it used to kill. Somehow, the irritating stabs of a thousand points of light are crueller than a brief roasting before release. Arthur's still human enough to appreciate the irony of being able to survive daylight, only to suffer after sundown, with his senses becoming less acute, and the hunting skills blunted. He's awake all the time now, more or less, and it's getting harder to tell the difference between night and day.

A mongrel drifts by, drifts back, cocks a leg, and unleashes a stream against the bottom step. Arthur attempts a growl, but the dog's not impressed. Don't worry, Arthur thinks, I'll see him later, and get my own back. Not that dogs are ever his meal of choice, but the way things are going, it'll soon be a feast. They do leave an aftertaste, especially the crossbreeds, and can affect the digestion for days afterwards. Still, dogs are better than birds, with swans being the worst of all. Thing is, though, they can be hard to resist, particularly when they're floating on the canal in the moonlight, shimmering and majestic – who could resist? But their blood is foul, and possibly toxic in the long run, if you have too many of them.

Dark clouds paint the sky, and the stings of irritation relent, but sleep remains elusive. He closes his eyes, but the slamming of a car door puts an end to that, as a rowing couple emerge from the vehicle barking insults at each other. Whatever else Arthur has to put up with, at least he's been spared the absurdities of the physical imperatives. He has a vague recollection of the time before, when he was lumbered with earthly limitations. It seemed so important at the time, it was everything, and he certainly had his fair share. Fatefully enough, it was a woman that did for him, that brought an end to his primarily human existence, in the shadow of the Beggars Bush pub just up the road, when she lured him outside with sultry promises, only to drain him of a different bodily fluid than he was expecting. He still occasionally strays around there of an evening, hoping to catch a glimpse of her – maybe she could take it back, or *give* it back, though of course that's never going to happen.

Jesus, the joints are stiff. He almost tumbles down the steps when he stands. His eyes peel towards the Pepper Canister church, where he sang in the choir as a boy. It always seems to be locked these days, not that he thinks he could make it across the entrance. He doesn't quite know *what* would happen, but he's not taking the chance – although if things continue on their present course he might just risk it.

The legs are like jelly. People give him a wide berth, thinking him a drunk, or worse. If only they knew. It's funny how, during daylight, he has no appetite, and he rarely gives them a second glance. Come the appointed hour, however, and he'd claw at their veins with rabid vulgarity. That too, though, has started to abate, of late. He crosses the bridge, and reaches the Beggars Bush, wary of entering, disliking crowds and cramped spaces, conscious of his ragged voice at this hour, and the prospect of being thrown out. And then there's the obligation to order in tiny quantities, one glass at a time, with decent intervals between each. Unless he orders a bottle, and drinks it down on the canal bank, where he assuredly does look the part of the drunken old sot. Straight gin, or vodka, or whiskey, consumed in sufficient quantities, he has learned, clears the daylight cobwebs, and perks him up. There are side-effects, unfortunately, later on, when dizziness and confusion can occur. Everything is mixed-up these days, and it all comes down to blood, the quality of which has slowly been disintegrating over the years, due to mass migrations, and the intermingling of different races. The purity of his food has dwindled to dangerous levels, putting his whole breed's existence in question. Will they – will *he* – become human again, if the pattern continues? Will he eventually learn to sleep at night, and function properly during the day, and exist on something *other* than human blood – or dogs and birds? No, he seriously doubts that. If he becomes human again, how long could be last? He doesn't want to be human if that's what he has look forward to, simply waiting for death.

The first glass is like a fire in the brain, thrilling and scary, but the feeling quickly fades, and he aches for another, though he's forced to wait. He doesn't have to worry about being bothered, as customers instinctively avoid him. He reckons he must smell, though it's not the normal unwashed odour, he knows that. Arthur sits at the bar, like he used to sixty years earlier, when Dublin was a much quieter beast, devoid of confidence or optimism. He lived on Henrietta Street then, and worked on the buses, his squiring days behind him, pondering retirement, which is when the siren waylaid him on a Saturday night, flattering an old man – and over the following days, the old man became a young man again, although not outwardly. Retirement was put on hold, indefinitely.

He was never sure what he had become – or what he still was. It wasn't as if you got a letter explaining what had happened, or an official badge of membership. It was left to him to make sense of it, and he found it best not to give it too much thought. It was a new lease of life, or death, with one kind of hunger fading as another developed. The early attempts were clumsy, like a young animal with no mother to teach him. He vividly recalls that young man on Bolton Street who squealed like a pig as Arthur tried, and failed, to puncture the veins with nervous, feeble bites. The career was almost over before it began, but he learned quickly, rapidly honing new skills as intense hunger drove him on.

There was a girl once, in 1935, from Fairview, a pretty, pale fragile thing with wonky teeth and thick ankles, who formed an unhealthy attachment to him. He initially resisted, sure he could do better, but during a dry spell he looked at her anew, and decided to give it a chance. There was an informal engagement, and a quick fondle or two, just for investigative purposes, which boded well. But Angela developed tuberculosis, and she was taken before her time. Who knew what might have happened if they'd married, and moved to Howth as they'd dreamed. He'd be long dead by now, but he may have left children to carry on the name, and happiness might have dropped in on him for a short time. Looking back, he didn't love her as such, but it wasn't that important at the time.

There is a girl now, on the other side of the canal, shaking with emotion, looking at her phone for answers, but it stays silent, and if she's not careful, she'll slip down the muddy bank, and into the canal. She'd think he was rescuing her, when he'd be doing anything but. He's glad when she moves, and that's most unlike him. Sympathy has no place in his armoury. His head starts throbbing – the drink from earlier – meaning he passes up two good meals. They might not come around again.

He doesn't seek it out, it comes to him, while he's lying under the bridge, his thoughts muddled. The fox creeps up on him, and starts nibbling at his ankle. Arthur breaks the neck with ease, and pierces the hairy skin with his pincers, drawing out a paltry reward, regretting it almost immediately. He should make a move, before the time gets away from him. Each night, it seems, takes more out of him, and he's rewarded less and less. He used to glide along the river banks, and now he trudges, easily losing concentration, losing the scent and wandering down blind alleys.

There's a helpless young man, hopeless with drink, veering wildly along Portobello, talking to the mute swans, and Arthur has no trouble taking him down. In the reeds, he drinks the well dry, carelessly letting the young man slip into the water, where he'll likely drown. Sated, Arthur lies down under the bridge near Harold's Cross. Two teenagers, out looking for trouble, make the mistake of thinking him easy prey. His sudden movement alarms them, and they run as if the devil himself is on their tails. Arthur heads towards Crumlin, coming across a homeless man snoring loudly in a clump of trees, who barely moves when Arthur takes advantage of him. Not that the sleeping man should be taken lightly, as a career-drinker, with a diseased liver, can often prove lethal to the blood-feeders. This one tastes better than some, and might mean that Arthur can take it easy for the rest of the night.

The unhealthy mix of his intake that evening will come back to haunt him during the day. His favoured resting place, under Baggot Street bridge, is thankfully clear of vagrants, and he nestles into the narrow space between wall and water, praying for an undisturbed sleep that he hasn't experienced in years.

Awake but dreaming, above the city, though he's neither flying nor floating. Looking down on Henrietta Street, and the house he was raised in, where he later lived alone. There's his older brother, Maurice, throwing a coin against the wall, huddled against the cold, waiting for their mother, who emerges in her dull-patterned coat, a clothes-peg dangling at the corner of her mouth, and grabs Maurice by the ear until he surrenders. She laughs like a braying donkey, until their father appears, and puts an end to the horseplay.

Arthur crawls out of his bunker, knowing it's early yet, not even midday, blinking into the stabbing sunlight that jabs at him mercilessly. He is unaccountably afraid this morning. He needs to move out of his territory, perhaps cross the city, even as far as the Phoenix Park. There is the stench of carcasses in his nostrils, though coffee has the same effect on him, and *everyone* drinks it these days, which mystifies him. Whatever happened to the good old cup of tea in the morning? Or a bottle of milk to set you up for the day – even a glass of porter now and again. His vision is slightly off today, flashes of white are starting to appear. It was thinking of milk that's done that to him. Constant exposure to sunlight will also do that. It must be doing irreversible damage. What if he ends up blind, what then? He'll perish in no time, no matter how strong his other senses are – and they are failing along with everything else.

Why is he in such a hurry? He'll draw too much attention to himself, not that anyone will come near him. The police have braved it on occasion, and questioned him, but not for long. The odour, and that other unpleasantness underneath, soon brought about his release. He gave them his name freely, and often wondered if they followed up on it. They'd find some interesting results putting *'Arthur Boyle'* into the system. The only man of that name disappeared back in the '60's – it *can't* be him, because that would make him - . No, can't be. He made it into the paper once, the Evening Press way back, when he was listed as missing, and people were concerned – not family, because he had none left by then, but neighbours and fellow-drinkers from various establishments around the city. The feeling was that he'd left the Beggars Bush, stewed from whiskey and Guinness, and fallen into the canal. They'd dredged it, with Arthur on the bank watching them. *I'm right here*, he wanted to call out. He was irrevocably sad in those first few days, as well as bewildered by what was happening to him. Why couldn't they recognise him? He just thought that he was sick, and that a visit to the doctor would soon sort him out. But it went deeper than that. His friends walked right by him, and ignored him. Those who did gaze upon him looked wary, and moved on quickly. He then felt increasingly inclined to avoid others, not to mention the fact that daylight was becoming increasingly uncomfortable. Within a week, he was staying permanently in the shade, then inside. Night was much more to his liking, and in fact, he felt stronger after dark than he had for decades, since he was a teenager, with the same uncontrollable desires and appetites. It dawned on him slowly what had happened, however impossible it was to believe. The reality of his altered nature told him everything he needed to know. Acceptance was slow and very difficult, and decades later he still hadn't fully come to terms with it. He supposed he never would, and maybe only death would bring respite. Strangely, he'd never had suicidal thoughts, and even the prospect of surviving for centuries didn't force his hand. And he wasn't even sure that he could kill himself. He could throw himself off the top of Liberty Hall, and simply wake up the next morning with a few cuts and bruises. He did consider handing himself in, confessing, and begging to be confined. A few days in a prison or hospital, they'd soon see what he was, or what he wasn't. And yet…and yet, here he is, still hunting, and being hunted, struggling to keep ahead of the pack, a lone wolf in more ways than one, destined, it seems, to follow a path chosen for him by the grossest misfortune. Why he had gone to the Beggars that night? He could have stayed on the Northside, drank closer to home, and saved himself this torment.

He's wilting, moving through Stephen's Green Park, where he has some shade at least, and can avoid the crowds. But the streets have to be navigated, the light to be suffered. It doesn't sting today, it hurts. The city hurts, *Dublin* hurts, as if angry with him for being so careless all those years ago. He should have left, he did think about it back then, but he knew he couldn't, he had to stay close to his home soil. An inner voice told him that if he left the confines of the place where he was born, he'd be fatally weakened, and not last more than a week.

Crossing the river, Arthur hears the unmistakable sound of one of his own kind, which startles him, for they rarely encounter each other. They know to keep out of each other's way, as the consequences can be deadly to both parties. This one's in trouble, he senses, and it doesn't take Arthur long to find him. He's an old creature, maybe 250 years or more, lying across the seating on the boardwalk running along the water. Like a beached whale, the body swollen, with breaths coming erratically in noisy wheezes. The poor creature shudders, and starts getting agitated, sensing that Arthur's close. He'd like to roll him into the river, and allow him a dignified death, instead of being brought to a morgue, and carved up. They'll have no idea what they have on their hands, no matter how many tests they do. But the rank odour will hasten them to a misdiagnosis, and an eagerly-closed file. Arthur sees the man under the curse, an old fat man with a Santa Clause beard, a rope for a belt, and three empty wine bottles under his seat. A seagull lands on him, but takes flight almost immediately.

Arthur is hurting, his temple is throbbing, and his eyes are blurring. He reaches the gates of the Phoenix Park, and heads for the nearest dark mob of trees. He rests against the bark, his fear partially receding, but a melancholy remains. He wipes his eyes, trying to clear them, but they pulse with pain, and patches of white spread across his vista. He gets to his feet, fighting against the strain, smelling the animals that are lurking in the next grove. The deer smell *him*, and become agitated, moving in unison to safer ground. Two stags, though, turn in his direction, and bark their contempt. He's not looking to hurt them, well, not now. Perhaps later, when the hunger returns, although deer have consistently proved to be the worthiest of foes, and practically impossible to bring down. Their young are vulnerable, but only if they're sick or injured, and unable to escape. Their blood, though, is rich in nutrients, and possesses a singular flavour unlike anything else. But that's not why Arthur has come here. And it's not as if he's had much success here before. He has bitten into dead animals, which is never recommended, and only once captured a live doe, the effort almost killing him. No, he's afraid of the city, of something in the city, something coming. He can't put a name to it, there's no shape or substance to it yet, but he hasn't felt this way for a long time, if ever. And finding that old, dying creature on the boardwalk, breathing its last. That man will be dead by sundown, if he lasts until then.

Arthur finds a sleeping man in a torn tent near the Cross. Shoeless feet sticking out, and unpleasant smells emanating. He'll come back for him in an hour or so when it's dark, if there's nothing better on offer.

There *is* something better, in the form of a security guard prowling the border of the Ambassador's residence, his torch giving him away. The guard is in rude health, providing more than Arthur needs, meaning he'll survive the attack, but get a terrible shock in the coming days, when he'll wish he hadn't recovered. There are some things worse than death, as Arthur could have told him. There is no natural imperative to increase the numbers, it's a matter of chance. Frequently, excessive hunger leads the victim to die, but not enough to halt the continuation of the breed.

Dawn, and grey skies, but the pain lingers. In fact, it hasn't left him all night. He hesitates at the gates, viewing the city as a sleeping giant that can't be disturbed. He mustn't go near Baggot Street yet - or ever again. As he leaves the park, an enormous weight presses down on his shoulders, and one eye sees only a wall of white.

He should go home...his real home, his only home. Henrietta Street. He can stay for a while, until he feels better, until things become clearer, and the fear passes. It starts to rain, but the pressure is now in his legs, turning them to concrete, making progress painfully slow.

Which way is it again? Going round in circles, turning back in on himself. He thinks it's just around the next corner, but then it's further away than ever. He could do with a drink. More than anything, he could do with a sleep, a long, vacant sleep. Maybe, just maybe...when he gets…home.

⌒

The present incarnation of The Kings Inn pub is one his father would like have approved of, being a dark soulless cavern, a safe harbour for battered ships. Arthur raises one, or seven, glasses of hard undiluted spirits, but they have no effect, so he sits in stark reflection at the bar, right where his father might have sat, eons ago. The man worked as a stoker on a steamship that ran out of Portsmouth, where he tended the furnace for weeks at a time, before coming home to stoke the fires there, too. Except that is, when he wasn't perched right here, hectoring, lecturing, falling, fighting, and choking his son who'd been sent to fetch him.

'*Another*?' the barman says, shaking his head. Normally, a customer imbibing that quantity of liquor would be on the way to hospital, and well on the way to having his stomach pumped. But this one's troubles must be severe if it's having no affect. Another it is, and Arthur looks crestfallen as he downs it like the others, knowing full well it's futile. He rubs his damaged eye, certain it won't repair itself at this stage. He only has to wait for the other one to follow, and then he's in lumber. They don't give out canes or guide dogs to the likes of him. He's had enough, and the light is fading quickly, but the surprises keep coming. There's a burning sensation in his groin, an area he's had no use for since he can't remember. He finds the toilets, and stands at the urinals. It's almost black down there, and the flaccid flesh leaks a blackish liquid into the bowl. All the signs are pointing downward, just when he thought there was no further to fall. A customer crashes through the door, and stumbles into Arthur, who can barely contain his weight. They struggle incoherently, with his opponent making guttural sounds in place of words, and flailing his left arm. It misses Arthur but hits the tiled wall, and that puts an end to the uneven bout. Arthur leaves him to it, momentarily thankful for his less-than-human metabolism.

A police horse fouls the pavement, and Arthur sneaks past, leaving the rider to his ancient transport, sweating his way to Henrietta Street, and home.

The building is no more just bricks and mortar than he is just flesh and bone. The façade has been retained, but he doubts the interior has been so carefully tended. The scaffolding is an ugly brace on beautiful teeth. It must be…fifty years, he reckons. The blink of an eye. His brother, Maurice, appears briefly, his fingers on the railing, but then he's gone, dust, the victim of a heart attack in a forgotten year. A *lonely* heart, more like, broken by the woman that left him, though not before beating him. They were not overly close as children, and the situation didn't improve as they got older. Arthur wonders where the workmen are, the *destroyers* of a precious artefact, but there's a document posted to the railing, legal nonsense that he can't make head nor tail of. The front door isn't locked, because there's no front door. There is a temporary wooden barrier further back in the hallway, which he opens by simply sliding back the bolt. A breeze hits him as he enter into the house proper – but *what* house? It has been eviscerated, hollowed out, until it's nothing but an empty bowl of dust and memory, with more scaffolding running up the walls and along the ceiling. Arthur can't see a way down, or at least a way down that will let him get up again. He doesn't smell any danger, no imposters or desperate thieves. He climbs down, a child tackling his first tree again. The scale of the devastation is overwhelming. The Boyles were nothing to write home about, but the building wasn't to blame. He has witnessed resurrections all over the city, mausoleums brought back to life, fresh blood in old veins. But why save the face, and destroy the insides?

The walls of his room have been torn down, and replaced with thin plasterboard. The floors have been stripped, relayed, and varnished. There are marks everywhere, indicators of further restoration – or destruction – to come. The brothers once slept there, at arm's length from each other, listening to the rows and the blows, before adding their own, until they finally slept, and then woke to start all over again.

It's night. There are no windows down here, but the tingling in his blood tells him the hunger is coming. His bad eye offers tiny breaks in the whiteness, his hearing improves immeasurably, and he can smell the rats under his feet. They are single grains of sand as meals, with venal blood of no discernible flavour.

There are peals of bells, perhaps miles away, car engines, and train wheels on tracks, nesting birds, and fidgeting spiders, breeding rats and barking dogs. But only one Arthur Boyle, and not a sound out of him. His hunger is for more than fresh blood, it's for his flesh and blood, his family that fought and scrapped, only to reach its end with him in the desecrated basement of their former home.

He gnaws at the floorboard, nosing the rats below, prepared to feast on a handful if he can catch them. But the new boards aren't for budging, and he's forced to look elsewhere, above, beyond. And to think he thought he was becoming human again, when it was, literally, a trick of the light. If he could just get back to a diet of purer blood, perhaps this unsettling period will pass, and he'll carry on for another few decades, who knows. Until he's beached on the boardwalk, a blubbering mass of fetid meat.

The hunger overwhelms him, and he starts to climb. The scaffolding buckles under his weight, and sends him crashing to the floor. Stunned, he arches his back and stares at the original ceiling high above him. The house continues to writhe and struggle, disturbed by his unhealthy presence. The scaffolding weakens further, with a metal tube becoming loose.

Arthur watches it break free and start to fall. Gravity turns it into a hurtling weapon, aiming directly for his rapidly-beating heart. His mother takes his hand. He squeezes it, and tells her he's not ready to join her. He asks the city for its forgiveness, for being so weak, and turning his back on it. His blood becomes a furnace, churning under the stoking hand of his father, who screams with furious impatience for him to stop.

The metal spear strikes him with ferocity in the middle of the chest, pinning him to the ground. Black blood spurts from his mouth, and both eyes drown under a blanket of snow. He spits and chokes, but to no avail – his human frailties lift the curse, and carry him home.

The Comedian Who Died

Everything was funny once. The taxi ride, the pissing rain, the shit on his shoes, his nagging wife. *He* was funny once. Anywhere but the hotel bar, and the Stag's Head will do just fine. As a rule, he wouldn't drink before a show, but every desert needs a sprinkling now and then. And who knows, after a few pints, fresh material might flood in, and he'll have them rolling in the aisles.

Stanley Porter is fit to bursting, and he can't get the zip down quick enough. That's not his only problem. The rolling wave beside him smirks and winks, giving him that *'I know you'* look. The perks of the job, fending off drunken fans with dripping cocks in their hands. Stan attends to business, but the arm is already around the shoulder, squeezing the life out of him.

'Can I finish here?' Stan says.

'Sorry, brov,' comes the offended reply, hands in the air, protesting innocence. 'Don't want to cramp a man's style.'

'Just not while I'm taking a piss, all right?' Stan says in a friendlier manner. Don't want to be making enemies this early in the proceedings. Not that it's that early. *Fuck!* Better be making a move. That's the trouble with these late-night gigs, too much spare time, when all manner of troubles can erupt.

'It is *you*, though, isn't it?' the man asks.

'It is *me*,' Stan replies. 'Least I hope it's me — otherwise I'd be someone else, and we wouldn't want that, would we?' See? There was a time when that would have come out funny, but now, it sounds defensive, sarcastic.

'Stanley Porter,' the man announces. 'What you doing in Dublin? Working?'

'Always working, mate. Never stop, me. Over the road — the Olympia, in about an hour from now. I should get going.'

'Wow. Cool. Wish I'd known. I saw you on that thing — on TV — what was it called?'

Stan shakes his head. He's forced to shake hands, and neither has cleaned them. Could he use that later, work it into the routine?

'I can't remember – listen, I have to go.'

⌣

      The Central Hotel is exactly that. He could open the window and do his act from there. Shout it across the street, above the massed heads of messy drinkers, clicking flamingo heels and stinking dossers. He feels like spitting it. The notes cover his unmade bed. He rarely studies them closely. They're like his children. He likes to keep an eye on them, know they're there, but that doesn't mean he has to engage with them.

Belfast tomorrow night, Newcastle the night after, then three days off, before heading north of the border. It's a sprint *and* a marathon, carefully planned and chaotically dizzying. Them Shakespeare boys don't know they're born - same script every night, it's expected. God, he'd love that, and he does his best to recycle wherever possible, but *he* is expected to conjure pearls of originality from his locker every night – and it is pretty much *every* night.

The Guinness won't let him be, and he decides to stay in the toilet until it's had its wicked way with him. And, of course, his wife picks that very moment to call and rant. She's like a kidnapper, ringing with a list of demands, regularly, and he generally pays up. That *should* be a funny line, and he would use it, if it didn't make him so monumentally depressed. He takes it out on her, because she happens to be there, and she takes it well, unless she's storing it up for future retribution. Things calm down, and he tells her he loves her, and he thinks he might mean it tonight. That last labour was a turning point for him – Elsie – sixteen hours, hard and bloody messy. The first two births hadn't bothered him, and the sex had returned to almost pre-marriage levels, but Elsie's difficult arrival, for some reason, affected him greatly, and he'd found it a struggle ever since to muster up enthusiasm with Julie. Should he tell her? Not now, perhaps.

The theatre calls. They're running behind schedule, but *'you are coming, aren't you?'* Two minutes away, he assures them. Always happens with a number of artists on the bill, especially comics. And the money is shit, although he'll only have to do twenty minutes or so, then he'll be back in bed five minutes after that – unless they persuade him to join the after-gig festivities, to which he's grown allergic. That's to say, his liver has grown allergic. Devon Wainwright, fellow artiste, cockney, and black as the ace of spades, calls to tell him what he already knew –

running late, but *'you are coming, aren't you, man?'* Right behind you, mate, don't worry. A conveyor belt of comedians, that's what it is. Friends for the most part, but also competitors, and Stan's now most definitely a veteran on the circuit. Respect for your elder is one thing, but that quickly fades.

His agent calls when he's flushing the toilet for the very last time. He's not going in there again, no matter what happens. Donnie Palmer asks him how Dublin is going.

'I'll tell you when I've done it, Don.' What kind of man calls himself *Donnie*? 'They work late hours here.'

'New of series of 'Just A Minute' next month. Can I put you down for a handful of shows?'

'Is Paul Merton back?'

'Wouldn't be the same without him, Stan.'

No, it wouldn't, unfortunately. Merton is the nicest man working in the asylum, and the least competitive, but Christ, he's good.

'How can I refuse, Don?'

'That's what I like to hear.'

That's what the agent likes to hear, the slavish devotion of the client, the willingness to do almost *anything* for a buck. A stand-up they call him, but he spends most of his time lying down, and being walked on.

'I have to go. I'm due on soon.'

Nerves maketh the performer, they are the blood coursing through the veins, if you don't have them, you're dead. Stan doesn't have them. He draws the razor down the cheeks, slicing the last of the bristles, pining for a single malt, and sleep. Sheffield without the steel, that's Stanley Porter, a slight fellow, blessedly younger looking than his forty-eight years, splashes of grey in the goatee, itself a middle-age cry for help, liked by *nobody*, particularly his wife. Not all Northern comics, he likes to tell people, have to live up to *Northern* stereotypes. He's never owned a flat cap, or bred whippets, or worked down a mine, or done anything manual, for that matter. A Labour man, though, certainly, left-leaning, absolutely political, and eternally cynical. But that's old currency these days. The era of the shouty, spitting comedian is past, and the present is…what? He doesn't know. He wishes someone would tell him, though he probably wouldn't listen.

He tucks the shirt in, hating the fashion for leaving the tail out, flapping like an untethered tent. The hair, what's left of it, is best left to its own devices. The thought of using gel always reminds him of grandad and his buckets of Brylcream. He pulls a few hairs from his nose, knowing they'll have grown back before he lands on stage – *crash-lands*, more like. He thinks he'll have that single malt, after all. The notes on the bed are like old girlfriends, hardly worth the effort. He picks a few cards at random – what harm can it do? Old ideas might trigger new ones. Unlikely, but miracles do happen. But all that comes to mind is the road he lives on, the estate he lives in, and the house where his present and future collide. The revolutionary socialist ends up in suburbia, putting the bins out right alongside the victims of his comic tirades. His wife fits right in, she'd never move, and the kids are settled, just as he is increasingly unsettled. All this was funny once. *He* was funny once.

The theatre calls.

Devon calls.

The theatre calls again.

Stan opens the window, and shouts, '*I'm coming!*' But nobody hears him. He'll have to put in an appearance. The bloody show must go on.

⌒

Can't tell one city from the other, one street from another. On any given night, packs of young men, snorting, rampant, chasing the tails of flighty mares. This thoroughfare is called Dame Street, if he has his geography right. The problem with the chase, lads, is that someday you catch something, and then you're really lumbered. He hauled down his prize on the streets of Manchester many moons ago, and look where that landed him.

There is a dearth of humorous anecdotes to be gleaned from the current tableaux being presented. And he's less than a minute away from the Olympia theatre. He should have checked it out earlier in the day, got the feel of the place, but what the hell. In and out, shake the old jokes about, and hope that half the set is taken up with hecklers, who should always be encouraged as far as Stan's concerned. The venue coming up has something of a vaunted history, a change from the latest hipster joints and their knowing clientele. Not that he yearns for the pissholes of northern England of his apprenticeship. But God save him from the arenas, and the polite wine-sippers out for a jolly evening with their grannies.

The lap-dancing club sits cheek-by-jowl with a newsagent and a pizza parlour, with a doorway leading down to a discrete sex-shop.

Lovely-jubbly, as Del Boy would say, the upward march of modern man, and woman, continues, progress viewed through liberal glasses. Freedom, Stan has learned, is *not* always beneficial. Constraints are necessary, or the ignorant masses will make a merry mess of the whole thing – too late, we're already there. People wants guns to protect themselves, but then they decide prevention is better than cure, and they 'jump the gun,' literally. No, nothing funny to see here, lad, move along now, be on your way – don't you have a gig to do? He certainly does, but how will he open? What's happening in Dublin, or Ireland, for that matter? What state are their politics in? Who *is* the Prime Minister, or the Taoiseach as they call him here? He should know. There was a time he would have known more than the locals – he would have enlightened *them* on their own plight. Isn't Ireland just England, but smaller, quieter, funnier? Nothing funny here. Dame Street doesn't look so grand in the garish evening light. People are hurling themselves recklessly into traffic. Young children hang onto parents, terrified. The *craic* is just a crack as far as Stan can see. A man spreads his sleeping bag out on the pavement, having an early night, oblivious to the madness, unless he knows more than they do.

What time is the train in the morning? Why not hire a car, and drive to Belfast? He could actually look at the scenery along the way, instead of sleeping off the night before in the rattling carriage. Belfast – he thinks he liked it the last time he was there. An improvement on the first time he visited, over twenty years ago, when he played to what turned out to be a fervently Loyalist crowd who were extremely sensitive about being described as *Irish*. And liked a red rag to a bull, Stan pushed and pushed, until tables were overturned, and he needed help getting out alive. Then he needed help getting back to his hotel, where he didn't get an ounce of sleep. The city had come on since then, but peace and prosperity had its drawbacks, in softening the edge of the crowd, making his style of mocking commentary harder to pull off.

Why is he thinking of tomorrow night when tonight has still to be negotiated? Far away hills are more interesting, is that it? It's not as if the Olympia crowd will be baying for him, not with a dozen or more on the bill. At least Alexi Sayle didn't show, as was rumoured. That had briefly scared them all witless. For those who had seen him back in his prime, there was none better, nor ever likely to be. Incendiary, dangerous, possibly insane – all the immoderate adjectives applied, and now he was selling insurance on TV to supplement his income. Stan didn't blame him, but the business, for losing its nerve, and keeping him out on the margins. Anger now deadens when it used to incite. Comedic offence is now just offence, and subject to the rigors of the law. If *one* member of the audience is upset, the comedian is guilty, even if the rest are braying with laughter. People are afraid to be angry, in case their anger spills out into their real lives, and wrecks their carefully-manicured mediocrity.

What makes them laugh? Stan has no fucking clue anymore. He's been around so long that his very existence guarantees a few laughs, regardless. They clap because he's survived, they appreciate the work he did five, ten years ago, and it doesn't really matter what he does now. Like a rock-star touring a new album, the crowd want the old hits, and barely tolerate the new material. But Stan was never quite a star, and the hits were few and far between. And as for new material, *where is it?* It's not here, not in the caked face of the young girl in the slip of a dress, or her stumbling friend, or the lights of a hundred phones glowing like deities, invoking prayerful devotion.

It's cold all of a sudden. He should have worn a jacket, or had another whiskey to ward off chills. Unless it's nerves, or more likely, boredom. It shouldn't be hard work – it never has been. He's lost his curiosity, that's what it is. Age has worn away his interest in the everyday, and his ability to transform it into comedy. He wants to visit all those towns and cities again, but not to work. He doesn't want to take notes. Then he wants to leaves the cities behind, and travel further out, to where the land still rules the population, not the other way around. He's been thinking of the Scottish Highlands, gloomy mountain ranges and peaty rain, dour pubs, and swirling mists. He's been thinking about his kids, and their difficult years, and how he'd like to leave all that shit to his wife. He loves them, but that doesn't mean he was ever cut out to bring them up. He wants to lead them astray, yet they invariably veer back to their mother. He misses them until he gets back home. Or maybe it's the home, the four-bedroom, and the bank loan, and the shed out the back, and the filthy gutters. Or it's the growing flesh of his faithful, nagging wife. Not this his own is anything to write home about. He's one of those skinny men with middle-age spread, and it's not a good look. Billy Connolly could make that funny, he can't. But if he left her, left *them*, what then? He'd find a flat in London somewhere, and try to recapture a youth he hated. He was one of those young men who wanted to be old, and found out that age brings nothing but recrimination. Everything was funny once – because there was time left to fix it. And speaking of time – if he doesn't hurry, they'll dock his paltry fee, which won't do his faltering reputation any good.

There's man smoking outside the stage-door, and it could only be Devon. He'd block out the moon if there was one.

'Is that legal, what you're smoking?' Stan asks.

'Well, look who it is – they're cursing you in there, man, better make a move.'

'You done? How did it go?'

'They're crazy, man, fucking crazy,' Devon says in his slow baritone. 'But I blew them away, naturally.'

'Naturally,' says Stan. 'Can I try some of that?' Devon regards the joint, and smiles.

'This? *You?* That is funny. You should save that one for in there.'

'I'm serious. I need something,' Stan tells him.

'You nervous, man? I never seen you nervous.'

'It's not nerves, Devon, it's…I don't know what it is. Come on, hand it over. You forget, I am a relic from the dark ages, when we were all permanently stoned. It was a uniform you had to wear.'

'But time weakens man, Stan, and you don't look like you in shape.'

'Just – hand it over.' Stan swipes the joint, and takes a drag. 'See? Constitution of an ox. I suppose I should be making tracks. Can't disappoint my legion of fans, can I?'

'Slay 'em, killer,' says Devon, grabbing Stan's hand, and almost crushing it.

⁓

A *mardy bum* is what his mother used call him. A moody bugger, and he's been all that, and more, most of his life. Stan left college with a third-class degree in Literature, and discovered there weren't many jobs for lads who'd read the Classics. He discovered he couldn't write, either, and those poetic teenage years were anything but. He signed on, joined the Labour party, swore a lot at meetings, and found that people laughed when he swore even more. There was money to be made for educated, angry blokes with left-leaning tendencies. He punched well above his weight. He also threw the occasional *actual* punch, though that never ended well, so he stuck to the verbals thereafter. Stan couldn't tell a joke to save his life – he could never remember them, but that didn't matter once you had a firm opinion, and could articulate it. There was suddenly money in comedy, and currency in being from the North, and having both an attitude *and* an accent.

Where am I again?   Oh, yeah…Dublin

He blags a whiskey from one of the stagehands, and juggles fruit backstage while he waits for his turn. He's lucky to still have a turn. And is it worth it? What with the flight, taxi, hotel, meals – *what* meals? – he's well on the way to making a loss on the trip. And Belfast won't be much better. Through narrow, claustrophobic corridors he wanders in search of an opening line, and can only find a closing one. The walls pulse with cheers and thunderous clapping. Tommy Tiernan has just walked on – and Stan has to *follow* him. How is he supposed to do that? Better not watch too closely, or psychotic envy will set in. Tommy has more than a streak of madness in him, a genuine gypsy spirit that sets him apart. What sets Stan apart? Apart from being old. Devon's weed has had no effect, unless he's too low to get high, but surely the point of weed is to put you on an even keel. Keeling over, more like.

He's never noticed the amount of *machinery* backstage before, the lights, wires, and curtains, and the shadowy puppeteers working the controls. Someone might have to plug *him* in. He hasn't yet reached that pre-performance stage called rapturous anxiety. *Any* anxiety would be welcome. The comedians on after him, the last two, acknowledge him without being overly friendly, which he puts down to their own anxieties. They're both a decade younger, at least, and firmly established on the scene. They're serving up a new kind of comic dish, tending towards the surreal, and the intellectual, as if they've been brought up on a diet of Woody Allen and David Lynch. *Come back, Alexi, we need you more than ever.*

Out front, Tommy is telling a rip-roaring tale about pulling the wings off moths in Salthill when he was a boy. A couple in the front row are bent double with laughter, and in danger of embolism. It's a theatre for tall tales, all right, Stan thinks, or dirty rock bands smashing their guitars on the baroque pillars. It's *not* a theatre for a throwback from across the Channel, trying to convince them that politics still means something.

The producer sneaks up on Stan, asking him if he's ready. Tommy's at fever pitch, approaching lift-off, and then Stan's up. He'll be up when he's down. He looks around for Devon. He could do with some support in the wings. He could do with some wings.

'You're on!' the producer shouts, struggling to be heard about the roar that follows Tommy off stage. The Irishman screams into Stan's face, still riding the wave.

You're on, Stan   *Where is he, again?*

On the occasion of his first gig, a seasoned pro reminded him that the audience *wanted* him to be funny, they *want* to enjoy themselves, or why else would they be there? So, all he had to do was let them enjoy themselves.

On the occasion of his last gig, Stanley Porter pulls off a first in his career – he silences the crowd as he walks to the microphone. He *does* hear a pin drop. Yeah, those Shakespeare boys have it easy, all right – same script every night, no imagination required.

Everything was funny…once.

Stan leans into the microphone, opens his mouth, and…

Nothing.

nothing

noth-

A Bang On The Head

Still the pipes. Holding court. Hagan's Court. She's nausing him up. Christy. Tracksuit. Packed, blister packets. Can't move. Yellows, blueys, you name it. *And* blisters. Pram, without the baby. Serves her fucking right, the stupid bleedin' cow. Lucozade – aah, bliss. Try injecting *that*, mate. Jackie and her jacked-up tits, try finding the milk in them. Ask Liam. Yeah, ask him, the poor mite. *My son!* Sucking on them cry grapes. Juice, and biscuits. No feed for a growing boy. He told her, he fucking told her – and he'll tell her again, if this fucking phone will bleedin' work! Load of shite, shove it right back up Teeno's arse, get his fucking money back. What is this place? *Hagan's Court.* It's a back passage leading to another back bleedin' passage – same shit as over the river. The dogs still mark their territory. Marks his own. Cock is stinging. Not red though, like Tony's. Piss was like blood too, poor fucker. Laughing then, not now. Nothing like Smoothie – now, *he's* on the fucking treadmill, all right. Told him his leg was dead – *dead.* But he's still pushing the needle in – the leg's fucking *dead*, Smooth! Maggots seen crawling…*from the wound.* Blind fucking bat, no flies on him. Soon will be. *Yellow.* Just one. Still the pipes. Nicely nice with the mare. She'll be riding the wave. She drops Liam – I'll baste her. Narky bitch, steals the hits, falling asleep. Killarney Street is a kip. Sooner they pull it down the better. *One more.* Yellow calm. Pray Ronnie doesn't count. He'll do more than cut his share. He'll cut. Wrist has no room left. Crane screaming behind him. Men in funny hats poking out of the skyline. Give a man some privacy. Nothing to see here. Look, no needs! Getting off that shit, away from those shitters. Needs both his legs. Can't let Liam have a cripple for a dad. A dribble of Lucozade, soon parched again. *No more.* Blister packs are cutting his groin. Feed them to the birds, that's what he'll do. Let's see them flap their wings after that. Clip *her* fucking wings, slap or two. She slaps *him*, after all. Fucking phone, fucking Southside, don't know shit round here, too busy drinking coffee and stroking pussies. Keep an eye on the lane, the gap onto Baggot Street – *faggot* street. No guards round here, no fucking crime, too many fucking pussies. *Okay – one more. still the pipes.*

Need to be calm. Seagull, and his mates. Begging from *me*, there's a novelty. Kick them over the wall, that's what. Swings, and misses. Swings and…dizzies, room is spinning. The wall's not much help. Hands on the sign. *Hagans fucking court.* No court here. And he'd know. He'll know next week. *is* it next week or the week after? Who gives a bollocks? A 'stern warning' best they'll do. *suspended* sentence. Whole fucking life is suspended. No ponies here – fucking Noelie and his information. Over the river he says they're *giving it away*, notes are overflowing from the pockets. Wanker. Wank*er*.

Phone, drilling. *Her.* Still the pipes, Christy. Or she'll drop Liam. Drop both of them.

Drowsy, fading, street. Where?

'Jackie?…where the fuck are ye?' Laughing. At him? Hard to tell. He knows – the South Circular, mother's. For a feed, and a kip. She'll park the kid, drop him in Una's lap. *'Jackie? Get over here now! bleeding waste of time, place is dead, fucking dead. not a scratch.'* Listen, Christy, she says. Coming through clear now. Slow, awake, taking her time. *'You're wha?'* Not coming back. *not coming back.* How many times does she have to say? Mother's. Don't follow. And by the way, someone called, at Killarney Street, looking for him. They weren't Dublin, she says. Like, *not human. 'JACKIE?'* Jackie stills the pipes. No street, no Liam. Has she dropped him? He looks in the pram, just in case. A tin of cream. Gets on his fingers, won't come off. Phone stone dead. Not Dublin? I don't know anyone from there. From *not Dublin.* Never been there. *Shush.* Woman walking her dog. Can smell her. *'Any change, love?'* Like he asked to fuck her. Cobwebs down there, need a crowbar to prise those legs open. Here's another one! Young man having a smoke – moves away sharpish. Christy barks at him. *still the pipes, boy.* Calm, think. Of the stink that is Hagan's Court. Pushes the pram into the wall. Won't be needing it. Any son of him'll be walking in no time. Two strong legs on him. Two strong lungs. Sings all night. Impossible to get him down. Smother the fucker some night, keeps that up. What's he got to be crying for? *I'm* the one should be. Don't hear me, though, not Christy. Puts up with it. Takes the shit, without falling. *Last last one.* A blue. Finders keepers. He's carrying, he can have the odd snack. South Circular is the other side of the planet. And that house smells of mould. *She* smells of mould. Una, what sort of fucking name is that? And what sense of man stuck one up her, and brought Jackie screaming and hollering into the world? Then there's Frank, *her* brother, the monk, the Mormon freak, never, never *anything*. One puff,

72

and he'd blow you down. Pop one in his tea, that's what I'll do. Watch him stew. Plant them all over South Circular, make a call. Call in Store Street, watch the show.

The wall. That *fucking* wall. Hagan's Court. Who the *fuck* was Hagan? Pisses on the yellows, and blues, and zimmos. What're they worth now? *not from Dublin*. Not from Dublin, not from anywhere. Wall is a wall is a wall is a –

Use the corner not the flat. More damage there. They'll send someone. A hearse, if there's nothing else. Stem the flow. Bed for the night. Out of harm's way. Let her find me then. The sky is yellow. One after the other, dull the pain.

Hold on tight   dig into them bricks.

Find the right angle. Don't hesitate. Pills better kick in soon.

Bang!

Reversal of Fortune

It's cold comfort, morning. There's light, but no heat. And now he has an audience. But the taxi drivers and delivery men are an unresponsive lot. It's not raining, but the water drips down. The gulls are trilling from their high posts, on the look-out, ready to dive for the slightest morsel. He has dirtier company closer to hand. A stained sleeping-bag, layers of cardboard, and a fierce aroma. The present is viciously alive. Here on Sackville Place, within spitting distance of the bleeding artery of the city. Homeless. Less. Least.

⌒

Earlier, darker, animals on the loose, human and otherwise. Foxes, rats, pissing passers-by, curious beasts, some indignant. The verbals are one thing, the assaults on the ribs are quite another. Showers of urine surprisingly warm on the face, and the quiet threats in the ear. And it's his first time out here. And his last, surely? No sane creature would choose to spend a single night on a concrete step under the steel canopy of a derelict building. So, he's lost his mind. Wonder where? Wasn't all at once. Tiny pieces shed in stages along the way. Did it begin at birth?

They're queuing up to take his place. But they haven't the energy for a fight, and move on. Civilisation is just around the corner. They're holding the end-of-the-world party, and he's just one step ahead of them. There's a hand under his bag, but it's not looking for money. He pushes it away, and slithers down the step. Later, there is a courting couple within earshot, grunting like pigs against the shutters, racing to the finish. They start arguing almost immediately after, and the man punches the metal in anger. A period of calm follows, under a full moon, and slender hopes of sleep. Roaring snoring from his neighbour, whose shuddering foot accidentally kicks the empty bottle onto the road. A tyre will burst going over the broken glass, just wait. Or the tyre will send a piece of broken glass spiralling into his face. He turns his back to the road. Faint hopes creep in with the dawn. He'll give the police station one more go. He'll refuse to leave until they help him. He was the victim of crime, not the perpetrator. Unless poverty, and stupidity, is now an offence. He'll make it. He *will* make it.

Out of Dublin, at least.

⌒

Earlier, there'd been hope. Visitors, do-gooders, bearing soup and a sleeping-bag. The latter is a godsend, but the soup is the killer blow, because once doled out, they look like they're leaving.

'Is that it?' he asks. 'I thought you were here to help me.' They look at him as if he's spoken in a foreign tongue. '*Help* me. Take me with you.' But that's not their mission, apparently. Soup, and a bag, that's it. They're going to leave him there, and he's not up to it. Can't they see that? He's not meant to be here. It's all been a terrible mistake. But they're moving on, heartless helpers off spreading their curious Gospel of sympathising without actually doing anything.

Oh my God.

⌒

Much earlier, in the Phoenix Park. Passing the time until his train is due. After missing the earlier one, which *was* his fault. But who could blame him, after that excuse for a job interview. Needs to calm down, and sober up. How many was it? He didn't drink, as a rule, but the lads, and lasses, wouldn't take no for an answer. He was the oldest of the lot, by a considerable margin, disconcertingly. But they took him in, and cheered him up. And he missed his train. And here he is, in the sprawling mass of grass and deer. Far as the eye can see, a man could get lost here, or live here, rent-free, trouble-free, dining on berries and squirrels. Couldn't be any worse than his present lot.

The space is enervating, and oddly frightening. The city at his back, but he's afraid of being swallowed by the emptiness. Except he's anything but alone. The first herd of deer scatter before he can get close, but this one stag has other ideas. The antlers are lowered in advance of the charge, but he's still startled by the animal's attack. He stumbles backwards through the long grass, aiming for the path, desperate to see another human being. The stag is only sending out a warning, and relents. He feels stupid for being so scared. And to think he came here to clear his head. And think about the journey home, and what's waiting for him there.

He stays close to the main gate, within easy reach of Heuston Station, though he has an hour or more yet to go. The sun comes out, and something approaching heat. He wanders over to a grove of trees, drawn by the solitude, and the carpet of bluebells, and the peace. He sits down against the base of a tree, and closes his eyes. He doesn't dream, he doesn't dare.

Two creatures, both human, on the move, undoubtedly coming towards him. He scrambles to his feet, torn between moving further back, and out of sight, or facing them, and heading for the gate. They meet half-way, and they're all charm and bluster, though their clothes and shifty demeanour are a giveaway. They ask for the time, he tells them the time. They offer him a drink, a can, but he declines, politely. They ask him his purpose, and he gives them a sketchy outline. There is a gap, and he thinks he might have the beating of them, in a race at least. They finally get down to it, and ask him for money. He pleads poverty, the cost of the train ticket, etc, but they're not for shifting. He wishes they'd just get on with it, and cut out the phony bollocks. They do get on with it, and block his miserable attempts to escape.

Everything. Every last fucking thing. Money, ticket, watch, jacket. Left him the shirt on his back. And a bruise on the cheek. The station staff are unmoved, and announce they're *not* a charity. And never a policeman when you need one. Dublin it is, then, for a while longer, until this mess is sorted out. His left eye is weeping, above the spot where they struck. That's all he needs. He rides the Luas back into the city centre without a ticket. Let them arrest him, if that's the only way to get his story heard.

Pearse Street is his best bet, or so he's informed by a kind stranger. The plastic chair provides no relief for an impatient, angry man. He's up and down to the desk like a Jack-in-the-box, but to no avail. The officer on duty is impervious to most approaches, and only a murder confession seems likely to provoke. Wait. The weight of the wait proves too much to bear. One last effort, appealing to the man's basic humanity. *I have no way of getting home. And if I can't get home – what then?* That's not, apparently, the sergeant's problem. The city is in the grip, it appears, of more serious crime, and resources are being stretched to breaking point.

He leaves, reluctantly. With nowhere to go. But's that impossible - isn't it?

⌣

Before the Park, morning. Mourning the lack of a raincoat. His one good suit is no longer good. He is immune to Dublin's charms, searching the barren quays for an address, but there's nothing but glass warehouses – and where *is* everyone?

Multitudes have gathered. There won't be many one-on-one interviews, or he'll be here for months. Most look as if they should still be in school. What chance has he got among the acne-scarred masses? High above the city, they're workhouse orphans waiting for their betters to lead the way. Or cattle being herded, with the majority set for slaughter. He'll be front of the queue. He's handed a form with a thousand multiple-choice questions. *What is this?* He came here looking for a job. Heard there were 'numerous openings' in this vast organisation. Work here, in this prison in the clouds? Look at the drop – no doubt the corporation are hoping that a few might take the leap into obscurity, and narrow the field. The questions are more senseless than difficult, making him hesitate, thinking they're trying to trip him up. Whatever they're up to, it works – he loses concentration, thinking ahead, and back – others are finishing up, and he's barely quarter of the way through. And his one *bad* suit is still damp, it's itching, as he is, to get out of there.

Typical, the sun is out, and he squints into the horizon – what an awful waste of time and money. Barely noon, and a few of the kids are talking about a drink to soak up their sad fates. The Ferryman is close by, a decent looking bar, and he has an hour or two until the return train. No harm greasing the wheels, and easing his passage home.

The kids are alright. And generous, too, to an old man like him. This early drinking thing is a lark, and without food, the pints *sting*, hitting the spot, and then, in the blink of an eye, his new friends are scattered to the four corners of the earth, and he has a long walk ahead of him, made trebly difficult by swaying, rubbery legs. Sleep on the train, that's what he'll do – but what train? It's gone, and his watch tells him a weird tale with a twisted ending. Okay, *food*, sober up. There's a pub over the road, where it's mineral water all the way until he rediscovers a semblance of reason. Coffee for afters, and he thinks he might check out the Park before he leaves.

He's been thinking of Dublin. Why not? What's left for him in Cashel? And the papers are full of announcements coming out of the capital, about multinationals proclaiming the next golden era, with glittering careers for people with ambition. *He* has ambition, doesn't he? Or is it just desperation?

The hardware store can't 'carry him' any longer, their very words. Being a farmer once doesn't mean he can sell farm produce, and he can't argue with the facts. Or the complaints against him.

He watches her wheel the pram by on the street below. She protests it's not his, and he's not about to take her to court. He can't afford her, let alone *him*. Still, the thought does occur to him, the prospect of being a father, having a son. The poor kid's better off without him, anyway. Lorna displays her wares shamelessly, practically sashaying like a peacock through the town. She'll be lucky, having that thing with her.

Love? Lust, loneliness. The farmer with only the beasts in the fields for company, he needs more than that, and he has other qualities, if he could only let them out. Riordan's is the hub of the community, and Lorna one of its stellar members, a regular, and a regular source of entertainment for the local men. She can drink with the best, and the worst, of them. She can also get her fingers dirty around the farm when the need arises. She picks him more than the other way around, and who's he to complain. Everything is sweetness and light, until the drudgery takes its toll. And the land extracts its price, as always. In this case, the cattle, heartbeat of the enterprise, are stricken with TB, and the consequences are inevitably tragic.

Lorna leaves before the cattle do. And she's barely out the gate before the land agent arrives. The offer is pitiful, but it's an offer, and there won't be another for some time.

He stays on the land but the land doesn't want him. He stays when others go. His father doesn't want him, but he needs him. Treats him like one of the herd, surprised he doesn't make him sleep in the shed. He does feel the same lash of the tongue, and hand.

Until the day one of the animals lashes back, and the father is felled. The old man lies in the yard, and the son bears complicated witness to a painful death.

The farm is his, if he wants it. So he stays on the land.

But the land doesn't want him.

⌒

He's all set for college in Limerick. He's heard good reports, and it means getting out of here. He hates leaving his mother alone with her husband, but she won't hear of him staying. Her bruises are inside, but he can still see them.

He finds her in the kitchen, paralysed down one side. She doesn't last long. Her sudden departure should have hastened his own, but the old man is broken, and begs the son to stay and help. There is a temporary thaw in the relationship that deceives the son, but he realises too late.

He stays on the land. But neither the land, nor the father, will thank him for it.

The Miracle of Phibsborough

The Joy behind, the joy ahead. The lads cheered him out with a chorus of *we'll be seein' you soon*. But he won't be back. He might reach the morgue across the road, but that's as close as he'll get. There are no forks in the road left for Terry Walsh. His route was chosen long ago, but there are ways of navigating it. No more burglaries, aggravated or not. Or next time do it properly, and kill the fucker. Or at least choose a property *not* owned by a fellow member of the criminal class. Terry should have done his homework, but he'd reached a point where he reckoned he could smell trouble a mile away. How wrong he was. The man had put up a struggle, and had a certain skill with the fists. Terry won, on points, or so he thought, but he was fingered within a week, and the rest was repeated history. The sentence was light, and confinement held no surprises for him. But the real trouble was outside, if he continued to be careless. Some found God inside, Terry found wisdom, which was, maybe, the same thing.

The street doesn't exactly welcome him with open arms. It says, if you can handle it, here it is, come on in, but we can't promise it will be easy. Fair enough, thinks Terry, he hasn't always treated Dublin right, no reason to expect anything in return. The bag won't sit easily on his shoulder, the strap keeps digging in. And his head's spinning a little. Only natural, just out, and getting back into the swing of things. A pint would settle him, but he wouldn't settle for just one. And not around here – too close for comfort. Although the Broadstone does an all-day breakfast, as well as a decent stout.

He knows that bloke on the corner, the one struggling to light up, in the camel-hair coat, and the dyed hair. What's his name again? On the tip of Terry's tongue, and just like that, the smoker looks up, and over at Terry, and the feeling is mutual. He knows Terry, or did, or is protesting the stare – or Terry is paranoid from the hunger, and the thirst. He turns back. The Broadstone can wait. Plenty of other fish in the sea. He doesn't want to pass the Joy again either, so he hangs a right, carries on a bit, then turns into Berkeley Street, with the church on his left. Where his boy was confirmed – how long ago was that?

The boy is a man now, but not much of a son. Terry's not one for flying, especially not half way around the world to a land of baking sun and venomous spiders.

He's heading in no particular direction, towards town, where there's more to look at until he makes up his mind. There's a car moving slowly alongside him, and he's not imagining this one. It's not the driver, but the lad in the back that grabs his attention. The face itself isn't familiar, but the look on it is. He knows a dangerous breed when he sees it, and this dog's snarling before he opens the back door. Terry's too slow to react, and next thing he knows, a blow on the side of his head sends him reeling, causing a ringing in the ears which ain't the church bells singing. The attacker is screaming something, but in his confusion, Terry can't make head nor tail of it. Instinct leads him to pull away, and throw a few flailing punches of his own, none of which land, but it looks like the episode is over – for now.

He staggers into the church grounds, wondering why nobody has come to his aid. There's blood on his hands which comes from his mouth. A tooth is loose, but that's the least of it. When he tries to stand, his stomach does somersaults, and Terry feels nauseous. As he kneels over the bushes, he spies his bag on the ground some distance behind, but it might as well be on the far side of the moon. He empties his empty stomach into flowering shrubs, destroying their summer bloom. He does feel better afterwards, although everything is relative. The bells won't stop ringing, and he wants to topple over the minute he stands. He resolves to stay down until the sickness passes.

He kneels, unintentionally, beside the grotto where Mary, he assumes, is keeping watch over her suffering Son. Plaster she may be, but there's a defiantly human quality to her serene face. Safe here, for now, he reasons, while wondering what treasonous bollocks is behind the assault. Then, like the flick of a switch, he knows. It comes to him, or comes *back* to him. The who, and the why. All's fair in love and recrimination. And if he's right, this is only the beginning, and far from the end. He won't have the chance to be more careful, or pick his way merrily through the minefield of petty vindictiveness.

Best not risk the flat. They're not about to give him an uninterrupted sleep first night home. *If* Barry has kept his word and held the place for him. There's always the Ma up in Dolphin's Barn. She may well give him a few home truths, but she'll cook him tea regardless. He looks into Mary's face, feeling her eyes upon him. No wrath, or judgment, but....pity. *Pity?* The blow to the head, that's what that is, turning him funny. Talking to statues – fuck – they'll have him in St. Patrick's next, not the Joy. But still, there's no harm in listening. It's not as if he's in any hurry. He has to think – who else beside the Ma? She should be the last resort. Maurice would put him up, but he's all the way out on the Long Mile Road. If only he had a phone. Time was, inside, the cells were packed ceiling-to-floor with so-called illicit material, and the screws turned a blind eye, but a new regime swept most of that away, and basics like mobiles were becoming rare treasures. How's he supposed to get by without a phone? He'll have to run the gauntlet back into town, and then try to get out of it again. But if Maurice is out, he's stuck on the outskirts – unless Tommy Peirce is still out in Walkinstown, and answering his door. There *is* a man who went straight, and straight to hell, by the sounds of it. Turned his life around, so he said, turned his back on petty crime, and walked straight into a wall of cancer, and stroke, and God knows what else. A cripple now, by all accounts, can't even drink, and his wife has to wipe his arse. But needs must, and if Maurice is a let-down, Tommy it has to be.

Mary is still looking intently at him. She's listening – but what is he supposed to say? He feels naked in front of her. Terry tries to stand, but his head is a block of concrete, and he has to sit before he falls. *I'm back*, he tells her. She reminds him of his wife – *ex-wife* – now living the life with a proper husband and two new kids, in Howth of all places. Like her other son, she doesn't keep in touch. Or maybe it's Terry that doesn't.

The sky darkens, and crackles, sparking thunder that heralds a tremendous downpour. He moves in closer for shelter. They are practically kissing. When did he last kiss a woman? On his wedding day? Normally, he fucked them like dogs, so he didn't have to look at their faces, or talk to them. It does, though, leave a bitter aftertaste, the *lack* of communication. Sometimes you need to talk, don't you?

I'm listening. Her voice is sweet and light, hypnotic, occasionally incomprehensible, but more and more words come through, and he begins to understand. An hour ago, or less, he was preparing to leave, craving his first pint, a proper feed, or just a lungful of air – and now he's hiding, still stunned from the blow. If that was the first hour, what about the second? At this rate, he'll be dead by sundown. He feels a kind of remorse. He had it coming. That's not her saying it – he doesn't need anyone else to explain it to him. He's done stupid things, but that doesn't make him stupid. You give it out, you get it back. That one *fucking* burglary, one of hundreds, is the cause of all this. The next house along, things would have been grand, more or less.

How do I stop it? He asks. He repeats the question, but her face is blank, plaster again. Can't stop it, too much bad history, too many footprints left. And if that's the case, then, the consequences are inevitable. The blood on his mouth has dried, but the tooth rattles under his tongue. How does he stop it? He looks over to where his bag was, and it's gone. A thief steals from a burglar - can't blame a man, or woman, for taking the opportunity when it comes along. Because it may never come along again. Break into another house? He doesn't feel like he could climb a fence. He was never a cat, more of an elephant, but he had a brain – *had* a brain – and that usually compensated for a lack of athleticism. No need to make a hasty exit if the prep is done right. Only amateurs made a run for it, and caused a ruckus in the process. Terry also had good hands, nimble fingers, though they weren't made for fighting. He'd been lucky to escape from the last job with just minor injuries – and a prison sentence - mainly on account of the owner been disturbed from sleep, and the worse for wear from drink, judging by the smell of him. But he'd lose the next one, if it came to it, and it was coming. It had already come. So – the choice was stark. Get into shape, and prepare for the worst, or get out of its way. But how to do that?

How to do that?   *I'm listening, Mary, I swear to you.*

⁓

The rain abates, but not the violence. The priest betrays his calling, dragging Terry across the gravel with surprising strength. The man's collar is not immediately visible, and the random whiskers, bad breath, and fury are temporary distractions. *Fr. Ignatius?* The one and only, wrapped up in righteous fervour, blind to Terry's pale protests. *Wasn't I only released today?* Did someone make a mistake, and open the gates of Hell, not just a prison?

He appeals to the priest, in vain, consciousness fading as they reach the road, where the priest loosens his grip, and looks in need of oxygen. Terry will let the man die where he lies, but Ignatius recovers sufficiently to allay concerns, and displays a hint of regret for his actions.

'Do I know you?' he asks Terry.

'Once upon a time,' he replies. 'I suppose I was what you'd call a member of the flock - but that's ancient history.'

'That's a nasty looking bruise on the side of your face.'

'Wasn't you, don't worry,' says Terry, 'I'm made of sterner stuff.'

'I thought you were…' the priest stutters.

'What? Building a nest right over there? I was sheltering, Father, from the rain…and everything else. I didn't think I needed permission. I didn't think I'd need sheltering from you.'

'I'm sorry…I didn't think, I just acted,' comes the measly apology.

'*Only clean, sober sinners need apply*, is that it? No people in serious trouble welcome – I see. Well, I'm not one of those, I can promise you that. I had me shower this morning, thank you very much, and a breakfast of sorts, so I'm not asking you to feed me. I've *done* my penance, Father – and I was hoping for a better reception than the one I've had. Do I just have one of those faces, is that it?'

The priest visibly shrinks before him, and retreats back inside the church gates, as if they'll protect him.

'Terry Walsh, Father…at your service. You don't remember me, but I remember you. All the boys remember you. I just come from the Joy, Father, in case you hadn't guessed – which is where the likes of you should be, if the truth were known. But don't worry, I haven't the time, or the inclination, for revenge. Not in my nature. I intend going peacefully from now on. Do you believe that? I was talking to the Good Lady over there, where I was resting. Yeah, she spoke to me, and I listened. I *listened*, Father. Perhaps you should do the same.'

'Terry Walsh?' says the priest, squinting into the watery sun. '*Fran* Walsh's Terry. Of course I remember…I didn't recognise you…'

'Changed that much, have I? Well, being locked up does that to you. Lack of sunlight, and Vitamin D. Lack of a lot of things. Oh, don't be mistaking me, I know I'm the one to blame for my predicament. But not anymore – if *She* wasn't lying to me. Look at me – just out, and I get a smack on the head, and then *you* decide to join in – charming. Maybe I deserved it, but I'm only asking for a chance to redeem myself. I asked Her to help me, and she said she would. And I believed Her. I've given Her a chance, though it hasn't started too well. Aren't you and Her on the same side, then? Obviously not. You need to fix that collar, Father, I think it's come loose. You don't want to lose it now, do you?'

Terry's overcome by the flood of words that came from his mouth – was that Her speaking through him? Jesus. He looks back when the church, and the priest, is well behind him. What kind of madness is occurring? He's hardly had time to draw breath since getting out. Under attack from all sides, it seems. He can't be watching everyone every second of the day – like that man over there, at the lights. They've turned, several times, but he's not moving. What's he waiting for? *Who?* Terry barrels past him, out into traffic, crossing Parnell Street at his peril, but he lands safely on the other side. That curious man is still back there, rooted to the spot.

O'Connell Street before him, an endless parade, a circus of roaring animals, cars and humans entangled in a dance of impatience. Terry's not quite up to it yet. Freedom is one thing, but too much at one time can kill. Doctors might have called it a panic attack, and he'd witnessed quite a few inside, especially from novices quickly breaking down at the prospect of incarceration. Terry puts it down to concussion, but not all of it. His legs suddenly have a mind of their own, and almost lead him under a bus. A woman pulls him back to safety, and leaves him parked up outside Mooney's bar. Maybe there is a God after all, he thinks. There is comfort, and unease, in the dark interior, where faces never quite fully show themselves, and tinny music plays relentlessly.

The glass shakes in his nervous hands, spilling some before it reaches his mouth. When it does hit the spot, it hammers it. But the shock to the system passes quickly, and the Guinness starts to work its magic. He starts to take in his surroundings. Characters emerge, and none too savoury. It's the time of day that determines the cast of any pub. There's a shivering wretch at the end of the bar, teetering on the stool, pouring lemonade into his brandy, but it has no effect.

He has enough for one more, or the soup of the day. There is – *was* – money in his bag, along with his few meagre possessions. Barry will sort him out – if he kept his word. There's money due, as well as owed, obviously, but the latter can wait. Remembering his promise to Her, he opts for the soup, and wishes he hadn't. The skin on the surface is tough to penetrate, and he sends it back, to the barman's indifference. Sweeping off the stool, Terry remains unsteady, and aims for the toilets, wanting to get a proper look at his injuries.

Condensation on the mirror clouds the reflection, but when he clears it, the results aren't much better. That *is* him in there, except…he can't put his finger on it. That bruise will get significantly worse before it fades. The eyes, nose, chin, all where they should be…but…what's wrong with them? He throws cold water on his doubts. He could do with a lie-down. He'd take his cell back if it was offered to him right now. How sad is that – Terry Walsh spurning the chances being presented to him. He's never felt this fear before. In and out since he was a teenager, he knew the drill backward, he was made of steel – wasn't he? No drugs, never, not one needle ever spiked his veins, and he could handle a drink or two, or twenty, without falling over. He broke houses, not bones. He knew his limitations. There were savings for a rainy day – in Barry's hands, as it happened, and he could be trusted – and retirement was on the cards. There was a future that didn't involve risking prosecution and further imprisonment. Maurice had a job for him, anytime he wanted. Okay, so it involved moving furniture, and laying carpets, for a paltry wage, but Terry had the resolve, and the nimble fingers, and the strong back. And the Lady's promise.

But that face – God, had the last few months done that to him? It hadn't been any tougher than the rest. He always managed to stay on good terms with the various factions, who competed for territory they could never own. And he was never anyone's property but his own. He was – at the last count – a fifty-two that looked sixty, but that was to be expected. He looked – different – altered, slightly, as if the earth had shifted off its axis by a degree or two. Barely discernible, but there *was* something...not right.

He blags his way onto the bus despite not having the full fare. He sits at the back, preferring to keep the other passengers in front, where he can see them. They take a meandering, interminable route, and then he almost misses his stop.

Feeling thrown in the deep end without the strength in his arms, Terry flounders around looking for a familiar landmark. The store was around here somewhere – where else could it be? How would he know where to come otherwise? It was a fleeting memory, but a strong one – him and Maurice having a Christmas drink right there in the showroom, the last customer having been shown the door, the shutters down, and the proposal being made again, in earnest – come work for Maurice, earn regular, legal money, before it's too late. Terry laughed, he recalled, right in the man's face, while downing his whiskey, mocking Maurice's heartfelt concerns. What a criminal Maurice might have made if he'd put his mind to it. Terry's not laughing at him now. If only he could find him.

He drifts onto the hard shoulder, getting blasted out of it. A Garda car notices him, and slows, but there's too much traffic to turn. He moves in off the road, and there's *Carpet World* right in front of him, practically tapping him on the shoulder. There are several cars parked outside, and it looks open for business.

The door whistles as he pushes it, announcing his arrival. It doesn't take long before a wary member of staff blocks his path.

'Can I help you, sir?' says the youth.

'I was looking for…Maurice,' Terry says uncertainly.

'Maurice? I'm not sure…who's looking for him?'

'Terry Walsh.'

'I'll see if he's available. Give me a second.' Terry is having doubts. Minutes pass, giving him time to study every item for sale. He couldn't afford one square yard of fabric, even if he had a stairs or hallway to furnish. Are they hoping he'll give up and leave of his own accord? He would, if he had anywhere else to go. Wasn't there someone he once knew in Walkinstown? An impression more than a memory, and receding quickly. Maurice he's sure about – but Maurice *what?* The surname escapes him for the moment. Never had much use for it.

Maurice finally appears, a shapeless mass with a shock of brown hair, and a look of displeasure on his face. Terry is about to embrace him, expecting the same in return, but hesitates.

'Well?' says Maurice. Terry waits for the punchline, but the other man doesn't appear to be joking.

Maurice – it's me – *Terry*. Jesus, have I changed that much?'

'I'm sorry,' the man says, 'I think I'm missing something here. Can I help you?'

'Can you *help* me?' Terry snaps back. 'Maurice, stop fucking messing about – I'm not in the mood. I'm just out a couple of hours, and you wouldn't fucking believe the morning I've had.'

Maurice looks behind him, and calls, 'Niall, come here, will you!' The young man hurries over, looking nervous. 'What's this about, do you know?'

'He – this man said he wanted to see you – asked for you by name. That's all.'

Maurice looks back at Terry. 'You seem to be under the impression that we know each other – but we don't. Least I don't recall meeting you. And that's some shiner you have brewing there. Now, I'm a busy man, so if you could state your business, maybe we could clear this up.'

Terry reels back as if punched. 'I came here…to find you…Maurice…it's me, Terry…Terry Walsh. What are you doin' saying you don't know me – we've known each other for twenty years.' He looks at the young man. 'Do you mind leaving us alone?' Maurice gives Niall the nod, who happily leaves. 'Now,' Terry continues, 'what is this shit? What are you doing to me? First I get a slap on the head the minute I walk out the gate, and now you're acting fucking strange. Is this fuck-over-Terry day, or something? Have I done something to piss you off I don't remember? If so, just tell me.'

'I'll tell you again…Terry…I've never seen you before. I don't know any Terry Walsh. I am, though, getting pissed off with this, okay? I have a business to run, in case you hadn't noticed. I don't know who sent you here, but they've given you the wrong address…and the wrong Maurice. I don't know, maybe that bang on the head has messed you up more than you think. You should have a doctor look at it. Now, I really have to go.'

'I *know* you…I've met your wife…I've stayed at your house…I…'

'Jesus. Okay, what's my wife's name, then? And where's my house?'

Put on the spot, Terry can't answer him. He can *see* them, the wife and the house, but they're vague, as if from a dream, and could be anyone's wife, anyone's house.

'No?' says Maurice. 'I think you're confused, mate. Or drunk, I don't know. Or care.'

'But I knew this place was here…I knew this was *your* business. I asked for *you*.'

'You said, unless I misheard, that you 'got out' today – from where, hospital? Prison?'

'Mountjoy,' Terry admits.

'Whatever about any Terry Walshs, I definitely don't know any prisoners, or ex-prisoners. Listen, I've been patient, but I haven't got any more time for this. I think you should leave – unless you want to buy some carpet. No? Well, I'm sure you can find your own way out.' Maurice is leaving, and Terry is still hoping, against hope, that this is a joke, and there's really a surprise party waiting for him in the back office, with acres of drink, and possibly an escort, or two.

'I don't even have bus fare,' he says softly. He runs after Maurice, grabbing him by the sleeve. 'I don't have bus fare – nothing – I spent it all getting here. Someone stole my bag.'

'Take your hand off me, will you?' Maurice says. 'I don't appreciate being touched by the customers – and you're not even a customer, are you? You're a fucking nuisance, is what you are. I have been nothing but polite up to now, but if you don't leave right away, I will have you escorted off the premises. And if that doesn't work, I'll call the guards, all right? Am I getting through to your thick fucking skull?'

Terry puts his hands up, and takes a few steps back.

'You've made your point. And don't worry, I'm leaving. No need to bring in the army.'

Maurice shakes his head and smiles, and turns away.

That's it, Terry. No punchline, no joke, no party.

⌒

Kicked off one bus, he waits for another. The next one is packed to the gills and blows right past him. He starts walking, his mind swirling, trying to make sense of the last senseless conversation. He knew Maurice, but Maurice didn't know him. If he was acting, it was the best Terry had ever seen. I *am* Terry Walsh. Who else could I be? I've been inside six months, and out of circulation, and then the blow to the head, remember that – these things all add up – but not to the extent of completely changing a man. And Maurice didn't know the name, not just the face.

The Long Mile Road stretches to infinity before eventually turning, and running alongside the Luas tracks, and the canal. He slides down the slippery bank to the edge of the water, where a family of swans floats serenely by. There's one man and his dog just ahead, making little progress, and a kid with a cheap fishing rod, catching little in the muddy channel. Terry steers away from them, and back towards the road, where a familiar car glides past, before slowing well ahead of the lights. The left indicator comes on, and the back door starts to open. Terry doesn't wait to see who emerges. He scrambles back down to the canal, heading for the protection of the low bridge about fifty yards away. He stoops below the roof, before needing to sit, ignoring the filthy ground beneath him. He wraps his arms around his knees as the cold kicks in.

It's dark when he emerges, his joints stiff, and his paranoia intact. There's no sign of the car, but he reckons they'll be back. They'll *keep* coming back until they find him. He goes into the petrol station on the corner, Crumlin village a stone's throw away. He used to know the place well. He lived with a girl there one time – didn't he? What was her name? The shelves in the station shop are heaving with goodies – he's fucking starving. He's had nothing since that soup he couldn't eat. There's a way to do this, and that is move stealthily and without hesitation, and don't take too much, and maintain a steady pace, don't give yourself away. His nimble fingers are swollen and clumsy, and he knocks packs of biscuits all over the floor. He utters an apology, before sneaking a pack inside his jacket. It's not near enough, but he loses his nerve, and leaving the shop proves as difficult as any job he can remember. He reaches the forecourt, and looks back, checking for pursuers. He makes it back to the canal, where, in his desperation to eat, he spills half the packet into the water.

There's Barry, and the flat, to consider. Terry has no keys. They're in the bag he lost. Was that only today? He could be there in twenty minutes if he put in the effort, but the streets in front of him don't look too pleasant. Plenty of predators in the Coombe and the Liberties, although he could skirt around them. Or there's always Dolphin's Barn. He can't bear the thought of his mother's face. He dreads making her open the door at this hour, especially when it's his face waiting on the other side of it. She's best approached in daylight, when he himself is more sorted.

A row of empty properties should pose no problem to a skilled artisan. And where's the crime in breaking into a house that's probably set for demolition. He picks the middle house, and there's no need to pick the lock as the back door is already open. Someone's been there ahead of him, and left their mark, but Terry has it all to himself now. There's no furniture on the ground floor, but there is a bed of sorts upstairs, a mattress without sheets. There's no need of electricity, and he couldn't use it anyway, certainly not the lights, though the heat would come in handy.

They're parked around the corner, in his weary mind. There's four of them, they'd need that many to subdue him. He kneels by the window and watches the street. He misses his cell, and even his cellmate – Parker, the Protestant, the talker, the wanker, the one who tossed and turned all night, and spat on the floor to clear the phlegm. Terry misses it, the certainty, the blankets, the set times, the schedule, the exercise yard, the gym, the library. He wasn't much of a reader, but he was forcing himself through an Ian Rankin – he can still see it beside his bed. Scratching behind the walls, even the rats want to get out. Was it only today? Why didn't he turn left instead of right? The eyelids fall like broken shutters, and She's right there in front of him. *Thought you'd abandoned me.* She has. Supposed to protect me, when all She's done is put me here, in this filth.

He falls asleep against the window, the bruised area leaning against the sill, and the pain wakes him at the crack of dawn. He gets a proper view of the room, and wishes he had left in darkness, without seeing it. The stairs don't have a full set of teeth. A misstep, a broken ankle, and he might not be discovered for months. He came in the back door, he goes out the front, not caring who sees him. He touches the bruise, knowing it will have turned overnight to a shitty brown-yellow. He moves quickly, before the hunters are lured from their lairs. Past a house he once turned over, when he was seriously out of pocket, and less than choosy about his targets. He might have left with something, but he lost it before he made it home. He'd rarely been out of pocket since then. He'd upped his standards, became more committed to his trade. The pockets were fairly light at the moment, though.

He is making good time, until he reaches Dame Street, and wonders where exactly he's headed. He smells coffee, and follows his nose to where a real breakfast might be had. But the pockets are empty, and there's nothing for free anymore. Barry better be up and about, and feeling charitable. Favours are owed. Barry was once lower than low, and Terry gave him more than a helping hand. It's not as if he'll be asking for much, just his flat, and a loan to tide him over. Although, now that – Maurice – is out of the picture, new plans will have to be drawn up. Retirement might have to be postponed for a bit, that's all.

Dominick Street – that's where he is, isn't it? Jesus, how could he have forgotten so quickly? Up and down, back and forth – but nothing jolts his memory. He can't think of the number, or the colour of the door. Unless it's not here. Across the street, the church doors open, and Terry recalls the flat being three doors up on that side. Number seventy-four, apartment 13B. He breaks out in a sweat. He feels like crying.

The street door is opened by an Asian girl leaving for work. Terry slips inside, and heads for the stairs, never having trusted lifts. On the third floor he creeps along the corridor like a burglar, about to break into his own home. He knocks gently on the door of 13B. If there's nobody home, he's in trouble, but if there is someone there, what the fuck are they doing there? Unless, of course, it's Barry. He'd give anything for it to be Barry, *any fucking thing.*

The locks are being turned inside. Terry only remembers one in his time. The door opens an inch, if that. A single eye appears in the gap.

'Yeah?' says the girl.

'Who are you?' asks Terry.

'Who are *you*?' she asks back.

'Who the fuck is it!' a voice hollers from inside.

'Don't know. Some bloke. With a bruise.'

'I live here,' Terry informs her.

'I don't think so,' she says.

'I *used* to live here. I've been away. But the place was being kept for me. By Barry. Barry....Whelan.' That last name was a struggle.

'Barry's our landlord,' she says, opening the door another inch or two.

'Good, now we're getting somewhere. He'll explain it to you. In the meantime, I just need to come in and collect a few things.'

'What things? There are no things here, except our own.'

'Marie, tell them to fuck off!'

That settles it – Terry forces his way in, looking for the heckler. The pair offer little resistance, both being nothing but skin and bone, living on what appears to be a diet of sleeping tablets. They live like scavengers at a rubbish dump. Terry doesn't fancy searching for anything of his own amidst the wreckage. He does, however, find a distressed twenty-Euro note lying under an empty water bottle. He could do with that, and they could do without. The male of the miserable pair thrusts a phone into Terry's face, screaming *hah!*

'What's this?

'The fucking landlord, man!'

Terry takes the phone.

'Barry?'

'Who's this?'

'Terry...Terry Walsh, Bar.'

'And what are you doing in my property, Terry Walsh – whoever you are?'

'Barry – it's me. Jesus!'

'Could someone please tell me what's going on? I'm afraid I've never heard of you, Terry Walsh. And I don't particularly like Luke there calling me in his druggy drawl. He makes less sense than you do.'

'But this is...*my* flat, Barry. I've been here two years almost, on and off. I...got out yesterday. I *told* you I was coming out.' But the landlords refutes knowing anything about anything when it comes to

Terry Walsh. And as for the flat's current residents, he admits that he may have made a mistake in letting it to them before doing a more thorough vetting.

'Where are you?' Terry asks, sensing the tide go out. 'Can you get over here?'

'Bit difficult, seeing as I'm in Spain. You sure you got the right place, Terry? You been inside, isn't that what you said? Maybe you knocked on the wrong door – it happens. I'll be back in Dublin in a couple of days – I'm sure I can sort you out with something. That is my business, after all. Give me your number and - .'

Terry ends the call and throws the phone across the wasteland of the apartment. The pair scurry after it like rats, scratching and clawing at each other in order to claim it. He leaves them to it, wrestling with his own demons.

The street offers no relief, as another familiar car is parked across the street. The man in the front is the one who smacked him earlier, but it's not the driver that interests Terry, it's the one in the back. *Nealon* – the man whose house he robbed, the low-level dealer who encountered Terry on that unfortunate night, and who obviously still hadn't forgotten, or forgiven. Wasn't six months inside enough? What now?

Terry decides to end it there and then. He wants his life back. He is sick of the fucked-up dreams he'd been having since the assault. Why hadn't Nealon finished the job the first time? He heads straight for the car, calling them out, demanding a word, with the organ-grinder, and *not* the monkey. The monkey, however, has a job to do, and puts himself in front of Nealon, protecting him.

'What the fuck?' says the monkey.

'It's *him* I want a word with!' Terry cries, and Nealon orders his guard to stand down.

'What can I do for you, son?' Nealon asks calmly. 'You have thirty seconds – I have business to attend to.'

'*I* have business to attend to,' Terry replies. 'Well? I'm here. Get it over with. What more do you want? I served me sentence, didn't I? I took that excuse for a beating this morning – what more do you *fucking want?*' To his surprise, Nealon frowns, and smiles at his colleague.

'I think,' says Nealon, 'there's a misunderstanding here. Do I know you? I don't recall the face. Is there a name to go along with it?'

Terry shakes his head in disbelief. 'Why are you fucking with me? Why are you all fucking with me like this? I'm Terry Walsh! *Terry*

Walsh!' Inches from Nealon's face, Terry is pulled firmly away, and goes sprawling in the road.

'Help the man up, Dennis,' says Nealon, but Terry manages on his own. He retreats to the safety of the path on the far side, in the shade of the church. *(...I asked for her help...and She listened......She....listened)*

'You okay, son?' Nealon asks as he walks over. 'I think you need a lie-down. Sober up, or come down, do whatever you have to do. You're having a bad trip, that's all.'

'And you seriously don't know me?' Terry croaks.

'Never had the pleasure – sorry to disappoint you. Wasn't me that gave you a beating, lad. That's not my style. Let's go, Dennis.'

The church is cold, dark, threatening. He sits, then kneels, in the back row.

Nobody knows Terry Walsh. Nobody's *heard* of Terry Walsh. It's as if –

I asked for her help – but what kind of help did she give me? What did I want from her?

If nobody knows him......they can't hurt him. He's free to go....he's been released.

~

He puts the stolen twenty to good use, filling up at the café on the corner of Parnell Street. Afterwards, feeling bloated, he examines his face in the toilet mirror. No sign of any bruising. No sign of Terry Walsh either – not the one he's been living with recently, anyway. He's in there, somewhere, etched in certain lines. He almost grasps it...but then it's gone just as quick. There's an anxious patron at the door, and he lets them in.

The walk to Dolphins Barn leaves him in a state of further confusion. The streets are familiar, but it's as if he hasn't seen them in years. What happened to the butchers, or the primary school? He knows, and yet, he knows nothing.

The house is there, thank God. But it's different. Been a while since he visited, he regrets, but it can't have changed that much, surely. The house is there, as is the woman of the house, bent over, using a crutch while she dusts the door fittings. She doesn't hear him at first, and he has to raise his voice to a near shout. His mother turns, and in turning...

Terry knows, before she speaks, what she will say.

Where have you been?

'Where have you been?' she asks, masking her astonishment with affected indifference.

'I…don't know.'

'We'd given up on you,' she says, her voice breaking. 'Terry……it *is* you, isn't it? I've seen too many ghosts to know the difference anymore…'

'Yeah, mam, it's me. I think.'

'Twenty years, it must be, and more. The rest all said you were dead…but not me. You've been missing so long I'd almost forgotten what you looked like…your own mother…how terrible is that? Photographs don't help none.'

'I been gone that long?' Terry asks.

'Don't you know yourself?'

'I'm not sure where I've been……or what I've done. But I asked someone to help me….and I think they did.'

'Are you back, Terry? For good, I mean?' She moves unsteadily towards him. 'You're not in trouble, are you?'

'I don't think so,' he tells her with a half-smile. 'Not anymore. I thought…I dreamt…I had a wife and son, all that stuff. But I don't think I do. I don't have anything, do I?'

'A clean slate, perhaps,' his mother says with infinite wisdom. 'You're in one piece…and you're home. It's a miracle, Terry, that's what it is.'

Terry swallows her in an embrace, afraid of breaking her brittle bones. But he's free.

He's been released.

Vonolel...(from the horse's mouth)*

My master wipes the sweat from my back. The land is a furnace, the soil is dust, the flowers are dead, and the spoiled roots are stained with our slain soldiers' blood. My brothers and sisters, the poor beasts, lie with their stomachs ripped open, torn by bullet and blade, and the buzzards sweep in under the low sun, picking at the boiling organs without shame. General Roberts, still suffering under the weight of the fever, slides off me, holding on to the saddle, and unsheathing his sword. He chooses his target, a wounded, writhing Afghan, and pierces the man's skull like a ripe melon, ending the soldier's misery, though my master shows no pity, and instead exhibits a maniacal glee. I will never fully understand man, only that I serve them. I once served many men, and earned many a whip across my hind. I suffered more scars outside war than in it. The general commands, but often stays to the rear of his men, for what good is a leader if he's first to fall – what kind of example would that set? My master is encouraged to retreat, for fear of enemy cowards cowering in the brush, feigning grave injury, or even death, lying in wait for the opportunity to strike him down. But he won't be persuaded, and seeks out those very cowards with broad slices of his blade, cutting and slicing like a careless butcher. Victory has been long assured, but the aftershocks continue. Desperate cries for help, from the living buried in the carnage. Horses, too, shudder in the heat, kicking out at the vengeful God that brought them down. I bow my head in the face of their distress. I halt, refusing to go on, but the master's spurs dig into my side. When will we ever leave this awful place? It was a field once upon a time, where crops grew, and farmers gathered the harvest, somehow scratching a living from the parched earth. Now the arid landscape is moist with the blood of men and horse. Wild dogs scavenge, and beggars put their own lives at risk by attempting to rob the fallen. Guards and medical personnel soon take care of them, adding to the casualties. Screaming men are borne through the hell on stretchers, soon to face amputation, and blessed relief through morphine, or death. The crack of a rifle startles me, and I rear up,

96

dumping the general on the ground. I have heard ten thousand shots and barely reacted, so why this time? Perhaps I thought the last gun had been fired. But the end of every battle brings that feeling. One battle ends, and the next one is just up ahead, in the next field, over the next hill, men against men, horse against horse, and no one can really remember why they are there. They only know they have to be there, they have to fight, and that's an end to it. Men, it seems, have to fight, or they lose their purpose, and consequently their way. I would be happy if this was the last man on my back. These days, I feel their weight even when they have climbed down. I dream of dawn charges over rough ground, heading into uncertainty, and violence. Often, of late, I am back in Bombay, in the maddening noise and stench, where I am daily beaten, for no good reason as far I can see. Then one day, the soldier arrives, and pays my owner a fortune, and I am on the move, forever on the move, but treated more kindly than I could ever have imagined. The general comes soon after, and I am to be his, and his alone. We are of one mind, we understand each other, and I trust him like no other man, before or since. Long periods of peace and quiet, plentiful food, and diligent care, are interspersed with bloody passages, lengthy battles where the aim is to kill as many men, and their animals, as possible. There is extra food in the celebration of victory. The men drink until they fall down, although the master always maintains his dignity. No real harm comes to me, except for the occasional brushing of a sabre, enough to sting, but not to bring me down. My master and I are protected at all times, and the general refrains, for the most part, from the killing. We cover vast distances in our search for fresh blood to spill, but once the land, and its people are taken, we move on. When will we rest? When will the men be satisfied, and find a place where they can live? I think it is over, the battle of Kandahar, on this sweltering day in the year of 1880. I feel the master settle on me, as the men gather to offer their congratulations. I, too, receive numerous slaps of admiration around my head and back. A few grab my ears, thinking I enjoy it, but I throw my head up, bare my teeth, and the master can read the signs. He urges me to be calm, and pulls on the reins to steer us away from the melee. I almost lose my footing in the splayed innards of one of our own, but I manage to stay upright, and we eventually escape the lunacy.

97

They hang pieces of metal around my neck, and the general bows for me in thanks before the regal lady. I try to shake them clear, but I am burdened with them for hours. My front legs are weary from the obligation to be still, and the music from the marching band sounds like a volley of booming cannon or rifle fire.

In the green pasture, my belly full, my playmates aren't for games, instead choosing the shade of trees off to the side. I need to keep running to keep warm. This is England, in the spring, but the sun brings little heat, and the thin blankets are kept for darkness, when my Arabian blood is already suffering. If I stamp and bellow, and kick the side of the stables, they bring me extra blankets, but I'm still cold. It's more than cold, though. I search in my dreams for the desert lands, for the smells and sounds, but the cold, and quiet, wake me in the dead of night, and I struggle to remember where I am.

The general visits, but doesn't ride. He walks with a limp, and one side of his face barely moves when he talks. So he whispers, and leans into my neck, running his hands through my mane, dreaming too, no doubt, of the past. He stops visiting, and then I know that he can't. His legs won't carry him, any more than my legs could carry him, or any man. The men here are peaceful, and sword-less, who don't seek battles, or the destruction of their fellow men.

We outnumber them, and hold dominion. They serve us, letting us grow fat, and old. For I am, assuredly, near my time.

⌣

The sea torments, as do the rough hands of the men bearing me off the ship. My box strikes the edge of the harbour wall, cracking. Inside, I stumble, grazing my leg off a splinter of wood, and the flies are quickly there, sucking at will.

Is this my last home? The Curragh, in Ireland, lush and green, and wet. My first few weeks, it rains with gentle persistence. My companions unsettle me, snorting their disapproval, not liking the smell of me. My head is full of spirits, whispering, asking me to come home. I resist the swathe of open space in front of me, refusing the gallop, as the others race off ahead without me. The grass makes me sick, the water tastes like dirt, the meal like dung. I lie down, and can't get up. They come and hoist me up, cajoling, as if I am to blame. A needle punctures the skin, and I float from side to side until I fall into a dizzying sleep. In the morning, they watch me, and I push with everything, surprised to find my legs have not abandoned me as yet. The men clap their hands, and treat me with a bucket of apples. I *taste* them, sweet and delicious, and soon after, I am anxious for the fields, oblivious to the rain that has returned with devilish intent.

At the corner of the field, I look beyond the fence, over the heather and bracken, and into the denser parts of the forest. I see myself in there, rushing through the trees, urgently seeking the other side, where the final peace awaits. I am nudged in the rear by the chestnut mare who won't leave me alone, and I turn and give in to her youthful teases. I am no danger to her, though I have a sense of what I might have felt in another existence. We return to the shelter, where we are dried off and fed, and where we rest in adjoining stables.

One day the white arrives, the men call it snow, and nothing can prevent the frightening cold it brings from poisoning my veins. I stand in protest against this new enemy, remaining indoors while I wait for it to disappear. It relents, the green returns, but the cold clamps its teeth into my side the moment I leave my shelter. The ground is unsteady, and the mare slides to her knees, and is lucky to survive. We try to huddle together on our enforced trek, but the men on our backs wrestle us apart, and push us along the icy trail. My instinct is to shake my man off. He is not my master, he has no skill with the hands or the feet. I don't think he likes horses, and horses certainly don't like him. Long before the end, my muscles ache with the strain. How much longer can I endure?

The heat has returned, and drinking from the trough at the edge of the field, something of my former energy returns. This rare morning is interrupted, however, by a booming gunshot from nearby. We scatter in fear, before the danger passes, but for the rest of the day, I am easily disturbed, and every sounds seems to herald the arrival of the soldiers, and the beginning of the next battle.

The next battle is my own. The heart is failing. The heart is racing to leave my body, and I foolishly try to catch up with it. My forelegs give way, and I fall, enveloped in exquisite pain, my face against the gravel in the yard, until release. A singular brief moment follows, a bitter sweetness on my tongue...the sweetest apples I ever tasted.

I am buried in the gardens of the Royal Hospital, Kilmainham, on the edge of Dublin city. I am alone here, hidden by the wall in a corner, out of sight and mind, the one deathly reminder in an oasis of flowers, of bloom, and life. The leaves fall, the petals drop, they die, but then they rise soon after, in the spring and summer, while I die, and die, my skin and bones becoming soil that nourishes new variations of plant, as if there weren't enough of them. It would cause quite a stir if *I* rose miraculously every spring, and sprouted from the earth in a gallop. It would scare the visitors, if there were any. A few patrons do stumble across me now and again, they strain their eyes to read the fading letters on the headstone, they struggle to pronounce the name – *Vonolel* – not realising my rich Arabic heritage. And as for me – I am there, of course, but only a part of me, the part that senses the changing of the seasons, and the indifference of the visitors. I am underground, but also out there, reaching back through the decades, looking for my master, searching for the torrid dry lands of the East, chasing the last herds of wild horses, drinking at the shrinking pools, and keeping a close eye on my kin. Mostly, and against my will, I find myself back at the morning of the battle in Kandahar, letting my sick master ease his way into the saddle. I feel his torment, and his resolve to command his army to victory. Trust, and love, are reciprocated, and with the gentlest urging, he orders me to move out. The battle is well in progress as we approach, and I hear the cries of my comrades as they ride through a sea of blade and rifle-shot. Limbs snap like twigs, and death rattles sing, but the General, *my* master, proclaims that the righteous will prevail. And those under him...*believe*.

*Vonolel existed, took part in the Battle of Kandahar in 1880, and is buried in Kilmainham, Dublin.

The Face In The Wall

It is a night for death, not comedy. The air is solid, and his lungs fight against it. Deacon Turner turns into Merrion Street, thankful for the short journey. In front of him on the road, a horse rears up as a stray dog runs across its path, causing a disturbance inside the carriage. A tall hat appears in the window, and the driver is suitably chastised. There will come a day, it is foretold, when the streets will choke with traffic, human and animal, forcing man to abandon his reliance on lesser creatures for their transport. The bicycle, too, is a menace. What's wrong with our legs, the Deacon muses? If they're not used, they'll wither, and future generations will be born without them. He cannot give voice to such blasphemous thoughts, although God has already heard them. He's in a foul mood, he reflects, on account of recent doubts about his vocation. But it's more than that. It's 1871, and the end of the century is galloping towards them. The Church of Ireland is no longer the official church of the State, and what will that mean for the likes of him? When the well of funding runs dry, he will doubtless be cast aside, and returned to the mainland – if he hasn't already left the church by then. There is always the farm on the Borders, he would be welcomed back with open arms, and, Lord knows, they could do with his help. Dublin has been a folly, he realises. Even now, he yearns to be back in his rooms, poring over his books, and living in a theoretical world. The outside has left him bruised and humbled. He has weakened in the face of the city's adversity. And his betters know no better, and do less. They spend their days organising evenings like this – attending plays in new theatres. *Theatres!* When just around the corner, families forage in the same bins as the rats. Yet – Deacon Turner accepted the invitation to attend, and that is where he is now headed, when he should be in his bed, or at his studies. Or something nobler. He *has* an idea, a project that he is considering putting into operation, if his courage doesn't desert him, if he can *find* his courage to begin with. He will attend to the matter at hand, be seen, shake the glad hands, but his thoughts will be elsewhere.

⁓

The great and the good are present, and probably a few bad. The rich, and the less rich, but definitely not the poor. *He* is poor, in material possessions, but he doesn't struggle to put food on the table, like so many, therefore it would be a sin to complain. He does feel the lack of proper clothing, having worn the same clerical garb for month after month. The weekly wash keeps it presentable, but it does wear the fabric down. They know him, but he doesn't know most of them. They can use his name, but he can't use theirs. There is a brief ceremony, and the Gaiety Theatre is officially opened. If he doesn't get out of the cold soon, he'll die before the opening act.

'She Stoops to Conquer,' by Goldsmith, is sublimely ludicrous, a confection of mistaken identity, and triviality. Deacon Turner laughs in spite of himself. The joy of unimportant things. There is room for levity, but surely everyone should have the opportunity to experience it, instead of the privileged few. He accepts a glass of wine at the interval, and joins in the merry conspiracy. The second act is more of the same, or less, if you want to think of it that way. Roars of approval from some at the end, though not, of course, from the high guests in the high boxes. They are spirited away in grand carriages, while the likes of him are cast out into the freezing fog.

He passes cacophonous dens of iniquity on his way home. He's curious about how long he would last if he dove inside. Would he emerge within an hour devoid of all moral direction, and money? Are his foundations that weak? A man stumbles out, reeking, laughing as he falls, rising momentarily before he falls again. Deacon Turner goes to help him, but pulls back at the last minute. He fears the swing of a drunken arm, or simply the anger of the common man. The *common* man? Who is more common than he? Take off the cloak, and there's nothing underneath. He steps into the road, failing to avoid the horse's dung that litters the capital. He scrapes his shoe on a step, and laughs at his misanthropy. Perhaps if he had a wife, and children, he would feel less put-upon. His selfishness has thrived in the absence of such responsibilities, and holds sway, for better or worse.

There is a man collapsed in Fitzwilliam Lane, a short distance from his home. Deacon Turner leans in closer, and hears breathing. There is no obvious injury, though continued exposure to this cold might inflict its own. He runs to his lodgings and procures a blanket, with which he covers the poor man. Returning home, securing the front door behind him, he lights the oil lamp, and begins a fire, all the while consumed with the image of the man he left outside. But, he reasons, help one and you have to help all, and if you don't help all, you'll go mad, and what use are you then to anyone? Sparks in the grate herald a roaring fire which quickly fills the small room with smothering warmth. He makes tea, and finds a few stale-ish biscuits in a tin. He opens Volume 2 of Gibbon's *History of the Decline and Fall of the Roman Empire*, and soon falls under its spell. He falls asleep with the book open on his lap, and the fire at full strength. He dreams of moving through sheets of rain on the Border farm, on his knees, trying to find a lost ewe. His fists dig into the mud, and he's on all-fours, resembling a lowly beast himself.

He thinks he hears a pounding at the door, but it's just the gusting wind. There's a man outside in that, he thinks, with nothing but a thin blanket to protect him. And across the city, he knows, there are many men, and women, facing the same storm.

Barley beef soup for breakfast, and a bracing wash with cold water and carbolic soap. He's not a purist in the absolute sense, but he believes in living sparsely where he can. The Bishop will be dining in his morning robes, no doubt, with servants tending to his every whim, and Deacon Turner won't descend to those depths.

The man under the blanket has not survived. Deacon Turner says a prayer over him, before hurrying to find a policeman, and absolving himself of all blame. *I did not wield the knife that killed him...but maybe I watched him perish in the aftermath.*

His church, on Leeson Road, is damp and overpowering. Rector Lavery is his usual polite, and distant, self, laying out the duties of the day like a worn tablecloth. There is satisfaction to be gleaned from routine, and service, but the battle, he feels, is out there, not in here. The Rector has heard his arguments, and grown resolutely deaf to them. If he pushes too hard, too often, Deacon Turner knows he risks banishment to a place where no one will hear him. He *has* an idea, though, and it's simply a matter of being prepared to suffer the consequences.

Over lunch with the Rector in the kitchen, Lavery recounts a story in the paper that morning, about the growing threat from so-called Fenians, separatists anxious for the British to relinquish their hold over Ireland.

'It will be the *church* next!' the Rector cries, in an unexpected show of emotion. 'As if we haven't enough to contend with. It's not enough that we have lost our status here to the Catholics — but it has given these *thugs* licence to use violence against us. We must look to our security, Deacon.'

'Or - ,' the Deacon suggests, 'we could encourage greater dialogue — open our doors wider, instead of closing them - .' The Rector looks aghast at the Deacon's suggestion, and refuses to discuss the matter further. The rest of the day passes in muffled tones, with sparse conversation, until the early evening service brings welcome solemnity to proceedings. Nevertheless, Deacon Turner heads home with pale, empty thoughts, searching for the strength to carry out his reckless plan.

Jesus didn't face his foes and vanquish them, he embraced and loved them. He used the weapons of forgiveness and empathy. Deacon Turner casts off his costume, tired of playing the part of a cleric, as opposed to actually being one. He puts on ordinary clothes, purloined from a charitable neighbour, and dons a cloth cap to complete the transformation. He steels himself against the night ahead with a brandy, and a hollow prayer. He's off to the theatre again, across the river, in the underworld of Dublin, where he must blend in, and be accepted, if he is to survive.

She swoops, and conquers, reeling him in, calling herself Maureen, or 'Mo,' if that's what the gentleman would prefer, and he has no defence against her, succumbing to her wishes, in the hope that she will think kindly enough of him to listen, at some point.

'I am the Queen of Monto!' she declares, cackling, and pushing up her voluminous hair, pretending to act regal. 'And *who* might you be, sir?' she asks. And there was he thinking he looked like a commoner.

'Andrew....Turner,' he says, unable to lie.

'Well, that's a lovely name, isn't it. Now, you just make yourself comfortable, and forget about the baby.' How could he make himself comfortable, let alone forget about the baby? The child sleeps peacefully in a lace-wrapped crib, the only decent item in the room, which is in the basement, where the smell of vegetables overwhelms, and the street seems very far away indeed. What is he doing here? He can hardly speak, and she's in the throes of removing her clothes, relishing his embarrassment.

'Stop!' he cries, 'please.' She hasn't even asked for payment, and here she is gleefully undressing in front of a stranger. She continues, albeit at a slower pace, and reveals her breasts, playing her game, teasing him until he can't resist, devoid of shame.

'Do I disappoint the gentleman?' she asks, adopting a childish voice. The baby then announces its presence with a wailing cry, and there's a knock on the door, a woman asking Mo if she has clean towels, and there's a clamour in Deacon Turner's head, he feels a prisoner, doomed to his fate, unless he can display some fortitude. He finds the coins in his pocket, and throws them on the bed. 'I only want to talk to you,' he manages to say. 'And I think the baby needs you.' She sees to the money before the baby, caressing both. The neighbour goes away, disappointed, and Mo covers up, laying the settled baby back down, and sitting on the bed, slumped.

'Talk?' she says. 'Am I that ugly, sir?'

'You are not ugly – not at all. But...I came here to talk to you, that's all. I have paid you, so where's the harm in letting me spend the time with you?'

'Who are you?' she says again, suspicious, almost fully dressed now.

'I am a Deacon,' he says.

'A priest?'

'Not quite, but something similar.'

'And you came here to cure me of my wicked ways, is that it? It's a little late for that.'

'No. I came here to talk...to understand....what it is that goes on down here....and if there isn't a better way for people here to live.'

'That's a strange accent you have,' she says.

'I live here, over the river, but I am originally from the north of England.'

'Aren't there no fallen women there?' she mocks him.

'No doubt there are – but my church sent me here. You are a Catholic, are you not?'

'I was born that way, sure. But God doesn't feed us, does he? Or care for our sick children, while the gents and ladies are blind to us, up there in their fancy houses and clothes.'

'These were once fancy houses,' he tells her, 'all along Gardiner Street, up to Mountjoy Square – maids and servants, nannies, and grand carriages.'

'I know – I scrubbed for the likes of them. They moved out to Kingstown, or thereabouts. But not before the gentleman of the house had his many ways with me, night and day, whenever he chose – that boy there has an aristocratic father, not that he'll ever meet him. And I've seen him back here, enjoying the company of several others around here. At least he pays them. He never did that for me.'

'How old are you?' the Deacon asks.

'Twenty-one,' she says with a certain pride.

'And you spend your days – entertaining – gentlemen, is that it? How many in a day, do you reckon?'

'I don't count them, sir – and only a few are true gentlemen. They have cold wives, and are in need of comfort.'

'And you are in need of money?'

'There you have it. He gets what he wants, as do I.'

'But how long do you intend to carry on? What about the dangers of infection, or disease?'

'Or when the soldiers move on,' she adds. 'They're the decent ones, to be honest. There's no thinking with them – no guilt or shame.'

'But what about your child – you do business right here in front of him?'

'Where else can I put him? Out on the step, or up on the pavement until I'm done?'

'But the soldiers *will* move on,' he tells her, 'and the gentlemen will be persuaded to relinquish their dubious habits. That is already happening.'

'And they are being persuaded by the likes of you, is that it? Tell me, *Deacon,* have you ever been with a woman? Or do you prefer each other, or young boys?'

'Yes – I have been with a woman. A long time ago.' The memory shudders inside him. On the farm, in the field, against the hedge, trembling, a girl from a nearby village, and both as clumsy and ignorant as the other, and neither sure at the end of it if anything had actually happened.

'It is like breathing,' Mo tells him. 'Where would the world be without it? We would have died out long ago. Why is it a mortal sin, Deacon? If it keeps my child and myself alive, where's the harm? You tell me that. I don't…' She breaks off, her voice cracking.

'You don't…want to continue in this way, is that what you were going to say?'

'Look at me, Deacon – my body, my face...my teeth.' She opens her mouth, revealing blackened molars. 'They look less and less,' she says. 'They can't bear to – and soon they'll give me a wide berth.'

'And that is my point, exactly. What future is there for you in this life?'

'But – what other life is there? Are you going to offer me one?'

'What about marriage?' the Deacon suggests, which prompts a derisory laugh from the girl.

'And do I hide the child while we're courting? Do I pretend to be a virgin on our wedding night? *He* can have been with a hundred different women before he lands on me, but God forbid the woman bringing the same. I think, Deacon......that you've seen enough. I'll keep your money, if you don't mind. That boy has had a cough on him that's lingering. I need the syrup, and that money will pay for it. I wonder...sometimes...what it would be like…without him…'

'Don't ever think that!' the Deacon cries. 'He is your flesh and blood, he is a miracle, the greatest of all miracles.'

'But I wouldn't be killing him…just letting him go, that's all.'

He *has* seen, and heard, enough. He bids her goodbye, and climbs the stairs with his mind reeling. The problem is beyond him. She is but one star in an ungodly heaven of millions. He can't save her, she can only do that for herself. Has he, at least, planted a seed of doubt in her mind? A doubt that already exists, and maybe, just maybe, she will arrest her decline – and bring others along with her. He is dreaming, his ideals are fiction. *Look around you.* The streets are clogged with base thoughts, the pavements thronged with every social class, faces he recognises, some from the play the night before, ones who'd shaken his hand, bishops and politicians, officers of every rank, each and every one in search of discreet ecstasy, pockets bulging with the money to pay for it.

His heart is close to bursting. He feels lightheaded approaching the river, welcoming the breeze coming off the water. He turns his head in the direction of shouts and cries coming from Sackville Street. He removes his cap, and throws it over the rail into the river, ashamed of his disguise, wishing he could pronounce his true calling in some way.

A small group of men are charging a line of police, unfurling a cheap banner that reads *Irish Republican Brotherhood*, throwing stones and bottles, angry and determined. The police have no option but to retreat, until help arrives in the form of a water-cannon pulled by steaming horses whipped up into their own kind of frenzy by the driver. Deacon Turner is compelled to intervene, pleading with each side to relent, to see sense, and talk. *Talk!* Is that his only solution to every social malaise? As with Mo, he is ignored, and pushed back to the sides, until they turn on him, and land some heavy blows before he can scramble to safety. He retches in a laneway, praying for forgiveness, bemoaning his failings. The Rector will hear of this, and do more than admonish him. He will be cast out without having made the slightest impression.

The warring factions have disbanded, though a handful of drunken republicans remain, delighted to find the Deacon back in their midst. They hurl obscenities instead of stones, and chase him over the bridge, laughing at his lamentable protests for reconciliation, and ordering him out of *their* country.

He pleads with the doorman of the Shelbourne Hotel to let him in, struggling to convince him that he's a member of the clergy. A party of ladies and gentlemen arrive at the same time, and the Deacon is recognised, and invited in as their guest. Once inside, he rushes to the bathrooms to clean himself up, before heading for the bar, and a brandy. Without money, he has no choice but to prevail upon the goodwill of the gentleman who had helped him earlier.

'Of course, my dear man. You look like you need it, by God!'

The brandy loosens his tongue, and he relates his adventures in Monto to his mortified listeners. They quickly make their excuses, and move to a more civilised part of the room. Deacon Turner is reluctant to leave the sanctuary, and comfort, of the hotel, but the manager suggests, discreetly, that it might be best for all concerned if he thought about going home.

'Home?' the Deacon cries, '...home? It is a damp, small hovel, unsuitable for a scholar such as I...such as I...I...'

'I think, sir,' says the manager, 'that it's time for you to get some rest. Perhaps we can arrange a cab for you - or do you think you can walk there under your own steam?'

The intolerable shame, the unsightly bruising, the aching limbs – anyone of these could have made the Deacon decide to stay in bed that day. He tries *not* to remember, but the nightmarish images come in abundant flashes, regardless, pinning him to the bed like a bug.

Thankfully, there are no callers, especially the Rector, whom he could not bear to face. As the day wends its weary course, Mo comes to him in broken sleep, converting *him* to her religion of futility. Why endure when there is not a single accomplishment he can point to? He follows the proper precepts, and obeys, and never strays, and feels nothing but empty at the core of his being. The farmer has the harvest, or his cattle's milk, to show for his labours. The carpenter has the simple table to proffer, the engineer a bridge – but the cleric…the cleric offers vague promises, and watches his flock dwindle, while struggling inwardly to retain his faith in the absence of proof.

He pulls down the sheets, and his hand finds the hard reminder of delayed lust. He closes his eyes, willing her to come back to him, and finish her striptease. But there is only the tease, and he imagines the rest of her with tortuous angst, spilling over, and spoiling the sheets. Strangely, he feels better, as if the worst is behind him. If he's going to take the punishment, he might as well do the sin. Rashly, he considers going back to her, and pursuing the real experience. After all, as she said, it is only…sex. They would cease to exist without it – and if both parties are willing, regardless of any money involved, where is the harm, if precautions are taken? This is…the Devil working his magic on him…*stop it!* The Deacon dresses hurriedly after a cursory wash, refusing to give his bruises too much attention. He needs air, and food, but *no* drink. There are medicinal benefits now and again from the port and the brandy, but last night was indulgent and self-pitying. Who were those people who brought him into the hotel as their guest? Might they recall his unpleasant testimony, and relate it to church elders? It will be used as an example of the decline of the Church of Ireland, and why its status needed to be fundamentally altered.

He keeps his eyes on his feet as he walks through town, settling on a café on Dawson Street for lunch. The thin soup burns his tongue, and the bread is rather stale, but he's not one for complaining, and the poor waitress looks worn to a frazzle. He is the only single diner in the establishment, and feels the eyes of the room upon him – the eyes of God upon him. The Rector will be cursing his absence, and Mo will be telling her neighbours about the cleric who wanted to *talk* – *ha-ha!* How will she spend the money he gave her – on food for the baby, or clothes for herself, to improve her prospects on the street? He did *nothing* – he relayed no Christian tenets, he didn't open her eyes to a different, better life. He must go back, and try harder, *press* the words of God into her soul, and then go next door, and do the same there, and on and on until the whole street is made aware of the plague that envelops them. And when that street is done, onto the next, and the next...

'I *must!*' the Deacon exclaims, banging the table, startling the other customers. He leaves, shaking, fearing further sickness, unless it's missionary zeal filling him up. Once back in his rooms, the tide of passion recedes, and he seeks solace in his books, keeping the bible until last, as it's invariably the most difficult to read, being a mirror that reflects back on him unfavourably. He retreats into himself again, retires to his bed, bemoaning once more his inability to carry through on his more ambitious plans.

He wakes in the middle of the night as if escaping from the clutches of an unspeakable monster. Bathed in sweat, he searches every inch of his lodgings looking for a nameless enemy. He opens the front door, certain there's a man waiting to take him on a long journey. Deacon Turner slowly shakes off the pitch black of his dreams, and senses a renewed strength within him. Before he can think it over too much, he takes his coat and leaves the lodgings, intent on returning to Monto, and facing up to his responsibilities. Day or night, the lowly trade continues apace, with pavements crowed by the fearful and fearless alike. Only the lights add a subterranean flavour, like spotlights over the stage, increasing the sense of drama. She is nowhere to be found, so Deacon Turner calls her out. He stands on Gardiner Street shouting her name. Getting no response, he moves out into the middle of the road, where he raises his voice even further, and intensifies his argument, widening his net, accusing every one of turning against God. They are falling into Hell, he exclaims, and nothing can save them. He appeals to those only *thinking* about taking a woman, calling them back onto his side, where he will shelter them. He holds a small crucifix in his right hand, and squeezes until it draws blood.

He moves from street to street, becoming more confident, quoting from scripture, and feeling rapture – when a blow on the side of the head sends him sprawling. A policeman looms over him, raising his truncheon, and prepared to continue the assault. He threatens the Deacon with arrest if he does not leave the area forthwith.

'What is the charge?' the Deacon demands to know, and the answer comes in another savage blow that dulls his brain.

The new bruises fire his holy spirit, and he resolves to continue his campaign that night, and the night after that, until the whole city rings with his cries. He is anxious to return to his job, and challenge the Rector to support his endeavours.

The Rector has received word of the Deacon's unsavoury activities from several sources, and proposes that urgent medical care is needed, and a prolonged period of rest.

'Rest!' the Deacon protests. 'I have only just woken up, for God's sake. The work has only begun – I *know* my cause now, I know my direction. God has spoken to me, He *is* speaking through me. I was hoping you might give me your support, or even join me one night when I venture out.'

'*Join* you, Deacon? You are insane, surely. You have a sickness, can you not see it? You cannot continue in this way, or you might never recover. And you will not pursue this madness in the name of *my* church, I can tell you that. Already you have made enemies – don't make an enemy of me. Do you not see? Our support is waning in this country. There is an increasing appetite for revolution, for violent change. Not only do they object to our presence here, they are willing more and more to do anything to force us out. You are an Englishman, Deacon, as I am, and we must be proud of that, but you must speak wisely, and softly, not shout and draw attention to it.

'So, Rector, we must cower like mice for fear of upsetting a few reckless individuals?'

'*You* are the reckless individual, Deacon – and I am warning you that if you persist in these tactics, this church will abandon you, and let you suffer your fate alone. Do you understand?'

'I understand completely,' the Deacon insists.

He stops bawling in the street like a madman, choosing subtler tactics, like gate-crashing meetings of so-called Republicans, and politely declaring his objections to their reactionary cause. He is chased out of each meeting, narrowly avoiding a heavy beating on more than one occasion, and warned to be careful, as both his face and name are now well-known in republican circles, and there is no guarantee that someone might take grave offence to his protestations, and take matters into their own hands. He is not afraid, he says. He is living and breathing his faith, taking the fight to the enemy, and there can be nothing to fear, not even death itself.

Each night in his rooms might be his last, he knows, if the church fulfils its promise to cut off its support. He considers the practicalities of finding alternative accommodation with no fixed income. He might end up living in the tenements, scraping an existence, and willing, like Mo, to do anything to survive. Perhaps that is his destiny. If he hopes to bring the most helpless up to the light, perhaps he has to go down into the dark with them.

He is refused entry to the finer restaurants, his new-found reputation having gone before him. He carries their insinuations on his back like a test, willingly sacrificing the occasional lunch, if that's what it takes. He is sustained by purer thoughts, and the prospect of making his mark before his inevitable defeat.

Nightly, he returns to his books, with increasing dissatisfaction – *words* – theories, flights of imagination, when he is now rooted firmly in the real, in the substance of daily life, in the breath of every living person that represents an obstacle that has to be overcome. He no longer reads for pleasure, as fiction only fuels his anger at frivolity. Every waking moment should be directed towards reaping God's rewards, and nothing else.

As he falls asleep, he thinks about burning every book in his possession, as a sign of his devotion.

Confined to bed with a persistent, and worrying, cough, Deacon Turner swims in feverish dream waters, unaware of the note being nailed to his front door. Only later that morning, when he sticks his head out the door for some air, does he notice the sheet with the red scrawl, the threat written in haste, and cowardice: *go back to where you came from! and take your god with you* He's not *my* God, the Deacon cries, he's *your* God, everyone's God – there is only one! The ground swirls beneath his feet, and cracks start appearing. His eyes roll back in his head, and he's helpless to prevent himself from going under.

The last face he expected is there to greet him – Beazley, the landlord. It wasn't *him* who put the note there, was it? No – the landlord may be many things, but he's not a common bully. He is, however, there with a similar purpose to his anonymous letter-writers. He doesn't threaten in so many words, but the meaning is obvious.

'The rent, dear boy!' Beazley declares in that florid, English, way of his. He has no more sympathy for the Deacon just because he's a fellow countryman. 'It's no laughing matter to ask for money, especially not from a man of the cloth. What has happened, Deacon? I thought you were solid? I was keen, as you may recall, to secure your tenancy. I felt sure that I would have no problems with you, sir. I have enough of those on my belt, I can assure you. I take my very life in my hands these days knocking on doors, when all I'm doing is asking what's due. There is no fairer landlord that Tankersly Beazley, and that's a fact!'

'I am not well, sir,' the Deacon says, 'as you can see.'

'Yes – what has you lying in the street? I had half a mind to call the constable, but then your eyes flashed open, as if you sensed me.'

'I have been stricken, Mr. Beazley, for several days – I simply came out for some air, and felt dizzy. I was barely out for a second before you came along. Can't we talk about the rent tomorrow, or the next day? When I am more sensible. I throw myself upon your mercy.'

'Tush, sir! We'll have none of that – I am not insensitive. No one can say that landlord Beazley does not have a heart – no, sir. And I will tell you this – I *will* accede to your request, and give you a few days to get back in the stir of things. How does that lie with you, Deacon?'

'It lies with me…very well, landlord….thank you.'

With the note still in his hand, the Deacon finds his bed again, craving hibernation.

He rides the hills, on the back of a dray horse, in a dense fog, before the arrival of dawn, and the cries of the sheep echo across the snow-topped fields. His every breath freezes in front of him, yet inside he is burning up, his blood boiling.

His bed sheets are like ropes tying him to the past, and he must escape them. He coughs blood in the lane, but continues forward, determined to break the fever. He chooses the first bar he comes across, on Baggot Street, asking for a large glass of porter before he finds out if he has the money to pay for it. He leaves a few coins on the counter, not knowing if it's the correct amount, and moves away to a quieter space. The bar quickly fills, and music strikes up in one corner, the temperature and the noise rising. Deacon Turner remains alone in that crowded room, reflecting on the friends he has so recklessly cast aside over the years. He made friends quickly in Dublin when he first arrived, but his single-minded refusal to tolerate opinions different to his own soon isolated him. He brushed their loss aside, thinking that God, and his books, were all the company he needed.

Several glasses in, the Deacon attempts to strike up conversations with anyone that comes near. But he tries too hard, and two men next to him, tapping their feet to the music, draw attention to his accent, and his heritage, questioning his presence in *their* country.

'Are you a visitor, sir – or do you intend *staying?*' says one.

'Sure, he's the Deacon!' another shouts, and a chorus of disapproval follows. Deacon Turner can read the signs, and bids farewell, apologising for causing any offence. It's more than their insults that follow him out.

He doesn't look behind, but feels them on his back. He fumbles with the key in his door, and he's close to tears when he locks it behind him. There's the threatening note from earlier – why hadn't he thrown it out? It mocks him. He makes strong tea, regretting the porter, and his belligerence in the bar. It is one thing to have passionate beliefs, it is quite another to force them on people. Maybe he should – leave, and take his God with him, if his God will come with him, that is.

He kneels beside his bed, coughing when there should be prayer. He will seek forgiveness from the Rector, and resign his position. He will face the landlord, and confess the truth. He will leave the lodgings to those more deserving. As for the next stage of his journey – perhaps a period of rest, and retreat. They will be glad to see him back at the farm, and he will be glad to walk the low hills of the Borders, until his mind has settled.

A commotion outside further interrupts his prayers. Are they in the lane, passing through, or is he the target?

He faces the door, unable to open it – if he gives them the opportunity, he will be lost. He thinks of his books, and the rooms, the landlord's property, and instead appeals to his unseen attackers through the barrier of the door.

'Please! I implore you – leave me alone. I am leaving, do you hear? Tomorrow, the day after – I promise I am leaving...Dublin, and Ireland, for good. I am going home, just as you want. But *please*...leave my property alone, I beg of you.' There is no response, there is low talk amongst themselves. Are they seeing sense, and considering the folly of their actions?

He hears nothing for several minutes, but still fears opening the door. What weakness! The fear abates, somewhat, and he retreats to his bedroom, clasping a bible to his chest. Laying down on the bed, he is soon overcome, and falls asleep.

It is not his sickly chest that induces the cough this time, but the smoke, spiralling through the room, bringing intense heat along with it, and flames in the rooms beyond. He imagines what might be beyond the bedroom door, but he can't afford to falter any longer. As he opens the door, he is blown back by the rushing flames – there is no way forward, there is nothing left. There is a backstairs that leads to an unused attic, a room he has rarely ventured into, and which he won't even use for storage. His precious books are now being destroyed by fire, their pages dancing as they blacken and rot in front of his eyes.

The attic has a small window that looks out on the lane, and the heat breaks the glass before he has to. He turns to watch the approaching flames, impressed by their unwavering ferocity. If only he had possessed such commitment, what he might have achieved. Turning to the window, he hopes to look, at least once, upon the faces of his executioners. He will forgive them. He will tell them that others will follow in his wake, as the cause is too great to ever be surrendered.

Deacon Turner pushes his face through the gap, and a piece of glass catches on his throat, tearing the skin, and pinning him there. As the house is consumed by fire, the Deacon's face stares out of the burning wall, his eyes looking towards home, his fate, and faith, determined.

The Loneliest House In The World

They prowl the blazing streets of Summerhill with malicious intent. Their target is the bleak house on the gable end, just off the main road, that juts out like a cold sore. Farlo's own house is not for the faint-hearted, so this one holds no fear for him. With his dad being handy with the fists, the ten year-old will stay out late enough for the drunken stupor to take hold.

The others knock and run, never daring to face the monster they came to meet. Farlo is made of sterner stuff, and has even brought ammunition, in the shape of a firework left over from Halloween. The old man inside, about whom rumours abound, and mainly on account of the fact that he's rarely glimpsed, can't compete with *his* old man, surely. And this time, Farlo will hit back. Most of his mates are nowhere to be seen – some of them have happy homes to return to – but he's not bothered. He approaches the front door, takes out a lighter, and fires the fuse. He pushes the firework through the letterbox, then kneels, and peers through the gap, into foul darkness, and screams, *'here's a present for ye, ye dirty fucker!'* He stands, or kneels, his ground, determined to do what the rest couldn't.

The firework is a damp squib, but Farlo's heart beats like a drum, as someone, or some*thing,* approaches. Where are the lights? How can a man live in darkness, unless he's not human? The stories about the owner are legend, with tales of desperate burglars breaking in, only to break out again without pausing to peruse the contents. There *were* no contents, it was said – but, Farlo thinks, it's a house, there must be something inside, furniture, cups, a bed, a TV. There's a shadow where the substance should be, breathing, wheezy, and then an old man's cough. Hah, he *is* human, after all! Farlo can't move, though a voice inside tells him to run, very fast, far away – but to where? Home? He'd rather sleep in the street. He's seen plenty of people do it, he's seen people that used to be neighbours do it. Because, first thing in the door, dad will slap him for being late, for being dirty, and just for being. And his mother – will – do – nothing. She'll whimper like a dog. And his sister, Alice, will sit mute on the sofa, bewildered.

'Come on, old man! You don't scare me!'

The door opens suddenly, and Farlo falls forward over the threshold. Before he can move, there are strong hands pulling him up – he knows what that's like, and resolves not to break.

'Come in, young man,' says the wheezing shadow. With his feet scraping along the floor, Farlo has no choice but to endure, waiting for a light to come on, *any* light. They're in a kitchen, of sorts, with red candles on the table, almost burnt down to their ends. He is deposited on a chair, as his captor slumps down opposite, his features somewhat clearer. He is human, though a desolate example of one. Large, unruly sideburns carpet the sides of his face, and wisps of hair spring up, as if reaching for the stars. He's out of breath, but he has the strength to light a cigarette and drag on it like oxygen. He coughs witheringly, and spits on the floor. Farlo could run, but he'd be blind, and something compels him to stay where he is, knowing he'll have a tale to share like no other. And it's not as if this *thing* opposite has hurt him yet – that's in his favour, at least.

'Welcome,' says the old man, 'to the loneliest house in the world. I don't get many visitors.'

'Don't you have any lights?' Farlo asks, remarkably calm.

'Don't have electricity,' comes the reply.

'And no TV?' the kid asks, prompting laughter from across the table.

'No – no TV. I do have a radio, though. The batteries run down easily, and I'm forever having to replace them. What's your name, son?'

'Farlo – just call me Farlo.'

'Pleasure to meet you – I'm Terrence – *not* Terry – Mulligan.'

'You live in the dark?'

'Not during the day.'

'Don't you ever go out?'

'At night – when I need stuff. My eyes – they don't take to daylight too well. It hurts them. So I go out when it gets dark.'

'They say you're weird,' says Farlo. 'Call you names. That you eat cats and dogs - .'

'And little children?' the old man teases.

'I don't believe that,' says Farlo.

'Good – 'cause little children upset my stomach. You're not little, are you? What are you, eleven, twelve?'

'Ten,' says Farlo.

'Are you? Big for your age. I was a fat fucker when I was your age. Couldn't run. Could barely walk.'

'Where's your family?'

'Family?' He coughs, worse than before, and crushes the cigarette on the table, before lighting up another. 'I know, I know. I was hoping these would have killed me by now. What's God keeping me alive for, that's what I want to know. What about your family, son? Will they be worried about you?'

Farlo shakes his head, oddly close to tears. 'He…hits me. Hits me when I'm late, or not.'

'That's terrible. Don't your mother do nothing to stop him?'

'She's afraid of him.'

'Are *you* afraid of him?'

'Not anymore,' says Farlo defiantly.

'And besides hitting you, does he…do anything else?'

'Touch me? Not me…my sister, though…'

'Family, eh?' barks the old man. 'You don't choose 'em. God just drops you in there at random, not giving a bollocks.'

'I'm getting cold,' says Farlo, missing the furnace of the streets.

'I suppose you are. I have no heating, I'm afraid. I wrap up tight, that's all.'

'Do you have any food?' Farlo asks.

'Nothing fresh. I have to go out later.'

'I'll go with you, then,' Farlo suggests.

'We'll see' comes the dark reply. 'Come on, I'll show you the rest of the house.' He grabs a candle and leads Farlo on a mystery tour. The stairs buckle under their weight, and there's scratching behind the walls. 'Mind the bags,' the old man says.

'What's in them?' Farlo asks, but he gets no answer. On a landing of sorts, choked with old furniture, the old man clears a path to a door that doesn't open easily. 'I wasn't expecting any guests, but it won't take long to make it habitable. Plenty of blankets, I can promise you that. And I do have a toilet, you'll be glad to hear. I haven't completely lost my senses. Other end of the landing, over there, see? Right next to my room.' Farlo is slow to understand. Why does he need a room? He's going home, isn't he? Dad will be well out of it by now. He misses the light, the heat. And he left his bike out there. Some knacker's bound to steal it. *He* would. And where are his mates? Are there any left outside? Dean, maybe. He'll get the word out, and call in reinforcements. Dad will nail this old fucker to the floor, pound him into the dust, drag him out into the sunlight, and watch him burn.

'Come on,' says Terrence Mulligan. 'Look, it's not too bad, is it? You'll soon settle. I'll head out for some food. What do you fancy? Has to be cold, I'm afraid, as I have no cooker, as you might have sussed.'

'I'm not hungry,' says Farlo, struggling to hide the nerves.

'Course you are,' says Mulligan, 'and I don't want to eat alone, not when I have a guest for once. Lots of people knock – kids, mostly – but none of them wait for me to answer. Except you. I forgive you for the firework, don't worry. And it didn't go off, anyway, did it, so no harm done.'

Farlo enters the room, shivering, his eyes adjusting to the gloom, and glimpsing more plastic bags, and a cracked mirror. Mulligan retrieves something from under the bed, revealing a small roll of notes.

'Never trusted banks, me. And I was proved right, wasn't I? A few have broken in here, but they haven't looked too hard. What did they think, that I had a safe?'

'I…have to get home,' says Farlo.

'Get *home*? So he can slap you around again? Oh, no, Farlo, we can't let that happen. 'Cause he won't stop there, I'm telling you.'

'Alice...my sister…needs me. I…I…left my bike outside…'

'I'll have a look for it when I'm out there – bring it in for you.'

He hasn't hurt me, Farlo thinks, *but I'm terrified, more than I've ever been.*

Mulligan locks him inside, promising to be as quick as he can, and telling him not to answer to *anyone* but him. As if anyone else is likely to come. Farlo listens at the door, wondering if a trick is being played on him. Has the old man really gone out? He tries the door, but it won't budge. There are sounds, from inside the room, scurrying noises, and the boy is frozen to the spot.

⌒

At home, Farlo would lock himself in his room and wait out the storm. Here, there's a strange kind of peace. He's not used to it. But there's a danger behind it, and he's conditioned to remaining absolutely still, until it's safe to move. Little or no light, the candle casts unfriendly patterns across the walls. There is a thin curtain over the window, a window he could break, and call for help. But – if nobody came, and Mulligan found the damage – what then? In this bitch of a summer, he's cold. There are blankets to spare, but he's afraid to touch them. Spiders are one thing, but rats are another. They're okay in daylight, when there's rocks to fire at them. He's in *their* home now, and best not upset them, or they'll bite.

How long has it been now? Does Mulligan really live here? How could anyone live in this shit? Better not to live at all.

He shudders as something runs over his foot. There's noise downstairs, coming closer. The lock must be tricky as the old man seems to be struggling with it.

'You look cold, son – here, let's get a blanket over you. It's warmer outside than in here. Maybe I should sleep out there.' The blanket smells, and itches. Farlo thinks of pushing him down the stairs, and watching the old man's neck snap like a chicken's. He did that once, before slicing the fowl's head off with a penknife. They're at the bottom, and his chance has passed. Does he *want* to leave?

Is it brighter, or are his eyes just adjusting to the murk? Mulligan unwraps the sandwiches and opens the bottle of water. 'There you are, son,' he says. He has wine for himself, a deep shade of red that he swallows in two lusty gulps. He holds the label up to the candlelight.

'*Polish*, do you believe it? No wonder it was cheap. What the fuck would they know about making wine? Still, beggars can't be choosers. I'd offer you some, to help keep out the chill, but you're a little young. Time enough for all that shit. I was drinking at your age – and look what happened to me. Come on – eat up! I'm not having a starving child on my hands.'

'Did you...see my bike out there?'

'What? Oh, I forget...sorry.'

'I think I need to - .'

'No, son, you can't. It'll still be there in the morning, don't worry. And if not, well, there's plenty more fish in the sea – hah-hah!' The wine has taken effect, and Mulligan starts humming, and drumming his fingers on the table, playing an imaginary keyboard. 'I could have been...,' he states, '...a contender. You don't get that, do you? And I know what you're thinking – *me* a musician. But I was, I'm telling you! I was even young. We had a drummer, and a bassist and a singer playing lead guitar. They were – *shit!* I should have left, I *did* leave.' He studies the empty bottle, wishing he'd bought a second. 'I left everything,' he adds with a sigh. 'You're not eating – what's wrong with it?'

'N-nothing. I'm not hungry.'

'Not hungry – I bet you're fucking starving. I bet the minute you get out of here you'll be down the chipper filling your gullet with shit!'

The words *get out of here* hang in the air. Mulligan calms down, and takes some of the water. 'Polish wine doesn't agree with me. I'll remember that the next time. I'm not much of a drinker these days – I get pains if I do – I used to, all right, sweet Jesus, did I or what? Holy fuck! We'd be on the batter for days.' He wolfs down the sandwich, and burps noisily. 'Yeah, I had friends back then, too. Well, *drinking* friends, which isn't quite the same thing.'

'When can I go?' Farlo pipes up.

'What? *Go?* But you've only just arrived – haven't I been kind to you? I'm sorry you don't like the food. If I'd known you were coming, I'd have made more of an effort.'

'I...want to go. My friends...will be looking for me...'

'Will they? Well, if they call, I'll let them in. Do you think they'll call?'

No, thinks Farlo, but doesn't say.

'I *won't* hurt you, Farlo,' says Mulligan. 'I promise you that. I haven't so far, have I?'

'No,' says Farlo.

'No, exactly!' Mulligan bangs the table. 'Never violent, me. Never raised a fist to anyone, even though...well...never mind. You're safe here. And you'll soon warm up – and I'll go out and get nicer food, if you like. I'll get better wine, for a start – no more of that piss from Poland.'

Farlo has that piss from Poland to thank for his eventual escape. Mulligan is in the middle of another instalment of his unremarkable history: 'My father built this house – and most of the ones around it. Pieces of *shit*. Just like him. Just like...' The bottle catches him on the side of the head, stunning him, so that there's a momentary delay before he keels over onto the kitchen floor. Farlo jumps up, running around to check the damage. Blood is pouring from the old man's ear, and he's groaning, desperately trying to grab the leg of the table, and haul himself up. Farlo snatches up the bottle, which survived the blow, prepared to use it again if there was a chance of Mulligan getting to his feet. The old man's legs jerk out, surprising Farlo, who drops the bottle, smashing it. He has another idea, one infinitely more insidious. He takes one of the candles, and holds it beneath the net curtain covering the back window. He waits until the material catches fire, and then he runs.

And then he runs. He stumbles in the hallway, but reaches the front door, and it opens at the first attempt. The warm evening air slaps him in the face, and he embraces it.

He ignores his bike, and his young legs, laced with adrenalin, bound along the streets as if on springs. He hears a siren, but they're never far away in his experience.

In sight of home, he pauses to catch breath. It was a dream, wasn't it? And anyway, who'll care about that old man living in that house? And using candles in this day and age? He was asking for trouble. Lucky it hadn't happened years earlier. Farlo feels no guilt – *he* was kidnapped, after all.

The extraordinary events are almost forgotten by the time he's walking up to his own front door. He's surprised to find the house key still in his jeans pocket. He pauses, and listens. Raised voices, but that was always the case. It didn't have to mean the worst.

The first thing he sees is Alice sitting at the end of the stairs with her hands over her ears. Frank Sinatra is blasting out from the front-room. That means that dad is mercifully stowed away in his bed, unconscious, but that mum has come out to play. And here she comes –

Cigarette dangling, her mouth works overtime as she berates her son for coming in at this time of night. She reeks of perfume and cider, and threatens him with dragging his father's lazy arse out of bed. Then she catches a whiff of *Strangers in the Night*, and she's off, swinging and swaying her way back to her music and drink and nicotine. Farlo sits beside his sister, and puts and arm around her, trying in vain to shield her from the onslaught.

You were wrong, Mulligan, he thinks – *this* is the loneliest house in the world.

31

'*Come on in, number 31, your time is up!*' An unremarkable number in itself, 31, but it's *his*, Frank recognises, and what's done can't be undone. Beauty is truth, and there is nothing more beautiful, or truthful, in Frank's eyes, than numbers. Their glorious, complex patterns, often mysterious, are everywhere, they *are* everything. That's why he makes his living studying numbers, albeit for rather profane purposes. To his employers, the numbers always have Dollar or Euro signs attached to them, and have no value otherwise. Frank often closes his eyes and imagines himself standing in front of a roomful of hungry students, baying for every morsel that he, the professor, will hand out to them, juicy cuts of information about *numbers!*

But Frank is on the 31 bus, in the depths of early morning, heading into Dublin city, reflecting on the fact that it's also his 31st birthday. *Coincidence? I think not!* He sets out to prove his point. He's been using his phone to accurately time the journey, in part to stave off the tedium, but mostly to add weight to his theory. He wipes the condensation off the window. There's a fair distance to go yet, and what seems like several hundred gloomy travellers to pick up along the way.

There wasn't much celebrating in the Harrison household that morning. His wife, Joan, had another uncomfortable night, which meant that he too had to suffer. She was a tempestuous woman *before* the pregnancy, but nothing had prepared him for the mood swings, which were more like savage blows, gradually eroding his already fragile optimism for the future. He woke that morning to the sight of her mountainous belly, fiercely alive and kicking, and ready to erupt at any moment. He hated touching it, but he felt obliged, and he also felt horny. He still had 'needs,' as the saying went, which she was loathe to satisfy. It was those *needs*, she'd say, that got her into this trouble in the first place. *This trouble?* Is that what she really felt about the child they were about to have? It was supposed to be the crowning achievement of their union, an heir to the throne, a testimony to their love – but the truth was there in the ugly distended pulsing stomach, up and down, up and down, making him sick, as if he was on a swaying boat, and he didn't like boats, or the sea. Anyway, he made her a cup of tea, gave her a peck on the cheek, and got – nothing – in return. Certainly not a *happy birthday, Frank.* No sign of a present around the house, and he wasn't really expecting one, but some acknowledgement of the day might have been nice.

They've arrived – Talbot Street – and he was right! *31 minutes exactly!* God, what does this mean? Is it a good, or bad, omen?

Heading for the café, and his regular double espresso, and his only moments of peace during any given day, Frank looks for any more 31's that might be scattered about the place. He knows he's not meant to look for them, or invent them, else the true meaning of the number will never be revealed.

He has a second coffee, his heart pumping, his mind reeling, as the first shreds of daylight appear outside, and his time ticks away. He'd better move, or he'll be late. The company don't like that, they don't like that at all. He pays at the till, takes his change, and then decides to count the money he has on him. In total - *€31*. Had to be, sweet Jesus! What's going on here?

He's a lion out of his cage, set free, he wants to charge everywhere at once, and devour everything in his path. He needs to calm down before he gets to the office, or they'll think he's on something. Word will spread, *Frank's on speed, or smack,* or whatever they call it nowadays. They'll haul him in for questioning, they're that low. They'll even call in a doctor, if need be. But he doesn't care, he has bigger fish to try. Should be buy a lottery ticket? If he fell into the Liffey, and without a swimming stroke in him, would a miracle rescuer be on hand? More than likely. He buys some water, and drinks the lot, hoping to douse the flames. He takes a few deep breaths outside his office, and then braves the gladiatorial arena. He thinks of the numbers he'll get to spend the day with, and that eases his mind.

Through the doors, and up the stairs – the stairs! He goes back down and starts again, this time counting as he goes. It can't be, but it is. It most assuredly is – 31 steps to his floor. If he rolled the dice, it would be 3 and 1, without a shadow of a doubt.

'You're late,' his manager barks, bursting Frank's balloon.

'Sorry – my wife – she had a difficult night,' Frank says, not lying.

'I have *five* kids, Frank,' says the manager, 'How many do you have again?'

Frank shakes his head, and heads for the relative safety of his desk, and his precious numbers.

⌣

Time has wings, but it doesn't just fly, it soars. There are 31 candles, of course, but there's no mystery in that, alongside a hollow chorus of *Happy Birthday*. Then there are the phone calls, 30 to be exact, and he's beginning to think the spell has been broken – or he miscounted, when the 31st comes through. It's Joan.

'It's coming!' she cries.

'What is?' he asks stupidly, his head wrecked after a manic day's work.

'The fucking baby!' comes the reply.

Oh dear Lord, Frank thinks. He was right. The numbers, they *weren't* lying. They've been trying to tell him all day, but he wasn't listening.

'Frank? Are you there? Did you hear me? THE BABY'S COMING!'

He hears her, the whole city hears her.

'I'll be home as soon as I can. I'll get a taxi…I'll -'

'No…I'll make my own way to Holles Street…it's not going to wait. Just be there when I arrive.'

'I'm on my way,' Frank tells her.

Numb. Legs are on stilts moving through a swamp, his head in the clouds, his thoughts awry. Pats on the back, shouts of encouragement, and a few *not.*

The air is good. That's better. Holles Street, sure, no problem, a ten, fifteen minute walk, and then – and then – he's seen the movie, he made himself watch a whole one straight through until the bitter end. He can do this! *I can't.* And even if he does – make it through – what then? He wasn't ready before, he's not ready now, he definitely won't be ready afterward. The baby won't be the only one screaming all night. And Frank will still be screaming long after the baby has stopped. Her swelling will go down, though, that's something to look forward to. Although the skin won't be as smooth and tight as it once was – there'll be folds and creases, that's what he's heard from a couple of lads in the office who've been down that road before him. Another thing – the wife might regain her appetite after a bit, but will *he*? And what if – God forbid – the first time they resume *things* after the birth, he gets her pregnant again *first time out*? It happens. They've talked about it, having more than one. Or, at least, she has. He went along with it, probably because he wasn't listening. Probably because he was in the saddle, on a nightly basis, and the ride was exquisite.

He needs a 'settler.' The Palace Bar is at hand. He orders a whiskey, and waits for the kick. It doesn't come immediately, but a warm glow runs through his body, relaxing him. Time enough, he thinks, she'll be ages waiting for a taxi, and then they'll be ages getting through rush-hour traffic. And who knows, maybe she'll have it in the back seat. That would suit Frank down to the ground. Let the taxi-driver deal with all the messy stuff. Let him have the nightmares afterwards. If Frank times this right, he can walk straight into the hospital, and - *hey presto!* – there it is, one healthy, clean baby presented to him on a golden platter, all wrapped up and ready to go. Okay, Joan will be upset, about the taxi, and the fact of his not being there, but she'll get over it, in time, and eventually forgive him. With the birth sorted, Frank turns his attention to the rearing of the child, the *years* that will take, and that's just for one of the bleeders. What if there *is* more? He needs a second 'settler.'

At the bar, a tall man in a long black coat and a bowler hat is holding court, gathering an audience as he invites them to hear a tale that will enthral and delight. Frank gets caught up in the scrum, hypnotised by the unusual rhythm of the man's voice. The story concerns a man's journey over land and sea, to every corner of the known world, by ship and train and plane, on foot, on knees occasionally, through blinding snow and tropical storms, unbearable heat and paralytic cold, and all for the purpose of unravelling the mysteries of the universe. Such a man, the storyteller informs them, must divest himself of material ambition, sever all personal ties, and be prepared to suffer alone, because only by being alone can he hope to discover the pure rapture of human existence, as revealed to him by God.

The storyteller pauses, takes a sip of rum, requests another, and then removes his bowler, which he offers as a receptacle for the audience's 'kindnesses,' as he calls them. Some of those present, including Frank, are too startled by his head to dig into their pockets. For his head isn't all there. It has the shape of a crescent moon from where Frank is standing, with a deep cavern from which scraps of hair sprout. Nobody dares ask the obvious question, and Frank has something else to worry about – two hours have passed since he arrived, and he thinks he hears the cries of his new child on the wind. She'll kill him.

⌒

Running, late. Tripping, grazing, shrieking, but not with laughter. Pausing on the hospital steps. An exhausted proud mother emerges, clutching her prize, her bundle of joy, with the father lagging behind. Frank moves past them, inside. *Holler* Street, the screams of witches and their cauldron offspring, he swoons until caught by an unimpressed nurse. She wangles the details out of him, and shows him the way, before he can even think of taking fright and turning tail.

Would it have been easier if he had arrived earlier in the proceedings, and caught the beginning of this horror show? He doubts it, as they, the staff, *and* his wife, doubt him, and with good reason. He's the second-lead in this performance, and he's missed his cue. There's no catching up – *the show must go on!* And go on, it certainly has. They're reaching a climax. It's not a surprise, but that doesn't lessen the shock.

The head – if that's what it is – is first to show, bloodied, and bathed in a mess of her *stuff*. Down there – down there – where – he can barely bring himself to think about it – he wants to close his eyes, but he'd see it regardless, it's already branded on his subconscious, and it can never be removed. Joan, to be fair to her, isn't screaming, but her face, contorted with ugly determination, is showing the strain. She looks at him for compassion, for a sign that she's not suffering alone. *No, love, I'm suffering too, believe me.* And it won't stop coming – how could something that size fit inside her? Did he do that to her? Oh God, if only he'd known. He takes her hand before he collapses, unable to look away from the monstrous miscalculation that's all his fault.

Almost there. Will someone shout *it's alive!* before it's all over? Except that it's never over. A smile is dawning on his wife's face, and it's dawning on Frank that the time for decision is near. *'I must be cruel only to be kind...'* He can't remember the rest of the quotation. Never much of a scholar, or a husband, or a –

'Oh, Frank, look!' Joan squeals with delight.

Fully formed, but still attached to her, Frank's son is held up for his astonished perusal.

'Would you like to cut the cord, Frank?' asks the beaming midwife. *Sever all connections*, isn't that what the man in the bowler hat said?

'What?...Yes, yes I would. There's nothing I'd like more,' he tells her. And with that, Frank lets go of his wife's hand, and leaves the room. And leaves the hospital.

And leaves the city.

With no plans but to wander the earth, unravelling its mysteries. He works out that he and Joan were married for nearly 31 months. *31!* That's an eternity, and long enough for any man to be able to say that he gave it every chance. She'll be all right. Strong as an ox, is Joan, and with a son to keep her company, she'll want for nothing. And maybe someday, if the mood strikes her, she'll pick another man off the rack, and tell him what's what. Good luck to the bloke.

Now. Departures. Where shall he go? The world is his oyster – until the money runs out. There, that's the one! Flight E231 leaving for Istanbul in three hours. He's delighted to find that they have a seat on the plane. Business Class only, though. Oh well, he thinks, what the hell. It *is* his birthday, after all. (And his son's birthday from now on, he realises)

Numbers, Frank decides, as he lifts off into the void, are beautiful, heartless empty creatures, who have taken him by the hand, and led him into madness. He holds his breath, and starts counting, wondering how long he can hold out.

…27

…28

…29

…30

…31…

The Moor of Moore Street

His huge frame threatens to collapse the narrow bed, as his mind swims in dark waters. He sees the man crushed under the train carriage, the wheels cutting him in half, the victim continuing to scream even after he's been severed. Men, including Linton, rush to his aid, but then they hold back. There but for the grace of God go all of them. The company will throw a few dollars at the poor man's family, and replace him with another desperate fool. The rest will whisper in the new man's ear, to take extreme care, but not to complain. The railways lines must be built, and quickly. The whole country must be connected if it is to grow, and drag its poor people out of their misery. Meanwhile, the men who build that network are treated like blind mice. They are plentiful, and worthless.

The grinding gears of the garbage-collector brings Linton to his feet, to the window, cursing them without real spite. They are doing their job, and can't be damned for that. The street is naked without its stalls, without its barkers and ballers, and creeping menace. He counts himself lucky each morning, and blesses himself in the face of such good fortune. Nigeria might plague his sleep, but it can't hurt him anymore.

He makes strong Brazilian coffee and waits for the staff to arrive. He does a sweep of both shops, finding hairs on the salon floor, and money in the till. The mobile-repair shop beside it bears no obvious evidence of neglect. He won't admonish the girls for their lack of diligence, not yet. Give them a week or two to feel more comfortable in their surroundings, let them get used to his ways, and *then* he will come down hard, and remind them that security comes at a price. They are guests in Ireland, he will tell them, they will always be guests no matter how long they stay, and they must act accordingly. They have been given a glorious opportunity, and must not forget it. Also, he himself must not move too quickly to gain their affections, or their gratitude. Both are fine women, one Somalian, one Nigerian, but he must tread carefully, or he will lose them. Anyway, it is not as if he is starved of company at the moment. Any more at this stage could be problematic, as well as exhausting.

It is still early yet, allowing him time to slip over the road for a porridge. He has grown addicted to the local dish, served with definite flirtation by the middle-aged owner. Normally, he wouldn't give a woman of that age a second glance, especially with that heavy ring on her wedding finger, but she seems so insistent that he might have to consider it. And if he can spread joy and happiness to Moore Street and beyond, where is the harm?

⌒

He is a man of his word. He is a man *of* words. He convinces the supplier that payment will be made by the end of the week, even eliciting a laugh from the man demanding money. Another friend easily charmed. In the salon below, the ladies are in full flow, singing along to the piped music, and performing miracles with customers' hair. The other shop operates at a steadier, quieter pace, overseen by Mahmud, a taciturn young man from northern Iraq. What he lacks in personality, he makes up for in technical genius. Linton steers a careful course through both shops, wary of stepping on toes, or getting involved. He gives advice when asked, though never about women's hair, or mobile phones, about both of which he remains blissfully ignorant. He imbues confidence, or so he likes to think, and of course, he pays their wages at the end of the week.

He often stands in the doorway, subtly enticing customers through the doors. He needs to attract more than African or Middle Eastern immigrants, if he is to grow his empire. He has discovered, since his arrival in the country, that his ambitions are somewhat greater than he had imagined. Finding his own piece of land, and stamping his authority on it, isn't, it seems, enough. He's capable of more, he knows, but he must not be fooled by his, admittedly, moderate success.

'Nice suit, Linton' the stall-holder remarks, winking at him. Now she *is* too old for him, but he gives her a dazzling smile, and smooths down the front of his azure blue three-piece. He is called back into the salon, to replace a light bulb, of all things, earning the admiration of the ladies who think he has tackled something difficult. He can't help it, he sizes each one up, knowing which one will surrender first. Mirella fixes him with a knowing look, and he holds her gaze. He returns to the street, satisfied with his morning's work. The stalls are ticking over, doing decent business on a fair spring day. The police scare a few tobacco dealers away, and some skeletons share a needle around the corner, but other than that, everything is on course.

He has a simple, solitary lunch in the flat upstairs, savoury soup and a selection of fruit, washed down with bottled water. His surroundings are spartan, a consequence of his uneasy upbringing, where nothing, not even lunch, was taken for granted. An ambulance outside shatters the peace, and he looks down as one of the addicts is carried off to an uncertain future. Linton remembers chewing *khat* with his fellow workers in the corrugated shelter that served as their home for months on end. The drug brought a kind of dizzy relief from the heat and boredom, which quickly wore off once their shifts began. He has no doubt that he could get his hands on some in Dublin, if he asked the right people. But that was behind him, unless he wanted to return to Nigeria, and in a sorry state, to face the lost friends he had abandoned.

His soup has gone cold. How easy it was to slip into a dangerous reverie, and drift off track. He goes down to the salon, engaging with customers and staff, and unblocking a sink stained with red dye. He checks the diary, marking the slight increase in recent trade, thinking of ways he can turn *slight* into *significant*. There is a vacant premises down the street for sale, which would be to his purpose. But what kind of business would be operate there? What's missing from the area that could be exploited? It would mean using the salon and repair shop as collateral, but where is the reward without the risk? He tells the ladies he's going out for ten minutes.

He cuts a colourful swathe through the monochrome street. He walks with a grace that belies his size, and gets noticed. There is envy and resentment in some of those looking on, but he just smiles at their jealousy. He reaches the property that might propel him on the road to greater prosperity. He envisages a window of mannequins dressed in vivid colours, capturing something of his own innate style. The street needs brightening up, before it's torn down. There is a history here that is treated in a most curious manner. Linton can't understand how the State can celebrate its past glories whilst letting buildings associated with that history fall into pitiful ruin. At the same time, if anyone suggests redeveloping the properties, there is uproar, and protest. Linton has been told that his own flat has a history to it, and that it might have to be reclaimed, and protected. Why, he wonders, have they taken so long to discover its importance? At least conflicts here are now fought without bullets, or violent confrontation. There is a decency at the heart of things that is remarkable to him, although he doubts how long it can last.

Was that *'nigger'* he just heard? He turns, startled at how his colour continues to amuse, and frighten, some. There are no obvious suspects, but a young woman is looking curiously at him.

'Can I help you, lady?' he says, scaring her off. A pity, he thinks.

⌐

She doesn't mean to stare, but it's hard not to notice a man like that. And he *wants* to be noticed, doesn't he? The clothes, the posture, and most of all, the confidence. No, she doesn't mean to –

'Can I help you, lady?' Flustered, embarrassed, she scurries away, pretending to be interested in puny heads of cabbage thrown across the table. No wonder they're cheap! *Is he following her?* She's afraid to look. The bananas are next, ripe and rotting, and they're a steal at that price. She should come down here more often, she's sure to save a few shekels. She heads into Arnotts, instantly feeling calmer, and more at home. There is something reassuring about department stores, they're comfortably numbing, as Pink Floyd might have said. She decides to have lunch there, against her better judgment, surrounded by pristine ladies with ironed hair and shiny handbags. Not quite as bohemian as Carolyn thinks she would prefer. She might dress like a gypsy, but that doesn't make her one. She wears second-hand clothes that retain their previous owners' perfume, and character. They're not really *her*, but then, what *is* her? She wishes somebody would tell her. It's exhausting trying to find out. She knows her husband isn't likely to tell her anytime soon. He wouldn't spot an elephant in their tiny front-room. In her head, she lives on the Portobello Road in London, circa 1967, in a fashionably decaying house where the party never ends, strangers crash in every available space, and David Bowie is just a pimply youth with delusions of grandeur.

The ironic truth is that the future is her present. She teaches, 'nurtures,' the next generation of young actors, preparing them for a life on the stage, or in front of the camera. Currently on secondment to the Gate Theatre, it may be 2019, but her focus is the winter of 2020 and beyond, and a slate of new productions, that may, or may not, see the light of day, largely depending on her. It's a heavy burden to carry, not helped by the latest crop of interns foisted upon her. Is she a primary school teacher or a producer, she'd like to know. There's no chance of a decent harvest unless the seeds are up to scratch.

Time to go, and sow. She skirts around Moore Street, just in case. But, she would like another look, soon.

⌒

The students don't lack for confidence, or talent, she'll readily admit. Talent is endemic, rife, but there is a lack of originality, a dearth of risk-taking. Her underlings treat acting like plumbing or carpentry, though. They have all the skills, they have ambition, but it's the wrong kind of ambition, in her opinion.

The sun bleaches the room, and her enthusiasm. *Am I a teacher, or a producer?* The iambic pentameter is a hurdle most can't overcome. They're learning by rote, like mathematics, and she's not getting through to them.

'Stop trying to *solve* it,' she tells them. 'Try to *understand* it. Don't just learn the words, *believe* in them.' She shows them a clip of Al Pacino from his *Looking for Richard* film. 'Look at him, listen to him. He's as New York as they get, but he *understands*, he *believes*. Watch, and learn. Now, watch Winona Ryder as Lady Anne in this next scene, when Richard woos her, after having had her husband killed. Unfortunately, Winona speaks Shakespeare as if she's been struck down with dysentery. She simply has no idea what she's really saying. She's not *listening* to the words.'

And on and on the afternoon drags, and drags every last ounce of energy out of her.

At home in Stoneybatter, she has several pots on the boil, and a couple of steaks waiting to go. Ray bounds in on the dot as usual, pecking her on the cheek, patting her on the behind, eager to hear about her day, before telling her all about his. The meat's a little tough, they both agree, but never mind, she can't be perfect every day, he tells her. A glass of wine will sort her out, he says. Sort *what* out, she asks. Oh, come on, love, you haven't been yourself lately – what is it? You can tell me, can't you?

She knows what he wants her problem to be – and he can help her with that, as he'll demonstrate in bed that night. She has to give him top marks for effort. He puts his heart and soul into the performance, seven times a week, at least, without once fluffing his lines. She sometimes thinks that she could go downstairs and make herself a cup of tea, and he wouldn't notice, he'd happily keep on pumping away on his own. *Make a baby* is the name of their production. Ray's the director, lead actor, and stagehand, whereas she – well, she's lost sight of her role. She knows her lines by heart – but they've lost their meaning for her of late.

Can I help you, lady? The voice pops into her head. Was he flirting with her? Or she with him? Ray measures up, as far as those things go, but she can't help wondering. *He* would crush her, he'd break her in two.

Towards dawn, she has an idea, a crazy idea that must not be articulated quite yet. It's a sketch, and she's no painter. She is, however, according to her list of credits, a producer, or was. And could be again, *if* she's careful, and does her homework. First things first, she must get another look at him, and figure out a subtle method of approach. Momentarily cheered, she surprises Ray by waking him and offering him a matinee performance. He's more than willing, she discovers.

Linton breaks stride, and apologises to Mirella. His mind isn't on it, or her. He can't admit it, but she reminds him of his mother. Various tiny gestures bear a scary similarity. He lost his mother when she was about Mirella's age. She's still, officially, *lost*. Taken, literally, from their home in front of him, by a group of masked and armed men, never to be seen again. He had to assume she was dead. He still hears her crying, though, her spirit wandering, deprived of a proper burial. She won't rest until he finds her, and prepares her for the afterlife, as only a son can.

Mirella says nothing, but dresses quickly, and goes downstairs, letting herself out of the salon, and slipping off into the night. He's not sure if she'll come back. He'll struggle to find a suitable replacement. His own stupid fault, and the subsequent sexual failure was probably what he deserved. She might spread the word, tarnish his hitherto unblemished record, and who knows, stem the steady flow of female traffic coming through the salon. Or perhaps he's overestimating his own standing in the community. And she *does* need a job, after all. No, she will be back. Time will heal the wound. He might have to spend less time in the salon in the next few days, but it practically runs itself, anyway.

He goes over the road for breakfast, but the porridge is not to his taste today. And the coffee is not quite up to his own. Then he crawls back into bed, unaccountably depressed, hoping that Thelonious Monk might mellow him. The music slows his heartbeat, and dulls his sorrowful memories, until they are behind him, and he feels strong enough to face the world. He chooses a suit of a more sombre colour, matching his mood, and, he reckons, making him less of a target.

There she is again – that woman from yesterday. Her blatant regard of him is both unsettling and insulting. He will speak to her, and correct her misunderstandings.

'Can I *help* you, lady?' he says in a harsher tone. This time, however, she doesn't shrink from his gaze, but moves toward him, with purpose.

'Forgive me – I - .'

'You're not the police, are you?'

'The *police?* Jesus, no. Do I look like one? Why, have you done something?'

'No, lady – I am, as you see - .' *black,* was that what he was going to say? 'You need something done with that hair? Step inside, why don't you, and let my girls look after you.'

Carolyn self-consciously pushes her hair back. She's not handling this as she'd hoped. 'No. I work for – *at* – the Gate. The theatre.'

'Yes, I think I have heard of it,' says Linton.

'Listen, is there somewhere we can talk?' she asks.

'There is my flat upstairs,' he says with a smile.

'I was thinking more of somewhere like a café. I could do with some coffee, to be honest.'

'And I make the best coffee this side of the river. Please, come. I will keep the doors open. My girls will be right downstairs, in case you are worried about my intentions.'

If she backs out now, it's finished, and she can go back to massaging the egos of the preening peacocks in her class.

'Okay,' she says.

His *girls* consider her warily as she follows him upstairs. His flat is not what she was expecting. It doesn't exactly fit with the man's dress. He can't live here, she decides. She introduces herself properly as he sets about making coffee on an ancient-looking machine.

'And I am Linton,' he tells her.

'Linton what?' she asks.

'All in good time, lady. First, you must taste this. Then you will tell me *precisely* why you are here.'

'Fair enough,' she says, taking the coffee. It almost blows her head off, and she's afraid she might have to lie down. But on *that* bed? She doesn't think so.

'You like it?' he asks.

'It's…strong.' Strongest coffee she ever tasted. She wouldn't even describe it as coffee. 'Is it legal?' she adds, drawing a bellowing laugh out of him.

'What, I am black, an immigrant, therefore I must be a criminal, is that it?'

'No…*no*, that's not what I meant. You could sell this stuff. People would get addicted.'

'You would like some more?'

'Oh, no. I need a clear head.'

'I am not insulted,' Linton says. 'Now, tell me, please, why you are here, theatre-lady?'

'I am responsible, partly, for the development of future productions at the theatre.' She pauses, unsure, wishing she had a script to read from. 'We plan months ahead of time, sometimes a year or more. In the autumn of next year, 2020, we are hoping to put on *Othello*. You have heard of it?'

'Of Shakespeare? Have I *heard* of Shakespeare? I think so, lady.'

'I'm sorry, I didn't mean to offend you. You'd be surprised how many people *haven't* heard of him. It has nothing to do with your….'

'Colour,' he finishes.

'Yes. Although, it is your…colour…that brings me here, so to speak.'

'Why are you dancing on hot coals, lady? I am black, it is no secret, no shame. It sets me apart, and I relish that, in truth.'

She clears her throat. 'Well, as you know, as you *may* know, *Othello* is one of those plays where it is necessary to cast a black actor in the part. There are no concessions to creative expression where the Moor is concerned. So - .'

'So,' says Linton, 'you are in search of a black man to play the Moor, is that it? Not many native niggers among the acting fraternity here, I would imagine. Except there is one problem – I am not an actor.'

'No,' she agrees. 'No, you're not, are you. So what am I doing here? I had this crazy idea of taking someone – an unknown, an amateur – off the street, and putting them on the stage, in the insane hope of capturing something, I don't know, raw, something original. Originality, you see, Linton, has almost become extinct in our theatre. I was desperate, I guess. I'm sorry for – treating you like an experiment. I should go - .'

Linton takes a book off the shelves, and hands it to her. 'Have you heard of this writer? Ben Okri – he is Nigeria's Shakespeare.'

'Yes, I've heard of him. I've never read him, though.'

'Then you have missed something important. If you read *The Famished Road*, I will read *Othello*. I will *read* it. I am no actor, lady. I am a businessman. I am a busy man, but I admire your courage in approaching me with your crazy idea. I, too, have crazy ideas. The world would cease to exist without them. I will read, you will read, and we will meet again. I am always here, or maybe I will venture all the way up to the Gate. Will we shake on it, lady?'

'Only if you stop calling me *lady,* and call me Carolyn instead.'

'That is a deal, *Carolyn.*'

'Your English really is very good,' she can't help saying. 'And you have a tremendous voice, very powerful.'

'Flattery will get you everywhere, but not racism,' he replies.

'I wasn't being racist,' she gasps, horrified.

'I was joking, Carolyn. You white people can be so sensitive. You need to relax. More coffee before you go?'

'Oh, I don't think so. I have to work this afternoon.'

'Well, then, until we meet again. You know where I am. And take good care of that book, won't you?'

'I will, Linton. I will.'

The Board listens to her proposal with astonished silence. But, Carolyn, they argue repeatedly, he's *not* an actor. He's not an actor, and you want to put him on the Gate stage playing one of the major roles in the theatrical canon – it's *madness.*

They're right, of course, but she's a dog with a bone, and won't let it go. She won't let *him* go. She reads the Okri book, and enjoys it, and is pleased she can report back to Linton with sincere positivity. But how is he getting on with the play? For beginners, Shakespeare can be daunting, and for him there is the added complication that he's not a native speaker. For any performance to work, the performer *must* have complete understanding of the text. They must know it upside-down and inside-out. She's afraid to go back to Moore Street. She's afraid Moore Street will come to her. Even Ray has noticed that she's not quite herself. She's not, in his words, *enjoying* their attempts to get pregnant as much as he is. I never have, she wants to tell him. It's work, just work, she says, I'm under tremendous pressure at the moment. She suggests a temporary hiatus in the making-babies project, so that they can rediscover their former ardour. She's never seen Ray so crestfallen. Is she losing him? And would she really mind?

Another Board meeting, bored senseless, and the question is asked – any other business? She raises her hand like the naughty kid at school – *Othello*, she says, trembling. *I'm not giving up on the idea. You should see him.* What is she doing? She hasn't seen him in weeks. He's likely to have forgotten her, as well as the play. Surprisingly, the Board come back to her with a counter-proposal. Before they could even consider backing her, they would have to meet her Othello – he must audition for them, two months from now, a piece of their choosing. That piece is Frank Hardy's opening monologue from Friel's *Faith Healer*.

'*What?*' is her response. 'You want him to do *what?*'

It is the night that she and Ray had agreed to resume activities in the marital bed, and she's well off the pace, to the point of inertia. Ray takes the unprecedented step of spending the rest of the night on the couch downstairs, but not before accusing her of having an affair.

'Well?' he demands to know. 'Is there someone else?'

'There is – and there isn't,' she says. And off Ray goes, stomping down the stairs.

⌒

They meet in the bar of the Gresham Hotel, where she downs her whiskey, and then blurts it out. Linton sips green tea, taking it on board calmly.

'They want to kill the idea, and this is their way of doing it politely,' she says.

'Unless I can pull it off,' Linton says.

'Linton, dear, I'm not sure if you understand what they're asking me – *you* – to do. *Faith Healer* is one of the most difficult plays any actor can tackle. It is all monologue. Frank Hardy's opening speech lasts *forty-five minutes*, without a break.'

'Do you have a copy of it?' he asks.

'Have you been listening to me? And did you ever get around to reading *Othello*, by the way?'

'*Haply for I am black, and have not those soft conversations the Chamberers have...*'

'Jesus,' says Carolyn. 'You have some fucking voice. A pity, then.'

'What is a pity? You are giving up before you've even started?'

'Does nothing scare you, Linton? It's impossible. It can't work. It was never going to work.'

'Get me a copy of *Faith Healer*,' Linton tells her. 'What harm is there in reading it?'

'Because – you're not an actor. You said it yourself. Doesn't it terrify you? You've read *Othello*, haven't you? Do you seriously think that you could learn all those lines? *Understand* all those lines? Understand them enough to be able to convince an audience that you are the Moor of Venice?'

'If you don't believe that I can do it, why are we having this conversation? Unless you have other motives? More personal reasons for being here?'

'Personal reasons? No, I don't think so, Linton.'

'Are you sure?' he says, beaming.

'Contrary to the myth, it is not every white woman's fantasy to sleep with a black man.'

'Isn't it?'

'*No*, it's not. And in case you've forgotten, I'm married. Happily married,' she declares.

'*Methinks the lady doth protest too much.*'

'Show-off,' she says, teasing. But, sweet Lord, that voice of his!

⌒

Linton is at home on stage. He grows visibly in front of her. She watches from the front row, letting him read from *The Famished Road*, hoping that it will make him feel more comfortable. His suit, of burnished copper silk, is the perfect costume, almost as if it was designed just for this space, for this performance. He closes the book, and fixes her with a determined look, before beginning: '*Aberarder, Aberayron, Abergorlech, Abergynolwy...All those dying Welsh villages. I'd get so tense before a performance...*' For a full ten minutes, Carolyn is pinned to her seat as Linton doesn't just speak the opening of *Faith Healer*, with its dense, packed prose, he *acts* it, giving the text depth and meaning. He stumbles eventually, and curses his own failings, apologising to her. She, meanwhile, wipes tears from her eyes.

'I saw Ralph Fiennes play Frank Hardy here,' she says. 'I thought *that* was something, but you, Linton...I can't believe it...'

'I bet he didn't forget his lines,' Linton shoots back.

'No, he didn't – but he's one of the greatest stage actors of his generation. That's the difference. What you did was remarkable. Truly.'

'I didn't hear you applaud,' he says, still hurt by his own sense of failure.

'That's because I'm in shock, Linton.'

'And that man at the back distracted me – I thought you said we'd be alone.'

'What man?' asks Carolyn, twisting in her seat, as Fergal Marron, the Artistic Director, makes his presence known. 'I didn't know you were...,' she says, fumbling her words as she stands. She's about to be fired, or - .

'This is the young man you've been talking about, is it?' says Fergal. He skips up onto the stage, facing Linton, sizing him up. Linton could crush him like an ant, Carolyn thinks. The men shake hands.

'As Carolyn said – that was remarkable, Linton. And you've *never* acted before?'

'I think I might have remembered something like that in a Nigerian school,' says Linton. 'That is, when I was in school, which wasn't often.'

'I – I was just showing Linton around, letting him get a feel of a stage,' Carolyn interrupts.

'He looks like he was born on the stage,' Fergal says, still regarding Linton with a degree of scepticism. He looks down at Carolyn. 'I don't think there's any need for that audition, is there?'

'No?' asks Carolyn, not sure what he means.

'No – I will recommend to the Board that we support the further development of *Othello* for next season, which will include, if he agrees, Linton here. There is still a lot of work to be done with him, regardless of how impressive he was today. Don't you agree?'

'Completely,' she says, giddy with excitement. Linton remains cautious despite the air of congratulation surrounding him. He has stumbled onto a road that might take him far, but with each passing mile, there will be less chance of turning back. Further handshakes, and a hug from Carolyn, cement the deal, and he vows to exceed their expectations of him. He will play the Moor. And more than that, he will *be* the Moor.

⁓

Her life is on hold. She watches it happening through a glass partition. Ray, and the rest, are on the other side of it. They can touch her, but she can't reciprocate. The words come out of her mouth, but she might as well be speaking in tongues. Her friends remark on her distance, her pale skin, her weight loss, her increased drinking. Is it the baby, they ask? That is, the *lack* of a baby? Ray is relentless in his quest to produce the miracle, while refusing the tests that might identify the real problem. A holiday is suggested, where she might relax, and regain her energies. A doctor is suggested, one that might alleviate her concerns, and ease her mental stresses, whatever they might be. Friends and husband alike regularly broach the subject of – infidelity – but she assures each and every one, and herself, that she has never been unfaithful to Ray. And she hasn't. But that doesn't mean she won't. Or hasn't thought about it. She cannot bend much further without breaking.

And then a break, in the form of email from a colleague in London, offering her preview tickets for *their* forthcoming *Othello*, with Idris Elba in the lead. She suggests to the Board that it would be good for Linton to see the production, and the trip is approved. Linton accepts the invitation, although not with the enthusiasm she had imagined. She is becoming concerned that the further into the process Linton delves, the scale of the task ahead of him is all too apparent. She has had that nightmare of the first night, when he freezes – and can't be unfrozen. It destroys him, and then it destroys her.

Ray is curious about Linton, but refuses to meet him. She can't do any more than she has to allay his suspicions. And, as she tells herself frequently, he has nothing to be suspicious about. She packs her bag for London, looking forward to seeing the play. It will do Linton good to watch a team of actors, and not just the lead. That must be the next stage, to integrate him into her classes, and not risk isolating him. She accepts his assurances that he works on the text every day, and has watched several screen versions. He seemed particularly taken with Orson Welles' take on the play, and does a fair impression of the actor's interpretation.

'Leaving me?' Ray asks on seeing the suitcase. There is a melancholy behind the levity.

'London, remember?' she tells him.

'How could I forget? You and your protégé.'

'My *what*? It's work, Ray, and his name is Linton. And I have asked you several times if you wanted to meet him – but you refused, remember?'

'I have no desire to spend time with any of your students,' Ray says harshly.

'I'll tell you what – Ray, are you listening? When I come back, we'll talk about that holiday you've been banging on about, okay? We'll organise it, I promise.'

'I haven't been *banging on* about it. I just thought that, as husband and wife, we might want to spend some time together.'

'We *spend* time together. Jesus. We fuck practically every night of the week. What more do you want?'

'I'd like you to be present at one of those *fuckings* occasionally.'

On that cheerful note, she leaves him, her taxi having arrived early.

⌣

Linton bears his burdens lightly, normally. But not this morning. He can't put on a brave face. He's leaving his comfort zone behind. What if he's not up to it? He's managed to convince them so far, but does he possess real magic or is it a trick? There is no secret to learning lines. They are songs without music, and repeated listening reveals the hidden melodies. Much of *Othello* is beyond his comprehension, but the Moor is a man after his own heart. His own experience. A man of colour in a black & white world, he understands. He has compromised, and seized the opportunities presented.

He leaves his bed. The day is hurrying in, and she'll soon be here. The girls, and Mahmud, are more than capable of looking after his enterprises. They will be here when he gets back. But will *he* be here when he gets back? He's not sure what that means, except that he has a feeling that something elemental is slowly being extracted from him. What if he is a success? What if he is the toast of Dublin? What then? Once he plays the Moor, once he *is* the Moor, there are no other parts, no greater parts. And what then?

The butchers across the road are first to open, laying out fresh cuts of evenly sliced meat in neat rows. In Abuja the meat was laid out on upturned crates, and the flies would be the first customers, and not the only ones who didn't pay. Linton starts to make coffee, but his fingers are clumsy, and the result tastes foul. He'll get some at the airport, which won't be much of an improvement. He hasn't been to the airport since he arrived in the country. His passport passed scrutiny back then, so hopefully there won't be any difficulty. Being with Carolyn should ease his passage, if not his conscience.

The taxi is waiting. He fears leaving, fears not returning. He's being foolish. Where is the Moor now? She will see him for what he really is – a shopkeeper, nothing more, nothing less. He will be cast aside when her mistake is realised, and they will bring in a professional actor to fulfil *his* task. His suit is on the dull side of green, though the shirt, a bright red, adds a dash of colour. He gives her the full set of teeth in the morning gloom, and settles in beside her on the backseat. He pats her hand, a gesture of intimacy that makes her blush. *Are you as scared as me*, his eyes say, and she responds in kind.

⌒

They miss the performance, preferring to attend their own. It was, perhaps, inevitable, she knows, from the beginning, from before then even. He overwhelms her, frightening her with the level of intensity she experiences. Sadness, too, assaults her. Her too predictable nature. *Infidelity,* there it is, then, as grim as the rainy dawn that greets her when she finally crawls from his bed, defeated.

They breakfast in confused silence, neither sure what to say. Their return flight is in three hours, an eternity in her mind, giving her time to calculate the enormity of the damage caused.

'We have six months yet,' he tells her.

'What?' she says, daydreaming in the departure hall at Heathrow.

'There is plenty of time to see other productions, to make up for this,' he says.

'*Make up for this,*' she repeats blankly.

'I *know* the play, the part, Carolyn. I will not let you down.'

'No,' she says. *But I have let myself down.*

Back in Dublin, she climbs into her bed mid-afternoon, and only wakes when Ray slips in beside her that evening.

'I'm sorry,' he says.

'*You're* sorry? For what?' He doesn't explain, but he holds her, and she holds him back.

'How was London?' he says afterwards.

'It was okay,' she says.

'Just okay?'

'Yes – just okay. Can we not talk about it?'

⌒

The Moor misses his Desdemona. He attends her classes, as requested, growing tired of the endless rehearsals. When will they actually perform the play properly, on a proper stage? And who is this girl they have given him as his wife? She is nervous, skeletal, childlike. He doubts she has ever been with a man. She flinches from his kisses, and trembles at his touch - while Carolyn fades into the background, her role receding as the play's official director takes charge. Linton transfers his affections to the latter, Marina White, an American, and a lady of colour. She proves more sceptical about his intentions, and his talents, but she weighs up the matter, and decides it's better to keep the 'star' on side. Also, they are both outsiders, with sad tales of intolerance to share.

Carolyn has retreated to the safety of the other projects on her desk, and the renewed sanctity of her marriage. She and Ray take that short break they argued about, and on their return are rewarded with the extraordinary news of her pregnancy. At first she bristles at Linton's continuing presence in her classes, where he lurks at the back, glowering. Their doomed passion has not, she comes to realise, derailed *Othello*, as by all accounts, he is blossoming under the pressure. There are niggling problems, as there always are, notably with the actress playing Desdemona. It is invariably so, with this particular play, that the leading lady is too timid in the role, in case she eclipses Othello. There's no danger of that happening here, especially with this slip of a lass. It's too late to recast. The girl, and the rest of the cast, will just have to manage. At least Linton *hasn't* been pursuing her outside of the ring, so to speak, if the rumours are true. The rumours point in Marina's direction, but she, more than most, Carolyn guesses, can handle herself. *Not* Carolyn's problem anymore, thank God. And there's the prospect of a nice little bonus if the production turns a decent profit. When the media campaign is launched for the Autumn program, *Othello* is bound to attract most of the attention, and therefore a decent run at the box-office. She should feel proud, and in quiet moments, she does, *but* – all sorts of things can go wrong in the lead up to opening night, not to mention the night itself. And then there's Linton – for all his strutting, and natural ability, he *could* freeze on the big occasion. That well of confidence could dry up in an instant. She has seen it happen to seasoned pros. No risk, no reward, though, she reminds herself, turning her attention to *Pygmalion*, and Shaw's savage wit. It, and the rest of Shaw's works, are in the planning for *2021*. She's forever running ahead, the future her present.

⌇

The Gate's coffers swell with the prospects of an unknown immigrant playing the Moor in the centrepiece of their autumn season. Linton becomes the subject of unprecedented attention, drawing small crowds to his Moore Street establishments. He basks in the glow, reciting Shakespeare from his doorway, and deflecting all talk of nerves ahead of his upcoming debut. One of the papers dubs him **'The Moor of Moore Street'** which leads to merciless taunts and teases from the other traders, who are secretly proud of one of their own making it.

Linton has to formally step back from business as the opening draws near. He calls in the staff, and puts Mirella in temporary charge. There is polite agreement about the arrangement, on the surface, but he has more important problems on the horizon. Now that the fateful hour is almost him, he betrays the first sign of apprehension, and doubt. It is not the words that will desert him, for they are embedded in his soul at this stage. His Desdemona remains a mystery to him, both the actress and the character she plays. Their embraces are deadening glimpses of mortality, and he fears displaying this on stage. He wishes he were playing Iago instead. That is *the* part in the play, perhaps in all of Shakespeare. The actor playing him is proving a worthy adversary, and Linton's sure that it comes from genuine animosity between the two men. And there is Marina, a mass of insecurities, looking to *him* for reassurance! He can't satisfy her, he doubts if any man can. He suspects she might be happier with another woman. Back home, she could be imprisoned for even thinking that way. He must admit, he misses Carolyn, and their infrequent encounters at the theatre never fail to rekindle his interest. Perhaps when the play has run its course, or he has, he might look to renew their former acquaintance.

The Moor of Moore Street is uneasy with the moniker, sensing a slight touch of sarcasm behind it. Do the media secretly doubt him, even as they plunder his privacy looking for pearls of wisdom? 'Haply for I am black, and have not those soft conversations....' has become his default reply, sending them off somewhat disappointed. There is one particular journalist, however, from the Irish Times, who has returned more than most, but his questions appear slippery, as if he's trying to trick Linton into saying something he shouldn't. The scribe, Linton learns from a quick perusal of the internet, is not a critic, but an investigative journalist. It must be slow-news season, Linton reasons. What else could it be?

'You are coming, aren't you? To the opening?'

'Of course I am. The question is – are you?' Ray pats her swelling stomach. 'Are you up to it?'

'It's not going to pop out during the second act,' Carolyn assures him. 'It's not due for months yet.'

'But the excitement might induce premature labour' Ray suggests.

'Premature? Jesus, Ray, that would be something of an understatement. But I *am* excited. I can't believe it's actually happening. I found him on the street, for fuck sake. What if he can't go through with it? Can you imagine how nervous he must be feeling right now? I mean, *I'm* shaking just thinking about it.'

'Hey, come here,' he says, holding her tightly. 'See, this is what I feared, you getting all uptight about this. It's not healthy, for the both of you.'

'I'm *going*, Ray, and nothing will stop me. I have to be there. He'll be expecting me. He'll look for me, I'm certain.'

'Then,' says Ray, 'you *shall* go to the ball, my dear!'

In the wings, Linton considers taking flight. Going back, home, Nigeria. Where he'll wake up and realise that it was all a dream.

He peers through the curtains, searching for her. There she is, in the second row, holding her husband's hand, the swollen belly clearly showing her to be well advanced. Her obvious contentment proves a welcome distraction, easing his nerves.

He kisses his Desdemona before the curtain rises, surprising her, making her blush, eliciting a rare, intimate smile. That might do the trick, he thinks.

He holds his breath immediately before his entrance, running along the railway tracks in the Nigerian night, and then chasing after his mother in the moments after she has been taken. Breathe, open your eyes, speak, believe . *'Tis better as it is,'* Othello begins.

His head is in the clouds, and it might never come down again. He is the talk of the town. He stares into Carolyn's eyes, and thanks her for proving that miracles do happen. She accepts a glass of champagne, and drinks it, much to Ray's disapproval. The reviews follow in the hours after, universally rapturous in their appraisal of Linton's performance. Even in the shadow of the first night there is talk of a London run, and then, who knows, Broadway. Linton spends the night with Marina in her hotel suite, summoning up reserves of energy he didn't think possible.

Carolyn finds sleep impossible, as Ray lies pressed against her back, snoring enthusiastically. Unearthing, and developing, new talent, is satisfying, up to a point. She has reached that point, and can see past it, to the inevitable void that comes from knowing that such talent will never be unearthed in herself. She can't act, or paint, or sing, or play, or – anything. Except, there is the baby. But that's only possible because of Ray. And it's not exactly a talent, is it, as practically every woman on the planet is capable of the same thing. The future is her present, but that too belongs to others, playwrights, actors, directors, each one more skilled than her.

Linton leaves Marina sleeping, anxious to return to his own bed. It strikes him as he walks down O'Connell Street in the early hours that he has to do it all again in a few hours. And every night after that, for months. And then – London, New York. The future stretches out ahead of him, but it's not his.

Carolyn leaves Ray sleeping, and goes to the kitchen, hoping to have a few quiet moments alone with her child.

His passion, and performance, diminish with repetition. He wants a new script, new surroundings, new companions. He tires of killing his wife. He grows increasingly envious of Iago having the stage so often to himself, while Othello is always attended by soldiers and courtiers. Linton desires his own space, his own private audience. His ambitions for change causes tensions, onstage and off. Discontent is soon rampant throughout the company, putting an extended run in jeopardy. Marina's relationship with Linton, an open secret, doesn't help heal divisions, forcing them to call it off. Crisis meetings are held, where Linton threatens to pull out altogether, and some of the cast urge him to do so, threatening *him* with getting in a professional actor as a replacement.

Carolyn remains unfazed by the difficulties, dismissing them as the usual strains that affect productions. Not that she cares much, what with the birth only weeks away. She's been thinking of the aftermath, revaluating her career, and the possibility of taking her talents elsewhere. Pastures new, and all that. Ray is up for it, still revelling in his achievement, and secretly hoping for a boy, an heir. She will take whatever God gives her, and hopes He doesn't surprise her with more than one.

For Linton and Carolyn, their time is near, although both have little idea of what upheaval awaits them.

Red sky at night, but there's no delight for Linton as he finds the journalist on his doorstep.

'We're closed,' says Linton.

'Linton Okador?' the man says.

'Who's asking?'

'You *are* Linton Okador?'

'Who else could I be?'

'Oh, I can think of someone – Mohammed Edu, for example. Does that name ring a bell?'

'Do you have identification?' Linton asks.

'I'm not the police, if that's what you're thinking.' He hands Linton his Press Card.

'If you're not here for a haircut, perhaps an autograph?'

'I am here, Linton, to offer you a chance to put your side of the story across, before it appears in the newspapers.'

'You are not a critic, therefore I don't have to talk to you.'

'Better talk to me than the police,' the journalist warns.

'Tell me your lies, and then get out of here.'

'You say you are Linton Okador – but according to my information, Linton Okador died in Abuja ten years ago, in a car accident. So, then we come to Mohammed Edu.'

'Yes, let's come to him,' Linton says, wondering how many people know that this dog has come to see him.

'He crops up first in a Malian prison, charged with terrorist activities, with links to Boko Haram in Nigeria. Then he disappears for several years, before turning up in Abuja working as a gun-runner for Somali pirates. His arrest is sought, but he disappears again. Until now – until right now…because I'm looking at him.' Linton howls with laughter, even as he howls with despair.

'And you are going to print these *lies?*' he spits at the journalist.

'I'm giving you a chance to deny the story before it comes out.'

'I *do* deny it!' Linton cries.

'I'll show you a photograph of the man identified by Interpol as Mohammed Edu.' Linton is afraid to touch it, and pulls his hands away.

'And *I* can show you my passport,' says Linton, 'and other documents proving I am Linton Okador.'

'I have no doubt you can. But how will the Gate Theatre feel about such adverse publicity? How long will your career last after this?'

'Why are you here?' Linton growls. 'Because I am black? An immigrant? A *success?* If you are so sure of your facts, why tell me beforehand? Why not print, and be damned?'

'*I* am sure. My paper is nervous, however. They are not fully convinced. But I told them I will get absolute proof. And I have that proof. I'm looking at it. At you. At Mohammed Edu. I'm the one taking the risk. I'm giving you a chance to run, before the authorities catch up with you. Or tell your side of the story.'

The red has faded to black, and they are shadowed in street light, the shops and stalls shut, the produce packed away. Linton unwittingly thinks of Nigeria, in the stormy days when he escaped by the skin of his teeth, and fortune threw him up on the shores of Ireland. Green, and lush, and wet, and largely incorruptible, he settled, and settled for moderation. And he might have remained, anonymous and harmless, if it hadn't been for that woman, and her crazy ideas.

'Well, Linton, will you talk to me – or do I leave, and let matters run their course?'

Linton stands up to his full height, looming over the journalist.

'I have done the State some service, and they know't. No more of that. I pray you in your letters, that you shall these unlucky deeds relate, and speak of me as I am.'

'And who, exactly, are you?'

Carolyn sleeps in late after a difficult night. The baby is anxious to see the world. The house is cold, and the coffee tastes especially bitter. Her mobile rings, startling her.

'Yes?'

No, she has *no* idea where Linton is – why would she? But where is he – that's what everyone wants to know. She assumes that the pressure has become too much for him, although why now, after everything he's accomplished? She has a day of strange conversations, with all manner of wild stories circulating. She decides to walk down to Moore Street, thinking he might have returned to hide out there. But she never makes it, interrupted by a phone call from Fergal Marron, telling her about the story that's due to run in the Irish Times. She can't take it in, but keeps heading in the direction of Moore Street, where some light might be shed on the mystery. But the baby has other ideas, choosing that moment to announce its impending arrival, *now*.

Holles Street – *holler* street – crashing forward, too soon, unprepared, alone, Ray running late, but hopefully running, she won't finish until he's there, despite the child's insistence, and the nurses' encouragement, but the pain, the *fucking* pain, unrelenting, with the midwife indifferent, *laughing* at her, only normal she says, bet she'd never been through it, Carolyn thinks, sinking into another wave of discomfort, begging for mercy, for drugs, for Ray, for *Ray!*

The future is the present, it has arrived, and it's alarmingly, and frighteningly, real. And empty, and alone, she's going to be left, literally, holding the baby –

'Ray!' He's there, at last, at the last, when she's nothing left to give, she can't push any longer, but never mind, it's almost here, it's coming, the head is coming, *coming*, out of her, the future has arrived –

'Ray? What – what's wrong?'

Carolyn strains to get a proper glimpse, through the blinding pain, and the sweaty tears in her eyes – no, wait, here it comes, they're about to hand it over – but Ray, what's wrong with Ray? Is there something wrong with –

Oh my God oh my ohmyoh

Linton may have gone, but a part of him will always be there, with her – with her child, *in* her child.

Haply......for I am black

Slump

Mister Bayliss of Bristol, businessman, makes his way steadily down O'Connell Street, squinting into the low sun, eager for breakfast, the essential ingredient of any successful day. The portly gentleman could have taken a taxi to his destination, the Metro Café on South William Street, but the day looked promising from his hotel room, and his wife had been badgering him about getting more exercise. Hah! She could talk, could Mrs. Bayliss, being rather large herself. They made a formidable pair, he'd be the first to admit, and cheers at the very thought of her. There's a crunching *snap* to his steps, as a heavy frost has turned sections of pavements into ice-rinks. One or two have already succumbed, and can't hide their embarrassment as they are helped to their feet. Bayliss reckons his weight carries an advantage in these conditions, securing him to the ground, preventing such accidents. He keeps a firm grip on his briefcase, containing as it does the tools of his trade. He is well prepared for his nine o'clock meeting, confident he can persuade them to decide in his company's favour. Bayliss knows he may not present the most dynamic image, but there's no more reliable man, he can guarantee that. He makes no false promises, sticks rigidly to deadlines, and provides an after-sales service second to none. Ah yes, the rest of the world may thunder on past Mister Bayliss, in its reckless desire to get to the finish as quickly as possible, but he won't be distracted, or stray from his steady course.

The Metro Café plays music too loudly for his taste, but the seats are comfortable, and the food to die for. Here it comes – sausage, mushrooms, bacon, with toast on the side, all washed down with piping-hot black coffee – heaven! He gets more good news in the form of his meeting being delayed, put back an hour. Normally, he hates it when his schedule is interrupted, but when there's a plateful of greasy food in front of him, and the hunger is upon him, reason goes out the window. He likes Ireland, and the Irish, but he doesn't know how they ever get things done. It's not that they're lazy, as such, but other things have a habit of getting in the way. Never mind, he'll still make his flight, still be home for dinner, and still get to spend the night with Brenda. And speak of the devil! - there she is now, calling him.

'Hi, love!' he says cheerfully. She babbles on, as she does, for the next ten minutes, updating him on everything that has happened in his brief absence. Mostly, she talks of their four boys, who range from seven to fourteen, spirited lads every one of them, although they have inherited their parents' genes, in the sense that he doubts there'll be any Olympic athletes among them. Still, nothing wrong with a healthy appetite, and their old dad hasn't done too badly for himself, has he? They could do far worse than follow his lead. He tells Brenda he loves her, and that he'll be home for dinner. As if he needed any encouragement, he devours his breakfast, and is tempted to ask for seconds. He settles on a pastry, and more coffee, which he enjoys as he goes over his presentation once more. He knows it by heart. Nobody knows more about the company's products that he does. He was in at the start, working from a draughty office on the outskirts of Bristol, over twenty years ago now. Progress was slow, and there were times when the business was staring into the abyss, but Bayliss and his partners soldiered on, stubborn and determined, until they finally started turning a healthy profit. And look at them now – look at *him* now. Yes, life is good, it has to be said. The secret, he thinks, is to enjoy the bad times as well as the good, and never start believing that you, or your business, have 'made it.'

He leaves a generous tip, and goes downstairs to the basement toilets. The mirror is unflattering to Bayliss, but he can't help staring. He looks paler than usual, though it's probably the light, and there's a redness in his eyes. He strokes his moustache with a degree of pride, knowing they're somewhat out of fashion, but it's an integral part of his identity, and could never be removed. Also, Brenda is extremely fond of it. She says it gives him an air of authority, and class, so sadly lacking in many others. She has nothing good to say about beards of any kind, strangely, and would prefer her man clean-shaven. So, the moustache it is, then. If he ever doubts, and who doesn't, that dark line above his lip invariably reassures.

The steps back up are hard work, and he's out of breath when he reaches the top. That mountain of food hasn't helped. He'll walk it off before the meeting, if there *is* a meeting. Are the clients having second-thoughts? It would be a shame to have come all this way, and put in all that work, and not get a chance to plead his case. He loves presenting. His company's products are like his children, and he loves nothing more than showing them off. He meets many businessmen, and women, who seem to dislike their work so much that he often feels like having a word with them, to remind them of what they're missing. You can't sell successfully if you appear to be desperate to get the product off your hands. You have to love the product so much that you feel obliged to share it with as many others as possible. His fervour, he's aware, borders on the religious at times, and he has to be careful not to give the impression that he's selling the secret to eternal life.

It's cold outside, he can tell from the solidity of his breath, and the brisk pace of warmly-dressed passers-by, yet he has to wipe sweat from his brow, and pause every ten yards or so. The indigestion strikes as usual, but with unusual intensity. He swallows a handful of Rennies, though they rarely provide quick, or adequate, relief. There's a burning sensation in his chest that resembles a fist closing around the veins. He puts his briefcase down on the ground for a moment, waiting for the worst of it to pass. He's unaccountably afraid in that moment, yearning to call Brenda, wishing she was here beside him, just in case. Nine o'clock, the meeting should have been underway, normality would reign, and he'd have help at hand. He knows his weight makes him an easier target for a heart attack, and sundry other illnesses, as his doctor regularly tells him. Maybe he *has* beaten the odds once too often. He feels the passage in his throat clearing, as if the lights have finally turned green, and the food can go down as it's meant to. He almost cries with relief, and decides he needs a sit-down. He can't go into a meeting flustered and flushed, that would be unprofessional. Stephen's Green park is in front of him, and he walks under the arch at the entrance, aiming for the nearest bench. The seat is wet from the thawing frost, but that's the least of his worries. *Big baby*, he scolds himself, taking out a handkerchief to blow his nose, and wipe his eyes.

Feeling much better, he walks over to the edge of the pond, calmed by the serene progress of the regal swans. Showing no fear, the birds float up to the tips of his shoes, obviously hoping for food from the large figure on the bank. Bayliss reflects on the fact that he never learned to swim, nor learned to feel comfortable near water. Now, looking out across the pristine surface, where the swans perform their ballet, he regrets not appreciating its qualities earlier. He and Brenda went on a cruise years before, where he spent most of the time hovering close to the lifeboats, and familiarising himself with the safety procedures in case they sank. A man of his size, he determined, would sink to the bottom of the ocean like a stone. A mother and child appear next to him, throwing bread to the birds, and attracting greedy intruders, mostly gulls in full cry. Bayliss moves away, feeling lightheaded, deciding that what he needs to do is focus on the task at hand, which is the client, and the potential revenue that could accrue from a successful negotiation. He looks back at the mother and child by the pond, but they've been swallowed up by the sun, rendering them just vague impressions of actual people.

Another call, a further delay, and the day is getting away from him. The sun has gone into hiding, perhaps permanently, and there's now the possibility that he will miss his flight, and his home-cooked dinner. He wonders if he's the cause of all this distemper, if there was something he did, or didn't do, which resulted in the world slipping, momentarily, out of kilter. His routine has been irrevocably disturbed, he'll never get back on track. He'll have to shorten his presentation, increasing the risk of mistakes being made, of crucial points not being emphasised. He's tempted to cancel, in order to regain control of the situation, even if it means returning home empty-handed. There's a sales conference in Plymouth the day after tomorrow, and he was hoping to have tied up this deal before then. Targets will be missed, his and the company's, to everyone's dismay.

Bayliss is out of sorts, walking aimlessly in a drizzle that's turning into sleet. That's all he needs, catching a cold on top of everything else. Dawson Street is a mess of barriers and cones, as the surgeons in hard hats cut into the concrete skin. Dublin, it occurs to him, is always being repaired without ever being fixed. He navigates his way through the minefield until he reaches the address.

He enters the meeting-room in the midst of a joke that isn't shared. Ironically, he's the last to arrive, and he hears himself apologising. He sets up his presentation to a wall of silence, and thereafter never quite finds his usual rhythm. He stutters, tripping over his words, before hastening to the finish line having omitted several key points. He sits down fuming, shaking his head, sure he's blown it. There follows another hour of dry discussion as each part of his proposal is pored over with forensic detail. He starts dreaming of Brenda's steak & kidney pie, with custard to follow. Then an early night, perhaps, though he's likely to be too tired. Still, Brenda's bountiful body is a sea worth drowning in.

'What?' he says, asking them to repeat the question. Not like him to lose concentration like that. However, they seem keen, and maybe they're willing to overlook his less-than-stellar pitch. His reputation, after all, precedes him, which must allow for the odd mistake now and then. They break for coffee, and normally he'd dive right in, but he's anxious about his flight, (…and his steak & kidney pie).

The clients are being unduly fastidious and diligent, wanting clarification on several issues. Bayliss is happy to oblige, back in his element. Can he possibly snatch victory from the jaws of defeat? Yes, he can, and yes, he does. Handshakes all round, even a slap on the back, and, more importantly, signatures on the bottom line. Another target reached – now, if only he can reach that flight, this will be a trip worth celebrating. He looks forward to the conference in Plymouth with a fair degree of excitement. Bayliss isn't one to blow his own trumpet, *too* often, but the Sales Director will *have* to say a few kind words about him: *Bayliss has done it again, gentleman! How does he do it?*

He snaps up the last of the croissants on offer before he leaves. He hates to see food go to waste. He sends a message to the office in Bristol: *mission accomplished, Dublin.* He can relax now. The indigestion has left him, mercifully, for the moment anyway. He'll be able to attack dinner with a hearty confidence.

⌒

Bayliss steps out of the building, and into a hole. Pipes are being laid, but the men are on a break – and the proper safety measures have been temporarily neglected. He's looking beyond where his feet are landing, and down he goes, hearing one bone snap, and then another, but where he can't be sure. He lies still in breathless silence, waiting for information, for someone to tell him what's happening. He hopes it won't take long, he has a plane to catch. A dinner to eat. A wife to sleep with. Out of the corner of his eye, spectators, at the edge of the hole. Why are they looking, and not *doing*? Will the sale still go through, even if – *what?* He's not there? But where else would he be? Company man, through and through, is Bayliss, of Bristol. There are voices in his ear, and in his head. There are sirens. His chest is tightening rapidly, closing in……shutting down. A man beside him removes his yellow helmet. That's not a good sign. And there was he, and everyone else, thinking that his weight would get him in the end….when it's a hole in the ground that proves his downfall…a *hole.* *That's Dublin for you…always being repaired…never fixed…*

Poor Mister Bayliss of Bristol, businessman, gentleman, makes his way steadily down a corridor of infinite brightness, practically floating, *soaring*. He can't remember eating, but he feels full. He doesn't think he could eat another thing, ever again. But he did reach his monthly target again, didn't he? He closed the deal – and that's all anyone could ask of him.

Time, perhaps, to put his feet up. He's earned a rest.

Pound of Flesh

Lighting a smoke in a bleedin' hurricane, story of his life. On Clyde Road - it doesn't want him there. There'll be alarms next, warning the residents of an intruder on the premises. Look at these fucking mansions, every one of them is a barracks in its own right, could carry a small platoon in every room, and *he* has one all to himself, while the rest have to suffer indefinite misery. Tommy can't find shelter, the rain is getting through the heaviest foliage, dampening his already low spirits, as well as putting out his cigarette.

This is a complete waste of time. He should have stayed with his wife, though watching her grasp for every breath isn't exactly pleasant. To be honest, he needed a smoke, he was gasping, while she was dying from the self-same thing. Sixty a day, both of them. He needed to cut down, before it cut *him* down. Jesus, bit late for that. It was funny, if you looked at it from a certain angle. Emphysema, they called it. Her lungs were shot, while his were unaccountably clear. It wasn't fair, but there it was. She'd be gone within months, and then where would he be? Look where he already is, hiding under a dripping tree, getting pneumonia on top of everything else. Maybe he'd be joining her up in James's hospital. They might even find him a bed right next to her. Least they'd be getting fed three times a day. Fact is, he's avoiding going back to the B&B on the Cabra Road, the one masquerading as a hotel. The State may be paying, but there's a good reason. Been a while since the establishment qualified for any stars, despite what the proprietor says. *Back in the day*, the man's always saying.

Where is *he*? – Seamus *fucking* Clifford, the reason behind it all. Cowering in his ten-bed palace, behind his lawyers, behind his protestations of bankruptcy. And in the meantime, Tommy's home, and that of a hundred others, lies empty, while the authorities decide who's to blame for the health and safety breaches which forced decent men and women to abandon the property. Clifford was quickly named, but not shamed. He blamed the electricians, and the plasterers, everyone but himself. Then, under threat of prosecution, he pleads poverty, and applies to be declared bankrupt. He could sell his fucking house for a start, Tommy thinks. He'll mention that when he finds him, *if* he finds him. He could barely find his left hand in this weather. He flicks the stupid stub away, and digs into his pocket for the next. Water runs down his neck, and he moves further back against the wall. He'll be in the garden next, and definitely trespassing. Dolores would love that, wouldn't she, him getting arrested, now of all times. Him in the Joy, and she breathing her last. Does he still love her? Did he ever, really? That's beside the point, she's his, and vice-versa, shackled together for life, that's all he knows. He couldn't leave her even if he tried. And he's tried. Long time ago, not going there again. He may not have kissed her on the lips for some time, nor anywhere else, but that's by the by. They have a daughter, don't they? They *had* a daughter, more like. In Sydney these past five years, rarely heard from her, but that's understood. Why would the girl want to be reminded of Dublin? Gone to shit.

Can't hear the rain, though he can see it. Slowing down, though. If he doesn't move soon, his legs will seize up. He *needs* a proper smoke. He checks his phone, the screen blurring with the drizzle, but there's no messages. Dolores, hopefully, is out for the count. She's permanently exhausted, so she won't waste her precious time chasing him. As if in sympathy, he starts coughing, excreting a sizable amount of phlegm. Thank God the rain will wash the mess away.

Where does the man live? What's he going to do, knock on every door, ask for him by name? There are embassies around here, what if one of them takes exception to his unexceptional appearance, and brings in the guards to question him? He's had dealings with them before, and they'll just hold it against him. Nothing major, some damaged property while he was under the influence. Only a fine, and well behind him, but it'll be on record. It will always be on record, and mark him out as one to be handled with care. What is this place, anyway? Who needs a house this size? He doesn't, for one. He needs a *quiet* house, for the most part, that's his, and his alone – and Dolores, of course. He's started thinking lately about *after*-Dolores. Will it be like losing a leg, or an eye? No more hospital visits, for one thing. No more listening to her wheezing and coughing all night – though he's more than contributed his fair share of both. And it's not as if she brings in any money – well, apart from the disability benefit – though driving buses hasn't made him rich, has it?

There's a break in the clouds, a splattering of blue. It's already feeling warmer. He can light up with confidence. Ah, bliss! He moves out from under the tree, and realises the scale of his task, if he means to go through with it. It's a mountain range of houses facing him, the Himalayas. He should have found out precisely where the man lived before coming down here. He's out of his depth. He'd be out of his depth if Clifford was presented to him on a plate, and with the State's permission, allowed to give him a slap or two. Truth be told, Tommy has never raised his hands in anger. He's been wise enough to keep out of harm's way all these years, so what chance of him finding the courage now? His head is getting clogged up with conflicting thoughts. A third cigarette fails to clarify things, and he starts walking, loosening his stiff joints, and studying each house in turn, hoping for a sign. He doubts there'll be a brass plate on a pillar with **Seamus Clifford** emblazoned on it, but you'd never know with people like that. Vain, *rich*, bolloxes do that sort of thing. He wants to see evidence of the developer's pronounced 'poverty' for himself. If it's true – he'll let him off with a stern word or two. Who's he fucking kidding? He lost his house once, and he did nothing then. Before the apartments went up, there were proper houses, and one of those belonged to him and Dolores. Okay, it was a tiny redbrick, in need of love and attention, but who had the money for that? A mild protest, and the whole row was demolished, and replaced by a gleaming pile of glass and steel, into which Tommy and Dolores moved. They hadn't really moved at all, just went up a bit. And it cost them nothing, part of the reward for losing the original. But this – this is different.

He's out in the open, feeling exposed. On the wide plain, vulnerable to attack, and he has no defence against this kind of creature. They eat their own, he bets. His brain is scrambled, and some kind of madness is pushing him into making a terrible mistake. But he can't stop – she has tubes and wires coming out of her, she's half-machine, and soon she won't be able to function without it – and they'll eventually ask him the question – on or off? He'll be tested, and sorely tempted – *off* – *off!* – and it's that man's fault, he pushed her over the edge, putting her under unnecessary stress, as if she didn't have enough to deal with. They wouldn't have minded moving out if they knew when they were moving back in. But the repairs could take months, *if* someone could be found to carry them out. Shoved, like refugees, into a B&B, but not with their neighbours - with *actual* refugees, from warzones and famines, blacks, Muslims, nothing against them, as such, but they had different ideas about things, didn't they, and some things weren't meant to go together.

Tommy finds his man when he stops looking for him. It looks like an old man putting out the rubbish, but on closer inspection it's clearly Clifford. He *is* an old man, Tommy realises, but that doesn't make him any less guilty. He's at the boot of his Bentley, looking like he's preparing to leave. Does he have any family? Tommy had been banking on fighting this battle alone. His cough gives him away, and Clifford turns on his heels, nervous as a kitten, and slams the boot closed before Tommy can get a look inside.

'This is private property,' Clifford declares in a weak voice.

'Some of us don't have any property – because of you.' Tommy's own voice betrays his doubts.

'I said – this is *private* property,' says the man, taking a few steps in Tommy's direction. 'Outside, now, or I'll call the police.'

'I heard the police have already called on *you*. And they'll be back, to arrest you.'

'Who the hell do you think you are!'

Tommy is shaking. 'Me? Nobody. Fucking nobody. I used to live in Inchicore until recently. Not as nice as this place, but we liked it. Until we were thrown out, and dumped in a B&B – because of you – *you*. Now, do you know who I am? Inchicore, that ring any bells? An apartment building, where a lot of ordinary, decent people lived – *lived* – but not anymore – because you couldn't be fucking bothered to do your job properly. People are thrown out on the street while you continue to live in fucking luxury. Doesn't seem fair, does it?'

'Nothing has been proven,' says Clifford without much conviction. 'It's in the hands of my lawyers. I have rejected the accusations, and will continue to do so – and, anyway, it's none of your fucking business.'

'I thought you told the papers you were broke, or did I hear wrong?'

'You wouldn't understand,' says Clifford.

'Oh, wouldn't I? Too fucking retarded, am I? Pleading poverty, are you, and all the while you're living on this road, driving that car. Is that what you consider being broke? My wife and I – our stuff had to be put into storage. It's rotting in some container somewhere, and you don't give a bollocks, do you?'

'No – I don't. Not really.' Tommy springs forward, not sure what he's going to do. Clifford puts his hand up to ward off an attack, startling Tommy with his cowardice. He can't do it, he can't hit another living soul. He doesn't want to fight. He wants a smoke. He wants to get back to Dolores. He wants to go back home, with everything in its proper place. Clifford shrinks back in fear, stumbling up the steps into his house. The street is eerily quiet again, crowding in on Tommy. He doesn't belong here.

He reaches Baggot Street, finds Searsons, and plants himself on a stool at the bar, ordering a pint, deciding the cigarette can wait. His hands are shaking. He drinks half without tasting any. He orders a second, and a third, and staggers out for a smoke as if he'd had about ten. Under the canopy, watching the rain and the failing light, he gets a call. It's the hospital. Bad news – the worst news. Dolores has been taken from him. Her weak body couldn't take any more of the strain, and her heart gave out. Tommy's heart gives out. He's shaking again.

He's still shaking when he returns to Clyde Road. He stands by the Bentley, trying to open the boot. There might be proof of guilt inside. The front door opens, and Clifford comes for him. They collide, and Clifford buckles under Tommy's greater will. He's about to kick the man when he's down, but the fall has dazed Clifford. There's blood on the gravel under his head. He groans, pleading with Tommy for help.

'Call an ambulance – for *you*? It won't do my wife any good, will it? Oh, that's what I came to tell you – my wife – she, how can I put it politely, she *passed away*. Passed away, just as I was having a pint. I was having a pint to calm myself down after talking to you…and she was…she was…'

Clifford manages to get up on his knees, where he crawls like a dog back towards the house. He finds keys in his pocket, but the effort is too much for him, and loses consciousness.

'I'll take those for you,' says Tommy. He thinks of dragging Clifford into the house, but the car is closer, and easier. He opens the boot, finding only bags of clothes and food. The man was obviously intent on staying away for some time. Tommy dumps the bags in bushes near the side gate. He grabs hold of Clifford's collar and drags him to the car, shocked by the weight. It takes a full ten minutes to get him over the lip of the boot. Exhausted, Tommy slides to the ground, crying for Dolores, figuring he might be joining her soon.

If he can drive a bus he can drive a Bentley, he reasons. Only one passenger on this ride, and Tommy is paying the fare for both. What is he doing? He doesn't quite know. They'll be waiting for him up in the hospital. *She*'ll be waiting for him. To take care of things.

'I'm *taking* care of things!' Tommy shouts, turning out onto the Stillorgan Road, driving out of the city to no particular destination. He almost loses control of the car several times, the engine's power taking him by surprise. He barely has to touch the throttle and it practically lifts off. Back towards the sea - he remembers a quiet road near the chimneys close to Poolbeg. Anyway, he needs a smoke.

He took Dolores here once or twice, in the dim, distant past. When they did that sort of thing. There are no lovers on the lane tonight. There's a skip nearby, overflowing. And a ditch, flooded from the earlier rain. He wonders how deep it is. How long before it would drain, or evaporate, and they'd find him? He almost chokes on the cigarette, flicking it away before lighting another. There's a noise coming from the boot, a dull thud.

Tommy opens the boot, and steps back, wary of a revived Clifford springing out. But the man looks like a fish left to die slowly on the harbour wall, slow heavy breaths that remind Tommy of his wife. He summons up one last mighty effort, and pulls Clifford out of the car. There's no struggle, except the one raging in his own mind. He rolls Clifford over to the ditch, kicking him over the edge, and the splash reaches the tips of Tommy's shoes. The body sinks beneath the surface, though only an inch or two. Tommy takes a filthy mattress from the skip and throws it over Clifford, though he knows it will do little to prevent discovery.

Tommy leans over the ditch further down, waiting for the nausea to pass. He stands, prepared to be sick, to get it over with. He throws the car keys in the ditch water, and starts walking back to civilisation.

⌣

In the hospital, he's greeted with pity and concern. It's past midnight. They were expecting him hours earlier, and in better condition despite the circumstances.

'Can I see her?' he asks.

The room is absurdly bright, and Dolores unnaturally pale. He wants to touch her...but he hasn't touched her in a long time. Instead, he whispers to her. He confesses. *As my mother used to say, love...I got my pound of flesh.* He doesn't recognise her without a cigarette in her hand, or a cough coming out of her mouth. The nurse pats him on the shoulder: his time is up. He could do with some fresh air, anyway.

And he could do with a smoke.

Red Cliff House

It isn't red, or anywhere near a cliff. It isn't even strictly a house. It's a *guest*house that once masqueraded as a hotel. How the mighty have fallen. How the street has fallen. This section of the Cabra Road was fairly quiet, and faintly posh, in its day. Now it's a clogged vein of crawling cars, from dawn till dusk, the residents unwilling spectators. *Red Cliff House* is on a precipice, though, of financial ruin, and infamy. The State, in its wisdom, decided to turn it into a refuge, a shelter for the homeless, and the stateless, offering paltry compensation to its owners in the process.

⌒

Daily, John and Breda Sullivan, proprietors, contemplate the error of their ways. Prisoners in their own kitchen. Tossing a coin to see who'll deal with the guests today. The Government's request had been a bolt out of the blue, and a blessing, or so they thought at the time. The regular income would tide them over, and they'd be doing some good. *Doing some good* are the words that will be etched on their headstones – and that day might come sooner than they think. A few years short of retirement age, they fell like a horse at the last fence, in sight of the finish line. They breakfast in sullen silence, neither particularly hungry. Breda, John realises, has been losing weight at an alarming rate, and he himself is nothing but skin and bone. They'll be found by one of the guests, and added to the menu, probably. There's a key in the back door, and the handle being turned. Nuri, their Indian cleaner, and only other member of staff, lets herself in, bowing good morning. They've stopped having conversations of any significance. Each knows what they have to do, and there's an awful lot to be done. John takes out a coin, and tosses.

'Heads,' she says. Tails it is. He'll play chef this morning, while she takes orders. Then, she knows, he'll hide in the office and bury himself in the accounts. In truth, he's welcome to it, as far as she's concerned. One look at the figures, and she'd run from the building screaming.

There's an idea. Not the screaming, but the running. It's not that she hasn't thought about it. She'd slip out while he thinks she's serving breakfast. Only thing is – where would she go? The car would take her so far, but even that would be a risk, given the Nissan's notorious history. No, she's trapped there, for good or ill. John's far from being the worst, she knows that. They have blazing rows, off and on, though lately it's been more *on* – but who could blame them for getting on each other's nerves? They've watched *Fawlty Towers*, and pined for a life that good. And unlike Basil and Sybil, they do show affection for each other on occasion. The frequency has diminished significantly, but the intensity has increased. They grasp at any chink of light in the darkness.

'I think I hear the enemies at the gate,' says John. He says it every morning, preparing himself for the battle ahead. There's a tear in the corner of his wife's eye. The strain is obvious, but what can he do to alleviate it? Unbeknownst to her, he has put their mobile home in Wexford on the market, hoping for a quick sale, and a pleasant surprise for her. They hadn't managed to get down for a couple of years, and the property was just sitting there – why not cash in, and give themselves a treat? He hasn't made up his mind how to spend the money, although there hadn't been a sniff of interest. He's thinking now that they could retire there, and end their days in poverty, where at least they'd be free.

'They're people – like us,' Breda says wearily. She doesn't know why she's defending them. They do nothing but complain, and *never* express their gratitude. Hard to believe now, but they once had regular, satisfied, guests who came back once, even twice, a year. She goes through to the dining room, which could do with a lick of paint, to put it mildly. As for the carpet, she can't bear to look down at it. The cutlery, too, once had a sheen to it. One table is occupied, by a Syrian couple, the woman wearing the full veil, while her husband berates their young daughter. Breda offers a smile and a tepid greeting, but they hardly reciprocate. They'll have cereal, milk and strong black tea, and argue through most of it. The child is forever trying to wriggle free, and Breda thinks she might help the girl escape one of these days. The Carmodys arrive on the scene, Irish, loud, a young couple with two children, the whole troupe is like a carnival, shrill and explosive, seeming to take up more space than the one table they occupy. They take the 'full Irish,' and invariably come back for seconds, filling their children up with the same crap, and dooming them to years of ill-health. They are 'homeless,' by all accounts, unable to pay the mortgage, but they don't appear too unhappy with their situation. And unless Breda's mistaken, Mrs. Carmody is pregnant again. Both parents have mobile phones, and each of the children has their own screen to keep them entertained, and supposedly quiet.

Nuri carries, and spills, plates. There's an accident every other day, but Breda hasn't the energy to ball her out, let alone sack her. If Nuri wasn't employed there, she'd likely be a guest, foisted on them by the authorities. It's a veritable United Nations of languages, and Breda has stopped trying. They all speak the universal language of despair.

In comes Terence, standing shyly in the doorway, waiting to be seated. He's the one grateful person under their roof, not having had a roof to sleep under for many years. He'd slept in most parts of the city in his time, mostly under the influence of whatever drug was available. Now clean, he's making herculean efforts to get back on the straight and narrow. He can't quite believe his current good fortune, and consequently doubts it will last. Breda has to reassure him every morning that nobody is playing a trick on him. She still can't give him the confidence to leave his room during the day. He doesn't think he'll be let back in. She's even asked him to go for a walk with her, but he flinched at the prospect. Let someone else have a go, she thinks. She's not a shrink, but she is shrinking. John's right, her clothes are starting to hang off her. She has to force meals down. And dishing out plates of greasy sausage and bacon for breakfast doesn't help.

She misses Tommy and Dolores. They were the only people for whom she felt genuinely sorry. They didn't want to leave their home, let alone move into *Red Cliff House*. And what a tragedy. It was beyond belief what happened. Dolores with those lungs of hers, and Tommy goes and gets mixed up in that ugly mess with Clifford. Whatever the reasons behind it, Tommy will get a couple of years for manslaughter, while Dolores is lying out in Deansgrange. At least Clifford got his just desserts, God forgive her for thinking.

Nuri keeps up her record, only this time she lets the dishes fall in the kitchen. John gives her a fair lash of the tongue, and she runs out crying. The guests return to their rooms, and Breda offers up her daily prayer, that that some of them might go out for a few hours, and give her a bit of peace.

Nuri comes back in, apologising.

'Don't worry about it,' Breda tells her.

'There are cameras outside,' Nuri then announces.

'Bastards!' John cries.

'John, please!' his wife says.

The cameras were camped outside *before* the tragedy of Tommy and Dolores Walsh. *Red Cliff House* was a story in itself, until God decided they hadn't suffered enough, so he heaped more misery upon them.

'We're trying to run a business here!' he cries. 'This used to be a guesthouse – but they've turned it into some sort of migrant camp.'

'Then let's stop this – now, today,' his wife suggests. 'We ring them up, and tell them, thanks, but no thanks. We don't want your refugees anymore, or your *contributions*. We want to go back to the way we were. We used to have a rating once upon a time, remember that? We were in the Guide. *Three stars.* We had a reputation, of sorts. This wasn't the Shelbourne, but it wasn't a dosshouse either. I - .' She can't continue, overcome by the outpouring of unexpected emotion.

'Nuri,' says John, 'you can continue clearing up in the dining room – please.' Nuri is only too happy to oblige.

'I know you're upset, love, but we have to tread carefully.'

'Which means what?' she asks.

'I don't know. We just have to grin and bear it. And hope the situation improves, that the Government sorts out the mess, as they keep promising.'

'We could sell,' she proposes.

'To who, exactly?'

'I don't know – there's always someone foolish out there, with money.'

'And that stupid?'

'Maybe the Government will buy it off us?'

'For a fraction of what it's worth – and where would we go, anyway?'

'I don't know – anywhere – Wexford, for a start. We have that, at least.'

'For now,' he says, without meaning to.

'What's that supposed to mean?' she asks.

'Nothing - I was going to tell you – not that there's anything to tell - .'

'*What!*' she screams.

'The mobile home – I put it up for sale – we never use it, do we? And it's not as if we can just pop down for a weekend, is it?'

Breda reels back, suddenly lightheaded. He catches her before she falls, but she wrestles free of him, demanding not to be touched.

'I thought the money would come in handy – but there hasn't been a single expression of interest – so, it's still there, nothing has changed.'

Breda takes a few deep breaths, and sits down at the table, not looking at him. 'But you were going to sell it without telling me – *without telling me*. I think of it every night, it's the only thing that lets me get to sleep. I dream of the fucking ocean, of drinking a glass of wine on the deck as the sun goes down. And *you* have been trying to take that away from me!'

'I've never heard you mention it,' he argues in vain.

'I kept it – inside – because I was afraid if I mentioned it – something might come along to take it away. The Government, somehow, they'd find out about it, and take it from us – and give it to one of *them*.'

'I'm – sorry.'

'You're sorry,' she throws back at him. The bell in reception sounds, announcing a pause in the argument. 'The enemy is outside,' she says. 'I'll let you look after this one.'

'Shouldn't we toss for it?' John says.

'I need some air,' she replies.

⌒

Sure, she tells the reporter, I'll talk to you, but not here. Somewhere more comfortable, away from *Red Cliff House*.

'You can buy me a drink, while you're at it,' she tells him. It's *nearly* noon, and she's been up since five, she deserves one. No need to tell John, he doesn't deserve such manners, not after what he's done.

A gin and tonic will do just fine, she tells her young suitor. He's young enough to be her son, but that wouldn't stop her if he made a pass. He won't, of course, but there's no harm dreaming. God, he's so earnest, and all he wants to talk about is homelessness and immigration, and Government policy, and all that shite. She's floating, giddy with her temporary freedom. He moves onto the terrible tale of Tommy and Dolores, and she starts getting upset, so he buys her another drink, and she puts a hand on his knee, and he freezes in terror. Guess she *doesn't* have it any longer, then.

'Do you regret agreeing to cooperate?' he asks, removing her hand.

'*Regret?*' she shrieks, causing her to spill her drink. 'Jesus, look at what you made me do – you'll have to buy me another one.' Now she's really flying, sliding down the seat. He offers to get her some food, sober her up.

'I can handle my drink, young man,' she declares. 'This – this is nothing. You should have seen me in my prime.'

Her prime was something to see, all right. Courted and escorted, by a succession of primates, until John Sullivan came along, and promised security. He had qualifications, which was a first for her, and impressed her with talk of running a hotel, somewhere along the north-west coast, where she imagined riding a wild horse on an endless empty beach, with *their* property sitting atop the cliff overlooking the strand, *The Red Cliff House*, as she would call it, and it would attract visitors from all over, surfers, posh folk, and everything in between. She had achieved one of those ambitions, at least. The only things left were the cliff, and the beach, and the clientele, and satisfaction.

'It seems I *can't* handle my drink, young man,' she says, on rising waves of nausea. 'Will you wait for me while I…I won't be long…powder my nose, as we say. And…you won't…*print* any of this?'

He shakes his head, smiling.

They part on the corner, and he heads off to write his piece, while Breda meanders home, wondering where the time has gone, expecting to see John waiting for her at the gate, disapproving. But there's no sign of him, inside or out, and she slips upstairs, where she lies down for five minutes that turns into two hours. There's something wrong, she senses, on waking, but she can't put her finger on it. Fixing her face, a temporary job, at the best of times, but not her conscience, she prepares to face the public. *Still* no sign of John, and there are new arrivals waiting to check-in. They are a melancholy couple with two clinging, frightened-looking children. They hand over documents, indicating they don't have much English. She doesn't have her reading glasses, or brain. The alcohol is still swishing around inside her. She grins and bears it. The papers show them to be from Eastern Ukraine, and due for transfer to a 'transition' centre in Tullamore the week after next. Poor fuckers, she thinks. She welcomes them as best she can, showing them to the room, finding it locked and hearing odd noises from inside. She decides to move them into what was Tommy and Dolores' room. It isn't exactly ready for new guests, having been neglected since the police were in there looking for 'evidence'. The Ukranians don't appear to mind, and given their situation, Breda doubts they'll complain about the sheets not being ironed to their satisfaction. She hands them their key, explains about breakfast, and the nearest places for dinner and shopping, if they're so inclined. They thank her in broken English, embarrassed by their ignorance, or just embarrassed. Breda has learned to keep an emotional distance, but the drink has loosened the reins, and she puts a hand on theirs to express sympathy.

She stops outside the locked room, listening intently.

⌒

John emerges from his cave, dizzy from staring at numbers, and numbed by the picture they presented. Breda told her she needed some air, but that was hours ago. She's done this before, but she has always come back. When lunch comes and goes, and there's no sign of her, he starts taking it out on Nuri as she performs her rudimentary tasks with underwhelming enthusiasm. The semi-decent weather has encouraged most of the guests to also get 'some air'. Perhaps they're all together, Breda and the Guests, having a laugh at his expense. He gets a phone call from his contact in Foreign Affairs, announcing the imminent arrival of more guests, later that afternoon. He accepts with a heavy sigh, knowing the paperwork that will inevitably follow, necessary if they want to get paid for their charitable act. He prefers the old days, and the old ways, when the guests paid themselves when they were leaving. He tells Nuri that a room needs to be prepared. He also tells her he'll give her a hand.

Terence comes downstairs, and considers going outside, but not today. John isn't going to press him.

'Don't want to cut the garden, do you?' John asks. Terence fears a conspiracy, and heads back to his room. 'I'll cut it myself, then.' He won't give Breda the satisfaction by ringing her. He'll get his own back tomorrow. He'll take the car, drive out to Howth or Portmarnock, sit by the ocean, and have a bag of chips. He might even tell her about it. That'll teach the stupid cow.

Mid-afternoon, he fears the worst – that's she's on her way to Wexford, to barricade herself into the mobile home.

Jesus, look at the time, better get that room sorted. He finds Nuri loitering in the back garden, and drags her upstairs. They may only be destitutes coming to stay, but he retains a pride in his establishment, even if his wife can't be bothered. He tosses a coin. 'Oh, look – me again. There's a surprise.'

He supposes it's Nuri or the wall, and the latter would cost more to fix. He locks the door behind him, and pushes her over the bed. He slips inside her, his hand over her mouth, although she knows not to scream. He knows from bitter experience that she has a tendency to squeal like a pig, in the throes of passion, so to speak, and she won't be told.

He's not completely stupid, and takes precautions. And never looks at her face. His behaviour has cost John staff before, but Nuri has been a blessing. She fears losing her job, and her right to stay in the country, or so he has convinced her. And, anyway, what real harm is being done? She enjoys it, deep down, as much as he does. As natural as breathing. And it's not as if he and Breda are rutting like animals anymore. There is the occasional meeting of minds and bodies, but it's purely because they happen to be in the same bed when their instincts get the better of them.

The key in the door is like a shot being fired into his chest. He untangles himself from Nuri, and thanks his lucky stars he thought to use the bolt as well. He looks through the spyhole, seeing his wife with four strangers. How could he lose track of time so carelessly! Nuri cowers in the corner, looking terrified. John puts a finger over his mouth, ordering her to keep silent. Wait – if she doesn't knock, that means she –

He looks again, and she's gone. He hears her, though, nearby. And then she's back, listening. Finally, she gives up, and goes downstairs. This *is* a scene from *Fawlty Towers,* but the audience isn't laughing. He unlocks the door, and lets Nuri go ahead of him. He sits back down on the bed, knowing he can't explain his way out of this one.

⌒

She's busy with the dinner, and doesn't acknowledge his appearance in the kitchen.

'Our new guests have arrived, I see?' he says.

'Yes,' she says.

'I only got the call around lunchtime. They're getting worse. They treat us with utter contempt. They probably won't even tell us before the next lot arrive. And then *we* have to beg for payment.' She puts a plate of stew in front of him. 'That looks delicious,' he says.

She toys with her own food, before pushing the plate away. 'I'm not hungry,' she announces.

'Where – where were you today?' he finds the nerve to ask.

'What? – oh, I, eh – a journalist. He was outside. He's been out there a fair bit. I decided to get rid of him by talking to him.'

'You did what? I thought we discussed - .' John decides not to continue in that vein.

'I made a mistake, John, okay? And I had a few drinks as well. There, I admit it. And I'm paying for it now. Happy? Haven't you ever done something you regretted?'

'Yes – of course I have. Why don't you go up and lie down, if you're not feeling well? I can look after things. It all seems fairly quiet, doesn't it?'

'Yes, it does. But you never know what really goes on behind closed doors, do you? I think I will have an early night, after all.'

⌒

Nuri doesn't turn up for work the following day. They don't waste time ascribing blame, as they have a more pressing problem at hand. There is a man in reception, in a grey suit, wielding a laminate badge like a handgun – he's from the Health & Safety Authority, making an unscheduled visit. Just a 'routine' inspection, the man calls it. He declines the offer of a coffee, preferring to 'get on with it.' Their staff shortages are the first item on the agenda, and their excuses echo unconvincingly through the building. Breakfast is over, thankfully – a more hellish experience than usual – but Terence chooses the wrong moment to come downstairs, running into the Grey Suit, and jumping, headlong, to the conclusion that *they* have come for him, so he rushes back up to his room, declaring that he won't leave without a fight.

'This is what we have to put up with,' Breda says with a shrug, trying to make light of it.

'I'm not here to pass judgement on the condition of your guests,' says Grey Suit, meaning he's here to pass judgment on *them*. John stays behind his wife, for the most part, letting her take the full impact.

'That's good to hear,' says Breda, struggling to remain cheerful. Grey Suit goes for a wander, promising not to get in the way. John and Breda stare at each other across the kitchen table.

'What is he really doing here?' asks John.

'Maybe we're due for an upgrade, at the State's expense. After all, look what we're doing for them, what we have to deal with.'

'I'll believe that when we see it. We normally have to grovel on our hands and knees for what's due to us. I doubt they're going to hand us over a bonus just like that.'

'What if he talks to the guests?' Breda worries.

'Jesus, I hope not, he'll be here for days, if that's the case. And what if Terence attacks him? I wouldn't put it past him.'

'Poor soul,' says Breda. 'He definitely shouldn't be here. He belongs in hospital.'

'*We* belong in hospital,' says John.

'Things aren't that bad, are they? And if they are, you – *seducing* – the staff doesn't help.'

At that moment, Grey Suit enters the kitchen, looking rather shaken.

'There's a......dead cat...in the upstairs bathroom,' he tells them. And he *will* take that coffee, after all.

~

There's no point launching an investigation into the mysterious case of the dead cat. One of the children, or perhaps even Terence, will be the culprit, and what's to be done with them? It's left to Breda, of course, to clean up the mess. She gives it a respectful burial in the garden, before being sick in the shade of the lone apple tree. John pretends to be busy with some new tax regulations, while she scrubs toilets and puts the washing machine on another cycle. The sheets, once white, are now a shade of yellow. Her skin, once a rosy pink, is now a paler shade of white. Lack of sunshine, she puts it down to, along with everything else.

She discovers her husband napping, and takes pleasure in waking him.

'Have you done anything about finding us some help?' she asks.

'Just getting round to it,' he lies.

'The situation won't magically improve all by itself. In fact, it won't improve, whatever we do.'

'Unless we do nothing,' John says, 'and force their hand.'

'*Force their hand?* What the fuck does that mean?'

'I hate it when you use that kind of language with me. It's ugly.'

'I *feel* ugly,' she tells him.

Soldiering on, each side digging in, digging deeper, while the guests roam the corridors like restless spirits, speaking in tongues, wary of each other, of their future, the children unhealthily silent. Something has to give.

⌒

The letter arrives on a Friday morning, opened by Breda after a fraught breakfast, when the electricity decided to throw a tantrum. She hands it to her husband the first chance she gets, unable to speak, unable to make sense of it.

'*Removed* from the list of approved accommodations under the Scheme?' John reads out. 'I don't understand.'

'We don't measure up, John. We're not good enough – even for refugees. Jesus, how sad is that? How bad does a place have to be if it can't even shelter the homeless and -.' She covers her mouth, too upset to speak. She thinks she's going to faint. John doesn't help by pressing her face to his chest, though he means well.

'This could be the best thing that ever happened to us,' he says, trying to comfort her.

'*How?*' she cries.

'Well…'

But he's right, when they both reflect on it. The burden has been lifted, they have been freed from the responsibility, and thrown back on their own initiative. They are filled with joy *and* sorrow.

It takes time, but it happens. The reporters decamp from their doorstep, and the guests are 'transferred' to further uncertainty. And the day comes when they don't have a single guest, not one. Peace reigns – it screams.

'We have our life back,' John says, pouring himself a brandy.

'A chance to start over, is that it?' she says bitterly.

'You want to go back to the way it was? Well, do you? No, I thought not. We can run the place the way we want to now.'

'The way we used to, you mean?' she suggests. 'Because that was such a success, wasn't it? In fact, correct me if I'm wrong, but isn't that why we accepted the Government's offer in the first place?'

'Doesn't have to be the frying pan or the fire,' he says.

'Doesn't it? In case you hadn't noticed, we have no guests. Nor ever likely to have.'

'If I may say so, you're being overly pessimistic.'

'Am I? You know, it's at times like these that I'm glad we don't have children – we wouldn't have much to leave them, would we?'

'So, what then? You want to give up, throw in the towel? Put it on the market?'

'I want – I want, more than anything to get out of this fucking house, and this fucking city – just for a while. Let's go to Wexford for a few days – while we still have the mobile home, that is.'

'Can't do any harm, can it?'

Are they being quiet in case *Red Cliff House* gets the idea that they might not be coming back? They pack lightly, and quickly, and slip out just after rush hour. Progress is still achingly slow, but they eventually reach the Stillorgan Road, and start getting their hopes up.

And then the unreliable Nissan…dies.

Interval

The drama is inside, the tension unbearable. Whilst onstage, a kind of ennui has set in, and it's spreading. The elderly couple in front continue to chat, mostly about the costumes. In fact, there's a veritable breeze of whispers throughout the auditorium. There's nothing wrong with the play, exactly, but that doesn't mean there's much right with it, either. Amy squeezes his hand, and gives him that smile that women use on such occasions. He wonders how the match is going. He works out how many hours are left before he has to get up, and drive to Kilkenny. Jesus. His bladder is acting up, and there's a danger he might not make it to the interval, but he's not disturbing the whole row. He prefers sitting on the edge, but he didn't buy the tickets. Neither did she, come to think of it. They were a Christmas present from her parents. *It's Arthur Miller*, they declared, as if that made all the difference. As far as Patrick was concerned, once you've seen one Arthur Miller, you've seen them all. The accents aren't helping, ranging as they do from Southern drawl to Dublin flat, and one or two in-between. The presence of one actual American, in the leading role, only serves to underline the problem with the rest of the cast. And the story? The father is a disappointed, disillusioned man, while his sons rebel against everything he stands for. The wife, of course, stands stoically by her man, even though she secretly sides with her sons. There's a yawning predictability to it, where its themes are rammed home with a sledgehammer lack of subtlety. *What has this got to do with me?* He's jammed into the seat, and there's insufficient legroom. Isn't that what's-his-name over there? That actor — why isn't *he* on stage? Couldn't do any worse. Patrick lets out a sigh, and he feels Amy's eyes upon him. He won't give her the satisfaction. Now her hand is on his knee. A very affectionate girl is Amy, forever touching and stroking. Normally, he's flattered, but right now she reminds him of an infuriating insect that just won't let him be.

The play is reaching some sort of climax. Does that mean the end of a scene, or the first half? Please God, let it be the latter. He's not up to these cultural outings midweek — or at any time, for that matter. All those books bought he hasn't read – each one recommended by the Guardian or Sunday Times as *essential reads*. Those obscure Polish films in the IFI. Museums like bad dreams. He smokes, but he doesn't inhale. He skates over the surface of things. Amy, possibly, goes a little deeper, as she's the one who starts conversations about art. Last time he looked, she was reading a Stephen King, and never missed *Coronation Street*. She has tonight, though, and all in the pursuit of intellectual stimulation. What would stimulate him is a pint, and then an early night. The bedroom is the one area of mutual agreement, and relative silence. Why talk about it when you can be busy doing it? Is that a tear at the corner of her eye? It could well be, as others around them are dabbing their eyes, or choking back tears. Has he missed something? He should pay more attention, and then maybe, he might get more out of it. On stage, there appears to have been a fight. Furniture has been overturned, clothes torn, and tempers frayed. Harsh words, too, have clearly been spoken. The second half, he knows, will be about the guilt and remorse, blah, blah, blah. He's seen this one before, or something resembling it. Are there no new plays, by new, *living*, writers? Why the constant revivals?

Loud applause, and a few cheers, heralds the end of the first half. People get to their feet, but mostly to stretch their legs. His hand is being squeezed again, and Amy's eyes are moist. She's loving it, and she'll expect him to feel the same. Compromise, he well knows, is part and parcel of any good relationship, but that doesn't mean he has to lie to her. Telling lies can be exhausting.

'Enjoying it?' she says.

'Yes,' he says. He *should* qualify that, but he doesn't want to hurt her.

'I think it's tremendous,' she adds.

'I'm glad,' he says.

'You're *not* enjoying it, are you?'

'No, it's fine, really. I'm just a bit tired, that's all. The father's very good. At least his accent is authentic.' Somehow, and he doesn't know how, he has managed to upset her.

'I need the Ladies,' she says. 'They'll be queuing out the door already, I bet.'

'I think I might get some air,' he says. 'Meet you outside, or back here?'

'Back here,' she says. 'And don't be late.'

'I won't.'

There is a cursory kiss. He'll have to make up for it in the second half – by paying attention. On stage, they're making changes to the set. Patrick looks at his watch. Still short of nine, which means another ninety minutes of this stuff. What he fears most of all is falling asleep. She'd never forgive him, though at least it might make her consider changes in their cultural schedule. This being Wednesday, there's bound to be one other excursion. There is tomorrow night to look forward to, Kilkenny, and a break from her. And to think this is only the beginning of it. The wedding in three months, and then God knows how many years together after that, *if* all goes well – decades, perhaps. Admittedly, he couldn't think of anyone else he'd rather spend the time with – but.

He appears to be the only one in a hurry to get outside. He'd love a drink, but the bar is packed, and he daren't risk it. He craves fresh air the way others crave a cigarette. He looks at his watch, and it's almost time to go back in. What would she think if he stayed out there for the rest of the show? She might give him the cold shoulder until they got home, but she'd soon forgive him once they were in bed – wouldn't she? They're ringing the bell, calling them back inside. Time enough yet – give the actors a few more minutes, he's sure they'll appreciate it. Amy would be back in her seat, clutching her programme, and looking at the empty seat beside her.

⌣

It's just him and a few hardy souls left outside. He can't make up his mind. Across the street from the Abbey, at the corner of the lane, a young couple are performing an act of their own. The young man has his tracksuit bottoms down, and his girlfriend is kneeling in front of him. But it's not what Patrick thinks, as the girl then produces a needle, and proceeds to inject him in the groin. He utters a grunt of pleasure, or pain, and slowly pulls up his pants. The couple start arguing, with the girl doling out most of the abuse.

Patrick looks around him. He's alone out there, and the lobby of the theatre is empty except for staff. The performance has recommenced, and Amy has obviously decided to stay. He looks back across the road, where the other performance continues. This one is far more compelling, because it's real. The rest of the city appears distant, mute.

He catches their eye, and his fate is sealed.

'*What are you fuckin' lookin' at!*' and other extremities to that effect. The girl makes a move in his direction, and Patrick moves back inside the Abbey. He is refused entry back into the auditorium, as the play is *in progress*. He doesn't argue the point – he's not that eager to see the second half. He *could* go to the upstairs bar, and have a sneaky pint – but he doesn't fancy drinking alone. Outside, there's no sign of his tormentors, and he's annoyed at himself for being so unsettled by them.

His patience, however, soon begins to run out. Through the closed doors, he hears the muffled voices of the actors. Is that *laughter* he can hear from the audience? If he'd known there'd be jokes after the interval, he might have stayed, although he doubts if Amy is finding any of it funny. He goes back outside, putting some distance between the two of them.

The girl comes out of nowhere, charging at him, and catching him on the neck. He feels a sharp sting, and sees her drop the syringe, before she runs away, squealing with laughter. One of the ushers comes out to help him.

'Jesus!' he cries, feeling his neck. 'Did you see that?'

'Are you all right?' the usher asks.

'I don't know,' says Patrick, unable to take his eyes off the syringe. 'She…*fuck*…I think she stuck that in me…*bitch*.'

'You should come inside, and sit down. We'll call the police.'

'No! I'm fine….I'm…' *Embarrassed*.

'If she stuck that needle in you, it's best to have it checked out. Let me have a look at it.' The usher tilts Patrick's head. 'There's some redness there…a drop of blood. You *should* get it checked out.' Too shocked to disagree, Patrick sits and waits, rewinding to before the interval, when he was in his seat, beside his girlfriend, and all was right with the world – more or less. So, what happened? What the *fuck* happened? Took his eye off the ball for a second, and…this.

Flashing lights, but no siren, for which he's grateful. A lot of fuss about nothing is his opinion, but the ambulance men have a different opinion, snapping on their surgical gloves as they prepare to escort him into the vehicle. There is a delay as the police arrive, the syringe lifted as evidence, and Patrick's case officially opened. He doesn't tell them about the woman he's left behind in the theatre. Has Amy wished this curse upon him? Has she that kind of power? He wouldn't put it past her. He'll never be so dismissive of Arthur Miller again.

'Lie down, Patrick,' he's told. 'We'll be there in no time.'

⌒

There is chaos and order, and he's not sure which side he's on. He's definitely more accident than emergency.

'What's the matter?' he asks the nurse when she eventually gets around to him. She put a plaster on his neck earlier, without saying a word.

'The doctor will be along to you shortly,' she says, before disappearing into the murky madness of the Mater hospital. *Shortly* clearly has a different meaning inside a hospital than out. The myth about the health service turns out to be true. And he feels *fine*, a little dazed, perhaps, but that's just from the shock of the whole experience. He reasons that the girl wouldn't have wasted precious product on the likes of him. Her boyfriend would kill her if she did anything that stupid, and she appeared to be the brains of that particular operation. Whatever was in the syringe was what she was injecting into his groin – was there any left? And would she throw it away on someone like Patrick?

They are lined in armchairs along the side of the corridor, actors waiting to go on and do their thing. He looks at his watch with incredulity. According to his Breitling, which is too valuable to lie, it's nearly midnight, and that's impossible. Where *is* she? Okay, he did desert her, but he was the real victim here, wasn't he? There's no message on his phone. It dawns on him that she would have come out at the end, and not finding him, she'd have gone home in a fury. He understands that, but wasn't she worried about him by now? True, *he* could have contacted her, but his grasp on reality seems to have slipped away. Better very late than never, he decides to text her, put her out of her misery. She doesn't have to come running, he wouldn't expect that – he's not at death's door, is he?

His finger is on the point of pressing 'Send' when the doctor arrives. They move to a cubicle where a proper examination is made.

'You'll be pleased to know, Patrick, that there was next to nothing in the syringe that she used.'

'Well, that's a relief,' Patrick says calmly. 'I didn't think she would have wasted anything on me.'

'There were minute traces of a substance within the syringe, but no sign of it in your blood.'

'What substance?'

The doctor pauses, before saying, 'Heroin.'

'Jesus,' says Patrick.

'But nothing for you to worry about. I think we can let you go, although I think there's a Garda here that wants a word with you. Best get it over with, and then you can get home.'

⌒

The Garda wants several words, but Patrick is having trouble concentrating, with Amy being in the room. Somehow, she's just *there*, and he never did send that message, and he didn't get one from her.

He remembers the girl, in his mind, but he finds it difficult to describe her. He'd recognise her if he saw her again, in a line-up of suspects, say, but that's not going to happen. Throughout the interview, Amy stays standing by the door, her arms crossed. What happened to the affectionate, tactile girl he used to know? The hardest part for him is explaining what he was doing out there in the first place. The Garda thanks him for his efforts, futile as they may have been, and leaves them alone.

'I'm sorry,' he says, expecting her to say the same, and rush into his arms. That doesn't happen. 'I'm *sorry*,' he repeats. 'I tried to get back in but they wouldn't let me. I just needed some air. I admit that I was – bored – in the first half. I know, it's a crime. How could anyone be bored with Arthur Miller? But I did intend waiting for you, didn't I? And then – this.' He rubs his neck, hoping the gesture might elicit some sympathy from her. 'And then, afterwards, I just assumed you'd find out, and follow me here. It was *madness* in A&E when I arrived. How do people stand it? How do the staff tolerate it? Anyway, the doctor said there were traces of heroin in the syringe, but none in my blood. That's something to be thankful for, isn't it? Amy? *Please* say something, anything.'

Amy closes her eyes at the onset of tears, arms still crossed, but shaking. Patrick thinks of that girl's devotion to her wreck of a man earlier. Admirable, in its way.

'I suppose Miller's not for everyone,' Amy says. 'I'll...see you at home.' Then she opens the door, and leaves.

Black Church

On the Western Way, in the shadow of the Black Church, Jim carries the body to its final resting place. It's nowhere for a young man to end up, but that's not Jim's concern. He doesn't even know the victim's name, nor wants to. The less he knows the better, and in this case he knows less than nothing. He collects from one address and delivers to another, and that's it. Weighs next to nothing, meaning he, it, was likely ravaged by the poison these people crammed into their bodies. There's little traffic, mechanical or human, and it's nearly noon. The area is not exactly a hive of activity, though he glimpses several suits entering the church. Long since deconsecrated, he knows, some business must have moved in, which makes him sad. Anyhow, God will still be watching him, regardless. Bearing the weight over his left shoulder, he opens the garage with his right hand, anxious to get started. He'd like to get some lunch before he hits the road again, especially after skipping breakfast. He's made that mistake before, nearly causing a head-on collision due to dizziness. He reckons he has thin blood, but a thick shell of fortitude. An even temper, too, a must in his part-time profession.

He removes the lid of the 200-gallon drum that will put an end to this particular episode. He regrets the necessity, but in an age of rampant technological change, desperate measures are called for. He dons the Tyvek suit, until he's dressed head to toe in white, feeling like one of those TV investigators come to have a peek at the remains. If he does his job right, there won't be any remains for anyone to peek at. It looks like a large sack of potatoes, making him think of home, the farm outside Tullamore that he has made home. Inside, it's just a youth, barely out of his teens, pale and skeletal, bones for arms, and blue-veined flesh. He removes the clothes, which he'll burn later, and hoists the body up to the lip of the drum, letting him slide over the edge. He lands with a dull thud, and Jim can't help but pause and consider the catastrophic decisions this boy managed to make in his short life. But he has no one to blame but himself, that's how Jim looks at it.

He covers his mouth and eyes before handling the acid, hydrochloric, vicious stuff, but the boy won't feel a thing. Jim fixes the lid, removes his paper suit, puts the boy's clothes in a holdall, and goes out to lunch.

⌐⌐⌐

In the basement café of the Hugh Lane Gallery, a five minute walk from the garage, Jim feasts on the special of the day, a Spanish dish that tastes like heaven. It'll save him binging on crisps and chocolate on the way home. He savours the quiet elegance of the surroundings, deciding he has time to look around the gallery. The acid needs time to work its magic, and remove all traces. In the meantime, there are the works of Francis Bacon to look at. He would never have considered himself an appreciator of art, or anything like it, and if his friends knew that he came here, they'd laugh in his face. But seeing Bacon for the first time was such a shock. The violence of it disturbed even him, and made him re-evaluate art, and those who made it. The recreation of Bacon's studio reveals a chaotic madness of mind, to which Jim could relate. The artist's ideas *erupted* onto the canvas - that was the only way Jim could describe it. There was perversion, too, which made Jim squeamish, but still fascinated him. Bacon was troubled, obviously, Jim reasoned, as were many, but he dealt with those troubles through painting. How many others articulated theirs through more direct, physical means? *Like me.*

Leaving the gallery, Jim feels momentarily disorientated, the result of the claustrophobic atmosphere, and the hypnotic impact of the works on display. The acid needs more time, he reckons, and heads down O'Connell Street. Dublin, like the Black Church behind him, Jim thinks, has been similarly deconsecrated, long ago. Stripped of its divine status, it chose a more agnostic path, resulting in its present condition. Troubled art has continued to erupt from its bowels over the decades since Bacon, but there'll come a day when there's nothing left. It's not far away, in his mind.

Jim knows few people outside his close family circle, so how does he know that man smoking outside the Gresham Hotel? He winks at Jim as he passes. He could be flush with drink, but he could also be putting it on. Jim *knew* a lot of unsavouries back in London, but he'd severed those ties over a decade ago. Is that man from then? Was he one of Lenny's mob? The boy in the barrel will be well past the point of identification by now, but he daren't risk it, not if this bleeder isn't a figment of his imagination. He's had a trouble-free run throughout his time in Ireland. There has never been a single set-back, though maybe that's about to end. But he never has any direct contact with his employers. He gets a message from one number, and any other is ignored. He never speaks to anyone, and is given a new phone every three months, but he never gets orders from anything but that one number. Payment is always made within forty-eight hours, with a little bit extra each time. He never questions, or disappoints. And in between jobs, he returns to the farm, and his new-found family, and works like any other farm-labourer, often doing long, brutal hours. It is, largely, a serene existence, a world away from the building sites of London, and the foul company he befriended there. On he walks, over the bridge, and taking a right, figuring to walk along the quays for a bit before circling back.

Did he secure the lid properly? Did he lock the garage behind him? He can't be sure, and he's always sure. And some bones are more stubborn, and resistant, than others. He sees his aunt open the door of the farmhouse, facing the police who've come to tell her the bad news about her nephew. He's never hurt anyone himself, she can rest assured about that. Never laid a hand on another human being. He'd be well capable of landing a decent blow, and his bulk has always kept threats at bay. There *is* a difference, he's always thought, between taking a life, and disposing of a body from which the life has already been taken. That argument wouldn't stand up in a court of law, but he doesn't foresee that ever happening. It shouldn't, if everyone does their job properly.

In the way of these things, he stumbles across a pub called *The Church*, on Mary Street, another deconsecrated establishment. He puts his head in for a look, and decides that one drink can't do any harm. Settle his nerves, which he didn't realise he had. There are two elderly women playing cards beside him, for peanuts, while drinking shots of rum. To keep out the cold, no doubt. He's now well behind schedule, and he'd been planning on being back in Tullamore by six. That could still happen, if he got a move on, and was lucky with the traffic. One of the card-players celebrates a winning hand by slapping a hand on the table, and loses her teeth in the process. For a moment, they're the boy's teeth, separating from the gums as the acid takes effect. Then his beer is acid, burning his throat until he can no longer breathe. This unease sits uneasily. Is it a portent, or a simple sign of tiredness? He's had an unusually busy month, now that he thinks about it. It's as if there'd been a spike in crime, a seasonal fluctuation, and it's only now that the impact is being felt.

The brown dog licks at his heels, and he feints a kick in its direction. He picks up the pace on Dominick Street, conscious of the time running away from him. He takes a shortcut through the flats, drawing unwanted attention from idle men, suspicious of his presence. He's through the other side, and in the shadow of the Black Church before they can react.

The first thing he notices, and it would be hard not to, is the yellow clamp on the front wheel of his van. Since when did you have to pay for parking here, and where the fuck were the meters? He definitely won't be in Tullamore by six. The second thing he notices is the garage door. The lock has been ripped right off, with some force, and there's noise coming from inside. There can't be anything left to identify, and there's no real reason for Jim to go in there, unless he wants a fight – and why change the habits of a lifetime?

He keeps watch from a short distance, and prays, in the shadow of the Black Church that is no longer a sanctuary. He makes a call, pays the fine, and then – waits. He reconsiders his chosen path. There will have to be a second clean-up job today, and he won't be paid for either. His space has been violated, and permanently spoiled. When they have left, someone else will come, next day, next month. Across the road, a hooded figure slips out of the garage, and scuttles away. Jim stays his ground, still wary of traps. Will he put up much of a struggle? Will they do unto him as he has done unto others? He hopes they do him the courtesy of killing him quickly first. Then they can do what they like to his body. The grave of the 'unknown soldier', that's what is waiting for Jim Steele. Will his aunt grieve for him? If so, she'll be the only one. The farm has barely scraped through the last few years, what with regular flooding, and spiralling feed and crop prices. He wishes he could continue to help them through the next few months, especially now when there was light at the end of the tunnel. But he couldn't put them under such risk. No, not even a fleeting visit to collect some of his stuff. Head south, maybe, West Cork – Skibereen, he passed through there once, this was his chance to renew the acquaintance. He'll turn his hand to – The clampers have arrived, that was quick. He uses them as cover to inspect the van for traps, but it appears untouched. The van is freed, and he jumps into the driver's seat, only pausing before he turns the key in the ignition. The engine catches first time, and he pulls carefully away from the kerb as proper darkness falls.

He pulls into a service station at Newlands Cross, texts '*compromised*' to the number, and pulls the phone apart, before throwing it into the undergrowth behind the toilets at the rear of the building.

On the radio, he listens to a snatch of the Rolling Stones' *Angie,* remembering his own Angela, not that she was ever really his – she was a brief infatuation in the grim part of Southend more than twenty years ago. And nothing more since. Each to his own, with some *on* their own. If he was Bacon, the canvas would be blank, or just black. If the church had still been a church, he might have asked if he could stay for a short while, until the storm blew past.

He turns off at the exit, and drives into Greenogue industrial estate in Rathcoole, depending on there being empty properties to allow him complete the job.

The carcasses of former factories line a whole stretch of road, before opening into undeveloped wasteland. This will do. It will have to.

He removes the plates, casts them amongst rubble, then tax and insurance discs, and sets about burning the van by leaving the engine running and blocking the exhaust. It was only a theory that he'd never had to put into practice, until today. It was turning into a day of firsts, and lasts. He keeps watch from a safe distance, until the diesel catches fire, and proves the theory correct.

There only remains finding a way back to the city centre, and then a way out of Dublin. In a more prosperous end of the estate, workers wait for buses back to town, and elsewhere. What about elsewhere?

Elsewhere, nowhere, no one, no more.

A Swim With Two Birds

Someday, he'll dive off the high board. He'll have to build one first, though. Like the one in St. Tropez – or was it the Blackrock Baths? The residents are sure to be impressed. It's bound to change their impression of him. Before all of that, of course, he'll have to learn to swim. He thinks he's ready to face the challenge after all these years. And to think he was a water-baby! – the result of having a gypsy for a mother, that is, a mother who *fancied* herself as a gypsy. She wore the uniform, the enormous earrings, the headscarf, the flowing robes, and drove around in a campervan that substituted for a caravan. Anyway, being eccentrically-minded, she decided to give birth in a bathing pool, and so, Barry 'King' Sweeney was born underwater – and spent a lifetime avoiding the stuff. Which he regrets now, and which he means to rectify before he shuffles off to meet his dead mother in gypsy heaven. Before his legs give out, not to mention his mind.

Blessington Street Basin is especially quiet today, the grey skies and persistent sleet keeping the crowds away. What makes it a basin, and not a lake or a pond? It's a question that bothers him every day that he comes here. As if it can't make up its mind, like the rest of Dublin, and thus it constantly gives the impression of being unfinished. The bench is damp, but he's come prepared, and lays the small towel beneath. He pulls up the hood of his anorak and sets to work on the *Mirror*. The sleet is an irritant, dripping down the pages like an unruly tap – so he shuts his eyes and dreams of something better. Maggie, for example – but as she was at the beginning, not the end. Try as he might, his mind wanders off to that unfortunate end, that otherwise unremarkable day when he came home to find the house on fire, and her still inside. He carried her out, despite the firemen's warning. Carried her out, and laid her down, and tried to suck the black smoke from her lungs. Thereafter, Barry hated fire *and* water in equal measure. Ringsend lost its appeal after that, not to mention the fact that the house had been destroyed. He moved to a one-room flat in Blessington Street, and found the Basin on his first day there. He thought of drowning himself in it, but it didn't look that deep, and he imagined

187

being rescued before he could get his wish. No, that's not the Maggie he wants to remember, it's that other one, the vibrant poetess who dabbled in all manner of creative endeavours, exhausting him with her adventures. And he a lowly teacher, a *bad* teacher, he'd readily admit, of mathematics, no less, a subject guaranteed to ensure his unpopularity in the school. They were both scholars, but only she had an imagination. He endured her dreamy doggerel, baffled by most of it, though others more qualified persuaded him of its literary merits. And another thing – she could swim, *really* swim. Not just swimming pools, but open water, in competitive races, after which she would take out her pen and tear into a few new verses that had come to her in the ocean.

What, he wonders now, did she see in him? He had a spirit, he supposed, once, and a curious manner that most people found off-putting, except her. She took him on as a project, rough material that might be shaped into something worthwhile. He thinks she died without completing her work. She did manage to move him off cigarettes and onto pipes, though her efforts to entice him into the water failed at the first attempt, the first which turned out to be the last. She encouraged him to see a psychologist, to exorcise whatever demons lay hidden. He never yielded on that one, to her eternal disappointment. He can't conjure her face, only a blurred essence. She resists being brought back for his entertainment. The sleet turns to snow, ruining the paper, and even the towel underneath him is failing. Apart from the odd stray dog, the Basin attracts no visitors, though the lake – or pond – vibrates with avian trade. A pair of mute swans look particularly down, and stick their heads in the water for something more interesting.

What day is it today? It's not that important, but little details like that keep slipping away from him lately. He *is* Barry 'King' Sweeney, he knows that for sure. A rather traduced version, but him nonetheless. As long as his identity remains, there's a purpose in all this. There's a rake of items on his agenda, such as the diving-board, for example. Why not? Brighten the place up a bit. The whole area could do with a lick of paint, to say the least. Too many foreign guests, for his liking, nomadic herds passing through, without a care for the local language, or keeping the place tidy. He pulls down his hood to get a taste of the rain. Be just his luck to get pneumonia, and end up in the Mater. He'd get fed, though. Three proper meals a day, and nurses on hand.

There's Dolly Moran, feeding the birds, leaning over the railing, almost falling in. She'll ignore him, as he'll ignore her. They're mirror images of each other, and therefore not to be trusted. She's a widower, like him, but they'd make poor companions. She draws a crowd of gulls, who disturb the peace of the morning, adding fuel to Barry's fire. He could sneak up on her, and tip her over the edge. She might slide under the water, and never be seen again. And if he was ever asked about the incident, his defense would be: *unfortunately, I can't swim.* Dolly suddenly looks over at him, scowling – and for a second, she's Maggie, as was and ever will be, a whirlwind, a tornado of life. He resists the illusion, closing his eyes against it, and when he opens them again, she's gone – both women are gone.

The clouds aren't for lifting, they've settled in for the long haul, making him miserable. The bookies should he opening, anyway, the dogs' prices being set. He'll come out ahead, barely, and that's all he wants. No horses for him, and definitely not humans, whether they're boxers or anything else. The greyhound has a grace and speed that's unique, making the gamble infinitely more exciting. Barry bought one, for domestic use, a few years earlier, but he lost the lurcher within a week, and decided he wasn't cut out to be a breeder. Maggie had decided the same thing, when she failed to get pregnant, despite refusing to have the tests to prove that the fault lay with him. If they had succeeded, his children would only be fussing around him, getting in his way. Barry banishes any infantile thoughts, returning to the present, the unremarkable present, which sees him approaching the bookies with a figure in mind, an amount he won't go beyond, not in his current financial situation. The sky cracks with thunder, and a flash of lighting scares the punters inside. He studies the form, even though it will come down to gut instinct in the end. His fellow travellers remain quiet throughout the afternoon, foolish young men, with families to support, risking everything with calculated stupidity. The occasional wife pops in, to take a pop, before popping out again, with diminished returns. Maggie often placed a bet, choosing the longest odds, against his better advice. But she knew when to stop, when to cut and run.

Barry cuts and runs, with the well truly dry. He finds himself on Berkeley Road, blaming the blizzard. There's nothing here that takes his fancy, unless he wants to make a confession, and ask for forgiveness. But now that he *is* here, this close to Phibsboro, he might as well have a pint. It'll put in the rest of the afternoon, and help him sleep later. His pockets are light, and he figures he might have to plead temporary poverty, and beg for mercy. Not easy for a man with no friends. Still, nothing ventured, nothing gained.

⌒

Kavanaghs proves fertile ground, with Mal Foster an unlikely source of generosity. Turns out, his daughter's just had a baby, and he's willing to forget and forgive. Barry stays for more than one, taking advantage, but keeping out of harm's way, and biting his tongue. Time was, he fought battles in bars, mainly fending off blows from offended women, who took exception to his wandering hands. It landed Barry in court once, but the judge took pity on him, as a result of the recent demise of Maggie. But that leniency only encouraged him to explore new, younger, more dangerous territories, resulting in Barry receiving several hefty slaps for his sins, though he avoided any more court appearances. Maggie used take the lead in the bedroom, as she did in most areas of their life together, meaning he never had to look anywhere else, though, naturally, his eye often roved.

There's a crush at the bar, with generation of Fosters packed in like sardines. It's not Barry's fault that his hand gets lodged where it does, down the short skirt of an intemperate teen. Either she doesn't notice, or chooses not to, but Barry takes his fill. He's no monster, and would never assault anyone, let alone a child. He forgets, though. His mind goes off on a tangent, sometimes, that's all, and his fingers take matters into their own hands. There's a Romanian girl in his building, and he knows for fact that she's a prostitute, but he'd *never* darken her doorstep. He'd never prey on that kind of animal, it'd be like burning his money.

'Hey!' he protests, as the barman escorts him off the premises. 'What have I done?'

'You know *exactly* what you did, Barry. So, take your filthy habits elsewhere.'

'I have no idea what you're talking about!' But he does, deep down, and is glad to escape. Where is he, again? I *am* Barry 'King' Sweeney, and that's the main thing. The Basin's closed for the night, more's the pity, as he fancied a sit-down, especially now the clouds have scarpered, and the stars are out in force. Bit chilly, though, and he should really get home and make himself some dinner.

Cottage pie, from frozen, with the potato forming a skin across the top. It's too hot to taste, which is probably the intention. On TV, there are quizzes, and bad news, and bad acting, and empty violence, and tepid pornography – when he could be making his own, with the girl next door. She sounds busy tonight, with a succession of visitors. He wonders what she charges, wonders if she does house calls. Maggie keeps an eye on him from the frame on the mantelpiece, an unflattering image that would offend her if she knew – and she *does* know. It was a blustery day, on the seafront in Bray, out of season, with high waves licking the promenade, and she in unusually subdued form, while he struggled with the camera. It's her, though not all of her. He leaves the dishes till morning, and lights a pipe in her memory. The drink has made him drowsy, and he's careful about dropping off and going up in flames. She'd like that, no doubt, but who'd carry *him* out? No, he's not ready to leave yet, far from it.

He locks the bathroom door for no good reason, and masturbates over a worn magazine. Keeps him from sticking it where he shouldn't, that's his reasoning. He finishes, and immediately feels the worse for it. He takes to his bed with a splitting headache, and opens his Flann O'Brien with little enthusiasm.

He falls over the cliff, lands on the bird's back, and they soar over yawning canyons before he's dropped on the roasting sands of the beach where multitudes race into the raging sea. His own bare feet are quickly stuck to the sand, the heat spreading quickly through his body, until his hair catches fire, and the eyeballs pop out of his head. Then his head is being held under the water, putting out the fire, but they're drowning him! He kicks out with his legs, and they propel him forward. He's cutting a swathe through the waters, without the need to surface and breathe, then he's part of a shoal of Barry Sweeneys, and they're heading for their winter breeding grounds, where each Barry will find a mate, and spawn a new generation.

There's a knock on his door, there's a ringing of his bell, but he can't move from his bed, he's tied down, and Maggie's crushing him, reciting her poems over and over, her voice growing louder, until it screams, and he screams, and he –

trips over the leg of a chair in the kitchen and bangs his knee off the cupboard. He's naked, and sweating, and blind, and the taps squirts water all over the floor when he puts his face to it and the kitchen is a lake or a pond or a basin and the mute swans are *talking* though not to him and he's climbing the ladder of the diving-board but it goes on for miles and when he reaches the top he can't see the bottom it's so far down – he's diving down there! but he has no say in the matter, and down he goes, likes a bullet out of the barrel and the ground is fast approaching he puts his hands over his face and braces for impact and he –

wakes to the sound of drilling – only this is for real, *thank God*. They're digging up the road. They're always digging up the road.

⌒

In winter, an old man's fancy turns to Glasnevin cemetery, and a resting place beside his wife. The pavements are lethal. The Basin is frozen over, though Dolly still throws bread onto the ice. Barry, skater extraordinaire, puts on his blades, and glides across the surface, putting on quite a show. At the end of his routine, the judges have no choice but to award him perfect '10s' all-round. Rising from the bench, and the reverie, he skids, and narrowly avoids toppling over. He leaves the *Mirror* where he drops it, not risking his back. He doesn't want to be found locked in that position, not by the likes of Dolly Moran, anyway. The seat of his pants is wet with cold. A Doberman-type dog, with a muzzle, strains at the leash, its owner also straining at the leash.

'Cold one, Barry,' the man says.

'Huh? Oh, yeah.' The dog has no inclination to stop for a chat, and pulls the man away, to Barry's relief, because he can't think of his name. It's been happening a lot lately, names, words, slipping away, only to return hours or days later, if at all. It's the cold, he reasons, messing up the machinery in his brain. This current ice-age is a blip, and the circulation will soon return to its normal speed once the temperature rises a few degrees. It'll have to, if he wants to swim the Channel in honour of his dear Maggie. That's his latest project, although he hasn't abandoned the diving-board for the Basin. Before that, of course, there's the swimming to master. He enquired about classes in Fairview, where they teach 'seniors,' and he made an appointment, only to then get lost when the time came. He found Fairview, all right, but he just couldn't remember why he was there. Why not learn in the Basin itself? It's on his doorstep, and there must be at least a dozen decent swimmers on his street alone. He'd pay them, obviously, if they asked. He rolls one arm over the other, mimicking the stroke, but his muscles ache with the effort. The cold, he reasons.

He can't find the bookies. It's not the first time, and he's too embarrassed to ask. He's bound to come across it at some point. Is he not eating right, is that it? Or is it the lack of sleep? His dreams have become increasingly vivid, and they can't be put down to a full moon. They're also bleeding into his waking hours, causing confusion, and no little amount of distress.

He can't find his car, and he can only surmise that it's been stolen. He'll be late for class, and the school Board will be on his case – as if he hasn't enough to worry about with them. Making outrageous accusations about him and several pupils. They're just jealous, though of what he can't be sure.

The flat is empty – his wife has left him! 'Maggie! Maggie!' he screams through the flat. He gets a response, from angry neighbours. He'll go out, wait for her, forgive her, ask for her to forgive him. They're lies, he'll tell her, whatever she's heard. The kettle whistles, the steam rises from the spout, and the tea calms him down. Then he notices the ring on the gas oven, glowing blue. He smells it, eventually, and knows that she's dead. Dead a long time. Never spent a moment in this flat, never knew it existed. It would never have existed if she hadn't died on him like that. He turns off the gas, and unplugs every device, fearing a spark, and an explosion. Three flights of stairs, they'd never make it up there in time, and he's not going out the window.

The bed is a priest, he whispers his crimes, he asks for penance, he starts the Our Father, but forgets most of the words. He's a baby, held over the font, wailing, as the blessing is made, and he's baptised. He can't see his parents' faces. Their wedding day – God, things are moving fast! – and her skin is porcelain, there's lipstick on her teeth, and later, she's an overwhelming force, guiding him through the murky waters of conjugal responsibility. They're in the middle of the ocean, she's well ahead of him, showing no signs of fading, while his arms are on fire, and his lungs are bursting, and he wants to scream at her to slow down, and wait, but each time he opens his mouth, it fills with salty water.

Three-fifteen a.m, the witching hour, his mother used tell him, and there's a hammering which might be the pipes. He turns on a lamp, riddled with panic, and flees the bed, dressing before it can get him. Is it at the door, looking for him? The simple act of opening his door brings him to his senses. The hallway is quiet, with only his heart making any noise. He's hard, and before he knows what he's doing, he's knocking softy on the Romanian girl's door, needing to ask her a question.

(is this a dream?)

She's not coming, she's not there, she's asleep, *he's* asleep – but then the door is unlocked, and dark eyes peer through the small gap.

'Is this a dream?' Barry asks.

She sits, childlike, on her bed, half-asleep, counting his money, as he undresses in front of her. He's not hard anymore, maybe he imagined it.

'Can I call you Maggie?' he asks, on the verge of tears. She nods, she doesn't care one way or the other. She bids him come closer. She uses her right hand to massage his tortured ego, without success.

'I can't,' she says. She gives him the money back, and opens the door for him.

In the corridor, he wonders what he's doing there. Has Maggie locked him out, have they had another argument? He needs his bed, he's exhausted, and he has to be up early in the morning. Busy day tomorrow, an exam to give, a dog to race, an ocean to swim.

There's a large black man in front of him, speaking in a strange accent. *Do I know him?*

'Come on, Barry, back to your bed. Do you know what time it is? I think you're sleepwalking.'

The bed is a coffin, he hears the nails being driven in. The sheets are concrete, his veins are ice, freezing the blood.

⁓

The two girls are skipping towards the Basin, dressed in spring shades, giggling. His seat is taken, and no amount of scowling on his part will remove the interlopers. The swans are being targeted by small boys with pebble missiles. He rolls up his paper, and slaps them around the head, teaching them a severe lesson. They stand down, but not before laughing in his face. He fancies a pipe, but he's nothing to light it with. He left the matches at home – but where is that again?

There's a skip at the gates, left by the workmen, where he finds a plank that will do just the job. It's what he's been searching for all this time. The only trouble is getting it out of the skip, and into the Basin, and then securing it to the railings so that it will support the weight of a man.

It scrapes off the ground, and his heart is threatening to bring a sudden halt to proceedings. If people would help instead of just gawping, he might survive.

There, done it! He has the plank leaning against the railings, and now it's simply a question of –

'Barry? Can I help you?'

It's a Garda. Just the man for the job, Barry thinks, and in the nick of time, as well.

'Yes, you can! I'm building a diving-board, and I have to find a way of securing it to the railings.'

'A diving-board? Do you have permission?'

'Oh, I haven't got time for all that,' Barry tells him.

'I need a word with you, Barry? Do you want to sit inside the car for a second?'

'What? *No!* I'm busy, can't you see?'

'We've had a complaint. Barry, are you listening?'

He listens, with a distracted ear – something about 'inappropriate behaviour,' and a woman in the Spar shop. What has all this got to do with him? The competition is about to start. Can't have a diving competition without a diving-board. And Maggie's over there, as one of the judges. She has high standards, so he can't afford to let her down.

Barry forgot his togs, so he'll have to make do with the shorts he has on. It's not the diver, it's the dive that matters. And he doesn't need to be able to swim, as such, does he, he won't be in the water long enough. He'll only be under for a few seconds, and then he'll be out, making way for the next competitor.

'Barry, are you going to cooperate?'

'I *am*, but not yet – can't you see I have a dive to make? I can't let her down.'

At the far end of the Basin, the two girls have had a similar idea, and are stripping down, preparing to go into the water. The Garda rushes off to stop them, leaving Barry to attempt his dive. He decides to do without the board, and climbs over the railings. On the muddy bank he loses his footing, and slides under the water. He swallows a mouthful of slime, and can't find his breath. His arms and legs struggle against each other, forcing him to the bottom. He digs his hands into the earth to stop himself drifting, but his throat is a wall through which nothing can pass.

Two mermaids come by, their golden hair flowing, their silver scales glistening. They each take a hand, and guide him to the surface.

He has no need for oxygen, or light, or strength to swim. Maggie swims for him, in him. She puts her mouth on his, and gives him new life.

He remembers. It had all gone on ahead of him, to prepare the ground for his arrival.

They reach the shore, and she pulls him up onto the beach, where he lies on the softest sand, where he will always lie.

He is Barry 'King' Sweeney, born under water, died under water. Nothing else was ever possible, was it?

The Fall

The Fool is Con, but Con is no fool. They're laughing with him, not at him. He's teetering on the counter of his brother's East Clare pub, the master-of-ceremonies, leading the celebrations for his niece's marriage to a fisherman from Kilkee. The doctor juggles responsibilities while he juggles pints of Guinness being passed up to him by all and sundry. After the formal congratulations, he leads the congregation in a macabre tale of a wronged young bride and her dreadful means of revenge. A cautionary tale, he warns the young couple, with a glint in his eye. Con wants a hand down, but the crowd wants more, another tale, a song perhaps, or even a poem. But he resists each and every tempting request, telling them his bladder has the last word, so, reluctantly, he descends from his throne, and takes his rightful place down amongst the ordinary people. His hand is shaken to the bone, while the bride and groom are largely forgotten. But he wasn't lying, his bladder *is* screaming at him, and if he doesn't get a move on, there'll be a new, legendary, tale to add to the canon of the village – the one about the doctor who didn't quite make it!

⌒

The magic road reveals new twists and turns in the moonlight, as Con considers his options. He could lay down in the heather, and let nature take care of him, or pull himself together, and call his wife. There'd be hell to pay – but when *isn't* there, where she's concerned? Mary, I'm lost, *again*. He'll plead and beg, and do whatever penance she thinks he deserves, which could be considerable. He's not a religious man, though he's had to say a few prayers throughout their marriage. Mary's no drinker, and there's the children to be looked after, hence her absence from the celebration tonight. She'll be well away, being a deep sleeper, which probably comes from having a clear conscience. He sees a familiar landmark up ahead, and if he doesn't stray too far from the path, he might just make it. The full beams of a fast-moving car behind startle him. He puts out an arm, hoping for a lift, but the teenagers roar past him, laughing faces pressed to the glass, music piping loud. Con continues on, watching the horizon appear out of the fading darkness. Jesus, look at the time! There'll be a Sunday of silence because of this, and only the kids will want anything to do with him – but he won't want too much of them.

His bed is heaven, with hell lying right next to him. He's hoping to slip quietly into unconsciousness when she moves, turning to whisper in his ear: 'Enjoy yourself, then?' She doesn't wait for an answer, and he's not about to give one.

The morning brings retribution on all fronts. Her distance is nothing compared to the hideous effects of simple daylight on his fragile constitution. The children don't take kindly to his less than enthusiastic attitude to life, and they, too, abandon him. He appreciates being left alone, but as he slowly starts to feel better, he starts to feel worse. It's no way for a man of his age, and prominence, to behave. He is, supposedly, a pillar of the community – a pillar of salt, more like. He shakes off the self-pity, sticking his head out the window for a dose of bracing winter. And as the day unwinds, his memory unravels, and his unfortunate antics come back to haunt him. Was he really *standing* on the bar? He could have done some serious damage, and where would the village be if the doctor himself was struck down, and by his own foolishness, at that? He resolves to do better, to make it up to Mary – *but* – last night, and the previous night, did prove that he does possess talents beyond medicine, that might be put to some better use. It had been said to him many times, inside the surgery and out – *you should run for office*. And politics was crying out for someone with real guts to expose the scandal that was the Irish healthcare system. Just look at Ennis General Hospital – empty wards due to lack of staff, due to lack of money, with patients forced to go to Limerick or Galway.

He appears at the dinner-table, revitalised, and infused with a grand determination to *do something*. He has to bite his lip, before he blurts it out to Mary, as she'd put an end to it before he'd even made it to the starting gate.

'Look, children,' says Mary, 'it's you father. He's decided to join us. Isn't that nice?' Con grins, and bears it.

He bears the morning surgery, his mind elsewhere – in Dublin, actually, leading a vast popular movement aiming to dismantle the status quo, and revolutionise the system. He turns to Mrs. Durcan to give her the prescription, and finds her on the floor, groaning. But he had only turned away for a moment! No patient had ever collapsed in his presence, let alone died. She *can't*, not now, not when he's about to embark on his great adventure. Thankfully, when the ambulance arrives, to take her to God-knows where, she has recovered somewhat, although her symptoms bear all the hallmarks of a stroke. Should he have seen the signs when she first came in? Had he been paying proper attention?

He studies each party carefully, before deciding that he has to run as an independent. He'll have support, but enough to carry him over the line? The established party machines are so deeply embedded in the landscape, how can he hope to compete with them?

He garners opinion among his patients, who all ask the same question: *but if you win, and take your seat, what will happen to the surgery?* They have a point. He's running in protest at the cutbacks in health services, but cutting back his own community's service in the process? He argues, though, that there must be a young doctor out there looking to set up his – or her – own practice, surely. Con O'Sullivan *is* replaceable, isn't he?

Mary *'won't stand in his way,'* if that's what he really wants. Not quite the ringing endorsement he was hoping for. His brother, Malachy, however, urges him on, telling him he should have done it years earlier. Rumours run before the facts, forcing him into a decision. If he turns back now, he'll be diminished in some eyes, but if he presses ahead, then there is no turning back.

Con announces his candidacy without a proper plan, no manifesto, and severe doubts. When the national media pick up the story, healthcare is the least important item on their agenda. They want to know about the storytelling, and the matchmaking, and the singing, and the poetry. *Who cares?* he protests, only escalating the scrutiny. *'Con is a con'* is the line from his opponents in the race. In their minds, he's a one-trick pony. Where, they ask, are his policies on the economy, and foreign affairs, and immigration, and crime – oh, and education? The man himself is stumped, a deer in the headlights, and fast becoming a national joke. Mary, oddly, seems quietly pleased, hoping that her husband will put these fanciful notions to bed, and return to being a country doctor. Once the Fool, now a fool, and they *are* laughing at him.

The *Daily Star* publishes a few lines of Con O'Sullivan's poetry:

'Fields of tawny brown,
Blades of rising wheat
Suffering the wet winds,
And brunt scythe
As the widow begs for mercy'

He can't find out who the traitor is, even suspecting his brother, knowing the man would sell his soul for an easy dollar. His wife, too, could have decided to scupper her own husband's hopes by betraying him. The ridicule shows no sign of abating. The numbers in his surgery slowly decline, and his spirits tremble at the humiliation being heaped upon him.

He sits on a stool at the end of the bar, cradling a whiskey, and reviewing his position. The viciousness of the campaign waged against him has been astonishing. Malachy refills his glass, 'on the house'. Con reaches for the *Irish Times* nearby, and reads the latest statistics on waiting-lists in hospitals up and down the country, the numbers at record levels, and set to rise like a tide that never goes out. There is a war to be waged, Con reflects, but no one is listening. What a waste, what a tragedy. Okay, he'll admit, he *doesn't* have any other policies. He's not sure he even has firm opinions on many other subjects – but isn't healthcare as important as any of the others, if not *more* important?

'Another one?' his brother asks.

'No – I need a clear head,' Con tells him. 'I have a lot of work to do.'

'Give it up, Con, can't you? Look what they've done to you so far. You want more of that, or worse?'

'That's all bollocks, Mal, and you know it. Who gives a fuck about my poetry? Well?'

'Nobody, apparently,' Malachy says, gently teasing. 'You're a doctor, Con, not a politician. They're wankers, one and all. Why would you want to join them?'

'*Why?* To kick all the wankers out.'

'And how, pray tell, are you going to do that, my dear brother?'

'I…don't know.'

The idle doctor is never idle for long. What ails this young lady, he wonders? He should know her, but she's at that age when the lines are blurred, and she could be fourteen or twenty.

'Angela?' Angela Carter, daughter of Ruby and Phil. Con knows, or *knew*, the mother quite well. 'I haven't seen you for a long time.' *I haven't seen her mother for a long time, either.*

'I know, I…' Angela studies him hard, making up her mind.

'So, how can I help you today?'

'I think…*I* can help you.'

'Help me? That's not the way it really works.' He's not especially practiced, or confident, when it comes to the problems of teenage girls.

'I know, I…'

'What is it, Angela? What's wrong?'

'I have…information,' she says nervously.

'Information?' Con says. *Not about me and your mother, I hope.*

'Yes…listen, everything I say here is confidential, isn't it?'

'Absolutely. It's called the Hippocratic Oath. Nothing you tell me will leave this room.'

'Good…Well.' She fixes her skirt, and brushes the hair back from her face. 'It's about Nealon.'

'Nealon?' Con asks. 'You don't mean…'

'P.J Nealon,' she confirms. 'Fine Gael TD for this constituency,' she adds with spite.

'What - what about him?' Con asks warily. He doesn't want to hear this, and yet…

'He – took advantage of me,' she announces, almost proudly.

'He…?'

'*Seduced* me,' she says. '…and more than once.'

'You mean, he…*raped* you?' Con can hardly breathe. This is *not* his area of expertise.

'Not exactly,' she says.

'What does 'not exactly' mean?'

'I mean, we were…involved.'

'You were having a relationship with PJ Nealon? For how long?'

'A while.'

'But – why are you telling me this? Why not a priest, or the police…or your parents?'

'My *parents?* Angela snorts with laughter. 'Why am I telling you? Because I want you to destroy that piece of shit. I want him to lose his fucking precious seat in parliament. Let him explain that one to his wife and children.'

Is she the same person who came into his surgery a few minutes ago? The lines of age are no longer blurred. She has, most definitely, crossed over into cynical womanhood.

'*You* should take his seat. Doctor. Teach that man a lesson. He had his fun, and then he just cast me aside when he got bored. That's not fair. I want justice. And you can help me.'

'You want *justice*? It seems to me you were both equally to blame. You did say it was consensual, didn't you? You were a willing participant – and now it's over. You didn't think he was going to leave his wife for you, did you?'

A fearsome look passes quickly over her face, before she regains her former composure.

'Don't you want to beat him?' she says.

'Yes – yes, I do. But through fair means, not foul. Each candidate presents their case, and the voters decide.'

'Jesus,' she cries. 'I thought you had something more about you.' She's about to leave, when she sashays over to him, playing the tramp. 'I've heard all about you, Doctor. Must have been lies, I guess. Pity.'

Con waits until she's gone before exhaling. He was sure she was about to sit in his lap – and he doesn't think he would have been able to control himself. Like mother, like daughter, eh?

Mal is more than eager to listen, and give advice. In the cellar of the pub, the two brothers assess the state of the campaign, and how to move it forward.

'How much do you want it, Con?'

'I want it,' says Con unconvincingly.

'And what are you willing to do to win?'

'I don't know. And how do we know that helping him lose will help me win. Putting him out of the race doesn't necessarily put me in it.'

'God, you're the most pessimistic creature on this earth, aren't you?'

'I can't just call him, and tell him I know about him and Angela, can I?' Mal rolls his eyes.

'For an intelligent man, you ain't half stupid. You don't go near the man. And let me make use of that information. He'll never know where it came from. He'll just be told that the information is out there, and ready to be exploited. We let *him* destroy his own campaign.'

'I'm not sure,' Con tells him.

'Then it's just as well that I am.'

One by one, the front-runners stumble, and Con, simply by staying on his feet, moves inexorably forward. Nealon announces his immediate retirement from politics, for personal reasons. O'Mara, the Fianna Fail man, *and* current Minister of State for Education, becomes embroiled in a row over a possibly racist remark he makes during an encounter with a black teacher in Kilrush. He furiously denies the accusations, but he's seriously wounded.

And so it is that Con O'Sullivan, doctor, raconteur, and *bad* poet, finds himself at the head of affairs leading into the last days of the campaign.

On the eve of election, Mary takes pity on him, and they have sex for the first time in months.

'Oh, by the way,' she announces afterward, 'if you win, I'm *not* moving to Dublin, if that's what you were planning.'

'I wasn't – I'm not. Why would I, or you, for that matter, have to move? *If* I win, and it's a big if, I'll only have to travel up a couple of days a week, at most.'

'Well, as long as you know where I stand,' she restates.

He tops the poll. He's borne aloft by his supporters, and carried from the Count Centre to his brother's pub, where the celebrations continue long into the night. Mary abandons him long before the end, staying true to her principles.

In the fading embers of victory, the problem of how to replace him at the surgery looms large. A locum is found, from Limerick, who will initially come in two days a week. Con aims to leave for Dublin before he's lynched. Mal takes a leave of absence from the pub to act as Con's adviser and confidante.

'I don't have any policies, Mal.'

'Hair of the dog?'

'What? No – I shouldn't. Oh, go on, then.'

'Good lad. You'll think better on this.'

Con doesn't. He's terrified, desolate.

'Listen, brother – you were elected to bring the fight for decent healthcare all the way to Dublin. *That's* your goal. The rest will take care of itself. You're a doctor, that's what they'll expect from you.'

'I *was* a doctor, Mal.'

'Glass half-empty, as always. And speaking of which - .'

'No. No more, for now. And I have to be careful when I get to Dublin, to keep away from this stuff.'

'And the poetry, and the tall tales,' Mal reminds him.

'I'll keep the poetry to myself,' Con assures him.

'Somehow, someone will find it – and let it out. And we don't want that again, do we? Do we, Con?'

'I guess not.'

First day of school for the new crop, and Dublin puts on a defiant show. Wind and rain lashes the fresh combatants, upsetting wives in their expensive outfits, and giving the media plenty of ammunition to portray the whole circus in an unflattering light.

Con holds Mary's hand, and smiles. Their children huddle close, shivering. Back home, he imagines, the villagers could be dropping like flies, as disease runs rampant, without him to protect them.

The formalities are endured, and soon it's time to say goodbye. Mary and the kids are returning on the afternoon train, while he and Mal will remain in Dublin, to 'set up shop,' as it were. Is that a trace of sadness in her face, or regret? Will she miss him while they're apart – will he miss her?

Mal leads him directly to Grogan's bar in South William Street, for a proper drink, as he calls it.

'I told you I was going to behave while I was here,' Con reminds him.

'Yeah, but you weren't serious about that, were you? You won't last a week on the dry in this town, I'm telling you. Dublin will take no pity on you – you have to give as good as you get.'

'I don't understand a word of that, Mal.'

'No, neither do I. Come on, to work.'

'Don't you miss home, Mal? And the pub?'

'Are you kidding? What's to miss? We're here now, and we're not about to waste the opportunity.'

The opportunity is not wasted. This one is for the record-books, for the memoirs, but not necessarily for the grandchildren. In the dining-room, or *dying*-room, of the Mespil Hotel, Con draws a blank on creating a new verse or two, an occasional hangover cure that rarely produces anything worthwhile, *or* cures him. There's Mal now, walking like an injured crab, his gills the colour of the Atlantic in a March storm. Neither is compelled to speak for a considerable length of time, until the ritual of staring-at-food-until-the-nausea-subsides is, thankfully, over.

'Let's call it a once-off, brother,' intones Mal, in a voice of a considerably deeper pitch than before.

'What am I doing up?' says Con, hearing his voice from across the room, or up on the roof.

'We have a busy day today – or at least you do,' says Mal.

'Do I? No rest for the wicked, then? Can't I sleep it off for a day, or a month?'

'Afraid not,' Mal informs him, braving a piece of toast.

'And if you mention a *hair of the dog* at any point today, you are no longer my brother – is that clear?'

'As if I would,' says Mal. 'What do you take me for?'

'The Dail's not in session today, is it?' Con asks.

'It's *Saturday*, in case you hadn't noticed.'

'Is it? Then *what*, I repeat, am I doing up?'

Con is up, and about, and in recovery, because Mal has a basement flat – *apartment* – to show him, in Haddington Road, a not unappealing area.

'What do you think?' says Mal.

'If I was a student coming to the big city after leaving home for the first time, I'd still have to think about it. You expect me to live here?'

'This is a very desirable neighbourhood – and beggars can't be choosers.'

Con takes a slow march around the flat, sighing, recovering, regretting, disbelieving. 'This is all wrong, Mal. It feels wrong, you know what I mean?'

'This flat, or - .'

'*Or*. What am I doing here, in Dublin? A fucking TD – *me!* I'm a doctor. I've always been a doctor, maybe before I was even born, who knows.'

'Give it time, Con. You've only just arrived. Bound to take time to adjust. Some change of scene, I'll grant you – but don't forget why you're here. Ennis General – the empty wards, remember those? The elderly patients stuck in there because there's nowhere else to put them. *Care in the Community,* remember that? Where is it! And you're the man to fight for it, Con.'

'But what if they start asking me about education, or economics – or the situation in the Middle East, for God's sake? I'm ignorant on all the rest of it, Mal, and they know it, and they'll keep picking at it like a scab until I'm exposed – as a con.'

'Okay, then, well if that's how you feel, we might as well head back today. You can pick up where you left off, running a small country practice until your heart gives out, and you die a disappointed man.'

'I was never – *disappointed.*'

'We're all disappointed, Con, all the time. But a privileged few occasionally get the chance to make a difference – as you have. And what'll they think of you back home if you crawl back today? What'll you tell them? *'It wasn't for me.'* And they'll say, 'after *one* day!' So, what's it to be?'

'I don't suppose,' says Con, 'you fancy a hair of the dog?'

The problem with politics, Con discovers, is that it's practiced by politicians, who are forever dreaming up new of ways of *not* getting things done. They form committees, and announce reviews, and clamour for public enquiries – because, deep down, they have no real power. They sit in the Chamber of Deputies, baying like the chorus in an amateur opera, waiting for the fat lady to start singing – except she never does.

Con finally, and fatefully, gets to his feet to make his maiden speech – introducing himself, describing his constituency, before getting to the meat of his argument, about the *savage* and *inhumane* cuts within the health service, which have resulted in wards lying empty in Ennis General Hospital, while A&E overflows, each new day bringing record numbers in, and record times reached before they get out. Con's voice trembles with emotion, and nerves, as he relates a tale replicated throughout the country. He sits back down, to silence – understandable when the chamber is practically empty. The next speaker is called, and Con sinks down into his chair, and into himself. He's offered a drink in the Dail bar afterwards, to congratulate, and commiserate.

He runs into Porter O'Halloran, Minister for Health, in the corridor.

'I hear congratulations are in order,' says Porter, 'maiden speech, and all that. I didn't hear it myself, unfortunately, but I hear you made some passionate arguments.'

'I was talking about the hospital in Ennis, where there are empty beds not being used, because of the cruel policies of this government. *Empty beds*, Minister, while there are people lying on trollies in the corridors.'

'Yes, it is most regrettable,' says the Minister. 'But you must remember, Con, that the healthcare system is like the universe – it's expanding, at an exponential rate, and there's nothing we can do about it, except try and make the best of it. Throwing money at the problem isn't going to solve it, in the short-term.'

'So, what is?' asks Con.

Porter smiles, as an adviser whispers in his ear.

'I have to go, Con. Always meetings to attend. It was a pleasure to meet you. I enjoyed listening to your point of view. We must do it again very soon.' A pat on the arm, and Porter is escorted away, like a prisoner being returned to the cells.

Con looks up and down Kildare Street, starts walking one way, before turning in the other. At the lights on Stephens Green, a young woman faints, and he offers his services, but she recovers quickly, promising to take his advice to rest and drink plenty of water. His most satisfying moment since arriving in Dublin, by a clear margin.

He's on his own, Mal having returned to check on his business. His base is a basement, what if it floods? He'd never make it out in time. He sits in, quietly, catching up on his homework, familiarising himself with the multitude of items on the government's agenda. Most of it makes his eyes glaze over. He's a tiny piece of matter floating in infinite space, dwarfed by billions of larger, more significant objects.

'What am I doing here?' he asks the room.

What am I doing here? he thinks, walking into the Beggars Bush pub down the road. Just in time for his one for the road, his *one*. The phone-call with Mary was the spur to his last-minute decision. He might have been cold-calling her, trying to sell life insurance, such was her distant manner. The Beggars is brimming, and revives his flagging spirits. He fancies a sing-song, or begging their indulgence, to spin a far-fetched tale from the far-flung corners of Clare. But they're a singular stew, happy to keep their own counsel, and guard their own territories. Each corner is packed, every seat taken, and there's conversation aplenty, but there's no merging of enthusiasms, the collective spark never catches fire.

The bed feels narrow, the mattress hard, and he's sure he hears water running down the basement stairs. How long can he hold his breath underwater? Can he swim if he has to, even though he's never had a lesson? *Please, God, let me rest – let me do the right thing.*

He's back in his 'surgery' – a backroom in his brother's bar - only this time he's attending to slighter matters. Fly-tipping, and nasty landlords, noisy neighbours, and vermin infestation. *Where* are the complaints about waiting-times in Ennis General, or maternity malpractice? He didn't sign up for this – or maybe he did. He promises, and then he *promises*, having no clue where to begin. Mal is only next door, but he might as well be in the next county for all the good he is.

And then there's home. And Mary. He feels like a burglar slipping in beside his wife when the lights go out. She's inches away, but protects her honour with astonishing skill. The whole, endless, night passes without a single moment of contact between them. In the sullen dawn kitchen, he scratches out a few phrases on a scrap of paper. *the gloomy paradox of marriage… a man in reverse, increasingly perverse.*

He'd hoped to leave before she woke, but there she is in the doorway.

'Oh,' she says, before seeing to her own breakfast, and heading back upstairs. One by one, the children, hardly children now, barrel in and out, greeting him in their own inimitable way. They don't resent him, like she does, they just don't really see him – or the point of him.

He eats up the miles to Dublin, yearning for his basement bunker, where he can plan his next move. On the outskirts of Portlaoise, roadworks divert him into the town, where he stops for coffee. In the café, a young boy nearly chokes to death, and Con does nothing. Nor does the boy's mother, come to that, but her excuse is blind terror – what's his? If he carries on this way, he'll be softened to the point of obsolescence, of use to no one, patient or constituent. He hits the road again, and then hits a brick wall, of doubt and uncertainty.

On the hard shoulder, with hazard-lights on, and head in hands, Con attracts unwelcome attention. He rolls down the window, and forces a smile for the Garda.

'Broken down, sir?' says the Garda.

'You could say that,' Con tells him.

'Have you called for help?'

'Yes – I have. They shouldn't be long. I haven't broken any laws, have I?'

'Not as far as I can see. You *are* all right, aren't you?'

'I'm fine – a little tired. And pissed off, I guess. But I'll be on my way soon.'

'Drive carefully, sir,' says the Garda, showing no sign of leaving.

'Anything else?'

'No – nothing else.'

Con has trouble figuring out the pedals, not to mention the gears. It takes a while, but he's soon on his way, staying well under the speed limit, and keeping an eye out for the Garda. He comes upon a hitch-hiker several miles down the road. Losing concentration at the last minute, Con almost kills him, and so has no choice but to offer him a lift.

'I thought hitch-hikers were a thing of the past,' Con says.

'I though people who gave hitch-hikers a lift were a thing of the past,' says the student, wearing a flat-cap, and on his way back to college in Dublin.

'Why not take the train, or a bus? Or can't you afford it?'

'Oh, I can afford it – but I thought it would be more interesting to try this.'

'And how's it been going, so far? How far have you walked, by the way?'

'About a hundred miles, I guess,' the student says with a sigh.

'A *hundred*? Am I your first lift, then?'

'You are indeed, sir,' he says with grave politeness. 'The milk of human kindness is in short supply.'

'Seems to be,' Con says. 'I suppose people are more wary these days.'

'They've seen too many bad movies, that's all it is.'

'Is it? Maybe. So, what are you studying?'

'Philosophy and Political Science.'

'Really? I myself am a politician,' Con confesses, to the student's apparent disinterest. 'An independent – no party allegiances for me.'

'Give it time,' the student tells him.

'What? Oh no, there's absolutely no chance of me joining one of the main parties.'

'You'll still vote to keep them in power, at some point, to keep *yourself* in power.'

'I resent the implication, young man. Some of us do have principles, believe it or not.'

'Principles? But aren't you a doctor? Or *were*.'

Con jams on the breaks, and then pulls over.

'You *know* who I am?'

'Of course. I study political science. I'd be a poor student if I didn't. I've seen you on TV. I've read about your plans to take the fight to Dublin, and bring about radical change in the healthcare system.'

'And I won't?'

'Of course you won't. You're no different to all the others that have gone before you. I'm sure you mean well.'

'But?'

'But – you're all so naïve. There's no such thing as influence outside the party system, or even inside it. Power and influence are wielded by a handful of individuals who tolerate individuals like you.'

'How can someone your age be so cynical?' Con wants to know.

'I have eyes and ears. I can read. I have read history, which repeats itself over and over.'

'At least I'm trying to do something about it. What are you going to do? *Write* about it in the *Irish Times*, or teach others about our mistakes in some lecture room somewhere? Easy to criticise from the side-lines. Let me tell you, it's a lot harder on the actual pitch, playing.'

'I think I can take it from here,' the student says, getting out of the car.

'Hey! Where are you going? Don't be stupid!' Con shouts after him. What have we done to the next generation, to make them so *weak*, he wonders? There are those who do, and those who talk about those who do. But if everyone just talks about doing, and never does, what then?

Time for a spot of lunch, and the *Foxhunter* on the outskirts of Dublin will do. He's at the back of the queue for the carvery, so he gets the leathery meat and the crusty potatoes. There's hardly room to swing a cat, either, and he has to join a table of beer-drinking golfers just in off the course. Lager is not his usual tipple, but its proximity is too much to bear. He also has to bite his tongue, and not pitch into the conversation. He has a great story about an old senile golfer playing alone on the wind-swept links of Kilkee on Christmas Day many years ago. It's a stormer, and he tells it well, if he says so himself – he even wrote a poem about it – but the lads finish their drinks with devastating ease, anxious to get back out for the second round. Con was a ten-handicapper once upon a time, until a slipped disc ended a promising amateur career.

The bar empties as the diners go back to work. He has another coffee to keep him alert at the wheel. What's his schedule for the rest of the week? In fact, what *day* of the week is it? He's lost without Mal. He's lost, essentially. Shouldn't he hire an assistant, to advise, keep him on track? Only one problem – money. And think of the reaction of his constituents to his hiring a 'servant'. He gets back in his car, and enters the muddy stream of city centre traffic. It's nearly three before he reaches Haddington Road, and looks for a parking space. There's a man coming up *his* basement steps, zipping up his trousers. Con finds the stain at his doorway, along with discarded wrappers and a handful of chips. *Bastards!* And there was he worrying about flood water, forgetting all the other shit that might be flung in his direction. He'll ask Mal to look for alternative accommodation, something *above* street level.

He locks his door, turns on the TV, and watches the Taoiseach stutter through another interview, defending his government's nervous majority, and their less-than-decisive start after the election. Con falls into a doze, and wakes to find a missed call from O'Halloran on his phone. It can wait till tomorrow, he decides. Today has been eventful enough, and he doesn't want to push his luck. He has a shower, fulminating on the policy issues he has yet to finalise a position on, fearing his honeymoon is well and truly over. It's not that far removed from his actual honeymoon, when he and Mary flew to the Bahamas for two weeks, and endured a hurricane, hotel fire alarms, and unremarkable sex. The markers had been laid down, and time had only confirmed those early doubts.

Midnight, and his policy paper remains a paltry document, short on detail, and even shorter on conviction. Noise outside, more would-be pissers, or litterers, this time he'd catch them in the act, and put the fear of God in them. It's only a cat that refuses to leave, and scratches at the door when Con closes it on him.

A full, mighty, breakfast, the latest in a long line of artery-clogging meals, gives him indigestion for the rest of the day, although Porter O'Halloran might also have something to do with it.

Con is cornered in the corridors of power, not by the Minister himself, but his minions, who request his presence in the Minister's office.

Con leaves his principles at the door, as the hitch-hiker foretold. He throws his hat into the pork-barrel ring, promising his support for the government in the upcoming vote on sweeping welfare changes, in return for a review of resources at Ennis General Hospital. A *review of resources* – that could mean anything, or nothing. It could last for years, if it even began. And what if the review decided that Ennis General had all the resources it needed? Con feels dizzy, rewinding to the moment he entered the Minister's office, and his senses deserted him. He can't take it back, he can't recant. *They'll slaughter me.*

They slaughter him, colleagues and media alike, until he's been flayed alive. The moment he steps out onto Kildare Street after the vote, he's attacked from all sides, and asked if he's sold his soul for simply the *possibility* of thirty pieces of silver. So that's it, he's worse than Judas, because at least he got the money. And what about the victims of the Welfare cuts, what can Con O'Sullivan say to *them* after what he's done?

'What *have* I done?' he asks a stranger in the Beggars Bush that night. He doesn't get a coherent answer. He does, however, get a sympathetic, though short, call from his wife, asking how he is. Things must be bad, he reckons, as he can't ever remember hearing that tone in her voice.

He can't hold out, and ends up pissing in his own doorway. *If you can't beat them, join them.*

His next 'surgery' back home is decidedly sparse of custom, and those that do attend berate him for selling out so cheaply. Mal is out of ideas, calling an official end to his leave of absence from the pub.

'I'm on my own, then?' Con laments.

'Listen, Con, it's Saturday – you need some time off. You need a night off, a night *here* – like old times. How about it?'

'I doubt if they want to hear from me anymore.'

'Bollocks' says Mal, 'you're still one of us. And you're my brother, my star attraction. No one draws the punters like you do. You're just out of practice, that's all. Forget politics for a while, and remember who you really are.'

'Maybe. I'll think about it.'

The bar is full but the cupboard is bare. He forgets the end of the one about the blind woman with the albino triplets from Fountain Cross. Now they're laughing at him, not with him, including PJ Nealon, looking smug, and raising a glass in Con's direction.

Unfortunately, he *doesn't* have a sore head the next morning, meaning he's fully conscious of the nightmare facing him, namely, a Sunday family lunch. The roast is a tad overdone, which can't be said for the conversation. He asks each of his children in turn for a brief summary of their recent activities, which they dutifully supply, without much embroidery. Mary clears the table, moving quickly onto dessert, a heavy trifle of sickly sweetness.

Later, Mary closes her eyes, and arches her back, moaning appropriately, though not exactly at the right times, as far as he's concerned. He pulls out, and then sneaks out, not waiting for morning, hoping to beat the traffic – that's his excuse, anyway. Running out of town before he's run out. They used to come to him to cure what ailed them, now he's part of what ails them. She will turn in the bed, and roll into the warm extra space, not missing who made it so. He can't turn around and make his peace. He can't turn his back on the government he vowed to support, or he'll never be trusted again. He can't turn his head without worsening the creak in his neck. Lying at a funny angle last night, that's what did it, trying not to disturb her, not after what had passed between them. It had passed between them like a gentle breeze, barely noticed, and quickly forgotten.

He drives too fast, or too slow, depending on his mood, which fluctuates wildly over the course of the journey back to Dublin. He cuts off for Athlone, and breakfast, where a slice of fatty bacon almost brings a sudden end to his political career, and his life. A fat salesman thumps him on the back repeatedly, and doubtless saves his life. He drinks a gallon of orange juice to make sure it's all gone down, and then as soon as he's back on the road, he needs to piss again. *it'll have to wait.* Only it can't, and he pulls over into a quiet space, and heads for the trees, where he trips over a branch and twists his ankle. He pisses in agony, as a curious fox looks on. Back in his car, the sprained ankle screams every time he touches the break. He lurches into Dublin, amusing and worrying other motorists in equal measure. He stops near the Grand Canal to stretch his legs, and examine his ankle. It has swollen alarmingly since the incident, and he curses his consistent misfortune. He suddenly remembers the end of the story, when the blind woman drives her three unfortunates over the edge of the cliffs of Moher.

He limps, literally, the last few yards to his flat, where a young woman is waiting on his doorstep.

'*Angela*?'

Angela Carter, in the flesh, angry and forlorn.

'Where have you been?' she cries through bitter tears.

'What are you doing here?' *and what have I done to deserve this?*

'I had nowhere else to go,' she declares.

'What the hell are you doing in Dublin, and, more importantly, how did you know where I lived?'

'I've been cast out,' Angela says. 'By my family, by *his* people.'

'Whose people?'

'His. Nealon, that fucker. Threatened me with all sorts of things, he did. And as for my *own* family...'

'Okay, but what are you doing...*here*?'

'You have to help me. I helped you, didn't I?'

He takes her roughly by the arm and drags her down the steps, and into his flat. 'Come in. I don't want people seeing you like this. Jesus. You had no right coming here.'

Inside, she makes herself at home, pouring herself a drink, and settling down on the sofa.

'You just treat this place as your own,' Con says sarcastically.

'I will, thanks,' she answers back.

'Should you be drinking that at this time of day? Should you be drinking at all?'

She laughs at him – not with him.

He calls Mal from his bedroom, asking for advice, and help. His brother sympathises, but that's all he's willing to do. Angela's in the doorway.

'Who was that? You trying to get rid of me? I'll tell. I'll tell lies, if I have to. Or I'll tell them about you and my mother.'

'Me and your *mother*?' Con says.

'Don't pretend there was nothing going on. She told me, a few years ago. We were very close – once.'

'And who are you going to tell?'

'Oh, I don't know – anyone who'll pay me, I guess.'

'Jesus. Listen to yourself. You're not even twenty, and you're already fucked up. Where, or what, will you be when you're twenty-five? Dead, probably, the way you're going. *Why*, Angela? What happened to you?'

She shakes her head. 'That fucking town. This fucking country.'

'Dublin is no better. I can tell you that from experience,' he tells her.

'Can I stay here tonight?' she asks in a softer voice.

'Maybe you should,' he says.

Like mother, like daughter. She bathes his swollen ankle, and moves her hand further up. He doesn't stop her. They have both been cast out, he reasons, and have been washed up on this barren shore, with only each other for comfort, so where's the harm.

He answers the door before realising that the knocking was in his head. The freezing night air slaps him fully awake. He can't go back to that bed, to her. He hadn't ruined her, but he might have ruined himself. He thinks back – what was it that made him stray so far off-course? Who, exactly, had persuaded him to take the plunge, and dive into deep, dangerous, waters before he was ready? The shadow in the bedroom doorway emerges into the light, Angela, naked, unadorned, un-self-conscious.

'I thought you'd run away,' she says sleepily.

'I thought about it,' he says.

'Come back to bed. It's cold.'

He obeys, and strays further from the path, just when he thought he'd reached the end of it.

There's a vote in the Dail. And a series of committee meetings. And interviews. And drinks in Buswells. And a throbbing, worsening ankle, and a dread of going back to the flat. She's a bad smell that he hopes might just disappear of its own accord.

There's a circus on Haddington Road – two Garda vehicles and an ambulance, with an expectant crowd. They're not to be disappointed, as the girl is carried out on a stretcher, still alive, apparently, judging by the mask over her face. Con watches from a safe distance, debating whether to intervene, and demand an explanation, while proclaiming his ignorance about the girl found in his flat. He lacks the courage of his muddled convictions, and retreats to the Beggars Bush.

The circus has left, more or less, when he returns later, but they're still waiting for him. He cooperates fully, and is taken to Pearse Street station for questioning.

'Yes, I know an Angela Carter. Or I did. I used to treat her, and her family, when I was in practice back home. I've known the family for years.'

'No, I *don't* know how she came to be in my flat, I've told you…I don't know. Perhaps, she thought I might be able to help her…I have *no* idea how she found my flat…someone obviously told her…why don't you ask her? She will be okay, won't she?'

It's dawn when he leaves, and there's a different kind of circus waiting for him at the flat. He's startled, and heartened, when Mal turns up, offering to help.

'It's a pity you didn't come when I asked,' Con says. 'None of this might have happened.'

'You haven't told them anything – that lot out there – have you?' Mal asks.

'No – because I don't know anything,' Con says.

'Are you sure about that?'

Con moves into the Mespil Hotel, still pursued by the pack of wolves calling themselves journalists, and, of course, the police, who continue to doubt his story. He repeats a tale about a tragic young girl who came to him for help, but he arrived too late to save her. Being the family's doctor, she, perhaps understandably, sought him out as a last resort, but it was not to be. He tells it well, digging deep into his well of experience, and starts to believe it himself. It has just enough truth in it to give him the benefit of the public's doubt.

Mary is downstairs, reception informs him, but she refuses to go up to his room. He goes down to her, and in front of prying eyes, she tells him of her intention to begin divorce proceedings.

'Now, of all times?' he asks her.

'It's because of now, Con,' she says. 'And because of Ruby Carter, and the rest of it.'

'What has Ruby Carter got to do with it?'

'Don't, Con, please. Why else would her daughter come to you for help? I've had my suspicions for a long time. All this has only confirmed it.'

By admitting one crime, he could get away with another. It was worth thinking about.

'I'm sorry,' he says.

'So am I,' she says after a pause. And then she leaves.

Con calls each of his children, telling them the news, taking some of the burden off her. They take it almost too well. Is this the end, he wonders? Is *this* the bottom of the well?

The Long Hall pub, on George's Street, it is, then. He'll go no further. There's a fair chance no one will recognise him in here, anyway. A small band is whipping up a storm, providing a diversion. Armed with a Guinness, he parks himself against a pillar, and tries to relax. A dark-haired woman and her mousy male friend begin to crowd his narrow space, clapping between swigs of spilling lager. Con's ankle lets him know that it's not happy, and being a doctor, he should know better. Angela was the last person to touch it. He can't remember the last time Mary did, if ever. The music is a dripping tap on his forehead, giving him a headache. He has nowhere to put his glass down, and he thinks about using the brunette's head. He's pushed from behind, and elbowed from the side. It's no different here than at the hotel, or at work, where the media has set up camp, hunters waiting for their prey. And now they've something very tasty to get their teeth into, for not only has Angela recovered, she's singing like a canary, inventing stories which Con could almost admire, if they weren't about him. She's claiming that Con, and PJ Nealon, it must be said, took advantage of her, *seduced* her, and then threatened her with serious consequences if she so much as breathed a word. Con had never *seduced* anyone in his life, not even Mary. They had sort of stumbled upon each other, and 'settled' for things, as it were. But – it had to be admitted – technically, legally, and any other way you wanted to describe it, he had *fucked* the girl, to put it plainly. Not that he had performed in any way satisfactorily, as she had gone way too fast for him, and his body seriously malfunctioned. He denied it of course, and would continue to do so for as long as necessary. The worrying thing, though, was that a part of him denied it to himself. It had happened, and – yet, it hadn't, in some strange way. It had, definitely, 'meant nothing,' emotionally, and therefore, he had quickly forgotten it. How was he to know she meant to kill herself?

He manoeuvres his way closer to the bar, and the stage, the headache clearing, and the melody striking a chord – *Like a Bridge Over Troubled Water* – fuelling his thirst, and his thirst for revenge – against who, though, he wasn't sure. Despite the crowd, he remains resolutely on his own, and, honestly, he misses the attention. Then an unexpected opportunity presents itself – the band take a break, to loud applause – and there it is, right in front of him, the stage, such as it is, the platform, the spotlight. It's about time he had a chance to put across his side of the story. He steps up onto the raised platform, takes the microphone, and clears his throat.

'Good evening…ladies and gentlemen. My name, in case you don't know, is Con O'Sullivan, from the banner county, Clare, that is, and I'd like to do a little something for you...' In the pause, as he wavers between one of his own poems and a weird tale, he is, firstly, jeered and booed, and then physically removed from the platform, to ironic cheers. Crestfallen, Con struggles to find his way back to his place at the bar, and his drink, when he has another idea. That's it! He proceeds to climb onto the bar, knocking glasses and bottles as he goes, and generally upsetting everyone.

'Please! Listen to me! Indulge me for five minutes, and let me have my say!' Someone has his legs in a stranglehold, the barman, most likely, and he's wrestled to the floor, where he cracks his head, and soon lapses into unconsciousness.

⌒

The white angel holds his hand, and gently encourages him to lie still. He believes her, and obeys. Other voices crowd in, and lights, and chaos. He is lying in his own bed, but many are sitting, some in great discomfort, waiting to be seen. He knows, he remembers, he closes his eyes in horror, and tears fill the corners. There is a bandage around his head, and the slightest movement brings a shiver of excruciating pain.

Magic pills pull him under into soft, comforting waters – heaven – will they let him stay here for a while?

In a private room, his angel leans over and whispers in his ear.

'Your brother is on his way, Con.'

'Really?'

Later – or before – who knows, he finds himself alone in the room, the curtains drawn around his bed, and he starts to panic. If he doesn't hurry, the curtains will open, and the surgeon will be there, armed to the teeth, and more than ready to operate. If he lets that happen, he is lost.

Where are his clothes, his modesty? The door is wide open, at least, so he has a chance, if he moves quickly. He walks out into the corridor, heading for the noise, and the madness, finding his purpose. It was here all the time, this close.

He approaches his first patient, an elderly woman in an armchair, attached to a drip, her sunken eyes staring into oblivion. Con puts a hand on her shoulder, startling her. 'Don't worry – I'm a doctor,' says the former politician. 'I *am*. Forgive the way I'm dressed. I had a minor accident, but I'm alright now.' The old woman starts screaming, and Con backs away, raising his hands. 'It's okay – I'm a doctor…I'm a *doctor!*'

The Man Who

Lost his hat.
Lost his way.
Laughed at the three-legged dog.
Kicked at the stray football that came his way, and missed.
Lived in Rathmines, alone.
Couldn't tell a joke.
Wrote for a living.
Made up stories.
Had never seen a pantomime.
Cried every time at the end of Hitchcock's *Marnie*.
Drank two pints of an evening, and no more.
Had two left-feet.
Followed Liverpool, but had never been to a match.
Read Stephen King with increasing disappointment.
Composed poetry in his head.
Dreamed of living in Florence.
Wore clothes until they fell off him.
Was afraid of teenage girls.
Never ventured too far.
Meant to visit the zoo more often.
Had nightmares about hungry lions.
Saw Meryl Streep on stage in New York.
Envied painters.
Had never been in a fight.
Let people walk over all over him.
Hated school, and passed every exam.
Played Gaelic football against his will.
Yearned to be old, and on the way out.
Lost touch with his siblings.
Wrote letters that he never sent.
Left a restaurant in Seville without paying for dinner.
Almost drowned in a Venice canal.
Never took risks.

Planted a tree that refused to grow.
Married a girl who died giving birth.
Buried a son he had never seen.
Bought a car he couldn't afford.
Sold the car at a considerable loss.
Considered taking his own life.
Watched his father beat his mother.
Was late for his own wedding.
Spent his honeymoon in a state of regret.
Found a publisher after ten years of nothing.
Woke one morning at the edge of a cliff.
Ran over a swan.
Had a book-signing where nobody came.
Hated the sound of his own voice.
Lied to the police about being drunk at the wheel.
Served on a jury, and voted to convict.
Squeezed from the bottom of the tube.
Hid from his landlord regularly.
Lamented the solitary existence.
Despised the company of other writers.
Sat in the same seat in his favourite cinema.
Found a lump under his arm.
Dismissed any thoughts of visiting a doctor.
Felt the disease run rampant.
Settled his affairs.
Was only forty-nine.
Locked his door for the last time.
Went to Merrion Square Park on his last day.
Made it to the corner of Grafton Street, and slipped.
Listened for the voice of his mother.
Saw the clouds pass over his eyes.
Struggled for breath.

Died.

The Town Without Cheer

Hoisted up, above the crowd, in her father's arms, facing into the teeth of the wind, and – waiting. The real parade seems to be happening *up there*, out of sight, around the corner – why can't she go up there and see it, instead of having to always – wait? She strains her neck to catch a glimpse, and nearly falls, angering her father, who threatens to put her down, where she *won't be able to see a thing!* She can't see a thing, anyway. Not that there's anything to see. Flags and frozen faces, bored policemen, and an alien voice on the loudspeaker. Her brothers are missing, messing, guaranteeing later punishment, while her father shifts his position slightly, his fingers red raw. An eternity of minutes, and the first of the floats arrive, and she thinks – *is that it? Where's the real parade?* 'Where's the real parade, daddy?' she asks, and he again threatens to put her down if she doesn't stop complaining. She *wasn't* complaining, she was just wondering. Dancing girls in gold skirts swinging poles, and huge pretend monsters waving to the crowd – but monsters don't *wave*, she thinks. She's about to tell daddy, but thinks better of it. She wants to get down, she's seen enough, which was nothing at all, but his hold on her is firm and unshakeable. The army marching band cheers her up, the brassy sound fighting back against the cold. The parade stretches as far as the eye can see, and maybe it isn't that bad, after all. She waves to St. Patrick as he waves at her. She can't see any snakes, much to her disappointment. She cries out with the rest, and gets a slap on the leg for her enthusiasm. She won't buckle, she'll be brave, even with the rain starting, and the wind blowing dust into her eyes. She will hold onto this for as long as she can, and use it against her brothers later on – he lifted *her* up, not them, though she knows that might have something to do with their being older, and considerably heavier. She is swaying, as the crowd swells, and pushes against them. His fingers dig into her, trying to keep her upright, but it hurts, and she's suddenly afraid of the sea of people around them. The sky above O'Connell Street turns black, and splits in two, ripped apart by lightning. She screams, and feels utterly alone. The crowd starts to disperse, and she wants to go with them. Why is she still up there, why won't he let her down? Does he *want* the lightning to find her?

'Down we go,' her father cries above the din, and she's deposited on the ocean floor, as waves of arms and legs move against her. It would be safer up high, she reckons, but isn't about to ask him. He's dragging her across the street, pulling her arm out of its socket. Her shoes scrape off the ground as she's pulled under the shelter of Clery's canopy. Her brothers are still missing. They're lost, but soon found, and duly clipped around the ears for their mischief. She clings to her father, burying her face in his coat, smelling him, dulling the sound of the rain and thunder, and closing her eyes against the flashes of light. The storm passes, and the street looks as if a bomb has landed, and exploded, on it. The parade is already just a memory, and fading fast. She yearns to hang onto it. The boys tease her, and punch her, and laugh at her, willing her to cry, but she refuses. What are they still doing there? She wants to go home. No, she wants to go back in time – and then freeze time.

She waits in the car with her brothers outside the Fairview Grill. The boys are arguing about which is the better car, the Hillman Hunter, or their own Cortina. She doesn't see the point, or the difference. Hooded shadows walk past, threatening, and she can't see her father inside the shop. Has he been hurt, or has he left them? He's always threatening the latter. Who'd drive the car if he never came back? They couldn't *leave* the car – she's not going out there, and it's too far to walk home. The front door is pulled open, and he's back, yelling at them to stop – stop *what?*- before revealing the treat inside the brown paper bag. The aroma of fish and chips, salt and vinegar, is almost overwhelming, and in the next few minutes, *everything* is forgotten and forgiven. *Don't tell your mother*, he tells them, winking. As if she won't know. As if she won't smell it on them. That wink, though, *that* just might be her favourite thing of the whole day. Where does that come from? Why does he hide it most of the time?

Galloping back to the suburbs, weary, nearly asleep by the time she gets home, he carries her into the house, where the mother is waiting in the kitchen, her face red and sweaty from the steam. She doesn't give her children enough time to explain, packing them off to bed, reminding them about *school in the morning*. No other words can so dampen a child's spirits.

She pauses in mid-sentence, taking in her surroundings, the exam-hall, the students bent over their papers in solemn concentration, the wandering teachers with their beady, suspicious faces, and the huge clock on the far wall. It ticks in years, not seconds, sending her teenage mind racing. There are *expectations* for her. College is assumed, naturally, but Trinity is *expected*. Her pen resumes its steady course, getting back on schedule, before finishing ahead of time, surprising even her. She raises her hand, needing the toilet, and then the freedom from this tedious pageantry.

She waits for her friends, dreading the post-match review. *It's over!* she'll cry, so what's the point of going back over it. Think about what's ahead, not behind. *Easy for you*, they'll reply, and it is, if she's honest. What does that mean, though? She breezes through exams, but that just means that her trials will come later, but in what fashion? She heads home, to prepare for the next exam, wondering what kind of state her mother will be in today. Cheerful, actually, which sets her daughter on edge, forcing her to search the house for the cause of that cheer. Bottles are 'hidden' in every room, mostly empty, with shopping still in bags on the kitchen table. Reclining on the sofa like an ancient queen, her mother struggles to keep track of the time of day, let alone the day itself.

The grass needs cutting, the lawnmower needs filling, the shed needs emptying, the neighbours need reassuring, her father needs to get his act together, her brothers need a sense of responsibility. She's carrying them for now, but for how much longer? Her mother misses a step on her way up to bed, banging her knee, but laughing it off. It's barely seven o'clock. There's a small window of quiet before it's shattered by the arrival of father and brothers. The chaos resumes, the madness, the noise, the rows, the banging. She cooks for her father, but the boys look after themselves. Then the children hold their breaths when their father goes upstairs, ostensibly to change. If she wakes, they'll argue, for hours, until peace breaks out some time in the early hours, interrupted by the occasional rattling of the bedsprings. How does *that* go on in the middle of a war? She'll never make sense of it, until she's married, and engaged in her own war.

The summer before college. Her mother has a sudden outbreak of sobriety, apparently brought about by a chat with the parish priest. The bins overflow with bottles, some of them full. And one evening, miracle of miracles, the five of them sit down for dinner together. The conversation is relatively normal, and even interesting at times. The boys, practically men, compete to announce plans for their dazzling futures, leaving the sister with the prospect of being left alone with their parents. In the following weeks, as the boys depart, their mother retreats back into herself, shutting down, and switching off. Their father grows thin and pale, and increasingly detached, foreseeing a solitary future.

She braces for the first breaching of her virtue, in a dingy flat off the Rathmines Road, by a skinny wretch reeking of cheap wine. She whines at the moment of impact, crying with relief, and then just crying. When she leaves, she vows never to return. The following day, she receives word of her acceptance into Trinity, and the securing of her immediate future. She also takes a part-time job in a Ballsbridge restaurant, waiting tables for puny wages. She breaks all of this news to her parents at once, prepared for the disapproval. Their sad, silent acceptance is almost worse. In for a penny, in for a pound, she decides, and moves out at the same time, a step too far for her mother, who vows never to speak to her again. Her father *can't* speak.

Independence paints the past in a different, softer light. Her home becomes a house, and even less when her mother is removed to a place of greater safety. She now has her own rather dingy flat in Rathmines, not far from the location of her 'downfall,' so to speak. Sharing isn't all it's cracked up to be. Her *flat*mates have their own particular notion of the concept, allowing anyone who happens to drop by to stay for a night, or two. She doesn't like locking her bedroom door, but sometimes the occasion necessitates it, garnering her a, somewhat, chaste reputation. *'Get thee to a nunnery'* is a phrase often tossed in her direction. She's forced, therefore, to open up her door, and her heart, to a succession of unsuitable suitors, none of whom grab her, although they do *grab* her. Is there something wrong with her, or did her maiden voyage scar her for life? It could have something to do with her inclination to study intensely, to the bewilderment of her fellow students. History to begin with, but she switches to the law, finding her 'family' history quite enough to deal with. None of her family actually visit the flat, a fact which both relieves and disappoints her. The brothers are missing, again, in Europe, apparently. Her father is her father, and her mother, well, she has moved from the drying-out clinic to the psychiatrist's couch. Flat-broke, she puts the blinkers on, and imagines the finishing-line a couple of years hence, when the shackles will be removed, and the world will be – her oyster?

Fridays in the flat are worst, when the pre-drink drinking begins, around six, and no excuses are permitted. Naturally cautious around the bottle, she sips while they drown, and inevitably ends up holding one of the others up at the end of the night, getting them home, helping them get sick, and putting them to bed. Oh, and then nursing them for most of Saturday, when she'd much rather be studying the law.

There's a brief period when she has to go home – because of the fire. A burning pan is found to be the cause, although none of them owns up. So the landlord blames them all, and kicks them out. She moves back to the suburbs, and her vacant father, now a habitual, and morose, drinker, who weeps at every opportunity, wondering where it all went wrong. He looks at her in earnest, expecting an answer. She eventually moves in with the restaurant manager, where she has continued to work. What appears to be luxury at first turns out to be nothing of the sort, and the manage*ress*, it seems, has designs on her guest. *'I'm sorry, I'm just not attracted to…women'* cuts no ice, and it's either surrender, or return to her father. Talk about the devil and the deep blue sea. She, to her eternal shame, surrenders – and what's more, she finds she enjoys it. Thereafter, she walks the streets, fascinated by her *lack* of interest in other women, even the most spectacular. She chalks it up, or down, to youthful experimentation, which will end when she graduates. She certainly hopes so.

Graduation is a chilly business, with only her father in attendance, in body if not in spirit. His nose is now a purple-veined train-wreck, and he slurs his words. She keeps him well away from her classmates, and even foregoes the class celebration for a private dinner with him, in the Shelbourne of all places, where his monosyllabic moan goes down a treat. She daren't ask after her mother, or even the boys, for fear of setting him off. At the end, he takes the bill, but forgets the pin number for his credit card, and asks her for help. She scrapes together the cash, forgoing the tip on account of being practically bankrupt. They leave under a cloud, which doesn't lift when they get home. The second he's in the door, the waterworks are on, and he's reaching for the brandy, and he's calling his wife's name. She can't stay, and tells him she can't stay, which is like stabbing a man who's already being kicked. *I…can't…*

Ballybough, less than salubrious, and not her first choice for a first office, but qualified solicitors, she realises, are as thick as summer fleas, even in winter. Her father pays her an unlikely visit, flush from the bookies where he spends a lot of his retirement. He looks happier, though. She hates his sentimentality, although he has every reason for it. He offers her money, and she runs him out of the building, albeit politely.

Business is steady, and steadily growing, although a crash is being forecast. Roll with the good times, she's advised, because they won't last. Her apartment, on the Stillorgan Road, is blandly minimalist, and nothing she does seems to warm it up. Maybe it lacks *human* embellishment, she thinks in quiet moments. Maybe. But how, and where, to begin?

In the *Galloping Green*, to begin with, where she sits alone at the bar nursing a red wine like an extra in a sleazy melodrama. This is no good, this will never – *'can I buy you a drink?'* he asks, and *he* is a marketing consultant, or something, and passably good-looking. *And* he lives in the same apartment building. Well, she reckons, that makes it easier, doesn't it? She can simply slip out of his bed and into her own, just like that! But she's getting ahead of herself – she's assuming he'll want to take it that far, and she's assuming that having gotten than far, she won't disappoint. Her track-record is spotty, to say the least. Even lesbianism gave up on her. But he's surprisingly gallant, and surprisingly shy in the bedroom, grist to her mill, allowing her to cover up a multitude of failings. To compensate for his shyness, however, he often resorts to dollops of cocaine, which so startles her, she can't respond. Not being a lesbian didn't stop her sleeping with a woman, however, and nor does her disapproval of hard drugs prevent her from giving it a try. She tries, and she flies, and she goes back for more. Soon, their relationship, and drug-use, is galloping ahead, to the point where she's no longer holding onto the reins, and she has no idea how she's still hanging on. The next time her father visits her office, after a win, she *does* take his money, and puts it to bad use.

Before the crash comes the crash. She knocks on his apartment door one evening, only to find it open, and every room empty, and an agent in the process of evaluating it before the sale. She's afraid to ask where the former tenant is. She's mightily relieved, in many ways, though she'll need a new supplier, and soon. Cocaine, according to the papers, is *endemic* amongst the professional class, so why can't she find any? And how does one advertise the fact? She doesn't experience 'cold-turkey' exactly, but she does endure almost a week of panic attacks and hot flushes, interspersed with raging thirsts and abnormal appetites. But it passes, and she emerges on the other side relatively unscathed, suitably chastened by the experience.

After the crash comes the crash, when the whole country is deprived of its hard drug of choice, namely money. She moves into her office, and Ballybough becomes her new home, bringing her closer to her father, whose habitual tendency is to get a bus into Fairview each morning, and pass the day 'pottering about' as he calls it. She joins him occasionally, buying him lunch, and even placing a bet now and then. Her number never comes up, though, and she has to rely on whatever legal scraps drop into her lap.

She crashes into her future one day after leaving her father to the bus-stop. The man berates her for daydreaming, and brushes himself down furiously. Almost immediately after leaving her, he calls back to her, apologising. She jokes that if he ever wants to sue her, he could do worse than hire her to pursue the case. He's nothing to look at, she muses in the days after, so why does she keep looking out for him? It couldn't be…love, could it? Or has her well run so dry that a single drop of rain is better than none? She's just about given up on him when he appears out of the ether, as if God had decided to take pity on her. He comes looking for her, which never fails to flatter any girl, although his clumsy attempts at asking her out almost scuppers the whole deal before it's even started. She does the asking for him, and sets in motion a series of predictable events.

First up, first date, a chaste picnic in Fairview Park, maybe the first of its kind. There's a blanket, and a wicker basket, which he opens to reveal all sorts of goodies. Then, as he's pouring the wine, the heavens open and they are soaked in seconds, leading to something approaching pneumonia for him, and just a heavy cold for her. From such inauspicious beginnings, it is a miracle that anything serious could develop, but develop it does, from that opening deep kiss, where his tongue acts like a demented snake, to her slow undressing in the bedroom of his Drumcondra apartment, where she gets her first hint that this might just be *it*.

It is interrupted by her mother's sudden, though hardly unexpected, death. A release, that's all she can think, although for her father, it's an almost fatal blow, as he suffers a minor stroke on the eve of the funeral. The brothers, grim, return from abroad, practically unrecognisable in their prosperity, lamenting the condition of Dublin as much as their mother. They meet her intended – for what else is he? – and voice their disapproval by having no opinion of the man. The wake is a tepid, brief affair in their father's local, even though he isn't present, with the brothers both pressed for time, and flights to catch. She doesn't try to persuade them otherwise, although there's a wrenching sense of emptiness when they leave. *'Good riddance'* she declares to the remaining guests, and they raise their glasses in agreement.

Beaumont Hospital stinks, and she pauses at the lift doors, vaguely intemperate. 'Let's get married,' she says to her boyfriend. 'Please say yes. It means we'll have some good news for my dad, and it might aid his recovery.'

Dad *is* pleased, though it's hard for him to speak. At one point, she fears that the news might prompt another, proper, stroke, but he squeezes her hand, and nearly smiles. She'll have to find a home for him, she realises. Jesus, is there *ever* a break from it?

'Did you mean it?' her boyfriend asks outside. 'About marriage? Were you serious, or were you just saying it for his benefit?'

'No – I meant it – unless you don't want to?' she quivers.

'N-no…I mean, yes…I do,' he says.

'And I do, too,' she says. 'We'll make a good team, you and I. The solicitor and the accountant. Can't get more solid than that, can you?'

'No,' he says, brightening, squeezing her hand.

⌒

The wedding is a small affair. It's what they both want. And they couldn't muster the numbers for a church affair, anyway. A Registry Office, in the heart of Dublin, witnessed by a few close friends, their only close friends, followed by a reception in the *Beggar's Bush* pub down the road, which finishes well before closing time.

The honeymoon consists of a week driving in West Cork, in driving rain, driving each other mad. They return to Dublin fairly bruised by the experience, and set about looking for a house, a project sure to inject some much-needed fun into the early days of their marriage. Is this what it's like for everyone at the beginning? But isn't the come-down, the dose of reality, supposed to come *after* the honeymoon? Maybe they're not honeymoon kind of people, preferring to skip the starter, and get to the main course. She finds relief, ironically, in visiting her father in his new care-home in Clontarf. He's recovered from the stroke, but not from his wife's death, which is surprising given that she'd been dead, more or less, for years. He's glad to have others look after him, because he hasn't the will to do it for himself. He won't last the year, he says, barely sixty, and prays that he won't be kept 'hanging around' for too long. She finds something in him that she never knew existed. Why now, on the brink of losing him, does she uncover it?

The house-hunting haunts her, as they can't agree, until it dawns on her that his stubbornness springs from his doubts about children.

'You don't want any?'

'I didn't say that.'

'But?'

'But…in the current financial climate…with *our* finances…' The honeymoon period is well and truly over, although she finds herself missing those tortuous days on the narrow roads around Skibereen. They thrash it out, batting arguments back and forth, for and against, until they reach a partial agreement, whereby they'll hold off on the kids to begin with, with *her* expected to take the necessary precautions. With that sorted, a house is purchased, in Killester, a three-bedroom, with a small garden back and front, and the potential to become a thoroughly normal family home.

The suburbs beckons, which is why she starts to panic, and search online for positions elsewhere. *No harm looking*, she thinks, and without warning, an opportunity arises, with a firm of solicitors in Belfast, headed by a former fellow graduate from Trinity. Yes, *yes, YES!* she wants to scream. She could be on the train from Connolly that afternoon – what's keeping her? Her father, for one thing. And, of course, there's her – husband.

The day arrives. The documents are signed, and the keys handed over. *He* takes them, of course, and drives slowly, solemnly, into their future. She wonders about the locks on the car doors, and if he controls them, and if she'd survive if she jumped out at this speed, and if he'd come after her if she *did* jump out. Too late, they've arrived.

He puts an arm around her shoulder as they stand at the gate.

'Well, this is it,' he says.

'Yes, this is it,' she agrees. She has no one to blame but herself. *She* was the one who asked him, simply to calm her nerves before seeing her sick father, and right after burying her mother. She hadn't been thinking straight then, and perhaps it's best *not* to do so from now on.

'Ready to go in, or do you want to drink it in some more?' he asks.

'No, I think I've drunk more than enough,' she tells him.

She drinks more than enough that night, dulling the dullness, and spends half the night kneeling over the toilet. A once-off, she declares, in celebration of their new life together, it will never happen again, she promises.

It is the curse of domesticity, the house making sure that it won't be abandoned anytime soon. He's especially enthusiastic that night, something to do with a new account at work, and anxious to share his good fortune by performing at a rather hysterical pace. Several times, she has to ask him to stop, to let her get her breath back. But he's possessed, and won't be dissuaded, and like the dutiful wife, she lies back and thinks of Belfast, and what might have been.

She gets her own back by getting pregnant, and traces it back to that very night. *Serves him right.* Pity she has to suffer as well. She presents the news as she presents his dinner, and he nearly chokes on the meat. He takes his time responding, and when he does, it feels rather forced. They do a dance of apprehension around the kitchen table. She has a momentary feeling of euphoria, which might well be her hormones, and therefore, strictly physical.

She swells, without necessarily blooming. Her business suffers. She tries to tell her dad, but she has difficulty getting the information through. His mind is slowing down, and he's happy to encourage it. Stomach pains turn out to be nothing, and the morning sickness doesn't last too long. Nothing, it seems, is going to prevent the inevitable, and to add to her woes, she's informed that she's having twins. *'When sorrows come, they come not single spies…but in battalions.'* She's offered seats on packed trains. She puts chocolate spread on her toast, and has a fried egg with her bread and jam for lunch. Her size doesn't put him off. If anything, it spurs him on, as if wants three or four, instead of just two.

The neighbours sympathise, and offer their own offspring as proof of what can go wrong. But, who knows, they say, you might just pull it off. She wants to pull it out, not pull it off. She wants to pull out, of town, like some teenage tearaway.

231

Her clients are disconcerted by her belly. It gives them the wrong impression, that she's careless, and therefore, maybe not the solicitor for them. Not that she can work for much longer, not with her husband pleading with her to stay home.

She sits uncomfortably down opposite her father, and the eyes pop out of his head.

'Oh my God!' he cries. 'You're…'

'Yes,' she says. 'Not long now.' He breaks down in front of her, weeping uncontrollably, and she has to call for the nurse. She leaves him in that distressed state, distressed herself for hours after, waiting for the phone call. He survives the attack, and recovers, hanging on against his will.

'Not long now,' her husband proudly tells her in the maternity ward at the onset of what promised to be a hard labour.

'I want a caesarean,' she says, but he's not listening, nor is anyone else in the hospital. 'I'm not sure I can survive this' she adds.

'Nonsense,' he says.

Is it? She rides huge waves of pain during the course of the night, with no sign of the shore in sight. 'Let me go,' she whispers, in her father's voice. She wishes he was there instead of her husband.

Passing out, passing time, enduring, stripped of every shred of dignity, they arrive, they are presented to her, and she's barely conscious – *they're your problem now*, that's what they appear to be saying. Her husband looks distraught, different. He has shed his skin, and become something wholly new, and not entirely attractive to her.

Home? We're going home? After everything she's been through, and they're just going *home?*

Her father takes it as a sign that he's done his time, and calls it a day, the day after seeing his grandsons. Yes – *boys*. She can't help it, she thinks that, somehow, her brothers have been reincarnated inside her, as if they're too busy to have kids of their own, and so have passed the problem on to her.

Monday afternoon, the curtains pulled to shield them from the sun, she daydreams on the sofa, exhausted, her breasts ruined, the twins blessedly quiet, recharging their batteries before battle is resumed once the sun goes down. She drags herself to the window, to watch the street in its regular hibernation. She knocks on the glass, hoping someone might hear her. She's considering taking them into town, to give them their first glimpse of the outside world, and to remind herself of what she's lost. Her business is on temporary hold, permanently, if her husband has anything to do with it. She could take a quick look while she's there, just to make sure. Then take them to Fairview Park – and have a picnic, maybe. She never makes it outside the door. The hours blink by, he arrives home, the boys wake, and the fun, for them, begins.

'I need a break,' she tells him in bed that night. 'Couldn't your mother - .' He cuts her off right there. Neither of them think that's a good idea. 'Okay, what about one of the neighbours? Or – we could hire someone - .' That, and every other idea, is dismissed.

'It'll pass,' he says.

Will it, though?

⌒

It passes. It passes her by.   She swells the ranks. *It's a girl!* Maybe she'll get it right this time. Is that why some women keep popping them out? It can't be for the joy of parenting. *He,* meanwhile, takes up golf, and hillwalking. Oh, and birdwatching, which presumably he can do while he's walking the hills. He has binoculars, and he's been known to stand for ages at the back door peering into the undergrowth. Or it could be he's looking at the handsome woman in the house behind them. She's prone to leaving her blinds up, so that she can blind the lost men of the neighbourhood.

There are holidays, like that week in West Cork(*again!*), when they're all squeezed into the car. Then they're all squeezed into a 'family' hotel room, where he tries his luck, with the kids just yards away. *Get off me!* she cries, in a whisper. She's been saying that a lot lately. Sex loses all its meaning after three children. What on earth does he find enticing about *down there* anymore? It's disgusting. Bantry Bay, and she watches the fishing boats prepare to leave. Would they take her with them? Drop her off at the nearest island, or Scandinavia, if they're going that way. She fancies a bit of Sweden after watching *Wallander,* unless it was only Kenneth Branagh that attracted her. The twins are wrestling, the girl is wailing, and *he* is practicing his swing, probably dying to get home. She, on the other hand, is just dying.

Speaking of which – she finds a lump in her breast not long after. It's benign, thankfully, but the effect is the same as if it were terminal. She stops eating, turning to skin and bone – and then she starts taking a tipple mid-afternoon. Gin, because it has no smell, and because, well, she likes gin. She's *not* her mother, though.

Hallelujah, they move – across the river, to a house they can't afford, but he keeps saying things like, *'we'll be fine'*. Maybe, she suggests, she could go back to work, but he looks at her quizzically, and says, but what about the children? They can fend for themselves, she argues ridiculously, well, the twins can, so she could take the girl with her to work in the short-term. *Why* would she want to go back to work, he wants to know? Isn't looking after the children enough? She might well have screamed manically into his face in answer to that one, fuelling his anger, which she didn't think he possessed.

It passes.

He can't play golf, or hillwalk anymore, because of a back injury, sustained in mysterious circumstances, which he never talks about. She can live without knowing. It means, though, that he's off work for extended periods, damaging the business, and their income, and their ability to pay the extortionate mortgage, and the timing is lousy because the second economic crash happens, forcing them into reversing roles. *She* becomes the breadwinner, setting up in practice again, and *not* in Ballybough, but in Stillorgan village, in a poky office above a hair salon. She couldn't be happier, and puts on twenty glorious pounds. She also cuts out the gin, although she starts to think that he has taken to it in her absence.

Their sex life resumes, up to a point, with her invariably taking the initiative, what with his bad back. There's not much he can do in terms of movement – *no change there*, she often thinks. The children in this period sprout like wild bushes, with personalities to match. She sides with her daughter most of the time, and comes to accept the fact that she doesn't really like the boys. She loves them, obviously. She just doesn't like them. Anyway, she only has to steer them along for a few more years, and they'll be off.

The parade. She hoists her daughter above the crowd, and waits.

'Where is it?' the girl cries.

'It's coming,' she tells her. The real parade is always happening elsewhere. He has the boys, and they're missing, thankfully, giving her time alone with the girl. Her shoulders sag under the weight. The girl's getting too big for this. There won't be a next year, she guesses.

They stop for chips at the Fairview Grill on the way home. It's out of their way, as *he* points out, but she ignores him. She's driving, after all. That back of his is getting worse. Knowing her luck, the children will leave, but her husband will be a cripple, and she'll have no choice but to look after him.

The boys compete to see who can fill their mouths with the most chips. One of them starts choking, and for a few seconds, it looks like he could be lost, until the airwaves are finally cleared, and he's back with them. Then the crying starts, *all* of them, and she starts driving home in the wrong direction, heading instinctively for Killester, even though it's been years since they lived there. He calls it a Freudian slip, that she really misses the Northside. She asks if they might move back, but his back goes into spasm before he can answer, and she has to pull over. The kids pile into the front seat as their father lies on the back seat. *Christ Almighty*, she thinks, he *will* be a cripple, and sooner than she imagined.

He undergoes several operations, but the medical people, as far as she's concerned, are whistling in the dark. He's worse than ever he was, and now depression is setting in like an early winter. The clouds don't lift for months. The children can't fail to notice, and keep out of his way. And she tries to keep out of *their* way, God forgive her. There's no other way – she needs help. She finds an unfairly pretty physiotherapist to come in twice a week, to run her tiny hands over her husband's back – and elsewhere, who knows. It seems to lift his spirits, at least, and soon he's able to join them for dinner. He calls the young woman a lifesaver. 'Thanks very much!' says his wife.

⌒

The daughter's first boyfriend, a clingy, sweaty squid, bows when she offers her hand.

'Be careful,' is the only advice she can give as they venture into the wide blue sexual yonder.

'*Mum!*'

Her husband shouts from the bedroom, demanding a glass of water. She gives him a vodka, and laughs when he sputters all over the sheets. 'Want me to wipe your arse while I'm at it?'

'Why are you being like this?' he asks. 'And where are the boys tonight?'

'It's a long time since they were boys. Jesus.' She holds a glass of water to his mouth, although he's perfectly capable of holding it himself. Later, she comes to bed, stripping off in front of him deliberately, and slipping in beside him. 'Oh, it's cold. Come on, warm me up.'

'What are you doing? What's *wrong* with you? You know I – can't'

'Yes, but maybe I can,' she argues, moving her hand into position, and massaging without success, only straining herself in the process.

'We have to accept, love,' he sighs, 'those days are over.'

'For you, maybe.'

'What does that mean? And where was this – appetite – when I needed it? When I was *capable* of it?'

'I'm scared – the advancing years, creeping old age. *Creepy* old age. No time to waste, that's my motto now.'

'Then you'll have to find someone who's better equipped.'

'Are you giving me permission to have an affair?'

He huffs and puffs, and shunts into his sleeping position like an old barge. He didn't say *no*, she thinks.

A client comes into her office one day, needing advice on power-of-attorney, and all that, and she decides – *he'll do*. The Stillorgan Park hotel is the venue, late afternoon, and he's nervous as hell, and not nearly as efficient as she'd hoped. In truth, it's not that much different than with her husband, albeit a few years back. The 'client' is first to leave, and she may have lost his custom.

Her daughter announces that she's moving out. Her father won't hear of it, and flatly refuses.

'That's fantastic news,' her mother says, rejoicing. 'What's his name? Can you both afford it?'

The twins are twenty-somethings already, but show no signs of shifting. They too are crippled, like their father, but by emotional immaturity. They have occasional, brief conversations, like passengers forced together on the bus. Fuck them, she thinks.

She visits her daughter's compact flat in Shankill, taking great pleasure in having helped create one viable adult human being. The girl will be all right.

The husband and wife will *not* be all right, it seems. The cripple makes the mistake of believing that he's on the mend, and attempts to get down the stairs all on his own. She had suggested that he might want to move his bed downstairs, but he refused, saying he wasn't an old man. No, she thought, you just look and walk like one. She heard him *bounce* down the stairs, and found him twisted like a rag doll at the bottom.

'*Pleeeeeeeeeeeeeeeeeeeeze*....'

She waits in the sitting-room for the ambulance, unable to look at his distorted form. If he survives, and if he remembers, he will never forgive her. But there's no chance of that, as the ambulance-men confirm his passing before they get him onto the trolley. They take his body, though, and she waits for the boys to come home. They arrive separately, both in their work suits, whimpering like young boys again. She cradles both of them to her breasts, oddly embarrassed by this show of emotion.

Her daughter meets them at the hospital, and is far more stoic about the whole thing.

He wanted to be cremated, she learns from his will. And so, he is cremated, and she carries his ashes through St. Fintan's Cemetary on a snowy day, the children marching behind her. None of them know a prayer through to the end, and they end up giggling, before retiring to the Marine Hotel, where they raise their glasses, and she offers up a toast to 'the love of my life'. *Where did that come from?*

She's curiously happy in the days afterwards, alone in the house, free as a bird, where she occasionally sneaks a gin or two, even though nobody's watching.

She's losing weight again, despite eating healthily, with several daily sugary snacks thrown in for good measure. It's not a lump, nor is it benign. It's a hidden, silent menace, slowly eating her from the inside.

And it doesn't pass.

⌒

Her daughter holds on tight, keeping her upright. She's wrapped in copious layers, but she's still freezing. And they wait.

'Can you see anything?' she asks.

'I thinks it's coming,' her daughter says. 'Won't be long now.'

The parade arrives, and the crowd surge forward to get a better look. She can't see a thing. She can't feel a thing. She takes off her hat, and drops it to the ground.

The parade passes.

And she passes, right there and then, on O'Connell Street, on St. Patrick's Day, in Dublin city. The town without cheer.

About the Author

Philip Boyle is the author of four previous novels – *The Body Politic, The Boxer's Dreams of Love, The Woman of Rivoli,* and *Limb.* He lives in Dublin.

www.theartofphilipboyle.com

Printed in Poland
by Amazon Fulfillment
Poland Sp. z o.o., Wrocław